# Eileen Goudge

# The Second Silence

## WHEELER
PUBLISHING, INC.
ROCKLAND, MA

★ AN AMERICAN COMPANY ★

Published in Large Print by arrangement with Viking, a member of
Penguin Putman Inc. in the United States and Canada.

Wheeler Large Print Book Series.

Set in 16 pt Plantin.

*Library of Congress Cataloging-in-Publication Data*

Goudge, Eileen.
    The second silence / Eileen Goudge.
        p. (large print)  cm.(Wheeler large print book series)
    ISBN 1-56895-902-8 (hardcover)
    1.  Real estate developers—Fiction. 2.  Kidnapping, Parental—Fiction.
3. Separated people—Fiction. 4. Divorced parents—Fiction. 5. Large
type books. I. Title. II. Series

[PS3557.O838 S43   2000b]
813'.54—dc21
                                                              00-039872
                                                                     CIP

# The

# Second

# Silence

# Acknowledgments

Many thanks to the following for their support and guidance:

Susan Ginsburg and Maja Nikolic at Writers House. Molly Stern at Viking. Louise Burke at Signet. My good friends Catherine Jacobes, who designed my Web site, Kathee Card, whose daily E-mails bring a smile and keep me going.

And last, but not least, my dear husband, Sandy, who's proven to be as good an editor as he is companion, helpmate, and navigator... and who brought home dinner every night while I was working round the clock.

Three silences there are: the first
of speech,
The second of desire, the third of
thought...

–Henry Wadsworth Longfellow

Burns Lake, New York, 1969

# Prologue

Mary Jeffers gaped in alarm at the man charging through the front door. She scarcely recognized him as her husband. For one thing, it was early afternoon and Charlie didn't get off work until five. And though he'd been driving their old Ford pickup, which hissed going up hills and got nine, maybe ten miles to the gallon—that was on a good day—his shorn black hair glistened with sweat and his face was stamped with color, like he'd run the whole way. As he jerked to a halt before her, she saw that the tips of his ears were red, too, a sure sign of something bad. It was exactly how Charlie had looked when she told him she was pregnant, what felt like a hundred years ago.

Gooseflesh skittered up her arms like tiny biting insects. Seated in the rocking chair by the woodstove, the baby asleep in her arms, she hardly dared to breathe. She hadn't the slightest idea what might have brought Charlie racing home in the middle of the day, looking like four kinds of bad news, but in a peculiar way she'd been half expecting it. That was how it was when you were poor: Every day brought some new piece of the sky crumbling down.

She clapped a hand to her heart to still its anxious thumping, asking in a soft, tremulous voice, "Charlie, my God, what is it?"

He opened his mouth to reply, then closed it again. The expression on his gaunt, troubled face was the one he wore when peering under the hood of their Ford at the balky fuel pump held together with spit and a prayer—as if wondering how much more she could take. Except for his lanky frame and the ink black hair pushed up in damp spikes, he might have been an old man instead of a boy of just seventeen. His shoulders were slouched in a permanent question mark, and a blackened groove stood out in his worn leather belt where it had all too recently been hitched in another notch. After a moment he straightened and took a step in her direction, adding a snowy boot print to the uneven trail leading away from the door.

"Corinne's dead." He spoke slowly, as if for the benefit of a foreigner who had trouble understanding English. She saw that his hands, chafed with cold and hanging loosely from the frayed sleeves of his hunting jacket, were trembling.

His words melted on impact like the snowflakes landing with a soft, sizzling sound against the window. Dropping her gaze, Mary noticed that there was a button missing from his jacket and that the plaid shirt underneath was badly creased. She wondered idly if flannel was the sort of thing you ironed. Not that it mattered; she hadn't ironed anything since they got married last October, the day after her seventeenth birthday, when she was already so big that standing for any length of time caused her ankles to swell. Then the baby came, and there was hardly a minute to—

It hit her then, knocking the wind out of her. She struggled to draw a breath, her chest hitching like an engine that wouldn't start. "No," she whispered. "No...not Corinne. There must be some mistake."

But Charlie was shaking his head. "Mary, I'm sorry. God, I'm sorry."

Her mouth moved of its own volition, shaping itself about the unspeakable. "How?" she breathed in a cracked whisper.

"They found her in a motel just off I-88, up near Schenectady. Her wrists were—" He paused to clear his throat. "They're calling it a suicide."

Mary's arms jerked up reflexively as if to ward off a blow. The bottle propped against her chest, its milky nipple grazing the baby's sweet little rosebud of a mouth, rolled away, landing with a muffled thunk on the braided rug at Mary's feet. Noelle twitched in her sleep, her pale pink eyelids like the insides of seashells fluttering partway open.

*Don't wake up. Please don't wake up,* Mary pleaded silently. The cold her three-month-old had come down with earlier this week had left Noelle cranky. She'd been crying on and off most of the day. *If she starts up again, I'll lose it this time. I really will.*

Mary remained frozen, the news of her best friend's death encircling her like barbed wire that would prick her if she moved even a hair. Oddly the image stuck in her mind wasn't that of Corinne floating in a bloody bathtub, but one from last Christmas. She and Corinne had been shooing the horses away from a trough while Charlie hacked at the frozen surface with a shovel, the three of them laughing idiotically at the uselessness of it; the stupid beasts kept circling back in an attempt to nudge him out of the way. She herself had been big as a house, due to give birth in just a few weeks, and Corinne, though tall, had seemed almost petite in comparison. Her thick, straight hair shone like polished oak against the turned-up collar of her navy pea-coat. Her cheeks were red with cold, her lips parted in laughter.

*As if she hadn't a care in the world.*

Mary's heart caught as if on something sharp. She began to tremble violently. Instinctively she reached for Charlie. "Quick, give me your hand." Feeling the grip of his long fingers with their knuckles like knotted rope, she felt her trembling ease. "Oh, Charlie. Say it's not true. Say you might have heard wrong."

"The newsroom picked it up off the band not more than an hour ago." His gaze cut away, as if he couldn't bear seeing what this was doing to her. "Ed Newcombe double-checked with the sheriff's office."

"Oh, God...poor Corinne." The words emerged as a sob.

"I wanted to tell you in person. I didn't want you to hear it over the phone." With his free hand Charlie reached out to stroke her hair.

She could feel the heat of his palm against her scalp.

She nodded slowly in appreciation, Charlie's hand and the warm weight of the baby seeming to anchor her in some way. When she spoke, her tongue felt thick and clumsy in her mouth, like after a trip to the dentist. "Does—does her family know?"

"Someone must have told them by now."

Mary rubbed a thumb over the back of his hand, feeling the rough spot where he'd scraped his knuckles on the corral gate trying to force it open in the foot of snow that had fallen the night before last. His angular features and pale skin on which every emotion stood out like a slap made her think of the faces staring with haunted eyes from Mathew Brady daguerreotypes, Civil War soldiers who'd been boys when they marched into battle and had come home men. She wanted to reassure him in some way. But how? What could she say? That it would be okay? Right now it didn't seem as if anything would ever be okay.

*I wasn't there for her.* The thought pricked hard enough to make her flinch. Mary was ashamed to realize how far apart they'd drifted these past few months. It wasn't Corinne's fault. *She* was the one who'd changed. Her days were no longer filled with school and glee club practice and endless hours of gossiping over the phone. She couldn't recall when she'd last concerned herself with split ends or a C– on a trig test...or even the Vietnam protest rallies in which she and Corinne had

7

begun marching last spring. When her friend phoned last week—or was it the week before?— Mary had been far too preoccupied even to chat. She'd promised to call back when the baby was down for her nap. But had she? Mary honestly couldn't recall.

*Oh, but you do,* a cruel voice injected. *You remember perfectly well. She sounded like she'd been crying. And secretly weren't you just a tiny bit annoyed? Thinking that whatever the reason— another fight with that creepy boyfriend of hers, no doubt—it was a molehill compared to the mountain* you *had to climb each and every day. So you didn't call back. You* meant *to...but somehow you just never got around to it.*

And now it was too late.

"I just can't believe it. I can't believe Corinne would..." The words melted from her lips like the snowy tracks darkening to a muddy trail on the rug. The truth was more painful in some ways than the simple fact of her friend's death: Mary couldn't even guess what might have driven Corinne to such a desperate act. Lately she'd been far too consumed with the mess she'd made of her own life.

Each morning she woke before dawn to her baby's hungry cries. In the beginning she'd tried breast-feeding, but Noelle fussed endlessly. Nervous milk the doctor called it, which meant she didn't produce enough: her first failure as a mother. So now there were bottles to be warmed as well as endless diapers to be changed and washed and hung out to dry.

Even when Noelle was down for her nap, there was the woodstove to be fed and stoked, meals to be cobbled together out of whatever was in the fridge. And oh, yes, let's not forget the spoiled little rich girls who boarded the horses she and Charlie fed and watered in exchange for rent. Twelve- and thirteen-year-olds in breeches and two-hundred-dollar riding boots who showed up regularly at the back door, needing everything from a Band-Aid to a glass of cold water to the use of the phone. By nightfall Mary felt as drained as the bottles Noelle greedily sucked dry.

But now that Mama and Daddy had turned their backs on her for good, Charlie and the baby were all she had. When her husband sank onto his haunches before her, Mary felt something flare in her chest like a spark from one of the frayed electrical cords strung like Christmas lights along the walls and baseboards of their converted bunkhouse.

Charlie was tall in the loose-jointed way of a long-distance runner so that hunkered down, he was eye level with her. Gazing into his long, angular face, she saw his Iroquois ancestors in its beveled planes and the high slashes of his cheekbones. In their sophomore year at Lafayette, when they first started going together, Charlie's hair, black as a crow's wing, had flirted with the collars of his shirts; now it was cut short as a marine's, orders of his boss, Mr. Newcombe. Charlie hated it, she knew, hated it because he'd had no choice. But secretly she approved. It set him apart from the boys with hair down past their shoulders who boasted of burning their draft cards...while at home their mothers made their beds and packed their school lunches.

His eyes were his best feature, though. Wide set and tipped down at the corners, they were an unusual ocher-green that made her think of sliding into the cool water of a shady creek hollow. Mary leaned into him, bringing her cheek to rest against his shoulder and curving her body to form a hollow in which Noelle could sleep on undisturbed. *We're like the two-by-fours propped against the barn,* she thought. *We kept each other from falling down.*

"What do we do now?" she whispered like a child lost in the dark.

Ordinarily she'd have phoned someone. But who? Since she'd dropped out of school, Mary hadn't seen much of her friends. Beth Tilson's parents had discouraged Beth from visiting— probably because they feared that whatever Mary had might be catching. Jo Ferguson was working after school and on weekends at the SuperSave to earn enough for college and never seemed to have any spare time. Even Lacey Buxton, the last person to desert a friend in need, had suffered her own fall from grace in the form of a visiting family friend with whom she'd been caught naked in the Methodist church choir loft—a man old enough to be her father—and been sent to live with an aunt and uncle in Buffalo, presumably to set her on the straight and narrow.

"There'll be a funeral, I'm sure. " A deep

line like a buried stitch had drawn Charlie's dark brows together over the bony ridge of his nose.

A picture formed in her mind of Corinne's mother and father and three brothers gathered in sorrow about the freshly dug grave. Then the picture morphed, and suddenly it was *her* grave with Mama and Daddy standing over it. Daddy, stoop-shouldered with sickness and defeat, his scalp gleaming white as bone through the thinning hair on top. And Mama, stolid and ageless as the house on Larkspur Lane, the house from which Mary had been forever banished.

The tears came then, rolling hotly down her cheeks as she gazed at the drowsing infant in her arms. Noelle's thatch of black hair that swooped up in a fat comma was the only thing she'd gotten from Charlie. Her gray-blue eyes and upper lip that dipped in a cupid's bow, the narrow nose from some blue-blooded ancestor: Mary might have been looking at a snapshot of herself at three months. She felt a rush of love that was immediately swamped by an even greater wave of despair.

Charlie, seeming to sense this, straightened and held out his arms. "Why don't you let me take her? I could look after her for a while, until you..." He let the sentence trail off.

A bolt of anger sizzled through her. "Until I *what?* Get a grip?" It wasn't fair, she knew, lashing out at Charlie, but she couldn't seem to help it. He wasn't just an easy target. He was the *only* target.

"Mr. Newcombe gave me the rest of the afternoon off." He went on calmly, as if she hadn't spoken. "I could make a run to the Laundromat, pick up some groceries on my way back. We're out of milk, I noticed." He spoke softly so as not to wake the baby, stirring fretfully in her arms.

"We're out of *everything.*" She had in her wallet exactly nine dollars and thirty-eight cents, which was supposed to last until Charlie's next paycheck a week from Friday.

Noelle began to squirm, making small, whimpering noises. Mary hoisted her over one shoulder and began to rock furiously back and forth. She buried her face in the sweet-smelling crook of her baby's neck to keep from drowning.

Once, at an eighth-grade swim party, one of the rowdier boys had pushed her off a dock into the lake with all her clothes on. She would never forget that panicky sense of being dragged under no matter how hard she kicked, which was exactly how she felt now. It had been months since she'd read a book or watched a TV show all the way to the end. Other than forays to the Laundromat and supermarket and helping feed and water the horses, she rarely went out. When she took a bath in the big claw-footed tub with its pipes that ran down a hole in the floor, through which a patch of the weed-choked dirt was visible below, she didn't always have time to shampoo her hair. It trailed in tangled auburn waves down her shoulders and back like something spilled that she hadn't had a chance to clean up.

It wasn't Charlie's fault, she knew. He was barely keeping his own head above water. He'd taken the first job he could find, as office boy at the *Burns Lake Register*. He swept floors and emptied wastebaskets; he jumped when fat old Mr. Newcombe barked. All for the princely sum of sixty dollars a week.

She watched him unfold to his feet, joints crackling, and for a fleeting instant felt as if she were being swept up in his wake. She yearned then for Charlie to hold her as he once had, unhindered by baby or by swollen belly. To feel once more that sense of teetering on the brink not of disaster but of something deliciously reckless. It had been more than a week since they'd even made love.

"I'll feed the horses before I go." His voice was dull and defeated.

"I could—" she started to say.

"No." He headed for the door. "You have enough of your own to handle right now."

Mary felt her panic swell until it was nearly choking her. Was Corinne's death going to sink without a trace in this fathomless lake she was treading with her shoes on?

"Wait!" she called after him in desperation. "What about Robert? *He* must have some idea why Corinne would—why she would do such a thing."

Corinne's boyfriend was the other reason she and her friend had drifted apart. In Mary's opinion, Robert Van Doren was the worst kind of trouble, the kind that doesn't advertise itself. A straight A student and the football team's star running back, he was the proverbial boy next door. Fathers, even those as strict as Corinne's dad, trusted their daughters with him. The Ivy League was courting him. Yet no parent or admissions officer knew about the time he and his buddies had gotten drunk and taken turns with poor, dim-witted, desperate-to-please Margie Rittenhouse.

She could see him in her mind now, boasting of the incident at Doug Eastman's barbecue out at the lake the summer after their junior year. She saw him perched on the nose of Doug's sleek new Sunfish—as tall as Charlie but built like a young bull with the looks of an Olympian god. Naked except for a pair of faded cutoffs and glowing in the way of rich boys doted on by their mothers, all buttery shimmer and blue ice. Robert was belting down a Rolling Rock with one hand while cupping an imaginary breast with the other. Corrine had gone off in search of more beer and Robert was reenacting Margie's rape (for that's what it was) for the benefit of his leering audience.

"Man, you should've seen the look on her face when Toomey walked off," he recalled with a sniggering laugh. Clearly, he hadn't spied Mary, standing just within earshot. "She was begging for more, man, *begging* for it. But he told her he wasn't into fucking cows."

"Beggin' for mercy is more like it," hooted fat, pimply Wade Jewett, the most worshipful of Robert's toadies. "I heard she was pretty wasted."

The smile dropped from Robert's face as abruptly as a sudden cold front moving in off the lake. With stunning casualness, he turned to Wade, sneering, "Like *you* would know. Christ, Jewett, if you weren't so busy jerking off at home you'd have seen for yourself."

That was Robert. Hot one moment, cold the next. Like ice that could as easily cause you to slip and break a bone as send you twirling deliriously in circles.

Mary shook free of the memory and looked up at Charlie.

He'd turned away from the door and was frowning at her in a thoughtful way. "Robert, yeah. Newcombe phoned him for a statement." Charlie's jaw was clenched and a look of disgust had deepened the buried stitch between his brows. "You know what that creep said? 'Jesus, the crazy bitch actually went through with it.'"

Mary must have jerked in surprise because Noelle's eyes flew open, and she immediately resumed the crying jag she'd been on since five this morning. Mary began to weep as well. Loose sobs that billowed up from her depths like the drowned creatures, squirrels and raccoons mostly, found floating in the lake after the heavy rains that descended on Burns Lake each spring like a biblical plague. Even Charlie was at a loss to console her. He stood awkwardly by the door, his fists stuffed so deep

15

into the pockets of his jacket she could see a white knuckle poking from its torn seam like a bone from a shattered limb.

Mary struggled to her feet, a hand cupped about the baby's head. Noelle had worked herself into a state, her shrieks coming in short, sharp bursts punctuated by strangled gasps. As Mary paced the floor, she felt weak with despair.

"Hush, it's okay, everything's going to be okay," she crooned as hot tears slid down her cheeks.

When her husband strode over to pry the baby gently from her arms, Mary was too tired to protest. Watching them, she was pierced to the core by the picture they made against the backdrop of the spartan living room furnished like a playhouse in castoffs: Noelle with her small red face bunched into a fist and her black hair standing up like an exclamation point...and Charlie, with a look of tender consternation on his old-young face, not unlike the expression he wore helping his mother upstairs to bed when Pauline was too drunk to manage it on her own. After several minutes of pacing, he stopped to put a hand to her forehead.

"She feels hot," he said.

"That's because she's running a fever." Mary marched over to show Charlie that at least one of them had a handle on the situation, however tenuously. An hour ago the baby's temperature had been only a little over a hundred. Yet when she felt Noelle's cheek, it was immediately evident things had taken a drastic turn for the worse.

Mary dashed into the bathroom for the thermometer. The bathroom had been tacked on in the early thirties, back when the bunkhouse was converted into living quarters. Consequently, the floor slanted at an angle where the supports on which it rested had sunk into the dirt below. As she fumbled with the drop latch on the old-fashioned medicine chest, Mary caught a glimpse of her reflection, canted at an angle in the speckled mirror: enormous eyes staring out of a stricken white face, like those on the evening news of people who'd survived some terrible devastation.

Awkwardly Charlie positioned their howling daughter facedown across his lap while Mary undid the snaps on her terry sleeper and removed her plastic pants and diaper. They both held their breaths as the silver line in the thermometer began to creep up. After several minutes Mary held it up to the light. The mercury had topped off at 104.

"My God, she's burning up! Charlie, we've got to do something. We've got to get her to a doctor." Mary dashed to the corner by the stove, where Noelle's crib was tucked alongside the lumpy foldout sofa on which they slept. She grabbed the crocheted afghan given to them by their landlord's kindhearted wife and frantically bundled the baby in it.

Yet Charlie remained motionless by the door. Slashes of color stood out on his cheekbones. "The heater in the truck's not working. She could—Christ, we could *all* freeze."

He didn't have to remind her that the nearest doctor was in Schenectady, twenty minutes away. But what other choice did they have? "If we stay here, she could go into convulsions and *die*," Mary shrieked in a high, nearly breathless voice.

Charlie thought for a moment, raking a hand over his head, front to back, as he'd been in the habit of doing when his hair was long. Its spiky ends bristled like the sleek pelt of some lithe, long-bodied animal. His face was as ghostly white as the naked lightbulb that dangled overhead. Then, as if coming to some sort of decision, he abruptly wrenched open the door. "There's only one thing to do," he said.

Mary followed him outside, the baby clutched tightly in her arms and a corner of the afghan dragging on the snowy ground. Her panic receded a bit. She told herself, *He'll borrow a car...or find someone to take us. Of course, why didn't I think of it?*

The light flurries that had been falling all day spun and drifted overhead. In the part of her mind that was still functioning, she dimly recalled the weatherman's reporting several more inches by nightfall. The trouble was they were still digging out from under the storm of two days ago. Ice-crusted drifts were piled up against the fence, and slushy ruts in the driveway had frozen over. Across the way horses with shaggy winter pelts nosed at clumps of frozen snow cake-frosting the rails of their corral. The truck, a '59 Ford pickup, once green but now the indeterminate shade of a moss-grown boulder, stood nosed up against the tractor plow in front of the barn.

He helped her into the frigid cab, then trotted around to the other side. "We're taking her to your mother," he announced, scooting in behind the wheel. His breath bloomed in the chill air as he started the engine.

Mary felt something lurch inside her. She grabbed his arm. "We can't," she said through clenched, chattering teeth.

Charlie shook her hand away and twisted around to look out the back window. "Your mother's a nurse, isn't she?" He ground the gear into reverse and the truck jerked backward.

"*Retired* nurse. She hasn't worked in years, not since Dad got sick." Which they both knew was neither here nor there. But the truth was simply too awful to face. "She won't help. She doesn't want anything to do with me or—or the baby. Charlie, please. We can go to *your* mom. She'll know what to do."

"Maybe. If she's sober." The knotted muscles in Charlie's jaw flickered with everything best left unsaid on that subject. Moments later they were jouncing over the deep pothole that marked the end of the driveway. Her jaws clacked together, catching the tip of her tongue between her teeth. She felt a bright burst of pain.

Mary sucked her cheeks in, tasting blood. "This is crazy. Have you forgotten what happened the last time?"

Christmas morning, with Noelle just a week old, Mary had phoned home in a flush of holiday spirit and optimism. Her parents were aware of the baby's existence, she knew, because a nurse at the hospital had mentioned something about a Mrs. Quinn's stopping by to peek into the nursery. Yet over the phone, Mama had been nothing more than civil. The furnace was acting up, she reported, but Mr. Wilson had promised to be out first thing tomorrow to fix it. And no, they weren't driving all the way to Binghamton for turkey dinner at Aunt Stella's. Daddy simply wasn't up to it; he'd been laid up all week with a bad cough. Trish couldn't come to the phone either, she said; wild horses couldn't separate her from her new transistor radio.

After a strained minute or two Mama excused herself to go look in on Daddy. Not once had she asked about her grandchild or how Mary was getting along. It was as if Noelle hadn't existed, and she herself were little more than a distant memory. It was worse, Mary concluded miserably, than if her mother had simply hung up.

"She can't ignore us this time." Charlie gripped the steering wheel, leaning close to swipe a clear patch in the foggy windshield.

Mary cast an anxious glance at her baby's flushed face peeking from the folds of the afghan. Miraculously Noelle had been lulled

20

to sleep by the rattle of the pickup as it lurched its way down the hilly, twisting road to town. *Charlie's right,* she thought. This was the only sane choice. And Mama wasn't completely heartless. Hadn't she at least cared enough to sneak a look at her granddaughter?

Five miles down the road, where Route 30A joined up with Route 30, the houses began to appear: large, square clapboard houses built in the thirties, with well-kept lawns and neatly trimmed boxwood hedges. The house Mary had grown up in occupied the corner of Larkspur and Cardinal. Nearly indistinguishable from the houses on either side, it was shaded by large spreading elms and maples and had a deep porch that wrapped around three sides.

As Charlie pulled up in front, Mary was stricken by a wave of nostalgia. It was all so blessedly, innocently familiar: the hand-painted sign over the mailbox, the nuthatches fluttering about the bird feeder, the porch glider with its memories of lazy summer afternoons spent with a book in hand and her feet tucked under her. She noted with a dull throb that the drainpipe was still loose, leaning away from the side of the house like a sentry nodding off at his post—one of the projects her father hadn't gotten around to before he fell ill.

Charlie reached over to cup a hand over hers. "Do you want to wait here while I ring the bell?"

Mary glanced again at Noelle, feeling her throat tighten. "No, I'll come with you."

Mama would have to be a monster to turn away her own grandchild, sick as she was.

As she made her way up the front walk, the baby in her arms and Charlie's arm firmly anchored about her waist, Mary forced herself to hold her head high. *I wouldn't be here if it weren't for Noelle,* she told herself. *I'm not asking for anything for myself.*

Nonetheless, as she waited on the porch, Mary's heart was pounding so hard she was certain it could be heard through the heavy oak door just as surely as *she* could hear the faint, measured tread of her mother's footsteps.

The door swung open. Mama stared at them in blank astonishment, as though she'd been interrupted in the midst of housework or preparing dinner. She wore an apron over slacks and a pink cardigan. Squiggles of hair the color of faded ginger strayed from the combs over her temples. Though still on the heavy side, she looked as though she'd lost weight recently. The flesh had begun to slide away from her square jaw and the knobs of her cheekbones. Her blue eyes squinted against the bright winter sunlight, as if it had been some time since she'd set foot outdoors.

No one spoke in those first few seconds. There was only their breath punctuating the frosty air, coupled with the hollow plink-plink-plink of icicles melting from the eaves. Then Mama brought a hand to the jutting prow of her bosom, exclaiming, "Good Lord, Mary Catherine. What in heaven's name happened to you?"

Mary, who in thirty-six hours of labor had not once, through sheer force of determination, cried out for her mother, opened her mouth now to say that a woman who hadn't turned her back on her own daughter would know such a thing without having to be told. But before she could get a single word out, she burst into tears.

She felt Charlie's arm tighten about her waist. "The baby's sick," he said. There was urgency in his voice but not a hint of pleading. He stood tall, looking her mother squarely in the eye. Mary had never felt more proud of him than she did at that moment.

Mama's eyes dropped to the tuft of hair peeking over the top of the afghan. Though her broad face remained impassive, she seemed to wrestle with some inner conflict. Then her mouth settled into its familiar line of disapproval—like a thin red line penciled in where a smile ought to have been—and she briskly stepped aside to let them in.

"I don't know what you could have been thinking, bringing a baby out in weather like this. You should have called." She berated them. "Here, give her to me. Why, she's burning up!"

Mary felt herself go limp, as if the bundle scooped from her arms were the only thing that had been keeping her from falling apart. As she trudged up the stairs after her mother, she felt the house wrap about her like a warm, comforting embrace. Even its familiar smells brought memories so vivid she could almost touch them: strips of bacon in neat rows on grease-soaked paper towels, line-dried sheets so crisp they crackled, deep drawers fragrant with the scent of dried lavender.

In her old room at the top of the stairs, which she saw with an almost visceral wave of relief was exactly as she'd left it, she watched her mother gently lower the fever-drowsy baby onto the bed. Mary hung back uncertainly, as if it had been her mother who'd been in command all along and were merely assuming her correct role. She watched Mama move about, brisk and knowing, in her sensible shoes and checked apron with its rickrack-trimmed pockets for stowing loose change and buttons and candy wrappers retrieved from between sofa cushions and under beds.

Mama peeled away layers of blanket and clothing until the baby lay naked atop the quilted pink spread. Noelle was wide-awake now, arms flailing, her face screwed into a small red fist of outrage. Mary instinctively moved forward, arms extended. But her mother, as usual, was one step ahead of her. Mama placed a hand squarely over Noelle's chest, and the baby at once grew still, seeming to sense that someone competent, someone who knew what she was doing even though it might be a little uncomfortable, had at last seized the wheel of this runaway bus. Noelle fixed her bright gaze on the stranger poised above her.

"Mary Catherine, run to the kitchen for some ice," Mama ordered. "We've got to get this fever down." She bustled into the adjoining bathroom and reappeared a moment later with towels, a washcloth, the plastic basin used for hand washing what she called the unmentionables.

Mary did as she was told. It wouldn't have occurred to her to question her mother's judgment in a matter such as this. In the kitchen downstairs her only thought as she filled a Tupperware container with ice was that *she* should have known what to do. What if Noelle had died because of her?

Faint with terror, she stared at the plate rail above the yellow Formica table, along which her mother's souvenir plates were lined up like shiny buttons on a sleeve. It was a moment before she could breathe normally again.

In the weeks to come, when she looked back on this day, Mary would see it as clearly as she saw the avocado pit propped with toothpicks in a jelly jar on the sill, the seed that had taken root in her that moment, fed by guilt and shame and simple exhaustion. Deep down she must have known, as she climbed the stairs to her room, that she was home to stay.

Charlie must have sensed it, too. She could feel his anxious gaze tracking her as she carried the ice over to the bed, as obediently as she'd once marched to the altar at St. Vincent's to receive her first communion.

Mary didn't dare look at him. She kept her eyes fixed on the baby instead. Watching Mama smooth a washcloth dipped in ice water over Noelle's tiny, feverish body, she flinched as if *she* were being assaulted. She could recall in precise detail her mother's hand against her own hot forehead as she lay in bed, home sick from school. The boiled egg and buttered toast cut in triangles brought to her on a tray. The sunlight slanting in through the lowered venetian blinds.

Her mother hadn't always been this way. Mary remembered when Daddy used to sneak up behind Mama in the kitchen and whisk her away from the sink while humming some old song they used to dance to. She would pretend to be annoyed, swatting him with a soapy hand and crying, "Ted, for heaven's sake!" But then she'd start to giggle and before long they'd be waltzing about the kitchen as if it were the Starlite ballroom.

Mary remembered, too, the day her parents found out she was pregnant. They'd all gone to noon mass at St. Vincent's. She hadn't eaten since the night before, and just after the blessings on the Eucharist, as she was sticking her tongue out to take the host, she fainted. When she came to, stretched out on the cool tiles of the vestry, Mama had insisted on taking her straight to the doctor. Mary, knowing full well what the matter was, buried her face in the folds of her mother's best Sunday dress—one Mama had sewed herself, navy piqué with white piping, crisp against Mary's cheek and smelling of lily of the valley—and wept. Christ might forgive her sins, she knew. In time even Daddy would come around. But as far as Mama was concerned, she'd be as good as dead.

It was Daddy who'd signed the consent form so that she and Charlie could be married. And her little sister, Trish, who'd helped her pack up her things, silently and with swollen red eyes. Mary hadn't seen or heard from her mother since the day she moved out, five months pregnant with fifty dollars in her pocket.

Now, as she stood on the threshold of her old life, looking down at her baby, pink and glistening like when she'd first entered this world, it was as if she herself had emerged naked and gleaming from some dark, submerged place.

Even the way Mama took Noelle's temperature, shaking the thermometer with an efficient snap of her wrist, was reassuring. When she held it up so they could see—down three whole degrees!—even Charlie breathed an audible sigh of relief.

Mary allowed herself to look at him then. Charlie was still wearing his Black Watch hunting jacket. Standing to one side of the door, he stuck out like a sore thumb against the faded wallpaper patterned in nosegays: a weary traveler who'd stopped to rest a spell before moving on.

His vivid creek water eyes seemed to beseech her. And despite all they'd been through, she felt the pull of something sweet and free and innocent. She thought of warm summer nights when they used to drive out to the lake. Once Charlie had clambered up onto the roof of his father's Impala, pulling her with him. Stretched out side by side, they'd gazed up at the stars while Mary pointed out the constellations. She'd been a virgin then, and he'd whispered in her ear that when the time came, he didn't want it to be in the backseat of a car. She deserved better.

The first time had been in this very room, on the very bed where their daughter now lay. One Sunday morning Mary had begged off church, feigning a headache, and Charlie had sneaked up to her room after everyone left. As she remembered how sweet it had been, not at all painful, but lovely and pure as a baptism, she felt a thread of longing pull tight inside her, one that was tugging her in his direction.

"One thing's for sure, you're not taking her back out into the cold. You can do what you like, Mary Catherine, but this baby stays put." Mama's voice behind her was crisp and firm. Mary didn't have to turn around to know that her lips were tight and arms crossed over her chest.

The invitation, however veiled, was clear: Mary and the baby were welcome to stay. But not Charlie.

He stepped forward at once, his eyes flashing, his voice carefully controlled. "Thank you, Mrs. Quinn. I appreciate everything you've done, and if you think Noelle should stay a little while longer, I have no argument with that. But she has a nice warm crib waiting for her back at our place. She'll be just fine."

Mama didn't reply. She didn't even look at him. She looked at Mary instead, as if to say, *You did wrong, but you're still my daughter. It's not too late to make things right.*

Mary wrapped the baby in the towel and picked her up off the bed. It was exactly six steps to the doorway where Charlie stood eyeing her expectantly; she'd counted it once, walking heel to toe. Six steps between her and freedom. The trouble was, she was no longer sure in which direction freedom lay.

Once she'd believed it was with Charlie. But that was before the harsh reality of caring for a baby had sunk home. Before she'd known what it was like to be poor. Before she'd been forced to drop out of school. Before...

*Corinne killed herself.*

With her eyes, she implored Charlie to understand. Why did this have to be so hard? She loved him, God knew she loved him. But it wasn't enough somehow. For that was the hidden truth, the trick snake springing from the can of fake peanuts, in all those sappy novels she used to soak up, and the movies where the lovers' embrace fades to black before disillusionment sets in: Love doesn't pay the rent. It doesn't keep the wind from whistling through the cracks in the walls or stop the bills from piling up in the mailbox.

"How's Daddy?" she asked, desperate to forestall the terrible choice ahead of her.

"He has his good days and his bad days." Mama shrugged and bent over to smooth the bedspread. In that instant Mary caught a flicker of something as deep and strong as the love she felt for Charlie. She saw fear, too: Daddy wasn't doing as well as Mama would like everyone to believe.

"Mary..." Charlie flashed her a stern look.

"What about Trish? Did she pass that algebra test she was so afraid of flunking?" Mary closed her eyes, blocking him from view.

"A C minus beats a poke in the eye with a sharp stick, I suppose." Mama didn't ask how she'd known about the test. And Mary didn't tell her about the furtive conversations with Trish, who used her baby-sitting money to call from pay phones.

Tears leaked out from under Mary's closed eyelids. "Mama? Did you know Corinne Lundquist killed herself? It happened last night. I just found out."

She heard her mother gasp. "Corinne? Good Lord. Why on earth would she want to go and do a thing like that?"

It took a lot to knock Doris Quinn for a loop, but that did it. Mary opened her eyes to find her mother standing stock-still in front of her, feet planted slightly apart as if squared against an oncoming blow.

"I wish I knew," Mary said. But in a way she did. She knew perfectly well how a girl of seventeen could run out of hope, how she could feel desperate enough to...

"Mary. Are you coming with me or not?" Charlie spoke sharply, but his eyes pleaded with her.

For a long minute she didn't speak. Even Noelle was quiet for a change. Mary could only sit there, shaking her head while tears ran down her face, knowing that whichever way she turned, there would be no going back.

In the end it was her father who pushed her into a decision. From the bedroom across the hall she heard him call weakly, "Mary Catherine, is that you?"

Mary turned a tearful gaze up at her husband. "I'm sorry, Charlie." There was no need to say more. No need for explanations or white lies about how long she intended to stay. Whatever was written in her face she saw mirrored in all its terrible anguish on Charlie's.

He wouldn't beg, she knew. He had too much pride. He stared at her in silence, his throat working. When he finally spoke, he sounded on the verge of tears. "I'll call you in a day or two, okay? We'll talk then."

She nodded. But they both knew that every day she remained under this roof would be another nail in the coffin of the life they'd foolishly imagined they could build together.

Even so, listening to his heavy tread on the stairs, she wanted to run after him, reassure him that she'd be back—in a day or two, as soon as the baby was well enough. As soon as she herself was rested (at the moment Mary felt as though she could have slept straight through into next year). And she *would* have gone after him, yes, despite everything, if she'd known then what was in store: that she would spend the next thirty years, nearly twice as long as her entire life until now, running after Charlie in her mind, endlessly running down those stairs without reaching bottom, forever chasing the dream of what their life might have been.

Burns Lake, 1999

# Chapter One

Noelle had rehearsed for days what she would say, the exact words that would set her free. Not just from her marriage but from the sense of obligation she now viewed as somewhat foolish, like her diamond ring that snagged on sweaters and pantyhose, and lately, because she'd lost so much weight, had a habit of turning on her finger. Once, when smoothing lotion over her leg, she'd even cut herself with it. A tiny cut, but it had drawn blood nonetheless.

Now, though, face-to-face with her husband, none of those carefully worded phrases came to mind. Only the plain hard fact of the matter.

"I'm not coming with you, Robert." She spoke as calmly as she could with her heart thudding like bricks being dropped one by one from a great height. "In fact, I'm not coming home at all."

They were standing outside her grandmother's house, where she'd been staying for the past three weeks, since Nana got home from the hospital. But Noelle had run out of excuses. Also, there was Emma to think of. Their daughter deserved to know the truth.

"That's ridiculous. Of course you are." Robert spoke sternly, as if to an employee who had stepped out of line. He glanced in irritation at his watch. "Now come on, get your things. You're supposed to be packed already."

"Did you hear what I said? Are you even listening?" Noelle felt suddenly panic-stricken, as if at any moment she would be sucked like a twig into the swirling eddy of his insistence. "I know this was only supposed to be temporary, but I—I changed my mind."

Now Robert was stepping back to eye her warily, a tiny dent of uncertainty marring his perfect Simonized exterior. He stood with his back to the boxwood hedge: a well-built man in his forties who appeared taller than his actual height of five feet eleven inches, with thick maple-brown hair that fell in a boyish swath over his forehead, reminiscent of JFK, and pale blue eyes that seemed to generate a cold heat, like the sunlight reflecting off his silver Audi 100 parked a few feet away. He was dressed in khakis and a lightly starched blue shirt open at his throat and rolled up over muscular forearms, yet there was a contrived look to it all, as if he were aiming merely for the appearance of being relaxed and casual, traits that no one who knew him well would ever associate with Robert Van Doren. Even the gray streaking his temples seemed the work of a skillful makeup artist.

One hand was in his pocket; the other clenched about his key ring. She watched him flex his fist repeatedly, knuckles tightening, easing, tightening. The tic in his right eye, which most of the time he managed to control, was acting up. It made her think of a twitching cat's tail—a reminder that with Robert you never knew quite what to expect. It was how he maintained the upper hand with friends and enemies alike: by keeping them off-balance.

"You're not serious." A smile flickered at the corners of his mouth, then died. "This is a joke, right?"

She drew in a breath that felt like something she'd swallowed that wouldn't go down. The sultry July heat seemed to close about her like a sweaty fist. "Eventually, of course, I'll be getting my own place. But for now I think it's best that Emma and I stay here."

There was a beat of silence in which the only sound was the chirring of insects and the faint chug-chug-chug of a sprinkler down the block. Then Robert spoke. "Is it Jeanine? Are you still punishing me for that? I told you. I'm not *seeing* her. I was never seeing her. It was just that one time. A mistake. One lousy mistake."

He was lying, of course. She could see it in his eyes. He'd been sleeping around long before she'd caught him at it. It was almost corny enough to make her laugh: a cheap affair with his twenty-two-year-old secretary. But hadn't she once been in the same position? A girl fresh out of college dazzled by her handsome, much older boss. Besides, Jeanine was no longer the point. She was just the excuse Noelle had needed to break loose. In a funny way she was *grateful* to Jeanine.

"It's not just Jeanine," she said.

"Everything was fine before that," he insisted.

"For *you,* maybe."

It wasn't just their marriage. It was the house on Ramsey Terrace and the Filipino maid who came four times a week. It was the country club and the Junior League teas, the committees and fund-raisers, the endless rounds of cocktail parties.

"Did the old lady put you up to this?" Robert's eyes narrowed.

"Nana had nothing to do with it." Her grandmother had never much liked Robert, it was true, but she was old-fashioned when it came to marriage. "In fact, she said I should talk it over with you before I made up my mind."

"It sounds as if your mind is already made up."

"Yes." She swallowed hard. "Yes, it is."

She dropped her gaze to his long shadow slicing the driveway into two neat halves. Late-afternoon sunlight lay in tiger stripes over the grass beyond, and the summer heat seemed to press down like a hot jar. Birds called from the feeder and she caught the flash of a cardinal out of the corner of her eye. When she looked back up at Robert, she was shocked to see that there were tears in his eyes.

"Jesus." He exhaled through his teeth, a faint whistling sound. "Jesus, Noelle, how the hell did it come to this?"

How indeed? When eight years ago her first thought each morning upon waking was, *How did I get so lucky?* Shy, skinny Noelle Jeffers, still a virgin at twenty-one, how had *she* managed to catch the eye of her much-sought-after boss? A man who might have been a movie star for all the whispered speculation around the office, all the hearts that beat faster when he was near. She remembered clearly the first time he'd stopped to chat with her. Her pulse had raced, and she'd become so tongue-tied she was certain she'd made a fool of herself. But two days later he'd asked her out to dinner.

"I don't know. Maybe we got off on the wrong foot to start with," she hedged. "I was so young...." Making excuses was easier than casting blame, she'd found.

"We didn't get off on the wrong foot. I did a stupid thing, that's all." He corrected her, almost angrily.

"I'm not punishing you, Robert." Maybe she owed him Jeanine. After all, it couldn't have been easy for him those first few years, living with a drunk. But that was beside the point.

"Really? Because that's what it feels like." There it was again, that nasty, grating edge, like a rusty tin can poking up from a neatly tended flower bed.

"I can't help that." In her head she heard the clipped no-nonsense voice of Penny Cuthbertson, her therapist at Hazelden: *Keep in mind, Noelle, it's far more difficult to reclaim power than to hold on to it in the first place.*

But Noelle couldn't remember a time when she'd taken a stand against Robert. From the very beginning he'd been in charge. First as her boss, then as her husband. She'd wanted the wedding ceremony to be held at St. Vincent's, but Robert had insisted on a grand outdoor affair at the country club instead. And when she was pregnant with Emma, he wouldn't let her near kindly old Dr. Matthews, who'd looked after her practically since she was a baby herself. (Never mind that the high-priced obstetrician in Schenectady was off skiing in Aspen when she went into labor.) Even when her drinking got so bad she could no longer hide it, Robert had stepped to the fore. He knew someone on the board at Hazelden, an old crony from Stanford. Within hours a room was available.

But now *she* was taking the lead, and Robert wasn't happy about it. Noelle could almost feel the seismic upheaval taking place in his mind, and as he moved toward her, she automatically took a step backward, edging off the driveway onto the lawn. In eight years of marriage he'd never once raised a hand to her but for reasons she couldn't quite put her finger on, she was afraid. She realized now that she'd always been a little bit afraid of her husband. Maybe that's why she had never dared to challenge him; she didn't *want* to know what he was capable of.

The hand he lifted, though, was conciliatory. "Noelle, please. If you don't care what it'll do to me, to us, think about Emma." His voice was low, cajoling.

She felt a hot flare of outrage. "Don't you *dare* drag Emma into this. That's not fair."

"Is it fair to tear a family apart?"

Suddenly Noelle felt tired. Her head had begun to throb. "Let's call it a draw, okay? It's not you. It's not me. It's everything. Maybe Jeanine was just the straw that broke the camel's back."

"It's not too late. We could start over."

She shook her head. "Oh, Robert, you know I was never cut out for that lifestyle. All those parties and committees. If I'd had to listen to Althea Whitehead drop one more mention of her ski lodge in Telluride, I think I would have screamed." She didn't add that her old friends from school, girls she'd practically grown up with, weren't exactly comfortable with her role as Mrs. Van Doren either. Over the years they'd drifted away, one by one.

He shot her a withering look. "How do you think my dad built our business? Working nine to five like the poor slobs punching time clocks? He threw parties, joined organizations, invited the right people to dinner. It's no different now. You think I'd have gotten the variances for Cranberry Mall without knowing Carl Devlin's golf handicap or that Reese Braithwaite prefers Habana Gold Sterlings to Honduran Excaliburs?"

"Stop." She put her hands over her ears. "Just *stop*."

Robert abruptly fell silent, scrubbing his face with a hand that appeared less than steady. He looked defeated all of a sudden. "Christ, Noelle, what do you want from me? Do you want me to get down on my hands and knees and beg?"

Noelle thought for a moment. What exactly

41

*did* she want from him? Suddenly she knew. "I want a divorce."

His mouth hardened, and he stared suspiciously at this new, possibly dangerous entity that had taken the place of his formerly quiescent wife. When he spoke, all pretense at cajoling had been dropped. His voice was harsh with controlled fury.

"Do what you want," he snarled, jabbing a finger at her, "but don't think for one minute I'm going to let you have Emma. I'll fight you, Noelle. I'll do whatever it takes." He loomed close, his face mere inches from hers. His right eyelid was twitching uncontrollably, and she thought of Dorian Gray, a handsome man whose real face, hidden in the attic, was monstrous. "You think any judge in his right mind would give *you* custody? A woman everybody knows is a drunk?"

Noelle felt the blood drain from her face. He was standing so close she could see the hairs in the nostrils of his perfect aristocratic nose, the tiny scar on his chin where his older brother had accidentally struck him with a hockey stick when Robert was ten. And those eyes, pale blue with a rim of black around the pupils, eyes that seemed to stare fixedly, like those of a Siberian husky. For a moment she was certain he *would* hit her.

She felt a flash of anger, cold and invigorating. It took all her control not to lash back, remind him it had been six years since her last drink, and not even six months since she'd caught him in the arms of another woman. That would have been giving Robert exactly what he wanted, the battle he was far better equipped to wage than she was.

She forced herself to reason with him instead. "You'd only be using her to get back at me, and—and I know you wouldn't do that to Emma. You're a good father, Robert. You'll still see her. We'll work something out."

For a long moment his expression remained stony. Then all at once it seemed to collapse inward. He blinked, rocking back on his heels. The fist in which his key ring was clutched unfurled slowly. He stared down at his open palm in wonder almost. Even from where she stood, Noelle could see the red welts in his palm where the keys had bitten into it.

"You're right," he said. "God, Noelle, I'm sorry. So sorry." Covering his face, he began to weep softly. She'd never seen him cry, not like this, and it stunned her into touching his arm lightly in sympathy. When he lifted his head, his pale eyes were bloodshot, his misery starkly written in a face filled with self-loathing. "It's all my fault. I screwed up. You have every right to hate me."

"I don't hate you," she told him, her own throat tightening.

He stared at her with that awful bleak expression, pleading softly, "Can I ask just one favor? Will you give me that much?"

She waited in silence, not quite trusting him.

"Have dinner with me tomorrow night. I'll reserve a table at the Stone Mill," he continued in a rush. "We'll talk about Emma, what's best for her. That's all, I promise. Like you said, we're her parents, both of us. Nothing can ever change that."

Noelle hesitated. She didn't doubt he truly cared for Emma. And if he was as sincere as he seemed, she owed it to her daughter to accept his invitation. At the same time a voice inside her whispered, *It's a trap. Don't fall for it.*

But that was silly, she told herself. What harm could there be in two civilized adults sitting down to a meal? They'd be in a public place, and if things turned nasty, she could always leave. Besides, Robert was far too careful to risk such a scene.

*That's what lawyers are for,* persisted the voice. *Can you honestly believe he'll give you what you want?*

Maybe not. But it was too soon for lawyers. How could it hurt at least to hear what he had to say? She searched his face for an indication, however small, that she was being set up. But the only thing she saw was raw, naked appeal.

Nevertheless, it was with great reluctance that Noelle found herself answering, "I'll see if I can get Aunt Trish to baby-sit. Nana's not really up to it yet."

Robert gave a wan smile. "I'll pick you up around seven, okay?"

"No, I'll meet you there." *If I take my own car, I'll be able to escape, at least.* For some reason the thought did little to dispel her uneasiness.

The Stone Mill, situated along Route 30 about five miles north of town, was where Robert had taken her on their first date. Over the years they'd eaten there often, and though she preferred its cuisine to the country club's, Noelle found it equally pretentious. Pulling into the tree-lined parking lot, she saw the usual assortment of late-model luxury cars, their hood ornaments twinkling like so many miniaturized trophies in the glow of the fairy lights strung from the wisteria over the mill's recessed entrance.

As she stepped into the vestibule, the hum of conversation floated toward her. She glanced about at the rough stone walls and low-beam ceilings lit by candlelight and nodded to an older couple seated at a table near the captain's station, a stout gray-haired man and his equally stout wife. They looked vaguely familiar. Where did she know them from? Robert would have been annoyed at her for not remembering, she thought.

She spotted him at a table by the window. Catching sight of her at the same time, he rose and began winding his way toward her. Despite herself, she was struck by how handsome he looked. His tailored charcoal suit hugged his muscled frame like a glove. His brown hair shone with gold and silver highlights as he ducked to clear a spotlit beam. And she wasn't the only one who'd noticed. Heads turned to follow his progress. Eyes flickered with admiration and envy.

For a brief moment Noelle felt as she had on their first date: privileged merely to be in the company of such a man. As if she, too, were bathed in the glow he cast.

But she knew what the others didn't: that the bright charm could be flicked off as abruptly as a light switch, followed by either silent coldness or a stream of criticism. Her dress was too short or too long. She was wearing too much makeup. At the party the night before she'd talked too much or hadn't been lively enough. And for God's sake, wasn't there something she could do about that *hair?*

"Grant, how's the rib eye tonight?" Robert stopped to greet the mayor, Grant Iverson, clapping him on the shoulder in a gesture of easy familiarity that wasn't lost on the diners who glanced their way. Iverson and his blade-thin blond wife, Nancy, beamed up at him, their smiles stretching to include Noelle.

"Bloody, the way I like it." The mayor chuckled, a stocky man in his early fifties with heavy jowls bracketing a toothy grin who reminded her of the Cowardly Lion in *The Wizard of Oz.* He nodded in her general direction. "Noelle, nice to see you out and about. Robert tells me you've been under the weather lately."

"Actually, it's my grandmother—"

But he was already turning back to Robert. Dropping his voice, he growled, man to man,

"Out celebrating, eh? You son of a gun. You actually pulled it off."

Robert shrugged modestly. "It could have gone either way."

"Like hell." Iverson winked broadly.

Nancy lifted her glass, square-tipped ruby fingernails twinkling against the deeper hue of the wine, wine that, in the old days, Noelle would have had to put away a whole bottle of to get through an evening like this. "Here's to the man of the hour."

Noelle fixed a smile in place, as if she'd known what they were talking about. Clearly some business deal had been successfully concluded. With Robert, there was always a deal in the works, one that depended on long-standing relationships with men such as Iverson, who, let's face it, wouldn't be sitting here—not on his fat expense account as mayor, at least—had it not been for the Van Dorens' support.

As they sat down at their table, she glanced out the window at the floodlit water sliding smooth as practiced lies over the millrace. She could see her reflection in the glass—hollowed eyes, a sharp-boned face surrounded by a cloud of black hair that seemed to flow out into the darkness beyond. Noelle offered up a tiny prayer: *God, help me get through this.*

"What was that all about?" she asked, arranging her features in what she hoped was a pleasantly neutral expression.

"The new superhighway. They voted on it up in Albany, just this afternoon as a matter of fact. Twenty million in state funds, with tax incentives for local linkups." He grinned in triumph.

"Congratulations," she murmured. She didn't have to ask to know the Burns Lake exit would be within shouting distance of the mall he was building.

"Iverson's in pig heaven just *thinking* of all those tax dollars. Look at him." She caught a note of scorn in his voice for the man whom moments before he'd been heartily clapping on the shoulder.

Noelle wondered what her father's reaction would be. Out of respect for her, Dad had been fairly restrained in the pieces the *Register* ran on Van Doren & Sons. But their brand of progress—the kind that razed historic buildings and erected lakeside condos and malls where unspoiled tracts of woodland had stood—had been chafing at him for years, she knew. Her divorce would be just the excuse he needed to begin firing with both barrels.

The waiter appeared, a slender young man with a crew cut so blond she could see the pink outline of his scalp. They both ordered their usual: diet Pepsi for her, scotch and soda for Robert.

While they were waiting for their drinks, Robert reached across the table and took Noelle's hand. "I would have ordered champagne, but it's never the same drinking it alone."

She frowned and withdrew her hand to fuss with her napkin. Why was Robert waxing nostalgic about her drinking? He'd poured her into bed too many times to remember those days fondly. And why was he acting as if yesterday's conversation hadn't even taken place?

She forced herself to hold his gaze. "This morning Emma asked how much longer we were staying with Nana, and I told her the truth: that we weren't going home."

The smile dropped from Robert's face. He picked up the knife beside his plate, idly examining it. Pinpoints of reflected light spun and flashed on its polished blade. "What did she say to that?"

"She was afraid you'd be mad." Noelle's throat tightened as she recalled her five-year-old daughter peering up at her in confusion, blue eyes filled with tears.

He cast her a sharp glance. "Christ, Noelle," he swore softly. "What did you expect? Did you think I'd be *happy* about all this?"

She hesitated before replying, "No, of course not. But is it really that big of a change? We hardly ever saw you as it was."

"What are you suggesting?"

"I'm not suggesting anything."

He glared at her, then let out a breath. "Okay, you have a point. I know I haven't been around much lately. Between the mall and Sandy Creek...well, you know how it is." He spread his hands in a helpless gesture. "But dammit, you're right, I *should* have been paying more attention to you and Em. Then maybe I wouldn't have had to get hit over the head to be reminded of what really counts."

His homespun humility was almost sickening in its insincerity.

She refrained from asking how much of his precious time had been taken up with Jeanine. Coolly she said, "Why don't we stick to discussing Emma?"

He sat back, clearly put out that she wasn't falling for the Hallmark routine. "What did you have in mind?"

"How does two nights a week and every other weekend sound?"

"Just dandy. For *you*." Robert bared his teeth in a cheerless smile.

Noelle shivered as if caught in a sudden draft. When their drinks arrived, she couldn't bring herself to pick up the chilled glass. Gathering her courage instead, she said, "I'm sure we'll want to discuss this with lawyers at some point. I just thought, well, for the time being..."

She dropped her eyes to the candle flickering in its ruby glass holder. It reminded her of when she was little, praying in church. Her prayer had never varied: that one day her mother would be there to tuck her in *every* night, not just on the rare occasions when Mary was around. It wasn't like that with her and Emma. Noelle felt a pang at the thought of being separated from her daughter, even for one night.

"You're right about lawyers—it's much too soon for that. So I guess that doesn't leave me much choice. If I have any chance of winning you back, I'll have to go along." His expression was smooth, considering. She must have looked surprised because he gave a short, mirthless laugh. "Were you afraid I'd make a scene? Really, darling, you know me better than that."

"Let's just say you're used to getting your way." It wasn't an insult. Robert took pride in the fact.

"I have no intention of shirking my responsibility toward either you or my daughter." He lifted his scotch tumbler to his mouth, eyeing her over its rim.

She felt her neck and face grow warm. Money was a touchy subject for her, mainly because she had none of her own. Noelle sometimes thought she'd been happiest as a teenager, working summers and on school holidays at the *Register*. But what had been the good of all those high hopes of a career in journalism when all she had to show for it was a handful of freelance articles published in magazines no one had even heard of?

"You've always been generous." She wasn't gilding the lily about that, at least.

"You're the mother of my child. Nothing could ever change that." He picked up his menu. "Shall we order now…or after you've checked up on Emma?"

She hesitated, uncertain how to respond. Was this a test of some kind? Noelle chafed at the idea that she had anything to prove as far as her mothering was concerned. On the other hand, Robert was used to her being overprotective—the legacy of her own mother's benign neglect, she supposed.

"Aunt Trish is baby-sitting," she said. "I'm sure everything's fine."

"I'm sure it is, too."

But the seed had been planted, and after a minute or so Noelle began to grow restless. "Maybe it wouldn't hurt. Just a quick call to say good-night."

She excused herself, but when she phoned home, it was her grandmother who answered. Nana reported that Trish and Emma were engaged in a heated game of old maid. Emma of course would be up way past her bedtime, but that was Aunt Trish for you. Noelle had to smile. In some ways her aunt was as much a kid as Emma.

By the time she returned to the table, Robert was already on his second scotch and soda. She hadn't touched her Pepsi and reached for it now.

"I should have saved my quarter." Noelle smiled, sipping her drink. "Emma was too busy to come to the phone. It looks as if my aunt is turning her into quite the little card sharp."

"She's a smart kid."

"Too smart for her own good sometimes." Noelle was remembering how when Emma was only three, she'd figured out a way to climb onto the kitchen counter where the cookie jar was stored: by pulling open the oven door to use as a stepstool. "She's a bit of a handful for Nana right now."

"Knowing your grandmother, she'd be the last to admit it." He chuckled. "Speaking of which, what's the latest word from the good doctor?"

She felt a prickle of irritation, not liking the tone with which he referred to Hank Reynolds—as if a country doctor were beneath his consideration. "She's doing about as well as can be expected." Noelle hadn't told him of her grandmother's decision to refuse further treatment. He wouldn't understand...and probably wouldn't care.

Several minutes later another waiter, a sallow-faced middle-aged man with an elaborate comb-over, appeared to take their orders. As Noelle peered at the menu in the dim light, its spidery print swam before her. She blinked, struggling to bring it into focus. All at once she felt light-headed, tipsy almost. A wave of panic, a knee-jerk reaction from the years when a night out had been little more than an excuse to get drunk, swept over her.

"Darling, are you all right?" Robert's face loomed close.

"Right as rain." One of Nana's favorite expressions, which struck her as silly all of a sudden. What was right about rain? It was cold and spoiled everything; it made her hair frizz. She began to giggle uncontrollably, clapping a hand over her mouth.

Robert eyed her with the same patient, long-suffering expression she remembered from the old days, but there was something different about it now, something she couldn't quite put her finger on. Absently she rubbed her arm, recalling his steely grip on her elbow, the thousand and one times he'd had to steer her out of a restaurant or party, all the while smiling and chatting as if nothing were out of the ordinary.

"Are you sure? You look pale," he said.

The room reeled. She had to clutch hold of the table to keep from tipping out of her chair. "It must be something I ate." But lunch was hours ago, and she hadn't had a bite since.

"Either that, or a bug you picked up. Half my crew is out sick with the flu." He covered her hand with his, and this time she didn't pull away. The room was revolving slowly, dreamily, like a carousel. "Come on, I'll take you home. Can you make it to the car?"

"I—I think so." But when she stood up, the floor rocked beneath her, and she immediately plopped back down again. She leaned over and whispered fiercely, "Robert, what's wrong? What's happening to me?"

"You'll be fine. We've got to get you home, that's all."

She nodded, her head bobbing like a balloon on the end of a string. It dawned on her that she'd heard those words before. It was exactly what Robert used to say when she was too drunk to manage on her own. Yet she hadn't touched a drop.

*He slipped something in my drink. He must have.*

In some small, still corner of her mind an alarm bell was going off. She opened her mouth to call for help, but it was too late. The room appeared to be closing in on her, as if she were viewing it through a rapidly narrowing lens. The light was fading as well, leaving only a velvety grayness pricked with starry points of light. The last thing Noelle saw, as she slipped from her chair onto the floor, was the all-too-familiar look of disgust on the middle-aged waiter's sallow, peering face.

# Chapter Two

"Mary, we've got the Channel Two van pulling up front, CNN at the door, and a lady with her head in the sink screaming that her scalp is on fire."

The cell phone sizzled with static, Brittany's voice fading in and out like the distant chirping of some frantic bird. Mary indulged in a moment's worth of panic. But when she spoke, her voice was calm. "Can you hold them off, Brit? Five minutes, that's all I ask. I'm at Park and Fifty-ninth, and it looks like the traffic is finally moving."

"Will do." Brittany's cynical laugh broke free of the interference. "Hey, I just flashed on tomorrow's *Post*. SOCIALITE SUES SALON. Talk about publicity!"

"Bite your tongue." Mary clicked off and jammed the phone into her outsize Prada bag. Half a block ahead the traffic light flashed to red. Leaning forward, she shouted over the radio tuned to the Yankees game, "Driver, let me off at the corner. I'll walk from here."

*Run* was more like it, but wasn't that the story of her life? The salon was at Madison and Sixty-first—one long block and two short ones. If the lights were with her, she'd make it in less time than it would take the cabbie to find out if Mike Stanton was going to strike out Sammy Sosa in the bottom of the eighth.

She was rounding the corner onto Madison, panting hard and praying her antiperspirant would hold out, when she spotted the Channel 2 News van. Her racing heart carried her the last dozen yards in what felt like a single bound.

Ernesto Garmendia was the hottest hairstylist around and the current flavor of the month; she'd already booked him for makeover segments on *Today* and *Live with Regis and Kathie Lee*. But negative publicity on this gig could make him a pariah—for which *she* would ultimately be held responsible. It had been Mary's bright idea, after all, to celebrate the opening of the uptown branch of his chic SoHo salon, Ne Plus Ultra, with an all-day "hair-a-thon"—open house to anyone willing to donate two hundred dollars for a haircut, with proceeds going to St. Bartholomew's pediatric burn unit. Mary had gotten Petrossian to supply caviar and blinis, and Sokolin & Co. the champagne. There was even a door prize: two tickets to the Andreas Schiff concert at Carnegie Hall.

Everything was set, the date locked in on her calendar. Then two days ago an author client, on the road promoting his somewhat unflattering Elvis Presley biography, had arrived in Memphis to find scores of angry Elvis fans picketing the store at which a signing had been scheduled. Several TV stations had canceled as well. Mary had had to fly out at the last minute to smooth her client's ruffled feathers and calm skittish producers, after which her return flight had been delayed, putting her into JFK with less than an hour to spare before Ernesto's event. Now this...

At the red-carpeted entrance Mary pushed past the crush of press and paparazzi gathered in anticipation of the celebrities due to arrive any minute, reporters whom Mary normally had to beg and cajole into covering an event, and whom her assistant, standing guard outside the plate glass door, was at the moment fending off. Brittany stood out like a torch amid the teeming horde, her pale cheeks flushed and her red hair flaming in the harsh glare of camera flashes and handheld lights. When she spotted Mary elbowing her way through the crush, her look of intense relief said it all: The marines had landed.

Mary clapped a cheerful expression in place. Holding a hand up to the reporters, she called out brightly, "Be patient, guys! Just two minutes, I promise!" Turning to her assistant, whose pretty young face wore the sheen of desperation, she whispered fiercely, "Hold them off a little while longer. I'll see what's going on."

Inside, Mary encountered a scene that would have struck her as funny had it been in a movie. A plump middle-aged woman held center stage in the elegant Louis Quinze-outfitted salon, her wet hair dripping onto the short black kimono cinched about her ample waist. She was shrieking at the top of her lungs.

"You call this a perm? I have third-degree burns on my scalp! I know lawyers who sue for less. You'll be hearing from mine, don't kid yourself." She waggled a crimson talon at the staff lined up motionless before a bank of baroque gilt mirrors.

Mary darted a glance at Ernesto, who was doing his best to calm the woman but who clearly had his dander up. His narrow nose was flared, and one hand rested on a slim hip that jutted in a stance bordering on insolent. "Señora, what you say ees...*impossible*. Never, never, never would such a theeng happen in my salon!"

Mary felt a fresh jolt of adrenaline kick in. If this tempest weren't brought under control, *immediately*, the lady's hair wouldn't be the only thing burned. At the end of it Ernesto would be lucky to have a single client left, and as for the account, well, Mary could kiss it good-bye.

But twenty years in public relations had taught her a thing or two, all of which could be contained in a single rule of thumb: In a world where Murphy's Law reigned, be prepared for all contingencies at all times.

She turned to the young woman tending the buffet table and ordered crisply, "Take some of this food to the reporters out front. Come back for seconds, if necessary." The girl, a waifish blonde, shot Mary a nervous look, then immediately snatched up trays of blinis and prosciutto-wrapped asparagus spears and began making her way to the door.

While the ravening pack outside was being mollified, Mary sailed over to the furious client, politely but insistently pulling her aside. "I don't believe I've had the pleasure." She smiled warmly, putting out her hand. "Mary Quinn. Quinn Communications."

"I, uh, Harriet Gordon." The woman was startled into shaking her hand. Yet her small, close-set eyes remained suspicious, and her short yellow hair sticking up like wet feathers brought to mind a timeworn expression: madder than a wet hen.

Mary guided her to a relatively quiet corner, where a gilt settee upholstered in bottle-green velvet was tucked beside an antique glass vitrine displaying hair products. "I can't tell you how sorry I am about all this. We'll make it up to you, of course."

"Well, I don't see *how*." Harriet Gordon's indignation, momentarily diverted, was once more gathering steam. "Money isn't going to buy me a new head of hair, is it? Look, you can see for yourself, it's absolutely ruined!" Grabbing a wet tuft, she held it out for inspection.

*Money won't buy you credibility either,* Mary thought. She doubted the woman had suffered anything worse than a mild burning sensation. Harriet Gordon, her instincts told her, was causing a scene because she knew that today, of all days, she could get away with it. At some point in her unhappy life someone had done her a terrible wrong, and now the whole world was going to pay.

Mary was familiar with the score. The thought of her mother flashed through her mind. Doris would have had a field day with something like this. Only with her, there'd be no way to make it up, no pound of flesh meaty enough to satisfy.

"You're absolutely right to be upset." Mary gave the woman's arm a sympathetic pat. "But I believe it's in both our interests to keep this as quiet as possible, don't you?"

Harriet Gordon eyed her warily. "I don't see how it would benefit *me*. Those reporters outside, they ought to be told what goes on in here. People ought to be *warned*."

Mary felt her panic mount and flashed a quick smile to cover it up. "Harriet. May I call you Harriet? I'm in public relations. Believe me, if there's one thing I know, it's the press. Ernesto isn't the only one who would look bad. I wouldn't be at all surprised if one of those gung ho reporters accused you of snatching medicine from some poor sick child." She shook her head as if in disgust at such sleazy tactics.

The woman's mouth fell open. "Why, of all the—"

"You know how things get twisted, this being a charity event and all," Mary rushed to add. "We've all got a lot invested, not just in making the salon a success, but in helping those kids at St. Bartholomew's. Did you know that many of them are now homeless? It's just so tragic. We really should do everything we can."

Harriet's mouth snapped shut. She blinked several times in rapid succession before peering closely at Mary as if to make certain she wasn't being had. Evidently satisfied, she cleared her throat. "Well," she said with considerably less vehemence. "Well, when you put it that way."

Quickly, before the woman could change her mind, Mary fished a business card from her purse. "Call me at my office on Monday. We'll talk then, okay?" Today was Saturday. That would give her the rest of the weekend to come up with some sort of compensation— free passes to a movie premiere perhaps?

Even so, it wasn't until she was ushering Hurricane Harriet out the door, laden with free hair products, that Mary breathed a sigh of relief. Her timing couldn't have been more perfect, as it turned out. No sooner had the obnoxious woman stepped onto the pavement than a black stretch limousine pulled up to the curb. Diverted by the promise of a celebrity sighting, the press rushed past Harriet to swarm about the limo.

Inside, the orchestra of blow dryers had struck up again. Above their furious whirring, Mary could hear Ernesto venting loudly to someone in Spanish. Two women seated before the mirrors were laughing as if the whole event had all been a skit staged for their benefit. A champagne cork popped. Beautiful young women in iridescent blue silk tops and black capri slacks began circulating trays of champagne and caviar.

Hours later, when Mary finally returned home, after treating her somewhat frazzled assistant to dinner at Jojo's, she was so exhausted she could hardly see straight. Dropping her purse on the table by the door, she eyed her answering machine, its red light blinking, as she would a small animal that might bite. She couldn't bear the thought of Simon's static-riddled voice calling from some airport. Or to listen to one more client bitch about everything she should be doing that she supposedly wasn't. Even her accountant calling to report that this year's estimated quarterly taxes wouldn't bankrupt her after all would have been too much to digest.

Mary drifted down the hallway and through the living room, hardly glancing at the spectacular East River view afforded by her thirty-fourth-floor penthouse. In the bedroom she stripped off her sage linen suit and cream silk blouse, her slip and panty hose, and finally her bra and panties, leaving them puddled on the carpet like stepping-stones leading to the king-size bed, on which she stretched out and promptly fell into a deep sleep.

*I*t seemed no more than a minute or two had passed before she was jolted awake by the phone. She fumbled for it, blinking groggily at the clock on the nightstand. Six-thirty. For the love of Christ, who would have the nerve to wake her this early on Sunday? Simon? She felt a flicker of anticipation before recalling that her boyfriend was in Seattle, where it was even earlier. Besides, he wasn't the type for such impromptu gestures. Simon was an investment adviser for blue-chip firms; that alone said it all.

She snatched up the receiver. "H'lo."

"Mary Catherine, is that you?"

No one but her mother called her by her full name anymore. Mary dragged herself upright, pulling the covers up over her bare breasts. Doris wouldn't approve of her sleeping in the nude, she thought. Not that she'd have any way of knowing. Besides, it certainly wasn't for show. Mary couldn't remember the last time Simon had spent the night; he was always off in Boston...or Chicago...or San Francisco.

"Who else would it be?" Mary couldn't keep the irritation from her voice. Wasn't that just like her mother? Not calling for weeks on end, even to thank her for the roses on her birthday. Then pouncing out of the blue. *No doubt hoping to catch me in the act of condemning my immortal soul to hell.* As if she weren't already condemned for all eternity.

63

"There's no need to get snippy. This isn't exactly a social call," Doris rebuked her, but her voice lacked its usual bite. She sounded old and tired.

At once Mary felt contrite. Her mother might be a pain in the ass, but she'd been through a lot lately—two surgeries in the last six months alone, not to mention the round of chemo and radiation. Something must be wrong. Why else would she be calling at this hour? Mary was suddenly wide-awake.

"Sorry, Mama. You woke me out of a sound sleep, that's all. What's up?"

Mary was aware of her heart beating very fast and the faint sighing of breath in her ear. Then her mother's voice, thready and querulous. "I'm fine. It's your *daughter*. Noelle." As if she needed to be reminded of her daughter's name.

"She's all right, isn't she?" Mary tensed, clutching the sheet about her. Maybe it was having been raised Catholic, but there was a part of her that lived in constant dread of her daughter's being taken from her—as punishment for her having been such a lousy mother.

There was a brief pause. Then Doris reported dully, "You'd better come see for yourself. She's passed out cold on the sofa."

Mary drew in a sharp breath, as if the mattress had been snatched out from under her. "Are you saying she's *drunk?*"

"That's not all." Doris hesitated, then said, "Emma's gone. Robert took her with him

64

last night after he dropped Noelle off. *Dumped* her off, I should say," she sniffed.

Mary shivered as if the air conditioner had been left on overnight. But the room was warm, sticky even, promising yet another day of temperatures in the low eighties. "I'm on my way...soon as I can throw some clothes on," she said, her feet already on the floor, rooting blindly for her slippers. It wasn't even light out, and already the day had begun to ebb, slipping from what it might have been into what it was: something she would have to navigate with extreme care.

"Drive safely," Doris cautioned. "We don't need you getting into an accident on top of everything else."

*No, we wouldn't want that,* Mary thought with a twist of old bitterness. *Haven't I caused you enough grief as it is?* It had been thirty years, but when talking to her mother, Mary still had the sense of an eternal, unpayable debt.

Wearily she promised, "Don't worry, I won't go a mile over the limit." What difference would it make? Burns Lake was a good three hours north, and even if she drove like the wind, Noelle was likely to have slept it off by the time she arrived.

The question was, What then? A hangover would be the least of her daughter's problems. Mary knew of her decision to leave Robert, and this certainly wasn't going to make things any easier. Suppose he had no intention of giving Emma back? A hard kernel of dread formed in the pit of her stomach.

Mary stumbled into the bathroom and cranked on the shower. Stepping under the steaming blast, she felt a deep chill that no amount of heat could dispel. Whatever she was walking into, she had a feeling it was going to be a lot more than she'd bargained on.

Mary took the First Avenue bridge to I-87 and drove steadily for two and a half hours until she reached the exit for Route 23. Twenty minutes later she was cutting over onto 145. Four lanes gave way to two, and tollbooths and rest stops to gently sloping hills and sunny pastures where cows and horses grazed. The towns seemed to blend together, each barely distinguishable from the next. Athens. South Cairo. Cairo. Cooksburg. Main streets made up of squat brick buildings interspersed with once-grand Victorians and white steepled churches that might have been built from the same blueprint.

Even the people looked alike from one town to the next: men and women oblivious of current fashion as they strolled to church or to their favorite eatery. Old people sipping coffee out on the porch. Passing through Preston Hollow, she smiled at the sight of a freckle-faced boy fishing from a wooden bridge set smack in the center of town.

At a service station just north of Livingstonville, where she stopped to fill her tank, a paunchy gray-haired man in overalls with a rangy mutt loping at his heels asked if she'd like her oil checked. Taken by surprise, Mary agreed to it, never mind that she'd had the Lexus fully serviced just the week before. Fresh from the city, where such courtesies had died out eons ago, she always needed a day or two to adjust to the fact that in this part of the world, time, though not exactly at a standstill, moved at a different pace.

The knowledge was at once comforting and disquieting. Because the slower pace only seemed to underline how much *she* had changed. Mary felt sure that were she to bump into her teenage self walking down the street, she'd scarcely recognize the girl. *I was so young,* she thought. Playing catch-up with a baby on her hip while her friends toted books and backpacks about college campuses. Rising at dawn to a dirty diaper after a night of studying logarithms and Longfellow, molecular formulas and Melville. And always, always, there was her mother.

She'd thought moving back home was the solution, but she only ended up trading one set of problems for another. *You should have listened to Charlie,* a voice whispered, words that over the years had become a chant. He'd believed in them, believed that if they stuck it out, their fledgling family would survive.

*Charlie.* Even after all these years the thought of him brought a dull pang of regret. Her memories, rather than becoming faded, seemed to have crystallized in some way. Charlie, on their wedding day in his ill-fitting suit, beaming as if he'd just been handed a prize. Charlie, cradling their minutes-old baby in his arms, tears of joy running down his cheeks.

One particular memory stood out from the rest. She would never know if that had been the night Noelle was conceived, but she chose to believe it anyway. For no other reason than that it made sense for something so wondrous to have resulted in their daughter. Mary let her mind drift back to that warm spring night, easily finding the path that had been worn to a groove from the countless times she'd trodden it. She saw herself racing barefoot down the creek bank in the moonlight to meet Charlie. Her heart in her throat, because she'd known perfectly well what was going to happen. The same thing that had happened twice before, once in her bedroom when her family was at church and once in the backseat of Charlie's car. Yet this time was different somehow. Maybe it was the moonlight or maybe the look on Charlie's face: one of love so pure she'd ached to bottle it—like perfume to be savored a dab at a time. *He'd never hurt me,* she'd thought. *No matter what happens, I can always count on that.*

Charlie had spread an old blanket from the trunk of his car beneath a weeping willow that shielded them like a tent fashioned of green lace. Pale light spilled between its drooping branches to dapple the sand with silver dollars. When he pulled her into his arms she was shivering, but Charlie's kisses had been warm and the air filled with the chirping of frogs that seemed to chorus their approval. She couldn't recall either of them removing their clothes; in memory they were always naked: Adam and Eve sprung from the clay. Charlie, a long silver blade in the moonlight, reaching out to smooth the gooseflesh from her bare trembling limbs. She, holding her arms out to let him know that she wasn't shivering out of fear. Though she hadn't known it then, the emotion that filled her like the beating of a thousand wings was desire. Not like the flame that had flared only briefly the first two times, but a grown-up urgency she had no name for.

Charlie, seeming to sense it, took his time. Kissing her until her mouth was tender and swollen before reaching down to stroke between her legs. Mary knew about climaxes from books devoured under the covers at night by flashlight—*Lady Chatterley's Lover* came to mind—and had experienced firsthand what happened with boys. But she herself had never climaxed, unless it had somehow occurred without her knowing it. In the view of the Catholic Church, it was a sin to even touch yourself.

Yet as Charlie continued stroking, the flame leaped higher and higher with each silken brush of his fingers. She found herself greedily arching to meet his hand. Her mouth open and her throat burning from the air sucked in to cool the rising heat. She was scarcely aware of Charlie's hardness pressed against her leg. For the moment the entire universe was contained in the white-hot point, like a star-burst, between her legs. Then she was crying out and Charlie was thrusting into her at the same time, and everything was dissolving into a blur like scenery rushing past the window of a speeding car, and she was...she was...oh yes...no question...oh God...she was climaxing.

Afterward, she collapsed on the blanket, as limp as someone drowning who'd been rescued from the creek. "How...how did you know?" she managed to stammer.

Charlie held her so tightly she imagined him bearing the faint impression of her naked body, like a ghostly thumbprint on a windowpane. "I just did," he whispered.

And that was the essence of Charlie. Somehow he'd known. He'd always known what was right for her...though she hadn't always listened.

The road before her blurred and Mary brushed a tear from her eye. Certainly she didn't feel that way about Simon. Nor had she been inspired to heights of passion by the men with whom she'd fallen in and out of love over the years. She told herself that one's first love is always the sweetest—if they'd met at another point in their lives, it wouldn't have been the same—but she knew better. Charlie was different. He was special. Countless times since then she'd wondered what her life would be like had she made a different choice that long-ago winter day.

Oh, she'd meant to go back, in a day or two or three, but somehow the days had turned into weeks, and the weeks into months. Her mother, though quick to play martyr, had looked after the baby while she earned enough credits to graduate. When Mary took a part-time job at the Hollywood Dress Shop, she told herself it was to set aside a little money so Charlie wouldn't have to break his back working sixty hours a week. They still saw each other, on weekends mostly, but seldom alone. Doris refused to baby-sit just so they could have a couple of hours together. Didn't she have enough on her hands the rest of the time, she complained, looking after a baby and sick husband to boot?

Mary hadn't had the strength to argue. She'd felt too beholden. Also, with her mother there was always a price to pay, and Mary had nothing left to give. So she and Charlie would sit in the living room, playing with the baby, while Doris kept an eye on them by every so often poking her head in as if vaguely searching for something misplaced.

Mostly what they'd talked about was Noelle. How big she was getting, her new trick of pushing herself onto her back, the noises she made that sounded like words. Charlie never spoke about how lonely he was. He didn't have to. It was written all over his face: pride and hurt and longing all wrapped up in a sharp-cornered package. He wouldn't beg, she knew. Mary would have to want him enough to come back on her own.

In the end, though, she didn't have the guts.

Mary remembered vividly the day she

learned he was seeing someone else. Six months after she moved back in with her parents, he took up residence in a rambling Victorian shared with two women and three other guys. There had been nothing romantic with Sally, not at first. That was Charlie's story, anyway, and she believed him. It was the Age of Aquarius after all. People of both sexes roomed together and even slept in the same bed without a thought to where it might lead. But there was Charlie, lonely and at loose ends. Looking back, Mary supposed it was inevitable that he and Sally became lovers, yet the blow nearly crushed her. It was as if a door that had been left open, if only a crack, had been closed forever.

The affair lasted less than a year, but by the time it was over Mary and Charlie were divorced. Then, in the spring of 1973, her father passed away. There was no more talk of her moving out after that; it was just assumed she would stay. In fact, Mary had the uneasy feeling that were she to leave, she'd be robbing her mother in some fundamental way. For though Doris complained about the extra work, bitterly and often, Mary's fall from grace had given her something nearly as precious as the granddaughter she doted on: a cross to bear.

Mary was so lost in thought she almost missed the turnoff for Burns Lake. With scarcely a glance in her rearview mirror at the empty lane behind her, she made a hard right into the exit. Rounding the bend onto Route

30, she was immediately welcomed by a patchwork of cornfields stitched together by the creek that meandered through them like an uneven seam. Along the horizon low green hills shouldered a scattering of clouds in a sky so blue you couldn't look at it without squinting. Minutes later the wheels of her Lexus were bumping over the wooden bridge that spanned the creek into town. Less than half a mile ahead, where the road crooked upward like a beckoning arm, lay the steep hill that climbed up toward Main Street.

*Home,* she thought...whatever that meant.

She rolled her window down, not so much for the breeze as for the familiar smells and sounds indelibly associated in her mind with Burns Lake. New-mown grass and the dry nose-tickling smell of alfalfa; the whirring of insects and friendly chugging of sprinklers. As she passed the Flower Mill on her left, she caught the perfumed scent of the rosebushes bundled in burlap and lined up alongside the greenhouse like bright rows of birthday candles. A farm truck laden with bales of hay was wheezing up the hill ahead of her, spilling bits of straw like confetti in its wake. As she mounted the crest onto Main Street, a familiar sight greeted her: eighty-year-old Elmer Driscoll, in his World War II uniform, standing watch on the lawn of the Golden Meadow Retirement Home and saluting as she drove past.

The sun had risen over the treetops, and the brass spire atop St. Vincent's, taller than all the rest, glittered as if newly minted. Driving slowly through town, she passed the American Legion Hall, with its jauntily fluttering flag and Civil War cannon that had served as a hobbyhorse for generations of children. On either side, squat brick buildings were lent a fleeting majesty by the lambent morning light, and in the town square, the bronze statue of horticulturist Luther Burbank, father of the Burbank potato, which for decades had been a staple crop of the region, gazed serenely from his perch, his hair and beard stained white by the birds that made their nests in the trees overhead.

In the park the playground stood silent at this hour, and with a quickening of anxiety Mary thought of her granddaughter. On her rare visits to Burns Lake, this was where she brought Emma. Her granddaughter especially loved the wooden fortress with its slides and tire swings. Whenever Mary tried to steer her onto what Emma scornfully called the "baby" slides, she would point to the biggest one, saying firmly, "I want to go on *that* one, Grandma."

Mary's chest tightened...as if she, too, were poised on the brink of something steep. What should she do about Noelle? Her daughter's counselor at Hazelden had cautioned against interference, stressing that alcoholics needed to face the consequences of their behavior; it was their only hope of getting sober. But did that mean she was just supposed to stand back while her only child committed slow suicide?

She sighed as she turned onto Bridge Road, plunging into the deep cleft of shade cast by the train trestle. Why did motherhood have to be so bloody complicated? It wasn't just this predicament. It was their whole long and bumpy history. Maybe it had all started when Noelle was a baby with Doris's assuming the role of mother. Or the move to Manhattan when Noelle was ten, a move her daughter had bitterly resented. Whatever the reason, they'd never been what you'd call close. On good terms, yes. But close? No, not really.

Mary made the left onto Larkspur Lane, where even this early in July summer had taken firm hold. The trees formed a canopy of green overhead, and sweet william and impatiens spilled onto sidewalks and walkways. Morning glories crept up over the railings of porches onto which sofas and easy chairs had been dragged to catch whatever breeze there was to be had. The air hummed with the wick-wick-wick of sprinklers. And in the Inklepaughs' garden, it looked as if a good crop of sweet peas and runner beans had established a beachhead. Doris's next-door neighbor would be busy with her canning come August.

Her mother's sturdy clapboard house looked exactly as it had the last time she'd visited, only then the trees had been bare, the lawn brown and crusted with snow. Now, with the maples and elms throwing a spangled light over the lush grass below, and the roses bursting with blooms, it was a Norman Rockwell illustration come to life. Mary half expected a white-haired grandma from central casting to step onto the porch bearing a freshly baked pie.

But when she pulled into the driveway, no one rushed out to greet her. She climbed from the Lexus and stretched to ease her cramped limbs before starting across the still-damp lawn. Mounting the creaky porch steps, she was struck by the unusual silence. At this hour, just past ten, there ought to have been the faint sounds of life stirring inside the house. The rattle of pipes and the hiss of running water, the radio tuned to WMYY.

She rang the doorbell, waiting with heart in throat for her mother to answer. Her response to this house never varied. Poised on its threshold at the end of a long absence, she always felt a conflicting sense of homesickness and despair. Nothing ever changed, but each time she couldn't help feeling she was about to embark on a journey from which there would be no turning back.

She heard footsteps, then the click of the latch. The heavy oak door swung open. An old lady stood framed in the doorway, peering out at her. At first Mary scarcely recognized her own mother. Doris, in her double-knit turquoise slacks and matching floral top, might have stepped off a tour bus filled with a group of similarly dressed seniors on their way to view the Acropolis or Old Faithful. Blinking in the sunlight, she fixed her gaze on Mary as if to get her bearings.

"Hello, Mama." Mary bent to plant a kiss on a dry cheek smelling faintly of talcum—and something else, something faintly and unpleasantly medicinal.

Seeing how much her mother had aged in just the last six months was a shock. Doris's ginger hair was now snow white and her illness had left her frail; the flesh on her face appeared to be melting like tallow from the bones underneath. Only her eyes were the same, sharp and blue as sparks from flint.

"You made good time," she said, stepping aside to let Mary in.

"Luckily there wasn't much traffic." Mary lowered her voice. "Is she awake yet?"

"Just. She's upstairs now trying to get Robert on the phone." Mary caught a flash of worry before her mother's expression settled back into its familiar groove: stoic perseverance mixed with a trace of scorn.

Moving more slowly than usual, with the crabbed gait of someone ailing, Doris led the way down the hall, her rubber-soled shoes squeaking against the old dark-stained floorboards. Mary followed with a knot of trepidation in her stomach. A glance into the darkened living room confirmed that Noelle had indeed spent the night there; the coffee table had been pushed aside, and a blanket was scrunched at one end of the brocade sofa.

In the kitchen Doris retrieved a mug from the drainer on the counter. "You look as if you could use some coffee," she said. "There's milk in the fridge. Help yourself."

"Thanks, but I take it black." It was a little game they played, her mother pretending she didn't know Mary took her coffee black and Mary acting as if Doris had merely forgotten.

She watched her mother fill the mug from the old-fashioned percolator on the stove. The kitchen was as tidy as ever, its speckled green linoleum and beige Formica counters gleaming. Even the souvenir plates on the rail over the table shone as if freshly washed. Noelle must have gone out of her way to keep it nice, knowing how much it meant to her grandmother. Mary felt a tiny stab of unwarranted jealousy.

She sat down at the table by the window. It looked out over the backyard, where an old tire swing hung from the stout branch of a linden tree, its shadow a flattened oval on the scuffed grass below. *Nothing ever changes,* she thought. Even with life as she'd known it about to erupt like a sleeping volcano, her mother moved about the kitchen exactly as she had on any one of a thousand mornings, wiping the stovetop where a few drops of coffee had spilled, carefully rinsing the sponge, then poking a finger into the African violet on the sill to see if it needed watering. Mary had the sudden uneasy sense of her past as something tangible, a book she could open at random, in which the story of her life was written, predetermined and immutable. It must have shown on her face because Doris paused to glance at her curiously as she carried the steaming mug to the table.

"You hungry? I could scramble some eggs."

*How could I possibly eat at a time like this?* Mary

wanted to scream. But all she said was, "No, I'm fine. I'll make myself a sandwich if I get hungry later on." Hearing the creak of floorboards overhead, she froze with the mug halfway to her lips. In a low, fraught voice, she asked, "Did she say anything about what happened last night?"

Doris shook her head. "No, just asked after Emma. When I told her that Robert had her, she went white as a sheet and rushed upstairs to phone him."

She lowered herself carefully into the chair opposite Mary. Sunlight poured in through the gingham curtains, reflecting off the gold crucifix that had snagged on the top button of her blouse. It seemed to wink like an all-knowing eye, reminding Mary that it had been years since she'd been to church. She felt like praying now, getting down on her knees and begging the Lord to make all this go away.

Mary sighed, cradling her mug with both hands. "Has she told him yet—that she's leaving him?"

Doris nodded. "They had dinner together last night to talk over what was best for Emma." Her mouth tightened. "I warned her not to. I had a feeling it would lead to no good. And I was right."

Mary felt a flash of annoyance. That was what counted most, wasn't it? Her mother always had to be right, first and foremost. Well, Doris wasn't the only one with a dim view of Robert. Mary recalled how horrified she'd been nearly nine years ago when Noelle announced that she was engaged...to Corinne's former boyfriend. A man old enough to be her father. A man whom Mary was convinced to this day had somehow pushed her friend into committing suicide.

In the shock of the moment she'd said something that had taken Noelle years to forgive her for. Stunned and disbelieving, Mary had blurted, "You can't be serious! The man's a monster. He'll destroy you, just like he did Corinne."

Her words had been like a sharp instrument puncturing her daughter's bubble. The rosy flush drained from Noelle's cheeks and her eyes glowed unnaturally bright in a face pale as ash. "I don't recall asking your advice," she'd said, her voice cold. "I learned a long time ago that it didn't pay to ask *anything* of you."

Mary's heart ached now with the knowledge that she'd been right all along. Unlike her mother, she'd have given anything to have been proven wrong. For years, she'd noticed how unhappy Noelle was and recently, when Noelle began confiding in her, she'd urged her to—

"He wouldn't even let me speak to her."

Mary swung around in her chair. Her daughter, white as chalk with dark circles under her huge gray-blue eyes, stood barefoot in the doorway. Her curly black hair lay in a tangled skein about her shoulders, and she was still wearing her dress from last night, a light blue silk sheath now hopelessly wrinkled. She glanced at Mary as if only mildly surprised to find her mother, who lived more than a hundred miles away, seated at the kitchen table having coffee with her grandmother.

Mary longed to jump up and embrace her, but something in Noelle's face warned her to stay put. "Oh, honey," she cried softly in dismay.

Noelle spoke as if in a deep trance. "He says I don't *deserve* Emma, that she'll be better off with him." The full weight of it struck home, and she collapsed bonelessly into the chair next to Mary's. Hoarsely she whispered, "He accused me of being drunk last night."

"Were you?" Mary forced herself to ask.

Noelle shot her a look of unadulterated scorn. "Would you believe me if I said no?"

"Of course."

Noelle's hard expression dissolved into one of confusion. "I don't know *what* happened. I started feeling dizzy at the restaurant, and the next thing I knew I was on the floor." She ran a trembling hand over her face. "I can't be sure, but I think Robert might have slipped something into my soda."

Mary had no doubt Robert was capable of such a thing. Even so, the idea was like something out of a soap opera. Sitting in this sunny kitchen with its African violets on the sill and Porky the Pig cookie jar on the counter by the breadbox, she thought it more than a little absurd.

At the same time she was acutely aware that a great deal hinged on her reply. "I wouldn't put it past him," she said crisply. "How do you feel now?"

"Like I got hit over the head with a croquet mallet." Noelle groaned.

"I'll get you some coffee." Mary started to get up, but Noelle's hand shot out with lightning quickness to fasten about her wrist.

It was her haunted eyes, though, that held Mary captive. "I know what it looks like, but you've got to believe me." Noelle's fingers tightened, digging into her flesh. "He *wants* everyone to think I was drunk. It's all part of his scheme."

"What about the police? Do you think it would help if we phoned them?" Even as she said it, Mary was dubious. The deputy sheriff, Wade Jewett, was an old buddy of Robert's.

"I already threatened to do that." Noelle dropped her hand from Mary's wrist and sat back, eyes brimming with unshed tears. "Robert just laughed and told me to call his lawyer. He claims to have gotten a judge to sign an order of protective custody."

Doris bolted upright in her chair. "Why, of all the lowdown, dirty—"

"Do you think he's telling the truth?" Mary interrupted.

"I don't doubt it for an instant. He planned the whole thing. He set the trap. And I—I walked right into it with my eyes open." Noelle's shoulders slumped, and she buried her face in her hands. When she lifted her head, her cheeks were wet with tears.

"You'll need a lawyer of your own," Mary told her.

Noelle's expression was dismal. "The only

lawyers I know are the ones who work for Robert." She caught her lower lip between her teeth, frowning in anger, not just at Robert but at her own naïveté.

Mary suddenly remembered her old friend Lacey Buxton. They'd fallen out of touch, but she'd heard Lacey was back in town, setting up practice. "I know someone who might be able to help," she ventured. "A woman I went to school with." She spoke carefully, so as not to arouse false hope. "Let's hope her home number is listed."

"I'll check." Doris rose to her feet and shuffled over to the phone on the wall, reaching into the drawer below to retrieve a directory that was thinner than Mary's address book at home.

"Look under Buxton," Mary directed. "Lacey Buxton."

Doris glanced up sharply, her mouth flattening with disapproval. "Well, if that's your idea of a life rope we might just as well call the undertaker."

"What do you have against Lacey?" Mary wanted to know.

"As if you didn't know," her mother sniffed.

A sharp ping sounded in Mary's head, like a taut string snapping. Anger, clear and bracing, swept through her. "You mean because thirty-odd years ago Lacey Buxton was caught naked with her father's best friend? Mama, with everything that's going on right now, do you really think all that ancient history amounts to a hill of beans?"

Doris's lips were buttoned so tightly to her teeth they quivered. Mary tensed, bracing herself for a blast of righteousness, but all at once her mother's expression softened into one of profound weariness. In a hollow voice she conceded, "I don't suppose it does."

Mary exchanged a look with her daughter. In that instant they were united, if only briefly. Two women who'd grown up in the same house, butting up against the same wall of hidebound beliefs and prejudices. However devoted she was to her grandmother, Mary knew it couldn't have been easy for Noelle either.

She felt a rush of protectiveness so strong it left her weak-kneed. Once before her child had been in peril, and Mary, too frightened and inexperienced to do otherwise, had allowed her mother to take charge. Now she knew exactly what to do.

"Why don't you get dressed while I make the call?" she suggested. "If Lacey's home and will see us, I'll drive you over there. Once you know where you stand, I'm sure we'll *all* feel better."

# Chapter Three

In the car Noelle watched Mary root about in her purse for the keys. *I ought to thank her,* she thought. For coming in the first place, for going to all this trouble. But something kept her from doing so. She didn't know why, exactly, but ever since she was little, she'd had this sense of withholding something precious from her mother, something you don't dare expose to the air for fear it might crumble. She reached over to touch Mary's arm.

"You don't need to do this." It came out more stilted than she'd intended, and she was quick to add, "I mean, I appreciate it, but I wasn't expecting—"

"Nonsense, I wouldn't dream of letting you go alone. Besides, I certainly didn't come all this way for nothing." Mary's voice was determinedly upbeat.

As they drove along Cardinal, the tension between them stretched to fill the silence. *We're like two ends of something broken,* Noelle thought. Forever butting up against each other in a useless attempt at a perfect fit. Maybe they weren't trying hard enough. Or maybe they were trying *too* hard. Either way, it could never be the way it was with her and Emma...

Noelle thought of her daughter, waking up in the house on Ramsey Terrace. Confused, calling out in panic. What would Robert tell her? That Mommy was sick? At least that part wouldn't be a lie. Noelle felt awful, her stomach rolling, her head like something that had been screwed on wrong. But she'd have walked barefoot over broken glass to get Emma back. She prayed this lawyer friend of her mother's could help.

Lacey Buxton lived across town on Egremont Drive, less than a mile from Ramsey Terrace. As they started up the long, winding hill that led past St. Vincent's and the Fin & Feather funeral home just beyond, she thought, *Suppose she can't do anything. What then?*

For a terrible moment Noelle wondered if it *had* happened the way Robert claimed. In the early days of their marriage there'd been too many mornings when she'd woken to only the fuzziest recollection of the night before. Mornings when panic would sweep over her like a dirty gray tide awash with the flotsam of shame and recrimination.

Then she thought, *No, I would have remembered picking up that first drink.* And the first thing she'd have wanted when she got up was a hair of the dog that had bit her.

*He's playing mind games. Trying to make me think I'm crazy.*

Realizing anew what she was up against, Noelle was flooded with despair. In this battle against Goliath she didn't even have a slingshot. How could she expect to win?

Mary glanced at her in concern. "Want me to pull over? You look a little green about the gills."

"No, I'm fine. I just need a little air." She rolled down the window. She was feeling anything *but* fine, but what was the use of explaining? Her mother couldn't begin to understand. Noelle was certain there had never been a time when Mary had felt this desperate over *her.*

With the breeze playing over her face, she felt her nausea begin to subside. But the stone of panic in her throat refused to budge. What if it wasn't as simple as hiring a lawyer? What if she couldn't get Emma back today...or even tomorrow?

It was unthinkable.

"You'll like Lacey." Her mother's voice drifted toward her as if from a distance. "I haven't seen her since high school, but even back then she stuck up for herself and didn't take crap from anyone. Not even when she was painted as the town Jezebel."

"Is it true she was seduced by a family friend?"

Mary chuckled. "She swore it was as much her idea as his, but I think she only said it to shock her dad." She slowed as they passed the Clover Patch nursery school, buttoned up tight for the weekend. "As I remember it, Mr. Buxton wasn't exactly the live-and-let-live type. Suffice it to say Lacey was sent to live with an aunt and uncle in Buffalo. I haven't seen her since, but when I heard she'd become a lawyer I wasn't surprised."

"I just hope she'll take my case." Noelle peered cautiously at her mother. "You believe me, don't you? About last night?"

They were making their way up Chatham Hill, past the Brass Lantern antique barn and Ferris Realty. Mary flicked her a glance and said firmly, "On my way here, I'll admit I had my doubts. But not anymore."

Noelle felt a welcome flash of relief. Not

counting Nana, that gave her at least one ally. With any luck she'd soon have another. The thought prompted her to reach for her purse. She'd thrown on some sweats but neglected to comb her hair. If she didn't make herself presentable, Lacey would think she was some kind of nutcase.

Her mother, on the other hand, was perfectly turned out as always in cream slacks and peach-colored shell, a matching sweater knotted artfully about her shoulders. Noelle braced herself for the inevitable comparison. People were always commenting that she and her mother looked more like sisters, but what they really meant was that Mary was prettier and more stylish.

"I just can't help thinking about all those people last night, what *they* must have thought." In the mirrored compact she held up to her face, Noelle's eyes were swollen and bruised-looking. "Not that I care as far as *I'm* concerned. But if this goes to court…"

"I'm sure the thought occurred to Robert as well," Mary observed dryly.

"Remember when you warned me that marrying him would be the biggest mistake of my life?"

"Nothing would have made me happier than to have been proven wrong."

"But you *were* right. Even so, I never imagined he'd go as far as this to actually *perjure* himself." Noelle clicked the compact shut and shoved it back in her purse.

"Suppose he didn't have to lie. Suppose this judge owed him a favor of some kind."

Noelle felt renewed respect for her mother. Mary sometimes acted as if she'd never set foot in a small town, much less been raised in one, yet she was clearly no stranger to how things worked around here.

"Everyone in Burns Lake owes him *something*." Noelle was so inured to it by now she might have been commenting on the color of the sky. "It's not just the subcontractors who bid on his jobs. He cuts deals on rents. He loans money. He even gets people elected. So, no, it wouldn't surprise me if this judge has a hand in Robert's pocket in some way." She sank back, overwhelmed by the thought of what she was up against.

"Let's see what Lacey has to say."

Mary pulled up in front of a modest ranch house painted a dark tan trimmed in green. Its shutters had begun to peel, and the older-model Datsun parked in the driveway clearly had some miles on it. If Lacey was any kind of a big-deal attorney, it certainly didn't show. Noelle felt a flicker of apprehension as she made her way up the path, noting the unkempt grass and pyracantha hedge in need of clipping.

A wave of dizziness swept over her, and when her mother tucked an arm through hers, she leaned into her gratefully. *Like a drunk nursing a hangover.* Those days weren't so long past that she didn't remember what it felt like to negotiate her way through the morning with a head stuffed full of oily rags about to catch fire. The memory caused her to straighten and pull away. Mary, misunderstanding, darted her a faintly hurt look.

*Step on a crack, break your mother's back,* Noelle thought. As a child, how many cracks had she cautiously stepped over? Oddly enough, it wasn't the thought of protecting her mother from harm; she'd known deep down that was just a silly superstition. Maybe what she'd been guarding was the fragility of the relationship itself. She'd hardly ever seen her mother, and on the rare occasions she was home, Mary never seemed to have much time for her.

Noelle didn't want Emma growing up that way. Living from one precious morsel to the next. Waiting for the magical day when the two of them could be together *all* the time, instead of just here and there. And what would *she* do without Emma? *Except for Nana, she's all I have.*

At the front door, noting the frayed welcome mat and cardboard boxes stacked at one end of the porch, she turned nervously to Mary. "How did she seem over the phone?"

"Like I'd gotten her out of bed. And I can almost guarantee she wasn't alone." Mary flashed her a crooked smile. "I guess some things never change."

Yet the woman who answered the bell wasn't at all what Noelle had expected. She'd imagined a bosomy blonde in a flowing silk robe, a sort of a cut-rate Mae West. But Lacey Buxton was petite and freckle-faced, with cropped dark hair threaded with gray and brown eyes that crinkled at the corners when she smiled. In her jeans and navy-striped T-shirt, she looked more like a PTA mom than a hotshot divorce attorney.

"Hi, you two. Come on in." She cocked her head to peer around them, letting out a piercing whistle. "Samantha! Here, girl! You leave that poor old cat alone!" The voice booming out of that compact little body caught Noelle by surprise; it was the bellow of a stevedore.

A huge, hairy beast hurtled past them into the house, and as Lacey led the way into the cluttered living room, the dog bounded up onto the sofa, muddy paws and all. Lacey didn't appear to notice. She was too busy eyeing Mary.

"Don't tell me...you have a painting stored in your attic, right?"

Mary rolled her eyes. "I appreciate the compliment. Especially since I was the only one in our class who graduated a year late with stretch marks."

The impish attorney laughed, turning to Noelle. "And you must be Mary's daughter. Goodness, it doesn't seem possible. I remember you when you were just a tiny baby." She stuck out her hand. No mention of their looking like sisters: Chalk one up for Lacey.

Noelle awarded another point for the businesslike firmness of her handshake. "Thanks for meeting with me on such short notice."

Lacey shot her a rueful smile. "Sorry it has to be under such lousy circumstances. We'll get to that in a minute. Have a seat, if you can find one. What can I get you to drink? Coffee, tea? That's about it, I'm afraid. I moved in exactly one week ago, and as you can see, I haven't gotten around to organizing things."

Noelle struggled against the urge to shout, *Are you out of your mind? My daughter is being held hostage, and I'm supposed to sit around making small talk?* Mustering a smile, she murmured, "A cup of tea would be nice."

"Coffee for me," Mary said.

Moments later Lacey yelled from the kitchen in her timber-rattling stevedore's voice, "Mary, I hear you have your own PR firm in the big bad city. Me? Twenty-eight years in Cincinnati—don't ask, it's a long story!— and I still couldn't seem to shake the small-town dust from my shoes. When my mother died and left me this house, I figured it was a sign from God that I should move back and try to make a go of it."

"Sorry to hear about your mother," Mary told her when Lacey reappeared a few minutes later, carrying a slightly dented metal tray on which three steaming mugs rocked pre-ciously. "What about your father—is he still alive?"

"Depends on how you define living. He's in a nursing home and most of the time pretty out of it." Regardless of any bad blood between them, Lacey looked genuinely regretful. "How about your folks?"

"Dad passed away when Noelle was little," Mary told her. "My mother's still going strong, though." She made no mention of Nana's being ill. Noelle wondered if she had any idea just *how* sick Nana was.

With a child-size sneaker, Lacey shoved her mutt aside to make room on the sofa. Plopping onto the seat-sprung cushion sprinkled with dog hair, she leaned forward, planting her elbows on her knees and directing her frank gaze at Noelle.

"Okay, let's have it. I know you didn't come here to listen to a lot of class reunion talk, so why don't you take a deep breath and start at the beginning?"

She sounded so warmly sympathetic, and at the same time so reassuringly businesslike, that Noelle had to fight to keep from dissolving into tears. "It's my daughter. She's five. Her name's Emma." She swallowed hard. "My husband and I—we separated a few weeks ago. I thought we could be civilized about it. But last night he came and got her while I—while I was asleep." Noelle held back from revealing every gory detail; it would sound too outlandish. She'd wait until Lacey decided whether or not to take the case. "Now he claims to have some kind of court order giving him temporary custody. I didn't know you could do such a thing without both parties present."

Lacey nodded thoughtfully. "It's called an ex parte hearing. And it's used only in extreme circumstances, when a child is deemed to be at immediate risk."

Noelle stiffened. "I'm a good mother, Ms. Buxton. I would never do *anything* to harm my child."

"Call me Lacey, please." She smiled reassuringly. "Look, I'll be straight with you. I don't know you from Adam, but I remember your husband from when we were in school together." She exchanged a knowing glance with Mary. "He had a habit of getting his way back then, too."

"The question is, Can you help me?"

Noelle sucked in a deep breath. What if Lacey refused? Where would she turn? As she glanced about at the boxes still to be unpacked and the books piled on every surface, it struck her that should anyone who knew her walk in just now, it would be assumed that she, Noelle, whose house had always been scrupulously neat, was the more together of the two. Yet here she sat, with her heart knocking like an engine on overload, hoping the woman who occupied this messy house, with its muddy paw prints and sofa covered in dog hair, would find a way to rescue her.

She watched anxiously as Lacey sipped her coffee, wearing a faraway look, as if weighing all the negatives of going up against a man as powerful as Robert. At last she set her mug down on the coffee table with a decisive thunk.

"I'm forty-seven. I've been busting my hump for almost as long as you've been alive. All I wanted was some peace and quiet, a nice little family practice. If I take this case, it'll be the Christians against the lions." She glared at no one in particular, then abruptly threw up her hands. "On the other hand, no one ever accused me of playing it safe."

Noelle let out a ragged breath. "Does that mean you'll take my case?"

Lacey abruptly turned to Mary. "Remember Buck, Robert's older brother?"

Mary frowned. "Wasn't he killed in some kind of accident?"

"His car went off the road into a ravine. He died instantly." Lacey shook her head sadly at the memory. "He was nineteen. Helluva way to go, huh?" Before Noelle could ask what Robert's dead brother had to do with any of this, Lacey explained, "We used to date, back in high school when he was a senior and I was a lowly freshman. Nice guy. Only the way his parents acted, you'd have thought I was the Whore of Babylon. Christ, we never even *slept* together. We only went out for a couple of months, but with all the pressure that was brought to bear I'm surprised Buck didn't break it off sooner."

Noelle could well imagine it. Look how long it had taken Robert's parents to warm to *her?* Even after nearly nine years it was more like a deep thaw. Lately, though, Gertrude had seemed more kindly disposed toward her. *Probably because I'm the mother of her only grandchild.* The woman absolutely adored Emma.

"My in-laws hardly ever talk about Buck," she confided. "I guess it's still too painful."

"The point is," Lacey went on, "I know firsthand what the Van Dorens are like. I know what I'd be going up against." She looked hard at Noelle, her brown-eyed gaze frank and unwavering. "I should have my head examined, but yeah, I'll take the case." She held up a hand. "Before you go thanking me, though, I should warn you: It won't be simple. It won't be cheap either. I don't even have to look into it to know that much."

Noelle wasn't sure whether to feel relieved or alarmed. "So what happens next?"

"First thing tomorrow morning I make some calls. Who's your husband's lawyer?" Lacey reached for the pen and yellow legal pad on the coffee table.

"Brett Jordan, of Jordan, Torrance and Sanders," Noelle told her. "But he only uses them for real estate transfers, that kind of thing."

"Most likely they referred him to someone who specializes in family law." Lacey scribbled something on the pad. "Soon as I get some answers, I'll call you. In the meantime, try not to worry. There's no point in pushing the panic button until we know the score." She glanced up sharply. "And however tempted you might be, do not, I repeat, do not attempt any further contact with your husband. You have enough problems as it is. *Capisce?*"

Reluctantly Noelle nodded. But the thought of her little girl crying for her in the night was etched in her mind like a tattoo. If she could *see* Emma, even for a minute, let her know everything was going to be okay...

"Can you give us an idea of what to expect?" Mary straightened, holding her coffee mug balanced on one knee.

"The *good* news is that an order of protective custody is strictly stopgap." Lacey absently patted Samantha, snoring away like a bear in hibernation. "As soon as a proper hearing is scheduled, you'll be able to speak your piece, believe me. The first order of business is to set a date, the sooner the better."

Noelle felt like someone starving who'd been thrown a mere crumb. Yet there was something else she needed to know, something that made her clutch hold of that crumb with all her might. "What are my chances of getting Emma back?"

Lacey offered her a rueful smile. "If I had the answer to that, I'd be a fortune-teller, not an attorney. We'll know more tomorrow. Hang tight until then, okay?" Rising to her feet she walked them to the door, where she squeezed Noelle's hand in solidarity. "Remember, we don't shoot until we see the whites of their eyes."

To Noelle, teetering on the outer edge of what she could bear, it sounded like a call to arms.


Doris Quinn, seated in her favorite chair by the window, struggled to poke a needle through her embroidery hoop without stabbing herself. Normally she'd have been napping at this hour. But these were hardly normal circumstances, were they? And however tired she felt, sleep was out of the question. With her granddaughter in trouble, she didn't have that luxury.

Besides, there was something she needed to do first. Something important.

At the sound of Mary's car in the driveway, Doris straightened, setting aside her embroidery. But when she tried to stand, her knees buckled, and she fell back with a sigh of forcibly exhaled breath. She was trembling, and her heart felt like a baby bird pecking its way through the fragile shell of her rib cage. A wave of impatience swept over her.

She loathed being sick. It made her feeble. Self-centered, too—each new challenge to her loved ones little more than a test of her own endurance. How would *she* hold up under the strain? Was this going to be the straw that broke the camel's back? As if her granddaughter's predicament weren't worry enough!

Doris fumbled in the pocket of her housecoat for her rosary. Her eyes drifted shut, and her lips began to move, reciting soundlessly: "Holy Mary, Mother of God, pray for us sinners, now and at the hour of our death..."

Yes, the Holy Mother would give her strength. When she was expecting her first-born, the doctor had warned that she might not carry the baby to term. She'd prayed hard then, and hadn't Mary Catherine come bawling her way into the world with all fingers and toes accounted for? In gratitude Doris had named her after the Blessed Virgin. Mary's middle name, Catherine, was after her own mother, who, even with five children to round up, dress and feed, had never missed a Sunday or first Friday mass. Yet a more willful child

Doris could hardly have imagined. Nothing at all like her sister, who was as easy as a kitten and just as uncomplicated.

It was that difference that had caused her to come down hardest on Mary, so determined was she to set her headstrong eldest on the straight and narrow. Yet somehow she'd failed. Not just as a mother but in the eyes of the Lord.

Oh, yes, she'd done the Christian thing, taking Mary and her baby in all those years ago. But hadn't she jealously hoarded her daughter's child? Encouraged Noelle in subtle ways to cleave more to *her?* Doris had been blind to it at the time, but her recent illness, coupled with the knowledge that her time on earth was drawing to an end, had forced her to see the error of her ways.

The worst of it was realizing that even given the chance to do it over, she would have done nothing differently. She'd had to face the fact that she was flawed in some fundamental way. Yet it was that flaw that had also put a roof over their heads and food in their mouths. Her husband, God rest his soul, had been a good man but spineless. She'd had to prod him every inch of the way. Bolster and berate him so he wasn't passed over when the time came for his boss at the plant, Mr. Evans, to promote him to general manager. And whose idea had it been to take out that insurance policy so they wouldn't be left penniless when he was gone?

But whatever damage had been done, she

had to try to rectify at least some of it. Mary Catherine couldn't go on believing she played only a minor role in her daughter's life. Noelle *needed* her. Now more than ever. It was time to set matters straight.

Hearing footsteps at the door, Doris hauled herself from her chair, wincing at the sharp pain in her side. Her gaze fell on the painting over the sofa, Christ on the cross, His face turned heavenward in an expression of almost rapturous agony. But there was nothing glorious about dying, she'd discovered. It was really quite...common. Even a bit embarrassing. Your stomach rumbled at odd times, and funny smells emanated from under your bedcovers at night. You grew cold easily and cranky at the drop of a hat. You spent half your time on the toilet, the other half in bed. You were forced to depend on people you might previously have done your utmost to avoid.

"Well, don't keep me in suspense," she piped as Mary and Noelle walked in. "What did the woman have to say? From the looks on your faces, it must not have been very encouraging."

Noelle's face was white as paper under that storm of black hair that had been the bane of Doris's existence since Noelle was little. "It went okay, I guess." She sighed, drifting over to the window as if any moment she expected to see Emma come skipping up the front path. "We'll know more tomorrow."

Doris snorted in disgust. "That husband of yours. I have half a mind to drive over there myself and give him a good—"

"Mama." Mary shot her a warning look. "Not now, please."

Doris's mouth snapped shut in surprise. How dare she! There was a time that kind of talk would have earned her daughter a smack on the backside. But Mary was no longer a child, and she, Doris, had to save her ammunition for the real battle ahead.

Swallowing her irritation, she said, "I have tuna salad in the fridge. Why don't I make us some sandwiches? There's a jar of sweet-and-sour pickles, too, left over from that batch I put up last summer."

Noelle shook her head wearily. "Thanks, Nana, but I couldn't eat anything if I tried. If you don't mind, I think I'll go upstairs and lie down for a bit."

"Nothing for me either." Mary glanced at her watch—slim, gold, expensive-looking. "I should be getting back. I don't want to run into any traffic on my way into the city." The hug she gave Noelle was full of warmth and motherly concern. "Call the minute you hear anything. If you need me, I'll be back in a flash."

Frustration bubbled up inside Doris. She had no doubt Mary meant it, but that wasn't the point. When her granddaughter replied, "Thanks, Mom. I will," she wanted to throttle them both.

*For heaven's sake, child, you've got to know enough to* ask *for what you need.*

Doris followed Mary out onto the porch. "Well, it was nice of you to stop by." There was a caustic note in her voice.

"I have an important meeting first thing tomorrow morning. A prospective client. I have to—" Halfway down the steps, Mary stopped and swung around to face her. "Why am I always apologizing to you? I'm going because for the moment there's nothing else I can do. It's not like I won't be back. For God's sake, Mama, what more do you *want?*"

"You could try being a mother for a change."

Doris watched her daughter's fine-boned face grow taut, as if being stretched to fit through some impossibly narrow space. Her cheeks glowed with indignation. Of her two daughters, Mary looked the most like Ted. She had his high forehead and guileless blue-gray eyes, his silky auburn hair that stubbornly refused to stay put, even his maddening habit of standing with one foot turned out, as if in preparation for flight. But there was nothing remotely spineless about her elder daughter.

She felt a moment's yearning to turn the clock back to the day Mary told her she was pregnant. If only she'd been a little more understanding. If she hadn't said those awful things...

"I don't need you, of all people, to remind me of the fact that I'm Noelle's mother." In the bright sunlight Mary's eyes glittered like ice.

She looked as if she wanted to say more, words that caused her mouth to pucker as if biting down on something sour. Doris almost wished she *would* spit it out; only then would they be able to put some of this behind them.

"Apparently you do," she said.

Mary's chin lifted in defiance. "This is where you like me best, isn't it? Between a rock and a hard place."

"This isn't about *you*, Mary Catherine. It's about Noelle."

"Are you still punishing me? Is that what this is about?"

Doris sighed. She supposed she'd had that coming. But, Lord, why did this have to be so hard? The pain that had started in her side was now thumping throughout every inch of her. And across the street Betty Keenan was practically falling out her second-floor window to get a look at what was going on. Doris felt a flash of irritation before remembering it was Betty who'd watered her yard and collected her mail the two weeks she'd been hospitalized.

"It's *you* who can't forgive," she said. "Oh, yes, I know, it's easier to blame it all on me, the fact that you feel shut out of your daughter's life. But that's not going to help." A tremulous note crept into her voice. "Come home, Mary Catherine. She needs *you*, her mother, not a sick old lady who's just one more thing to worry about."

Mary stood her ground. "You seem to have forgotten I have a busy life of my own, not to mention a business to run."

"You don't need to answer to me. Tell it to Noelle."

"You've always known exactly what was best, haven't you?"

The hate in her daughter's eyes caused Doris to reel. So this was how Mary *really* felt, beneath the studied politeness, the carefully chosen gifts on birthdays and Mother's Day. This was her legacy. Wearily she replied, "I know I didn't always do right by you, Mary Catherine. That's why I'm asking you to do the right thing by *your* daughter. For her sake, please…come home. She needs you."

The moment stretched between them. Mary was the first to break it. "I have to go." Her voice was cold. She hitched her purse onto her shoulder and spun about.

Doris watched her walk quickly down the path, stiff-legged, shading her eyes against the glare. In the hot July sunlight the yard appeared bleached of color. Mary might have been an image from long ago, a faded snapshot from their family album.

Then she was gone, the dull slam of her car door seeming to reverberate in the stillness. Doris drew in a breath of air laced with the scent of honeysuckle. Only then did she allow herself to collapse in the wicker chair by the door. She was breathing hard, holding the heel of her hand pressed to her side. Yet she was glad her daughter couldn't see. Mary had no idea how sick she really was. She thought they'd gotten the cancer all out. But if she'd been told the truth, it would only have made her feel obligated to Do the Right Thing, whatever that was.

*I don't want her coming back for all the wrong*

*reasons,* Doris thought. Which was silly, really. Because hadn't her daughter made it perfectly clear she wasn't coming back at all?

Mary had chosen the scenic route, which looped about the lake before linking with the road into town. In the past, whenever she'd felt out of sorts, it had acted as balm, a cool hand against a hot forehead. But today it wasn't having the desired effect. The lake slid past unnoticed. The narrow road, lined with alders and scrub pines, its cool green light flickering amid the branches overhead, might have been the Midtown Tunnel.

*How dare* she, *of all people, accuse me of letting my daughter down!* It was beyond unfair; it was outrageous. Of course Mary would do everything in her power to help, but did that mean putting her entire life on hold? It could be weeks, months even. In the meantime, how was she supposed to run a business from more than a hundred miles away?

Noelle wouldn't have asked it of her; in fact, she'd have been horrified at the idea. Much of the time wasn't that why Mary hung back? She was never certain how her overtures would be received. It wasn't that Noelle bore a grudge. That was too simplistic. No, their relationship was like a plant that had been given too little light. Pale and a bit stunted. It would live and was even capable of bearing fruit, but it would never flourish.

The thought brought a pang of regret. She

should have done more for Noelle back when it would have made a difference. She *would* have…if she hadn't been so hell-bent on getting ahead. Her only means of escape had been to work hard and study even harder. So she'd done what she had to. At her daughter's expense, as it turned out.

But was it fair to put all the blame on herself? She'd been so young. And back then she'd honestly believed it was as much for Noelle's sake as for her own. Too late she'd realized that having a child wasn't like owning a cat or a dog. Children couldn't be placed on hold.

She saw things more clearly now. She saw a grown-up daughter who'd forgiven but could not forget. She understood that some things can be repaired, others merely glued together. And one truth stood clear amid the haze of if onlys and might have beens: There is simply no remedy for time with a child not spent.

Her mother, dammit, had a point. Noelle *did* need her, however reluctant she might be to show it. Mary wouldn't let her down.

*Don't forget, she has her father, too.*

Mary's thoughts turned once more to Charlie. She hadn't seen him in years, not since Emma's christening. She recalled how distinguished he'd looked in his dark suit and tie, the newly appointed editor in chief of the *Register*. Bronwyn, his daughter by his second wife, who'd been a little girl at the time, would be—what? Sixteen? *Only a year younger than when I had Noelle.*

She remembered the moment their eyes had met over the baptismal font. There had been wry amusement in Charlie's, as well as a touch of old sadness, as if acknowledging how young they'd been when *they* became parents, and now, while many of their contemporaries were still raising families, here they were grandparents. In that instant she'd longed to reach over and take his hand. But of course she hadn't.

Mary drove on, soothed by the memory, the country roads gradually turning to two-, then four-lane highways. She wouldn't think about Doris, she told herself. She would do what *she* thought best. She knew a divorce lawyer, one of the best in Manhattan. She could call him for advice....

Back safely within the city limits, she was turning off the FDR onto Thirty-fourth Street, the East River a sullen glint in her rearview mirror, when her mother's words returned to haunt her. As if on cue, her head began to throb. The traffic became a straitjacket tightening about her.

*Does Doris have the slightest idea what she's asking?* In her line of work, she couldn't just disappear for days and weeks on end. Her business depended on having an ear to the ground and a finger on the pulse at all times. Her clients would feel abandoned; some might even jump ship. And though her staff was more than competent, it was far too much to expect—

Horrified to realize she was actually considering her mother's outlandish proposal, she paused in midthought. The notion was so startling she began to laugh weakly. *I must be insane,* she thought.

Years ago, when she left home for good, she'd vowed never to return. If she were actually to go through with this, it would mean sleeping under the same roof as her mother, not just for a night or two but indefinitely. Was *either* of them ready for that?

On the other hand, what if her mother was right? What if she'd be letting Noelle down otherwise? *It's true there's only so much I can do from a distance....*

Mary didn't realize she was crying until she reached up to brush away a stray hair and felt hot tears against her palm. Why did she have to choose at all? Why was it that the only choices that truly mattered were the ones you felt least prepared to make?

# Chapter Four

Monday came and went with only a brief call from Lacey. She reported merely that she'd spoken with Robert's attorney, who'd faxed over a copy of the emergency protective order signed by Judge Ripley. Robert wasn't bluffing, that much was clear.

"According to your husband, the night before last wasn't an isolated incident. He claims you've been off the wagon for months." Lacey's voice was dry, noncommittal.

Noelle's heart sank. Leaning against the wall at the top of the stairs, she slid slowly to the floor, landing with a thump on her tailbone. "He's lying."

"Trouble is, it's your word against his. He has affidavits from two unrelated witnesses who claim to have seen you passed out cold on several occasions while your daughter wandered about unattended."

A sudden cramp caused Noelle to double over, clutching her knees, the heavy black receiver pressed hotly to her ear. "My God, who would make up such a thing?"

"You tell me."

She thought for a moment, a hand balled against her forehead, her sleep-deprived mind tipping and whirling like a carnival ride. "Jeanine." She spoke through gritted teeth. "One of them must have been Jeanine. I'll bet he put her up to it."

"Who's Jeanine?"

"Secretary. Girlfriend. Take your pick."

"Hmm. The plot thickens." Noelle heard a drawer slam shut, followed by the rustling of papers. "How about neighbors? Anyone who would have had occasion to observe you at home on a fairly regular basis?"

There was Judy Patterson—she and Noelle had shared car pool duty and served on the block association's landscaping committee—

but that was like trying to imagine Kathie Lee Gifford robbing a convenience store. "I don't know anyone who'd be that vicious."

Lacey sighed. "Well, whoever the culprits are, this is shaping up to be a real can of worms. You up for a fight, kiddo?"

"Do I have a choice?"

"I withdraw the question." There was silence at the other end as if her lawyer were weighing various options. "Okay, where do we go from here? I'll tell you. Listen good, because this is going to seem like the toughest thing you've ever been asked to do."

Noelle tensed. "I'm listening."

"I want you to swear you'll stay as far from your child as humanly possible for someone living in Burns Lake, population of eighteen thousand." Lacey's voice was stern. "At this point the last thing we need is to give your husband any more ammunition."

Noelle didn't answer at first; she *couldn't*. Lacey's words were like a bone caught in her throat.

How on earth was she supposed to get through the next few hours, much less days or weeks, without seeing or holding her daughter? Robert wouldn't even let her speak to Emma over the phone! At least a dozen times since yesterday Noelle had found herself reaching for her car keys. Once she was halfway out the door before she thought better of it. Even then the effort of turning back was like being physically restrained.

"By this time tomorrow I should have a

firm date for a hearing." Lacey went on briskly. "We can discuss visitation then."

Noelle's chest constricted. "Visitation? I don't want visitation. Emma belongs *here*, with me. I'm her *mother*."

"I know that. Believe me, I'm doing everything I can to make that happen." Lacey's voice was somber, like that of a doctor informing her she had only six months to live. Gently she added, "In the meantime, kiddo, you've got to trust me on this. Can I count on you not to do anything stupid?"

Noelle hesitated. "Yes," she breathed.

"Good. I'll call you as soon as I have a date." Lacey hung up.

Noelle sat listening to the empty hum of the dial tone for a moment before pushing herself to her feet. She was trembling so badly it took several attempts before she was able to fit the receiver snugly in its cradle. *It's real,* she thought. *This is really happening.* It wasn't just a matter of going before a judge and setting the record straight. This was going to be a long and bloody battle.

By the following afternoon, when there had been no further news, her anxiety slipped over into despair. Since Sunday she'd slept only in brief snatches, waking with a start to find her heart racing and a dull throbbing behind her eyes. Hunger was a thing of the past. When she forced herself to eat, she became sick to her stomach. Worse, for the first time in years, she found herself longing to dull the pain with a drink.

Then the same siren's voice that had whispered silkily that a brandy—just one, for medicinal purposes only—would be oh-so-lovely began asking what would be so wrong about taking a drive to her old house. She hadn't even officially moved out. Her clothes still hung in its closets, and the keys to the front door were still on her key ring. If Robert was there, she wouldn't make a scene. She'd merely ask calmly to see Emma.

*Oh, sure, and while you're at it, why not ask for the moon on a string?*

Ironically, what kept her from acting on the impulse wasn't the threat of what Robert might do or even the promise she'd made to her lawyer. It was her daughter, who would be six in October, who still believed in the tooth fairy and Santa Claus. How would Emma feel, seeing her mother turned away at the door?

On the other hand, what must her little girl think: no word, not even a card or phone call?

"Nana? Am I doing the right thing?" Noelle stood at the stove, warming a pan of soup. It was lunchtime on Tuesday, and her grandmother had just gotten up from her nap. "I feel like I'm going out of my mind. Like if I don't get to at least *talk* to Emma, I'll die."

Her grandmother sat at the table, hands folded loosely in her lap, her hair sticking up like wires from a smashed circuit. Her pale, spindly legs, below the hem of her purple velour housecoat, were riddled with veins.

"At times it *does* seem the good Lord gives us more than we can bear." She sighed.

"This has nothing to do with God."

Nana straightened, replying smartly, "God's hand is in *everything*. And don't you forget it." After a moment she hauled herself to her feet and crossed the kitchen, the worn soles of her pink scuffs whispering over the linoleum. Without Noelle's being aware of it, the soup had started to bubble, and Nana switched off the burner, observing, "The Lord also helps those who help themselves. If you ask me, it doesn't appear to be doing much good, you sitting around like a bump on a log."

Noelle set down the spoon with which she'd been stirring the soup. "What I'd *like* to do," she said fiercely, "is give Robert a taste of his own medicine."

"So, what's stopping you?" Nana's blue eyes, nested in their papery folds, flared with some of her old fire.

"My lawyer, for one thing."

Nana snorted in disgust. "Lacey Buxton might chase after everything in trousers, but what does she know about being a mother?"

"Nana..."

"Why, I have half a mind to drive over there myself!"

Noelle felt a flash of irritation, tempered by the thought *At least she's predictable.* Growing up, she'd always known she could count on her grandmother. Unlike Mary, who'd dashed in and out, forever running to catch a bus or simply running late. Always with a good excuse, a breathless kiss...and a promise that things would soon be different.

She put her arms about her grandmother, bringing her head to rest against the sharp blade of her shoulder. Nana smelled of Ivory soap and fresh ironing.

"Remember the time the living room curtains caught fire and you put it out with the garden hose?" Noelle recalled softly.

Nana made a hmmphing sound. "Who needs a bunch of swaggering men in muddy boots making a mess of everything? Anyone with half a brain would've done the same."

Noelle refrained from pointing out that the house could just as easily have burned to the ground. "That's how I feel when I think of Emma. Like the house is on fire and she's inside...and I can't get to her." Her throat tightened.

Nana drew away to place her hands on either side of Noelle's head, as if to force such thoughts from her brain. Her palms felt smooth as polished stones against Noelle's cheeks. "Well, then, honey, you'll just have to put out the fire."

"But Robert—"

"He's only a man. I never met one other than your grandfather who didn't think that what's between his legs gave him the right to lord it over the rest of us. That doesn't mean you have to give in."

Noelle stared at her grandmother in surprise. She'd never known Nana to use a profanity, much less refer to a man's private parts. Her world really *had* turned upside down. Then a voice whispered, *She might be right, you know. Maybe you've been going about this all wrong. Maybe you* ought *to take action.*

Noelle was filled with a sudden reckless abandon, every fiber of her being pulling her in a single direction, toward her daughter.

She snatched up her car keys, conveniently parked on the counter by the back door. "I'll be back in time for your appointment with Dr. Reynolds," she promised. "Can you manage on your own for an hour?"

"I'm not completely helpless. Not yet at least." Nana sniffed. But her eyes were worried—not for herself but for Noelle. "You take care now, hear?"

As Noelle drove across town in her safe gray Volvo, staying safely within the speed limit, she felt as if her knuckles, clenched about the steering wheel, would pop right through her skin. Her lawyer's admonitions flashed like a yellow light inside her head, but the primal urge to protect her child was even stronger. *I can handle this,* she told herself. *If it starts to get ugly, I'll just...leave.*

She was rattling across the bridge onto Iroquois Avenue when a new fear burrowed its way in: What if no one was home?

With her own life on hold, it hadn't occurred to her that as far as the rest of the world was concerned, this was just another day. Robert would be at work at this hour, and why not? *He* wasn't the one chewing his fingernails. Nor would he have been careless enough to leave their daughter with a sitter. There was only one person to whom he'd have entrusted Emma.

Pulling up in front of 36 Ramsey Terrace, Noelle fully expected to find her mother-in-law's white Cadillac parked in the driveway. It came as a mild shock when she was confronted by Robert's Audi instead. As she stepped onto the curb, she eyed the path of wide flat stones leading up to the front door as she might have a tightrope.

The sprawling Tudor, with its mullioned windows and rough-hewn timbers set in stucco, seemed to mock her. Why hadn't she moved out sooner? Why had she needed an excuse? Noelle recalled the countless meals thrown together at a moment's notice after Robert had phoned to say he was bringing a few business associates home for supper. And the Sundays after church, when her in-laws would come for brunch and linger most of the day. If she complained of feeling tired or overwhelmed, Robert would remind her impatiently that she had a maid and a gardener to do most of the work. She could have a nanny, too, if she didn't insist on shouldering the entire burden of childcare herself. As if Emma were a burden!

It was her own fault, she knew. No one had held a gun to her head. And in some ways hadn't she *conspired* with Robert to create the passive creature that had so foolishly walked into his trap?

*Maybe so, but I won't let him get away with it this time.*

Striding up the path, she felt suddenly weightless, as if too forceful a step would send her bounding upward. She scanned the windows along the top floor, hoping for a glimpse of her daughter. But they glowered back at her, yielding nothing. From the Pattersons' backyard came the sound of children splashing in the pool. Was Emma among them? Her heart soared at the thought. Noelle imagined plucking her small daughter from the water, bare-limbed and gleaming, like the very first time she'd held her, moments after her birth.

Robert must have heard her pull up, for no sooner had she set foot on the porch than the front door swung open. A tall, well-built man in tan slacks and yellow polo shirt, regarding her with irritation, as he might have a salesperson or uninvited guest, stood framed in the doorway.

"What are *you* doing here?" he asked coldly.

"I should think that's fairly obvious." Noelle was mildly astonished to hear her grandmother's tart voice coming from her mouth. She peered around him into the house. "I'm here to see Emma."

"She's asleep."

"I'll wait."

"There's no need for that. She's fine."

"I'd like to see for myself, if you don't mind."

"As a matter of fact, I *do* mind." In her husband's handsome patrician face a storm was brewing. Looking into his pale Siberian eyes, she felt the temperature, hovering near ninety, drop suddenly and drastically. She shivered in the sultry July heat as though standing before an open meat locker.

In her head a voice urged, *Be strong...for Emma*. She didn't have the luxury of backing down. Not this time.

"How dare you." Her voice trembled with the effort to keep from shouting. "How dare you keep me from my own child."

"*Someone* has to take responsibility." Robert's cruel gaze raked over her, his mouth twisting in disgust. "Christ, Noelle, when was the last time you looked in the mirror? You're off the deep end, and you don't even know it."

She flinched but didn't back down. "You can have it all. This house and everything in it." She threw out her arm in a wide sweeping gesture. "Just let me have Emma."

He gave a short, dry laugh. "I have it all anyway. You don't see me begging on anyone's doorstep, do you?"

"What I *see* is a man who thinks he can get away with murder," she hurled back. "But you won't, Robert...not this time."

He smiled coldly, but she could see that her words had found their mark. His right eyelid began to twitch. "Look, I don't have time for this. If you have anything more to say, tell it to my lawyer." He started to close the door.

"*No!*" Noelle's shrill cry rang out obscenely in the stillness of the suburban cul-de-sac where voices were seldom raised and car horns rarely honked, where the last hint of scandal had been the parcel wrapped in plain brown paper, addressed to the Whitleys' teenage son, that had found its way instead into the hands of eight-year-old Lindsey Amberson next door. When Robert hesitated, she seized the opportunity to leap forward and wedge her foot between the door and the jamb. "I'm not leaving until I've seen Emma."

"You're drunk," he said, louder this time.

Noelle reeled, and with her foot still rammed firmly in the doorway nearly lost her balance. She hadn't expected this. Was he trying to convince her she was crazy? Or was *he* the one who'd lost his mind?

*He's crazy, all right. Crazy like a fox.* Noelle glanced over just in time to see Judy Patterson step out onto her porch. Across the manicured swath of lawn separating their houses, she caught the wary expression on her neighbor's face. At first it didn't occur to her that *she* might be the one Judy was eyeing with mistrust. They were friends, weren't they? Okay, not *close* friends…but still. When Judy's mother died last winter, who had spent the better part of an afternoon consoling her, not to mention caring for her boys the four days she and her husband were in Boston for the funeral? It wasn't until Robert lifted an arm in Judy's direction, as if to signal her—*don't worry, she's basically harmless*—that brutal realization kicked in.

"It would suit you if I *were* drunk, wouldn't it?" she said in a low voice, too low for Judy to hear. "The other night you slipped some-

119

thing into my soda, didn't you? You wanted everyone to think I was plastered out of my mind. But it won't work, Robert. Even *you* aren't above the law."

"The law will decide what's in Emma's best interests. And from what I've heard, Judge Ripley takes a dim view of negligent mothers."

"Negligent?" Noelle nearly choked on the word. "Robert, this is crazy. You *know* it's crazy. Stop this. For Emma's sake, please."

Robert's expression softened slightly, and Noelle wondered if she was at last getting through to him...until she saw him glance out of the corner of his eye. *He's putting on a show,* she realized to her horror. In fact, it wouldn't surprise her if this whole scene had been staged. Why else would he have stayed home in the middle of a busy workweek? He'd known it was only a matter of time before she showed up.

"Go home, Noelle. Sleep it off. You don't want Emma to see you like this." His voice, deep and authoritative, carried above the lilac bushes over which Judy Patterson peered.

Noelle wanted to hit him. Yet despite the rage that roared through her, she might have heeded his advice, turned away before it got ugly. If it hadn't been for the cry that pierced the air just then.

*"Mommy!"*

Through the partially open doorway she could see into the living room, where she was afforded a glimpse of dark pigtails, a small face alight with surprise. Her heart swooped up into her throat. "Emma! Oh, sweetie. Are you all r—"

Her foot slipped. The door slammed shut.

Noelle began to hammer at it with both fists. In its polished brass knocker she caught the distorted reflection of a mouth stretched in outrage. Like a madwoman's.

"Let me in! Dammit, Robert, open this door! Open it…or I'll—" She broke off. *What? Call the police?* The irony of her predicament brought the frenzied hammering to a halt.

Then she remembered her keys. She fished them from her purse and tried the lock. Unbelievably the knob turned. The door was halfway open when she was abruptly shoved backward and the dead bolt rammed home. Noelle stumbled and fell onto her side, scraping her elbow against the rough concrete porch. Inside, she could hear Emma begin to wail and the muffled sound of Robert trying to quiet her. Through the bushes alongside the house Noelle caught a flash of movement.

For a wild instant she thought, *Judy. She's coming to help me.*

But her neighbor was only retreating into her house.

Noelle pulled herself to her feet, sagging against the door. Tears streamed down her face. "Emma? Sweetie? It's Mommy. I'll come get you as soon as I can, I promise."

There was no sound on the other side except the faint tread of retreating footsteps. Noelle was engulfed by a wave of despair. She imagined Robert secretly smirking in triumph even as he wiped away their daughter's tears. How many lies had he told? How much more damage would he cause before this was over?

A savage fury overtook her.

"You won't get away with this!" she shrieked, beyond caring what the neighbors would see or think. Beyond all reason. "Robert, do you hear me? You can't do this! I won't let you!"

She threw herself against the door, pummeling it until her knuckles were scraped raw, kicking it so hard she felt something—*a bone?*—give way in her foot with a painful wrench. Flecks of saliva flew from her bared teeth. Her voice, barely recognizable, skirled up into the hot blue sky. "You *bastard!* Let me in. *Let me in!*"

*You're playing right into his hands. You know that, don't you?*

A voice in her head, eerily akin to Lacey's, brought a cold slap of reality. Abruptly the fight went out of her. Noelle tottered backward, suddenly aware of her painfully throbbing foot. Her knees buckled, and she sank onto the grass, shivering uncontrollably. *What have I done?* she groaned inwardly. *Oh, God, what have I done?*

"*You*'d best have Dr. Reynolds take a look at that ankle." Nana peered down at her as she lay stretched out on the sofa.

Noelle put on a brave face for her grandmother. "I will, as soon as I can hobble back out to the car and drive us over there." She shifted her foot, propped on a plump throw pillow, wincing at the pain. Her sandal had cut deep grooves in the swollen pink flesh around her ankle, but she didn't dare slip it off. She'd never be able to get it back on.

"Nonsense," Nana clucked. "You're in no shape to drive anywhere."

It wasn't just her foot. Noelle didn't have to look in the mirror to know she was a wreck. It was a miracle she'd made it home in one piece. "Well, one thing's for sure, I'm not walking."

"Let's ask him to come here instead."

"A doctor who makes house calls? Nana, those days went out with the horse and buggy." If she hadn't been so miserable, Noelle would have smiled at her grandmother's worldview that had stopped evolving somewhere around the Truman administration.

"Maybe so. But Hank Reynolds isn't like other doctors," Nana stubbornly insisted.

"Because he's not browbeating you into another round of chemo?"

"Among other things."

"Name one."

"Well, for one thing, he sure isn't in it for the money. If he'd wanted to get rich he'd have gone to work in one of those big city clinics where they charge an arm and a leg just to look at you. I wouldn't be at all surprised if he didn't charge one dime extra for coming all the way out here."

Hank Reynolds had taken over the practice

several years ago, when old Dr. Matthews retired, but it wasn't until Noelle began accompanying Nana on her doctor's appointments that she'd met him. The young internist had impressed her so much she'd even begun thinking about switching over from her doctor in Schenectady.

At the moment, though, all that was a distant concern. She couldn't think about anything except how stupidly she'd behaved. Ignoring her lawyer's advice, walking into Robert's trap—*for the second time*. What in God's name could she have been thinking?

"Never mind my foot. It's my *head* that needs examining." She groaned, pulling herself upright. "Oh, Nana, I've really made a mess of things, haven't I?"

"You did what you had to do." Her grandmother's tone was sharp. She wouldn't tolerate the suggestion, even by Noelle herself, that she was in any way to blame. "If there's a way of fighting that *isn't* messy, I don't know it."

"Did you ever feel this way about Mom or Aunt Trish? Like you'd sooner cut off your arm than see them suffer?"

"I never lost a single night's sleep over Trish. Your mother, though, *she* was a different story...always one step ahead of herself even while tripping over both feet." Nana's mouth pursed in recollection. "But, yes, there was a time when it just about did me in, knowing what she was going through and not being able to do a blessed thing to help."

"You mean when she was pregnant with

me?" Noelle perked up. She'd heard only her parents' version of the story. Nana didn't like revisiting that particular chapter. The way she talked, anyone would have thought her baby granddaughter had been brought by the stork.

Nana nodded distractedly, her eyes elsewhere. "I thought I was doing the right thing, keeping my distance, waiting for her to come 'round on her own. Now I'm not so sure...."

"In the end, though, she *did* come around."

Nana absently fingered the top button on her blouse. She'd gotten dressed for her doctor's appointment, even putting on lipstick. But her powder blue pantsuit hung on her newly shrunken frame, making her look even more frail.

"It was winter, the winter of '69, a particularly nasty one, as I recall. Your parents didn't have two nickels to rub together. What else *could* she do?" Nana shook her head.

*She could have stayed with my father,* Noelle thought. That was the trouble with her mother; the only thing she'd ever fought for was to get away. Maybe she should have tried harder to make a go of things here in Burns Lake, with Dad.

With an effort she hauled herself to her feet and limped to the door. Her swollen foot thumped with dull, hot pain. Glancing at her watch, she announced, "It's two-fifteen. We'd better hurry if we want to make that appointment. Afterward, if he has time, I'll have Dr. Reynolds take a look at my foot."

"I'll drive." Nana wore an expression of feigned innocence.

"Nothing doing. Remember what the ophthalmologist said."

"The cataract's only in one eye. I can see just fine," she insisted.

"All right then"—Noelle countered with equal stubbornness—"if you can see so well, what does the sign on that truck say?" She pointed out the window at the van parked in front of the Keenans' house across the street, on which was painted in bold letters FIGUERA POOL MAINTENANCE.

Nana squinted hard, her lips pressed tightly together. "It's those pest control folks. I remember Betty saying something about having termites."

"Get your purse, Nana. I'll wait outside."

Her grandmother knew when she'd been outwitted. With a snort of disgust, she clomped off down the hall to retrieve her purse, the same boxy black handbag she'd been using since Noelle was little, a traveling medicine chest from which had issued an endless supply of Kleenex and Band-Aids, nickels and Sen-Sens.

*Oh, Nana, what remedy do you have for me now?* Noelle thought in despair, her heart aching. What was the cure for having stupidly allowed your child to be snatched from under your nose? For a lawyer's sound advice not taken?

A short while later, seated in Dr. Reynolds's small shabby waiting room, Noelle began to wonder if maybe she should have taken her grandmother's advice as well and stayed at home. Was it her imagination or was everyone staring at her? Yvonne Lynch wasn't even making an attempt to disguise it. And Mona Dixon, pregnant with her second child...they'd gone to school together, but from the way Mona was acting you'd have thought they barely knew each other. When Mona's two-year-old wandered over in her direction, Noelle was certain she hadn't imagined the abruptness with which he was snatched up— as if her former classmate thought he'd be harmed in some way.

Mona and Yvonne weren't the only ones. Yesterday at the Shop 'n' Save, Noelle had bumped into a neighbor from down the street. The whole time they were chatting, Karen Blaylock kept sneaking glances at Noelle's laden shopping cart—as if she expected to see a six-pack of beer or a bottle of wine tucked in among the groceries. It didn't matter that the people whispering behind her back had absolutely no proof of anything. In a town the size of Burns Lake, you were guilty until proved innocent.

Noelle suddenly felt too warm. The waiting room, though air-conditioned, might have been a hundred degrees. She was reaching for one of the well-thumbed magazines on the coffee table with which to fan herself when she stopped short. Sylvia Hochman, seated directly across from her, was eyeing her narrowly. Round, no-necked Sylvia, who reminded her of a fat old tabby, with stiff hairs that poked like whiskers from the moles on her face. As proprietress of the town's one and only gift shop, appropriately named The Basket Case, she'd be quick to fan the flames by whispering that Noelle Van Doren had been sweating like a prisoner on the way to her hanging.

At that moment the door to the examining room swung open and Hank Reynolds stepped out into the waiting room, looking a bit disheveled in creased chinos and rumpled doctor's coat, but wearing a smile a colicky baby couldn't resist. Even Sylvia's sour old face lit up.

Noelle judged the doctor to be in his midthirties. Medium height, with light brown hair just beginning to recede at the hairline. A slight overbite kept him from being classically handsome, but his face was so kind—the gentle mouth that curled up in permanent bemusement, the intelligent brown eyes that crinkled in a sunburst of fine lines when he smiled—that was all you noticed.

Noelle had a sudden keen desire to go into the next room and hop up onto the examining table. She remembered how when she was a child, Dr. Matthews would hold his stethoscope pressed to her chest, a large spotted hand resting on her shoulder. She longed for it to be that simple now, for the cure to everything that was wrong with her life to be as uncomplicated as a scribbled prescription, a soupçon of advice, a cherry sucker from the jar on the counter.

Hank glanced about the room, his gaze falling on Noelle's grandmother. "Mrs. Quinn, I believe you're next."

But Nana shook her head, remaining firmly seated. "Thank you, Doctor, but I'd appreciate it if you'd see to my granddaughter first."

His gaze shifted to Noelle. "What seems to be the problem?"

Noelle held out her foot, which was beginning to purple where her sandal's straps had cut deep into her swollen flesh. "It's probably just sprained. I don't think anything's broken." She was conscious of every eye in the room being fixed on her and even more horrified to realize she was on the verge of tears.

"Let's have a look." Hank stepped forward to help her to her feet and held her elbow as she limped through the doorway.

The examining room was exactly as Noelle remembered it. The same brown leather table with a fat roll of paper attached at the foot. The same gray metal filing cabinets and salmon-colored Formica. It even smelled as it had in Dr. Matthews's day: of rubbing alcohol and cherry suckers.

"I would have phoned ahead for an appointment," she apologized, scooting onto the table. "But since I was on my way over anyway, I—"

She broke off, wincing as he unbuckled her sandal and gingerly probed her ankle. Hank was seated on a low stool with his head bent over her foot, and she stared down at his neck, which was pale, except for the line of sunburned flesh along the collar of his light blue oxford shirt. His brown hair was shaggy in back, she noted, the downy triangle at the nape making him seem oddly vulnerable somehow.

When he lifted his head, his brown eyes were twinkling. "Which do you want first, the good news or the bad?"

"If the bad news is a broken bone, believe me it wouldn't be the worst I've gotten today," Noelle assured him grimly.

Hank didn't press for details. "In that case maybe things are looking up. I could take an X ray to be on the safe side, but I'm ninety-nine percent certain you're suffering from nothing worse than a bad sprain." His smile broadened. "The bad news is that whatever you kicked is probably beyond repair."

Thinking of the ghastly scene with Robert, she felt her stomach pitch. At the same time, Hank's smile was so warmly sympathetic she found herself smiling back ruefully. "It was a door," she confessed. "Unfortunately it's still in one piece."

"Lucky for whoever was on the other side."

She eyed him warily. "I didn't know you practiced psychiatry as well."

"I don't. Just common sense."

Noelle became uncomfortably aware of how she must look. On her way out of the house she hadn't done much more than run a comb through her hair and splash water over her tear-stained face. Had Hank chalked her up as unstable, someone crazy enough to kick a door in? *The patient, a thirty-year-old white female, appeared to be suffering from a psychotic episode, possibly drug- or alcohol-related.*

But no, that wasn't the case. Hank was regarding her with genuine interest, even a hint of admiration. Taking a leap of faith, she confided, "It was my husband. We're in the process of getting divorced."

"It's not amicable, I take it."

"You mean this?" She raised her foot. "I'm not out to get him if that's what you mean. Actually it's the other way around." She heaved a shaky sigh. "It's a long story."

"Divorce is tough, I know. You have a little girl, right? Sorry, I know that hurts." Hank grimaced in sympathy as he eased her sandal off. "How's she taking it?"

Noelle hesitated, debating how much to reveal. "It's too soon to say. She's only five."

"During my residency I saw a lot of kids that age." He spoke gently, seeming to understand her need for reassurance. "It's surprising how resilient they can be."

She seized at the opportunity to switch subjects. "Where did you do your residency?"

"Columbia Presbyterian."

Noelle was astonished. Such a prestigious hospital! Before she knew it, she was blurting, "Forgive me for asking, but how did you end up in Burns Lake?"

She immediately regretted her presumptuousness. Besides its being rude, it was none of her business.

But Hank didn't appear offended. He merely

smiled like someone used to such questions. Up close, she saw that his eyes weren't so much brown as hazel, the color of strong brewed tea. In the glare of the overhead fluorescents, his thick lashes cast faint shadows over the lightly freckled ridges of his cheekbones. He looked as if he spent a fair bit of time outdoors and she found herself wondering about that, too, about the sorts of activities a busy family practitioner without time even for a haircut might enjoy. Fishing? No, he didn't look the type. Jogging maybe.

*He's certainly in good enough shape.* She blushed at the direction her thoughts had taken.

"The best way to answer that is to ask what I was doing on Park Avenue to begin with." Hank gave a rueful laugh. "I gave it nine years, nine not-so-terrible years, but it just wasn't me. I grew up in a small town in Kansas, a town I spent my whole life trying to escape from. And now I've come full circle. How's that for a cliché?"

"I guess that makes two of us," she confided. "I was born and raised right here in Burns Lake, moved to the Big Apple with my mom when I was ten. Don't get me wrong. In a lot of ways it was a wonderful experience. But the whole time I couldn't wait to move back." Noelle was surprised to find herself smiling. "Any children of your own?"

He shook his head. "My wife didn't want any."

Noelle felt absurdly disappointed to learn he was married.

"Motherhood isn't for everyone," she offered weakly.

"We'd planned on a family, but after we'd been married a few years, she had a change of heart. Actually it's one of the reasons we got divorced." This time his smile didn't quite reach his eyes. "Kathryn's a professor of women's studies at NYU. Needless to say, she's very political. At some point she became convinced that children were little more than devices by which men make chattels of their wives."

"What an awful way of looking at it." So he was divorced. Not that it should matter, but the knowledge left her lighter somehow.

"My sentiments exactly." Hank rose and walked over to the counter, where he began rummaging in a drawer. "This won't take long," he said. "I'm just going to wrap that foot in an Ace bandage. Keep an ice pack on it. The swelling should go down by tomorrow. If it doesn't, I want you to come back and see me. In the meantime"—he paused, his eyes crinkling—"don't go kicking down any more doors."

Noelle fought the impulse to confide in him. The thought of being just one more patient crying on his shoulder was more than she could bear. Forcing a smile, she replied simply, "I won't."

With her ankle snugly bound, she slid off the table, careful to rest most of her weight on her good foot. She was limping toward the door when Hank reached into a supply closet and pulled out a stout wooden cane. He handed it to her with a wink. "Here, you might need this. It's good for braining ex-husbands, too."

By the time she and Nana were on their way home, the throbbing in Noelle's foot had miraculously subsided. She wasn't sure how much of it had to do with the Ace bandage or Hank himself. She replayed their conversation in her mind. Was he just being nice, a doctor with a chatty bedside manner, or had his interest been genuine? She could certainly use a friend. Especially now. But if he wanted to be more than that she'd be forced to tell him that right now there was no way on earth—

She was turning onto Larkspur Lane when all thoughts of Hank Reynolds were pushed from her mind by the sight of her mother's dark blue Lexus parked in the driveway.

Mary, dressed in slim-fitting jeans and a white cotton blouse, was struggling to lift a cardboard carton from her trunk. At the sound of Noelle's car she straightened and turned around.

Noelle clambered out to greet her, wincing as she stepped down too hard on her bandaged foot. "Mom, what are you doing here? What's all *this?*" She gestured toward the luggage and cartons piled on the lawn.

She must have sounded less than welcoming because her mother stiffened slightly. "What does it look like? I'm moving in." She gave an airy laugh that wouldn't have fooled a child.

"Not for good, of course. Just for the duration."

Noelle was too stunned to reply. Her mother cared enough to put her career on hold? Swallow her differences with Nana? It was incredible. Amazing. Almost—

—*too good to be true.* Her exhilaration was replaced by a rush of familiar doubts. She had no doubt Mary meant well, but how long would it last? Until the first crisis at the office? Until a client squawked loud enough to send her running? An awkward silence fell. When Noelle finally spoke, her words came out sounding flat and insincere. "Wow. That's great."

Mary's smile was equally forced. "My computer is already set up in the guest room. I can work from here, take trips into the city when I need to."

Noelle nodded toward the cartons. "I'd help you carry in the rest of your stuff, but I seem to have sprained my ankle."

Mary looked down at Noelle's foot. Her expression of forced cheer was instantly replaced by one of genuine dismay. "Oh, honey, how in heaven's name—are you sure nothing's broken?"

"I'm sure." Noelle's tone was curt.

She glanced over at her grandmother. If Nana knew anything about this sudden descent out of the blue, she showed no sign of it. Nana stepped forward to greet her daughter with a peck on the cheek. "You look as if you could use a nice cold glass of tea. How was the traffic?"

"Not too bad." Mary seemed to relax a bit. "And, yes, I'd love an iced tea."

When her mother had finished carrying everything upstairs, Noelle hobbled up to join her, leaning heavily on the banister. Mary had taken the bedroom across from hers, the one that had been Mary's growing up. Noelle sank onto the bed, watching in silence as she arranged her clothes in the closet with an almost military orderliness: dresses at one end, slacks in the middle, blouses arranged according to hue. After several minutes the brittle tension became too much.

"I'm sorry if I didn't seem more excited to see you," she blurted. "You caught me by surprise is all. When you said you wanted to help, I never expected—" Noelle stopped, afraid of saying what was really on her mind. It could be days, even weeks before all this was resolved. Could she really count on her mother to stick around until then?

"I'm here. That's all that matters, right?" Mary pried open a carton and lifted a shoebox from inside, dark blue, with the unmistakable Polo logo. A leather suitcase lay open on the bed beside Noelle, smelling faintly of suntan lotion. A reminder of Mary's recent vacation to St. Maarten.

Noelle glanced around the room at the chintz curtains and matching quilted spread, the built-in shelves lined with back issues of *Reader's Digest* and *National Geographic*. On the dressing table an assortment of fancy cologne bottles was displayed on a mirrored tray, one for every Christmas that Aunt Trish hadn't been able to come up with something more imaginative.

For her sophisticated mother, this room, this house, would be like a pair of shoes that no longer fit. Except for the Curlycu Café, which was the antithesis of fancy, there wasn't even a single decent restaurant in Burns Lake. Even for a caffé latte, you were looking at a twenty-minute drive to the Starbucks in Sche-ectady. How long before she went running back to the city?

"Well, it was nice of you to come," Noelle replied awkwardly.

"I'm not doing it to be nice." Mary's tone was pleasant, but her gaze remained care-fully averted. She moved from suitcase to dresser to closet in a seamless rhythm eerily reminiscent of Nana's.

"There isn't much any of us can do until we hear back from Lacey."

"You'll need help with this house. And with Nana. You're not going to be able to get around very well on that foot." Mary spoke briskly.

"The swelling should go down in a few days."

Mary turned slowly to face her. In that instant she might truly have been Noelle's older, more glamorous sister. Then Noelle took note of the tiny lines about her eyes and mouth, like creases in fine linen stationery, and the strands of silver glinting amid her chestnut hair. She looked sad.

"Oh, honey, I know I haven't always been"—Mary faltered—"all that available. But I want to be here for you now. Will you give me the chance?"

What Noelle wanted at that moment was to be a child again, curled up in her mother's lap. She longed to feel Mary's hand against her brow and to hear the lilt of her voice reading aloud a bedtime story. Her mother *had* loved her...in small, sweet bursts like flowers that bloomed, then were gone. Maybe it was good that she'd come. Maybe she *could* help. Tears filled Noelle's eyes, and she quickly dropped her head so Mary wouldn't see.

"I'd like that," she said in a small voice. She was glad when Mary didn't try to hug her. It was enough for now to be sitting in this room with an open suitcase between them.

Down the hall the phone began to ring. Noelle grabbed her cane and lurched to her feet to answer it.

It was Lacey, thank God. "We've got a date." She sounded out of breath, her voice nearly lost in a sea of static—*damn cell phones, it should be a rule that all important calls be made from a* real *one*, Noelle thought. "Thursday morning, first thing. We'll meet in my office Wednesday afternoon to go over everything."

"Lacey, I—" Noelle started to tell her about today's dreadful episode, but all she could manage was "Thanks."

Her mind and heart were racing. Two days, she thought. Two more days without Emma. Would she survive until then?

# Chapter Five

Mary stared in dismay at the open cardboard carton on the floor. What on earth could have possessed her to come here? In her Madison Avenue suite, as she'd been laying it out for her staff, the decision had seemed just short of reasonable. But here in her old room on Larkspur Lane, seated on her childhood bed, with its maple headboard that still bore the moniker Mrs. Charles Jeffers—carved on the underside with a penknife when she was just fourteen—it struck her as just shy of insane.

Hers wasn't the kind of job from which you could simply take a leave of absence! She had accounts to oversee. Clients who depended on her. Lucianne Penrose, for instance. Lucianne, with her twenty-five diet centers and another one opening next month. The very first time Lucianne had trouble reaching her in a so-called emergency, she'd have a royal fit. On TV the formerly obese housewife, now a trim size eight, might appear to be the patron saint of the overweight, but in reality she was hell on wheels.

Lucianne wasn't the only one. There was Madison Phillips of Phillips, Reade & White, a white shoe investment firm specializing in "intergenerational transfers." It was her job to publicize the firm without appearing to do so, mostly through carefully planted items in the *Daily News* and *Wall Street Journal*. Madison, with his silver mane and fondness for Cuban cigars, who had once, while gazing out the window of his thirty-fourth–floor Wall Street office, remarked to Mary in reference to the Staten Island ferry terminal, that "it was a damn shame something wasn't done about that eyesore." The old man would not be amused, she thought, to hear that she had temporarily relocated to a town that, as far as he was concerned, wasn't even on the map.

And she wouldn't allow herself even to *think* about the potential (make that probable) pitfalls of orchestrating the Rene's Room banquet from afar. Hollywood mogul Howard Lazarus had founded the charity in the name of his beloved wife, Rene, a victim of breast cancer, and its annual fund-raiser was the fall season's hottest ticket. This year more than two thousand socially prominent New Yorkers were expected to show, along with a number of Hollywood movers and shakers. And guess who was in charge of planning the affair, soup to nuts? One false move, Mary thought, and the whole apple cart could overturn, bringing *her* down with it.

The only person who seemed to understand was Simon, but what did that say about her life? "Take all the time you need," her boyfriend had purred over the phone from Seattle. "I'll be here until the end of the month anyway, and who knows where after that. At least this way I won't feel I'm neglecting you." He gave a wry chuckle.

"Do you think I'm crazy?" she'd asked.

"No crazier than most," Simon was quick to reply. Which did nothing at all to reassure her.

*Crazy?* She indulged now in a dry, mocking laugh. *If insanity were incorporated, I'd be its majority stockholder.* When was the last time she'd taken her mother's advice? At the very least she should have first discussed it with Noelle, who'd made it abundantly clear she wasn't exactly thrilled with the idea. Had Mary done so, she wouldn't be sitting here feeling like the world's biggest idiot.

*What did you expect, a brass band marching down Main Street?* a voice scoffed. Thirty years weren't going to be reversed in a day. Anyway, her heart was in the right place, even if *she* might not be. As her father always said, there's no substitute for seats in the saddle.

She would simply have to weather the storms to come. Not all of which, she thought gloomily, would be of Robert's making. And the first order of business was to leave the unpacking for later and find out what was going on.

Mary rose with a sigh. She was sweaty from the drive and thirsty enough to drink a whole gallon of iced tea. The prospect of a long, hot summer in Burns Lake was about as welcome as a trek through an Ecuadorian jungle. To make matters worse, her mother had an almost pathological aversion to air-conditioning. According to Doris, all that "canned" air was nothing more than a breeding ground for germs. Growing up, Mary and her sister would take turns with the fan on sticky summer nights when they couldn't sleep, positioning it on the sill to send a sluggish stream of air blowing over one bed or the other.

Mary thought about calling her sister. Or better yet, driving over after lunch to say hello. Trish was at least one person who'd be genuinely glad to see her. And the bookstore was air-conditioned. Trish might not have made it out of Burns Lake, as she'd talked about doing when they were young, but at least she'd managed to shake off many of the antiquated notions with which they'd been raised.

Mary was descending the stairs when she was brought to an abrupt halt by a deep voice drifting toward her from the kitchen, a voice she recognized at once. *Charlie.* Her heart lurched. She closed her eyes, leaning into the newel-post. But why should it surprise her? He was Noelle's father. Naturally he would want to help. Charlie wouldn't need to be told the right thing to do.

Making her way down the hall, Mary was as acutely aware of each deliberately placed step as she had once been, aeons ago, crossing a creek on stepping-stones to meet Charlie on the other side. In the kitchen doorway she paused for a moment, struck by the sight of her former husband seated comfortably at the table, his chair cocked at an angle and one long blue-jeaned leg propped on the rung of the chair beside it. Doris and Noelle sat opposite, leaning in as instinctively as weary travelers to a warm grate. They were talking in low voices, a family sharing a problem, weighing options. With a sudden, swooning sense of despair, Mary felt like an outsider, an *intruder* almost.

Then Charlie glanced up, and their eyes met. The moment seemed to stretch out and out. At last he cleared his throat and spoke.

"Mary."

There was the scrape of his chair against the worn green linoleum, and he was on his feet walking around to meet her. Taller than she remembered. Still lean and loose-limbed, too, though thicker about the chest and middle. His black hair, clipped close to his head, was dusted with gray. The years were evident, too, in the deep lines scoring his narrow, angular face. Only his eyes were exactly the same, an arresting ocher-green, the color of a shady creek hollow.

"Hello, Charlie." It was the only thing she could think of to say. Maybe it was the long drive or the strain of wondering what the coming weeks would hold...or maybe it was Charlie himself, a reminder of her youth—the happiest time of her life, and the most terrible— but she suddenly found herself tongue-tied.

Charlie hesitated, as if wondering whether or not to kiss her cheek. He put out a hand instead. His clasp was firm and dry. "I saw your car in the driveway. Noelle tells me you're planning on staying awhile."

"That all depends." Mary cast an anxious

glance at Noelle. "Was that Lacey on the phone?"

Her daughter nodded, looking tense. "We go to court on Thursday. But even if the judge decides in my favor, it'd only be temporary. There's still going to be a full custody hearing, Lacey says. Robert meant what he said—he's not going to let go without a fight."

Charlie's large hand fell on her shoulder. "Don't forget, honey, the scales of justice tilt both ways. Besides, it's not just you he'll be going up against." His hard expression made Mary wonder what he would do if Robert were to walk in right now. He looked over at Doris. "I believe I'll take you up on that offer of iced tea, Mrs. Quinn. No sugar, just plenty of ice."

"I believe I know by now how you like your tea." Doris's tone was tart, but she was clearly pleased to be of use. She pushed herself to her feet. In her powder blue pantsuit, with her white hair smoothed back in a bun, she might have been on her way to a meeting of the Ladies' Altar Guild. And though she moved about the kitchen more slowly than in years past, it was with a kind of creaky dignity.

How ironic, Mary thought, that Charlie, once banished, was now more at home here than she. Doris even knew how he liked his tea. But it was only natural in a way. The years Mary had been shuttling back and forth to Danville College, forty miles each way, Charlie had been right here in Burns Lake, planted in one place like a sturdy tree. He'd worked hard, yes, but there was always time for Noelle. Even now that she was grown, they remained close. The same was true of Emma. At the christening Mary had been struck by the way their baby granddaughter had lit up when he took her in his arms. A little envious, too, since she herself had been little more than a stranger to Emma.

Even Doris seemed to have formed a queer sort of affection for him. Was it Charlie's easy charm? Or her mother's mellowing with age? Either way, Mary didn't doubt they both were better off for it. From her point of view, though, it would take some getting used to.

"Does Lacey have any sense of how it will go?" she asked.

Noelle shook her head and turned a harrowed face up at Charlie. "Dad, I'm so scared. Emma must think I've abandoned her."

He squeezed her shoulder. "No, honey. She knows you too well. Anyway, you'll still see her. Even if"—he cleared his throat—"things don't go your way at first."

His words hung in the still, muggy air. Noelle didn't reply. She didn't have to. Her frightened look said it all. Mary's heart twisted in her chest. She knew that face. It was the face that once upon a time had looked back at her in the mirror.

"The important thing to remember is that you're not alone," she soothed, reaching out to lightly stroke her daughter's arm. "Your father and I, Aunt Trish and Nana—we'll be with you every step of the way."

"Not to mention your sister." Charlie gave a small, wry chuckle. "When Bronwyn heard you sprained your ankle trying to kick Robert's door down, I had to practically tie her up to keep her from going over there and finishing the job."

So that's how it happened. Mary felt a surge of motherly pride, and thought, *Good for you, Noelle.* At the same time, it hurt that her daughter had confided in Charlie before her. In fact, this whole tableau seemed a cruel cosmic joke. She'd pictured it so many times—the three of them gathered about the kitchen table like any ordinary family—that the reality, *this* reality, was more painful than all their years apart.

Mary took a deep breath, fixing a bright expression in place. "Speaking of sisters, I was thinking of driving over to see Trish." She turned to Noelle, adding casually, perhaps *too* casually, "Feel like coming along for the ride?"

"Thanks...but I'm a little tired." Noelle dropped her gaze.

She *did* look tired, Mary thought. And why not, considering the day she'd had? In fact, maybe it had been insensitive of her to ask.

"Well, I guess that's my cue to shove off." Charlie gulped down the rest of his tea and set the glass down on the table. "Thanks, Mrs. Quinn. Sorry I can't stay for seconds, but I want to make it back in time to fill in the headers for tomorrow's edition."

"I'll walk you to the car, Dad." Noelle started to get up.

Charlie gently pushed her back in her chair. "No, honey, you rest that foot. I'll call you tonight after I've done some more of that digging we talked about."

Digging? For dirt on Robert? An old memory prickled at the back of Mary's mind, nothing concrete, just a vague sense of something amiss, like an itch she couldn't quite reach. She longed to ask Charlie what he'd meant, but he was clearly in too much of a hurry. She walked him to the door instead.

"See you on Thursday?"

"Unless you'd care to accompany me now on a quick tour of the *Register*," Charlie offered lightly. "I doubt you'd even recognize the old place."

"This whole town has grown," Mary observed.

"It's those new condos tacked up around the lake. It's brought in a lot of summer folk." A bitter note crept into Charlie's voice, and she remembered that Van Doren & Sons was behind this recent building boom.

"Well, anyway, I'd love a tour." The words were out of her mouth before she realized she'd said them. "I can walk to the bookstore from there."

Not until they stepped outside did she realize how tense she'd been. Mary released her breath with an audible exhalation.

Charlie, walking along the path just ahead of her, turned to cast her a knowing look. "It still gets to you, doesn't it?"

"What?"

"This house. Your mother."

"Only when I look down."

"Give it a few days, it won't seem like such a tightrope."

"Says who?"

"I've had my share of experience with this kind of thing."

Mary knew he was thinking of his parents. "I heard about your mom," she said softly. "I'm sorry. I hope she didn't suffer."

"Mercifully, no. In the end she went peacefully. More important, she died sober."

Mary thought what cruel twist of fate it was that after ten years in AA, Pauline Jeffers had died of liver failure. Six decades of hard drinking had clearly taken their toll. "How's your dad doing these days?"

"Spends most of his days at the senior center fleecing old Kiwanis buddies at poker, but he's hanging in there. Dad's like your mother in that sense, a real survivor." Charlie jerked his head in the direction of the house. "She seems a little better, don't you think? For a while there we weren't sure she was going to make it."

"Doris? She'll outlive us all." Mary gave a dry laugh that didn't quite mask her tumult of conflicting emotions at being once again at her mother's mercy.

Charlie wasn't fooled either. He seemed to sense what was on her mind and opened his mouth to respond before abruptly changing his mind. "This lawn could use some mowing," he noted as he cut across it to where his car, a mud-spattered Chevy Blazer, was parked. "I'll send one of the boys to take care of it."

It was a moment before Mary understood he was referring to the office boys at the *Register*, the same job Charlie himself had once filled. Watching him stride across the unkempt grass as if to meet the long blade of his shadow, she was struck by the irony.

"I'll follow in my car," she told him.

He shrugged. "You know the way."

Minutes later she was pulling up in front of the familiar brick building on Chatsworth Avenue. Five years ago, when Charlie bought out Ed Newcombe, the place had begun to look run-down. Since then the old bricks had been power-washed, the shutters and trim painted a glossy hunter green. Even the pallid ivy that used to trail dejectedly from the planters in front had been replaced by bright geraniums and nasturtiums.

Inside, too, what had once been a sleepy operation was now a bustling hub of activity. In the newsroom on the second floor there were at least a dozen desks, with a row of glass-partitioned offices along one wall. She remembered the old days, Charlie telling her about the veteran reporters who'd thought nothing of taking two- and three-hour lunches. What she saw now, though, was a crew of energetic-looking men and women, most of whom looked fresh out of college. As they bustled about, the noise was almost deafening, a cacophony of rattling keyboards, jangling phones, and voices shouting to one another over cluttered desks. She tried not to imagine what it would be like later on, with the volcanic rumbling of the presses below.

"There was a fire down at the Mackie Foods warehouse last night." Charlie raised his voice to be heard above the din. "There's talk it might be arson. I sent two of my best and brightest to cover it. Stan!" He waved over a stoop-shouldered young man with a thatch of hair the color of a rusty pipe. "What did you get from the night watchman? He pick up on anything suspicious?"

The kid shifted from one foot to the other, scratching his freckled nose with the eraser end of his pencil. "I spoke with *both* guards. The guy who works the five-to-twelve shift and the one that comes on at midnight," he reported. "The first, a Mr. Bluestone, claimed he had his eye on the security cameras the whole time and didn't spot a thing out of the ordinary. The second, a Mr."—Stan consulted the notebook in his hand—"T. K. Reston, friends call him Tuck, told me on the QT that Bluestone is fond of napping on the job."

"See if you can get copies of those cam tapes from the fire marshal," Charlie ordered. "They might turn up something interesting."

"I'm already on it, Chief." Stan tossed him an airy salute and sloped off toward his desk.

Inside Charlie's fishbowl of an office it was somewhat quieter. "Have a seat." He gestured toward the chair facing his battered oak desk, a remnant from the previous administration, stacked with newspapers, its trays overflowing with paperwork. To the right of the computer sat an ancient Underwood type-writer.

Mary pointed to it. "Don't tell me you still use that thing."

Charlie chuckled. "You'd be surprised. Last winter when the power was out during that big storm, it came in pretty handy. But mostly I keep it around for sentimental value. Reminds me of when I was just a lowly copyboy."

"I'm impressed. And I don't impress easy." Mary looked about in open wonderment. "You've turned this into a real newspaper, Charlie. Hot dog reporters and all." She smiled. "No more pieces about cats rescued from trees, I take it."

"There's plenty of real news, even in a town this size—if you know where to find it." He picked up a paperweight, a geode sparkling with crystals that made her think of tiny, sharp teeth. He examined it without really seeing it, his gaze turned inward.

She recalled his earlier remark to Noelle. "Speaking of which, what's this about your doing some digging? Is it something I should know about?"

With a sigh Charlie replaced the paper-weight and leaned back against his desk, folding his arms over his chest. She couldn't help noticing that his wedding ring finger was bare. A new woman in his life? Or had he merely decided it'd been long enough? His wife, after all, had been dead eight years.

"I don't know yet. It might be nothing." His expression was remote, unreadable. "My first impulse was to march over there and kill the bastard. Luckily I thought better of it and decided to do some nosing around instead. Anything I could pull up on Robert Van Doren, going all the way back to high school."

"And?" Her heart quickened.

"What I've come up with so far raises more questions than answers, I'm afraid." He swiveled around and pulled a file from atop an overflowing basket. "Here, take a look."

The file contained a series of newspaper articles copied off microfiche. The top one, from the *San Francisco Examiner,* was dated April 12, 1972:

### YOUTH CHARGED WITH MANSLAUGHTER

Yesterday morning, police in Palo Alto arrested a student at Stanford University, 21-year-old Justin McPhail, for the alleged rape of 18-year-old coed Darlene Simmons. Both had attended a party at the Kappa Alpha fraternity. When Simmons left the party with McPhail and two of his friends, all were reported to have been drinking heavily. Simmons identified her attacker as McPhail, claiming to have been raped as she walked back to her dormitory.

When questioned by authorities, McPhail's companions, neither present at the time, 21-year-old King Larrabie and 20-year-old Robert Van Doren, said they knew nothing of the alleged crime. McPhail's only statement was, "We'd both had a lot to drink and started fooling around. I didn't force her into anything." He is currently being held without bail. Meanwhile, campus police at Stanford have launched an investigation.

The thought that had been tickling at the back of Mary's mind materialized suddenly: Corinne's suicide. What if they could find a way to use it against Robert? Coupled with this article, it would cast a pall of suspicion if nothing else. People might begin to wonder, as she had all these years, if he'd had more to do with Corinne's death than met the eye.

"Why didn't we hear about this at the time?" she asked.

"For one thing, it wasn't local." Charlie ticked off the reasons with his fingers. "For another, there was no proof that Robert was directly involved. I remember hearing something at the time, a rumor about some trouble at Stanford. But I don't have to tell you the Van Dorens are a pretty tightlipped bunch."

"But if he wasn't guilty of anything, why all the secrecy?"

"Good question."

"You think he's hiding something?"

"Maybe, maybe not. Could be just a coincidence. I don't know yet what happened with McPhail, but the interesting thing is where Larrabie ended up." Charlie pulled another clipping from the file, this one from the *Burns Lake Register*, dated November 16, 1998. The headline read:

*REP. CANDIDATE KING LARRABIE ELECTED TO STATE SENATE*

Mary looked up. "What makes you think the two are connected?"

"Like I said, too many coincidences. And I'm not a big believer in coincidences." He tossed the clipping back into the file. "You hear about the new superhighway that just got voted in up in Albany? Take a wild guess who its biggest backer was."

"Larrabie?"

"Bingo. And who in Burns Lake will benefit most when that highway goes in?"

Mary didn't have to ask. Cranberry Mall was all their son-in-law had talked about for months. The highway would provide the crucial link to outlying areas, which in turn would spur more growth in Burns Lake itself. But other than the usual corporate payoffs, where was the smoking gun? Her mind groped for a connection.

"It sounds a little fishy, I agree," she said. "But that doesn't make it illegal."

Charlie cocked an eyebrow. "No, but what if Robert and Larrabie have been in cahoots since way back when? What if they knew more about that girl's rape than either of them admitted to? They'd have reason to look out for each other."

154

A memory came to her then, like a draft of cold air finding its way through a crack. The night of Corinne's death Robert claimed to have been at home with his family. But what if his parents had lied to protect him?

She remembered something else, a comment her friend had once made. They'd been sitting on the bed in her room, talking about Robert, and Corinne had gotten this funny look, as if she were bewildered, but also maybe a little scared. She'd said, "Nothing ever gets to him, Mary. I don't mean stuff doesn't bother him. It doesn't even *touch* him."

What exactly had she meant? That nothing bad ever happened to Robert? Or simply that he was without conscience? On the basis of his recent actions alone, she'd go with the latter. But underhandedness in a divorce was one thing, murder something else altogether.

Nevertheless, Mary felt the hairs on the back of her neck stand up. It was the same feeling she got when a major opportunity for publicity presented itself. "I was just thinking of Corinne," she mused aloud. "Do you remember her funeral? How cold Robert acted. Almost like—like he was trying to distance himself from the whole thing."

"To be honest, the only thing I remember clearly is the day we heard she'd died." He shrugged, spreading his hands.

Of course, she thought. How could *either* of them forget? That was the day she'd walked out on Charlie. And however unwitting her actions, there was no getting around the suffering she'd caused. She thought she saw a flicker of that old pain in his eyes just now.

Mary fought the urge to look away. "What if Robert knows more than he's telling, not just about the rape but about Corinne?"

Except for a barely perceptible tightening of his jaw, Charlie's expression remained neutral, considering. "I thought of that, too. But even if we're right, we have no way of proving it."

"Suppose we *could* prove it, though?"

It had been this way with them from the beginning. Whenever one expressed an idea, it was only to find that the other had been thinking along the same lines. They used to laugh about it. Now it made her uneasy to realize how little had changed.

"Speaking as a newspaperman," he said, "I'd have to see some pretty compelling evidence. And after all these years, frankly I don't see much likelihood of anything new coming to light."

Even so, an idea was taking shape in Mary's mind. She leaned forward in her eagerness. "Let me help, Charlie. I'll have plenty of time on my hands. And God knows I'm familiar with the territory."

Charlie shook his head. "Look, I don't mean to sound harsh, but you'd just be getting in the way. Anyway, like I said, it was a long time ago. Whatever trail there might have been is stone cold."

She bristled. "I may not be in the newspaper business, true, but one thing I *do* know is spin-doctoring. It's what I do for a living. If Robert has something to hide, believe me I'd know where to look."

He regarded her thoughtfully. In the dusty light that slanted through the blinds, his angular face appeared to have been chipped from the same hard stone as the arrowheads of his Iroquois ancestors. Was he wondering about the two of them working so closely together? Was he apprehensive, as she was, of the old feelings it might dredge up?

*It's been thirty years,* a voice scoffed. *What makes you think he still cares?* He was the one who'd remarried, not she, with a child to show for it. Anyway, this wasn't about Charlie and her. It was about their daughter. And Emma. *That* was the reason she'd come back. Not to pick over old bones.

She knew she'd won when Charlie inquired casually, "Just for the sake of argument, where would you start?"

Mary thought hard, the noise outside fading to a distant hum. But oddly enough, what came to mind was a memory of Charlie and her at their junior prom. She'd been wearing a blue satin dress with a lace overskirt, she recalled. The auditorium had been showered in silvery coins of light from the glitter ball twirling overhead. They were dancing to the Righteous Brothers, and Charlie was holding her tight, saying something she couldn't quite make out over the music. There was only the feel of his lips brushing her ear, his warm breath against her cheek. She remembered loving him so much at that moment it hurt, a sweet ache that traveled all the way down to the quivering muscles in her calves as she strained upward in her high heels.

There were other memories, too: of her breasts swollen with milk; of her baby's hungry cries in the night as she dragged herself out from under the warm covers into the icy cold. Memories that made the earlier, innocent ones seem no more substantial than dreams. But she would never forget that night, the way she'd felt slow-dancing in Charlie's arms.

Rousing herself from her reverie, she was momentarily unable to meet his gaze. For if he could read what she was thinking, he would also know how often over the years she'd relived those memories, how many times while making love to other men she'd imagined them to be Charlie.

Briskly she suggested, "I could start by talking to Corinne's mother. Nora might remember something."

Charlie nodded thoughtfully, tapping his chin with a loosely clenched fist. "It's a long shot."

"I'll phone her as soon as I get back to the house." She rose and started for the door, suddenly impatient to be on her way. "It's been a while. I owe her a visit anyway."

"Let me know if anything comes of it. We can decide then if it's worth having you pursue this." Charlie followed her to the door, touching her elbow lightly as she turned to say good-bye. "And, hey, just for the record, I'm impressed, too. I've heard how successful your firm is. Whenever I ask how you're doing, it's all Noelle talks about."

Mary started, heat rising in her cheeks. She didn't know what flustered her more: Charlie's asking about her or the fact that Noelle boasted of her accomplishments. An awkward silence fell; she rushed to fill it. "Thanks, Charlie. Like you, I've worked hard."

"We'd make a great team then."

His eyes seemed to hold hers a beat longer than necessary, a corner of his mouth hooking down in a small, ironic smile. Then the moment passed, and he was once again a concerned father, nothing more.

"She's our daughter, Mary, yours and mine." He spoke slowly with emphasis on each word. "I know you love her as much as I do. Emma, too. Whatever happened with us in the past, *they're* what counts now."

Shaken in a way she couldn't have explained, Mary replied in a low voice, "I wasn't always there for Noelle the way I should have been, I know. But I'm here now. And I'm not going anywhere until Emma is back home, safe and sound."

It was only a five-minute walk to her sister's bookstore, but as Mary trudged along Main Street, she felt as if she were wading through the heat that shimmered off the pavement in serpentine waves. Its familiarity was comforting nonetheless. The pink ginger-bread-trimmed Curlycue Café, as incongruous among the stolid brick storefronts as a lacy Victorian valentine amid flyers for a sale. And Cochran's Deli, which advertised the "World's Best Doughnuts" that really *were*. She noted the cluster of sleekly tanned men and women in tennis shorts out front—weekenders brought in by those new condos of which Charlie had spoken so disparagingly—and wondered how long Burns Lake would remain a sleepy backwater.

The Hollywood Dress Shop where she'd once worked, on the corner of Main and Fremont, reassured her that fashions at least hadn't changed. Displayed in the window were the same fifties-era mannequins, sporting dress styles that had gone out with the Hula Hoop. The shoe store next door too was exactly as it had been when Doris used to take Trish and her shopping every fall for back-to-school Buster Browns. Even the Benjamin Franklin across the street, the last of a dying breed, continued to hold its own with the tenacity of an aging dowager decked in rhinestones. The last she'd heard, you could still sit at its soda fountain and order a root beer float.

Her sister's bookstore occupied a narrow storefront wedged between the Snip-Shape Beauty Salon and Peterson's Grocery. Ten years ago, when The Dog-eared Page first opened, local cynics had predicted it would fail. Why pay $19.99 for a hardcover when you could take your pick from the rack of paperbacks in

Peterson's? But Trish had proved all those naysayers wrong, carving out a niche for herself, selling both new and used books. With no family of her own, she'd poured all her devotion into promoting her favorite authors and pet causes.

When Mary walked in, the first thing she noticed was the easel next to the cash register, displaying a handmade sign. Large bold letters across the top read: HELP SAVE OUR ORANGE-CROWNED WARBLER! Photos of the endangered bird, clipped from magazines, were taped below. On a small table beside it was a stack of leaflets and a clipboard holding a petition half filled with signatures. But before Mary could take a closer look, her sister came rushing over.

Trish, looking a bit like a small brown bird herself, with her soft round face and baby-fine hair that fluttered in wisps about her temples, stood on tiptoe to hug her. She smelled of something faintly fruity, like the lemon drops she'd liked to suck on as a child. A book tucked under one plump arm dug into Mary's ribs.

"I don't believe it. So it *is* true!" Trish cried. "Mama phoned to let me know you were on your way over, but seeing is believing. And look at you. Two hours behind the wheel and not a wrinkle in sight."

Mary drew back with a breathless laugh, glancing about at the shelves of lovingly displayed books and walls hung with framed needlepoint samplers. Nothing had changed since her last visit. Browsers perched contentedly on step stools and where there was room sat cross-legged on the floor. In the children's section, which had its own carpeted play area, a curly-haired toddler was happily absorbed in yanking books off shelves. Even Homer, the store cat, looked perfectly at home. The tabby lay curled on an easy chair, regarding Mary sleepily with one slitted eye.

There was only one new addition. Gesturing toward the easel, Mary observed dryly, "I see you're still trying to save the world."

Trish frowned, brushing a stray lock from eyes the cloudless blue of a newborn's. "No way, you're not getting off that easy. Mama told me you'd moved back into your old room lock, stock, and laptop. Come on, I want to hear it—every gory detail—was this your idea or did she twist your arm?"

"Actually, it was a little of both." Mary dropped her voice. "But don't go spreading it around that I'm back. I wouldn't want people to get the wrong idea."

"Heavens, no. Who in their right mind would stay in Burns Lake if they didn't have to?"

There was a note of wistfulness buried in Trish's jest and Mary instantly felt contrite. "I didn't mean...oh, you know what I meant. Look, the truth is, Noelle's not exactly thrilled with my being here. I don't know that Mama will be, either...once the novelty wears off."

"So you don't think this will blow over in a day or two?"

"Knowing Robert, no, I don't."

Standing there, wringing her hands, Trish looked like a character from one of the glossy paperback romances lining her shelves, lady-in-peril variety. "Poor Noelle. I wish there were something I could do to help."

Mary felt a flash of annoyance, and wanted to snap, *If you'd stood up to Robert the night you were supposed to be looking after Emma, we wouldn't be having this discussion now.* That was Trish for you—terrific when it came to passing petitions, but put a *real* crisis in front of her and she instantly turned to jelly.

"The hearing is Thursday at ten," Mary told her. "Can you make it?"

Trish didn't hesitate. "I'll be there with bells on."

Mary felt ashamed for being so quick to judge her. Trish had a big heart. Her trouble was she didn't always know where to put it. Though patiently waiting out the longest engagement in history—eight years and still counting—she had no children of her own. There was no question about Gary and her living together out of wedlock either. Not as long as Doris drew breath on this earth.

"I'm not so sure Mama will be up to it, though. She *says* she's better, but..." Mary let the sentence trail off.

Trish shrugged. "You know Mama. She could be trapped under a car with both legs crushed and be thinking about what she was going to serve for dinner that night."

The two sisters who looked nothing alike shared a wry laugh. Trish, in her plaid jumper and Birkenstocks, and Mary, in her eighty-dollar jeans and bench-made loafers.

"Speaking of dinner, what's on the menu for tomorrow night?" Mary picked up a book off the display table, idly flipping through its pages.

"I don't remember inviting you."

"I accept anyway. *You're* not the one who has to sit across the table from Mama every night." Mary looked up to find her sister's eyes dancing.

"No big deal. I'll throw some steaks on the barbecue."

"Since when do you eat red meat?" Mary couldn't remember a time her sister hadn't been a strict vegetarian. Hold the beef, pass the tofu: That was her motto.

Trish shot her a quizzical look, as if to say, *Where have you been all these years?* But she only shrugged good-naturedly and said, "You know Gary—Mr. Meat and Potatoes. I got tired of eating just the baked potato."

"Speaking of Gary, how is he?" Mary arranged her features in an expression of pleasant interest. The truth was, she'd never much liked the guy. Not since the time he'd groped her under the table at Noelle's rehearsal dinner.

Trish turned away to fuss with a stack of books. "Oh, you know how it is. We're both so busy. We don't see each other nearly as often as we'd like."

Mary swallowed the smart remark on the tip of her tongue, *What is so hectic about being an elementary school PE teacher?* Instead, she only commented mildly, "Business must be good."

Trish glanced up. "It's okay. I'm holding my own at least. To tell the truth, though, I'm a little worried about the new store that's going in at the mall." Trish had her head down, but Mary could see her chewing on her lip, a nervous habit from childhood.

"What store?"

"Bigelow Books. I thought I told you."

Mary felt a flicker of alarm. "How many square feet?"

She knew from promoting authors that Bigelow Books owned fifteen hundred stores nationwide. If her guess was right, The Dog-eared Page would be facing at least thirty thousand feet of competition, at prices that would undercut her sister's by more than 20 percent.

Trish grew flustered. "I...I don't know. When I first heard about it, I was so upset I didn't think to ask. And Robert didn't say."

Mary felt slightly sick. She should have known who was behind it. Was there nothing that man wouldn't stoop to? "Well, there's no sense worrying about it now. The mall is still months away." Her attempt to reassure Trish sounded false even to her own ears. Eager to change the subject, she pointed at the sign by the register. "In the meantime, what's the story with the birds?"

Trish quickened in a way Mary recognized all too well. She sensed an attack of political correctness coming on. "As you may have heard, the Sandy Creek reservoir is slated for development by you-know-who. Which is bad enough on its own, but that's also where the orange-crowned warbler nests. Unless the town council puts a stop to the development, its entire bird population will be wiped out." Bright pink flags of indignation stood out on her cheeks, and in that moment she looked ten feet tall. Then abruptly her shoulders sagged. "The trouble is, the orange-crowned warbler hasn't officially been declared an endangered species."

In college, Trish had been active on campus protesting the Chilean junta and U.S. intervention in Nicaragua. In the years since there had been a number of such causes, most recently the Green Earth recycling center, for which she'd campaigned heavily, and the fight to restore the Victorian-era train station that had been on the verge of being torn down.

Now, with her own livelihood at stake, she'd chosen to concentrate on saving a creature that would no doubt survive long into the next millennium, with or without the aid of Patricia Ann Quinn of Burns Lake, New York.

But despite their differences, Mary loved her sister dearly. Without missing a beat she marched over and scrawled her signature on the petition. "Long live the orange-crowned warbler." Peering closely at a photo of a small olive drab bird dusted with gold, she added dubiously, "Not much of a looker, is he?"

"In a way that makes it more special," Trish

replied staunchly. "Think what this world would be if only the beautiful and exotic were allowed to exist."

"That's one way of looking at it, I suppose." Mary wondered if her sister thought of herself the same way, as an ordinary woman making a stand in a world that too often looked the other way.

Just then a heavyset man in a denim jacket and bill cap sidled up to the cash register, clutching a copy of the Living Bible. Trish shot Mary a regretful look. "I have to go. Can we talk later?"

"I'll call you tonight," Mary said. "Are you going to be home?"

Trish rolled her eyes, as if to say, *Where else?* and hurried off to wait on her customer. There hadn't been any mention of either a night out or a quiet evening at home with her fiancé. Gary Schmidt clearly was in no rush to tie the knot, Mary thought.

As she stepped out onto the sidewalk, a huge man loomed suddenly into her path. Startled, she looked up into a beefy red face that looked vaguely familiar. A middle-aged man with strawberry-blond hair and eyebrows so pale they stood out like strips of adhesive against the shiny pink of his skin. It wasn't until her eyes dropped to the badge gleaming on the front pocket of his sheriff's uniform that recognition kicked in.

"Wade. Wade Jewett," she recalled. "My goodness, it's been a long time. I hardly recognized you." She hadn't seen him since high school, but when she'd heard he was a deputy sheriff, it hadn't surprised her.

"Hello, Mary," Wade greeted her casually, as if running into an old classmate from out of town were an everyday occurrence. "It has been a while, hasn't it? Guess you couldn't make it to our last reunion." Was that a note of resentment she detected in his voice? Or a snide reminder that she hadn't graduated with the rest of the class?

Mary told herself it wasn't worth getting annoyed. Wade Jewett had been a pompous ass back then, and clearly nothing had changed. "My work keeps me pretty busy," she replied pleasantly. "I don't get back to town much these days."

"What brings you this time?" His eyes, flat and brown, regarded her with a curious intensity.

It wasn't her imagination. *He knows exactly why you're here.* She remembered something she hadn't thought of in years. In high school, Wade Jewett had been somewhat of a Goody Two-shoes. When their principal, Mr. Savas, found a plastic Baggie of pot in his locker, the general consensus among the student body was that it had to have been planted. Nevertheless, an investigation was launched. It wasn't until Robert Van Doren, a student to whom no school official in his right mind would have given more than a mild reprimand—not unless he or she wanted one of Coach McBride's size twelve cleated shoes down his throat—stepped foward to claim jokingly it was *his* stash, that

Wade was let off the hook. Robert hitherto became the object of abject hero worship. Mary could see fifteen-year-old Wade in her mind now, fat and pimply, trotting after Robert like an overgrown St. Bernard puppy.

Was Wade still trotting after Robert, eager to do his bidding? She eyed him warily, thinking it was an arrangement that would suit them both.

"Family business." She made a show of glancing at her watch. "Oops, I have to run. Nice seeing you, Wade," she called over her shoulder as she dashed off.

Her car was parked in front of the butcher shop several doors down, where from this distance the slabs of meat displayed in the window resembled a splash of blood on a white shirtfront. All the way down the street she could feel Wade Jewett's cold eyes on her back.

# Chapter Six

On the south side of the square adjacent to town hall stood the Burns Lake courthouse, an imposing Italianate structure dating back to the late 1800s. In 1964 the old city hall had burned to the ground but the fire had been put out before it reached the courthouse, miraculously preserved alongside the ugly modern sprawl of its rebuilt municipal parent. Virginia creeper festooned its ornate brick facade. Pigeons roosted in its bracketed eaves, and oak doors thick as a medieval dungeon's guarded the entrance. As Noelle mounted the wide granite steps, she half expected to hear the creak of a drawbridge being raised. She had never felt so terrified in her life.

Before this she'd never seriously questioned the System. The freedom guaranteed by the Constitution was like the air she breathed, an odorless, colorless form of sustenance she took entirely for granted. It wouldn't have occurred to her that she might one day be robbed of that freedom. That she'd be found guilty without any evidence of having committed a crime and forced to pay the ultimate price. Even for fighting to protect her child, she was being punished.

Bright and early on Wednesday morning, she had been served with a restraining order that barred her from within a hundred feet of Robert's residence or office. Nothing more than a legal ploy designed to paint an even blacker picture to the judge, according to Lacey. But it had hit hard. Noelle was no longer certain, deep in her heart, that justice would be done. Beneath her calm surface and demure navy linen suit, her carefully rehearsed responses lined up in her head like rosary beads, she felt on the verge of a nervous breakdown.

Inside the courthouse, as she limped her way

down the cavernous corridor, which smelled of dusty crevices and ancient timbers, her dread mounted with each step. She kept her gaze on her father, walking ahead of her, his broad shoulders and proudly erect back a bulwark shielding her from the storm ahead. From behind came the rhythmic clacking of footsteps against the marble floor: her mother and Aunt Trish, her half sister, Bronwyn.

In the oak-paneled courtroom at the end of the hall, they all filed forward to take their seats. Her mother, sidling past her, pressed something into her hand. "My lucky fifty-cent piece," she murmured. "I found it under the lining of my top dresser drawer. Can you imagine? After all these years."

The coin felt warm and heavy against Noelle's palm. She blinked hard and bobbed her head in a fierce nod so as not to give in to tears. Mary looked stylish and sophisticated in a narrow below-the-knee saffron skirt and matching peplum jacket. Too sophisticated? Would it look to the judge like city slicker overkill?

She glanced at her aunt, the opposite of stylish in her dirndl skirt and short-sleeved blouse. Aunt Trish squeezed Noelle's hand in sympathy, her blue eyes bright with tears. "Don't tell Nana, but yesterday I lit a candle for you in church," she whispered. It was a sore point with her grandmother, Noelle knew, that her daughters no longer attended mass. Aunt Trish wouldn't want to give her false hope.

Noelle remembered how when she was

little, her aunt used to read aloud to her from children's books. A character from *Treasure Island* came to mind now: Ben Gunn, the old hermit who'd been consumed with thoughts of cheese, to the exclusion of all else. *That's what I have to do,* she thought. *Focus on Emma and block out everything else.*

It shouldn't be hard. For the past five days she'd been able to think of little else. She'd ceased being aware of what was going on around her, whether it was cloudy or sunny outside, warm or hot inside. She didn't dare leave the kettle on to boil, or she might wander off and forget it. If the TV or radio was on, she barely noticed. Most of the time she could scarcely bring herself to eat. Perversely, she was glad for her sprained ankle; it reminded her that she was capable of fighting back. It reminded her of Hank Reynolds, too, of his quiet support that had left her bolstered in a way she couldn't have explained.

She caught her father's eye and forced a wan smile. He winked at her in return, but his face was haggard with worry. In the dull light even his hair seemed more gray than usual, its crow's wing black faded to a dusty charcoal. She noticed, too, that he'd nicked himself shaving. Suddenly she loved him for that—the tiny cut on his chin like a badge of his concern.

Bronwyn stepped up alongside her, growling under her breath in imitation of a gangster, "Anybody gives you a hard time, I'll break both their kneecaps."

Noelle couldn't help smiling. Her sister, at

sixteen, was more of a handful than Emma at times. A real heartbreaker, too. Limpid dark eyes and long dark hair, full lips curled in mystery. A teenage Mona Lisa with the spirit of Huck Finn.

"Thanks, but I'll settle for a fair hearing," she whispered, oddly touched for some reason by her sister's attempt at proper courtroom attire: black skirt and clunky black lace-up boots, denim jacket over white button-down shirt.

At the petitioner's table, Noelle lowered herself into the chair next to Lacey. Nervously she glanced over at Robert's lawyer, Everett Beale, seated at the table to their right, a thin, intense-looking man in his late forties or early fifties, with one eyebrow split in two by a scar and tortoiseshell spectacles perched on his toucan's beak of a nose. But where was Robert? Was this another of his tricks—a continuance that would further delay Emma's return? She felt her stomach clench at the thought.

"What are the chances of his not showing?" she muttered.

"Relax, he'll be here." Lacey offered an encouraging smile and reached into her briefcase. "Here, have one." She held out a roll of Life Savers. "It's something to pulverize in the meantime." In her dark gray suit, she looked small and fierce, like an alley cat poised to pounce.

Noelle heard the door in back creak open. She swiveled around and was confronted by the sight of her husband strolling in as if on a red carpet, flanked by his parents. Cole, a silver-haired version of Robert with his regal bearing and aging movie-star looks, paused only briefly to flick a haughty glance her way, while Gertrude kept her eyes carefully averted. Noelle's mother-in-law was dressed to the nines in Chanel, her coiffed champagne blond hair lacquered with enough spray to withstand a mortar attack. Her gloved hand was tucked into her son's arm, her chin held high as if to ward off an unpleasant smell.

Robert played his part to the hilt. In his tailored blue suit, bronzed and confident, he might have been the new CEO striding into a boardroom following a hostile takeover. At the same time, his boyish smile and the swatch of hair that dipped over his forehead made him appear ingenuous, trustworthy. Why would anyone doubt his word? How could she hope to show what he was *really* like? Noelle began to feel dizzy and short of breath. Pockets of sweat formed between her breasts and along the insides of her thighs.

When her husband slid smoothly into the chair next to his lawyer, leaning over to whisper something in his ear, something that brought a smile to the older man's thin, pale lips, she had to bite the inside of her cheek to keep from crying out, *He's a fake and a liar! Can't you see that?*

Robert didn't even glance her way.

Just then, the bailiff stepped forward, a heavyset man with three strands of hair combed over his balding head and, inexplicably, a generous dusting of dandruff sprinkled over the shoulders of his too-tight uniform. "All rise for the Honorable Calvin Ripley. Court is now in session," he intoned.

The judge, a small, round figure draped in black, stepped from a side door. Noelle rose to her feet with the rest of the courtroom, staring in surprise as he bounded up onto the bench. She'd braced herself for a monster, but here was a rosy-cheeked elf straight out of Santa's workshop, with merry brown eyes and snow-white hair that rose in tufts about a plump face creased in permanent amusement. Judge Ripley simply radiated good cheer.

When the formalities were dispensed with, he leaned onto his elbows, his alert, twinkling gaze moving with almost fatherly concern from Noelle to Robert. "Well, now, you both seem like decent people. Frankly, I don't see any reason we can't resolve this like civilized ladies and gentlemen." His high, reedy voice made her think of Barney Fife on the old *Andy Griffith Show*. "I know it's a bit unorthodox, but I'm going to ask Mr. and Mrs. Van Doren to step into my chambers. Don't have a heart attack, Mr. Beale. You and Miss Buxton are welcome to join us." He waggled a mock chiding finger at the two attorneys. "I want to remind you both, however, that this is a *preliminary* hearing. Save your theatrics for the courtroom."

An alarm bell went off inside Noelle's head. She couldn't have said why, but she had the sudden sense of being lured into yet another trap. As she rose to her feet, the blood rushed from her head and everything turned a little gray. At that moment Judge Calvin Ripley might have been the proverbial stranger offering a pocketful of candy and a ride, the wolf in sheep's clothing on the path to Grandma's house.

Even Lacey looked apprehensive. Standing up, she gave Noelle's elbow a little squeeze of encouragement. "Let me do the talking," she murmured.

Noelle silently took up the rear, thinking that if her heart were to beat any harder, it would knock a hole right through her chest. Yet the moment she stepped into the judge's chambers, she felt her fears subside. Except for the impressive display of leather-bound volumes lining the walls, it was like any office, only handsomer. Light streamed in through mullioned windows, casting diamond-shaped shadows over the genteelly faded oriental carpet. A stained glass lamp stood at one end of the antique partner's desk. A grandfather clock ticked sedately in an alcove beside a built-in glass case in which various trophies and memorabilia were displayed.

As she and Lacey settled onto the worn plush sofa, Noelle sneaked a glance at Robert and his lawyer, seated across the room in a pair of matching oxblood leather chairs. Serenely confident, he smiled back at her. She trembled with the urge to lunge at him. *This is all a game to him. He doesn't care what it's doing to Emma.*

She focused on the judge, praying he would see through Robert's phony facade. With a nimble backward hop, Ripley scooted up onto his desk so that he was perched on its edge, his smallish feet—shod in dapper two-tone oxfords—dangling a good six inches off the floor. His pink hands folded in his black-robed lap made her think of a pair of nestled piglets. A hysterical giggle clawed its way up her throat. *This isn't happening,* she thought. *It's a Monty Python skit. Any minute now the* real *judge will walk in.*

"Mrs. Van Doren, I'll get right to the point." Ripley beamed at her with his relentless good cheer. "There's been quite a bit of concern expressed lately about the state of your health, concern that quite frankly has brought to question your ability to care adequately for your child. I must confess I find it all rather disturbing."

Lacey leaned forward indignantly. "Your Honor, we're not here to discuss my client's health. I move that—"

The merry elf silenced her with a scolding waggle of his finger, as if chastising a naughty schoolgirl. "Now, now, Miss Buxton. You seem to have forgotten this isn't a courtroom. Yes, I know, I'm taking a few liberties here, but bear with me." He returned his fatherly gaze to Noelle. "Mrs. Van Doren, your husband tells me that prior to this you spent several months at a rehab facility. Have you considered further treatment for your unfortunate, ah, lapse?"

At first Noelle was too shocked to reply. She just sat there waiting for the joke to be over, for this impostor to clap his hands and say that they could all go home now.

"No—I mean, *no*, you've got it all wrong— I'm perfectly fine," she stammered. "My only problem is that my child is being held hostage." She glared at Robert, who merely shook his head pityingly.

"I'm a little confused." The judge frowned. "Are you saying I wouldn't be correct in stating you're an alcoholic?"

"Don't answer that," rasped Lacey.

But Noelle couldn't help it. She *had* to explain. "I'm a *recovering* alcoholic," she corrected him. "It's true I was at Hazelden, but that was six years ago. I haven't had a drink since."

"Your Honor, this goes to prior prejudice." Lacey persisted, her freckled tomboy's face growing darker by the second. "Any health problem my client might have suffered in the past bears no relevance to this case."

Ripley paid no more attention to her than if she'd been a fly buzzing at the windowpane. "Six years? Well, now, Mrs. Van Doren, that's certainly commendable. I take it you attend AA meetings?" He crossed his legs and leaned back, one knee cradled in his fat pink hands.

A scalding rush of blood left Noelle's cheeks stinging. "I—well, no, not for some time," she was forced to admit. "I stopped going after my third year. I just...didn't feel the need anymore."

"And you haven't had a drink in all that time? Six years, didn't you say?"

"That's right, Your Honor."

"Well, now, that does present somewhat of a dilemma." The snowy peaks of his brows drew together in an expression of deep consternation. "I was going to suggest you volunteer for treatment and that we reconvene at some future date to decide what's best for your little girl. But I can see that's not where we're headed."

Noelle felt a flicker of hope. "I've been *trying* to explain, Your Honor. This whole thing is"—she caught Lacey's warning look and barreled on regardless—"a terrible mistake. I would never do *anything* to harm my daughter. In fact, it's the other way a—"

"Your Honor," interrupted Robert's attorney, "my client isn't out to malign his wife. He's genuinely concerned for her welfare. But we've got to keep in mind that the state of Mrs. Van Doren's health isn't our primary concern. We have to think of what's best for the child."

Ripley's frown deepened. "Thank you, Mr. Beale, but I don't believe I need to be reminded of my duty," he replied testily, his expression softening as he turned back to Noelle. "No one is suggesting you would ever *purposely* harm or neglect your child, Mrs. Van Doren. But might there have been times you weren't entirely, shall we say, *cognizant* of your daughter's needs?"

"You mean, like a blackout?" Noelle's heart was beating in great, lurching thuds. Things had gotten off to a bad start, but she felt powerless to reverse them.

"Precisely." Ripley brought the tips of his fingers together under his chin as though fairly clapping with glee, as if she were a dull pupil who for once had gotten the correct answer.

Noelle felt sick. "But I *told* you. I've been sober for six—"

"Noelle, for God's sake!" Robert erupted. "Everyone in that restaurant *saw* you. I practically had to carry you out to the car! If that were all, believe me, we wouldn't be sitting here. But when I think of all those other times, what might have happened if our little girl had wandered into the street, or—" He stopped, as if too choked up to continue.

Noelle was engulfed in a hot flood of panic. In her drinking days she'd never had what you would call a true blackout. More like brownouts, where she'd been only vaguely aware of what was going on, like the outlines of solid objects sketched amid a thick fog. Nevertheless, her first waking thought the morning after was always: *Oh, God, what did I do?* She had the same feeling now, a hollowness in the pit of her stomach coupled with prickly unease. The ticking of the clock seemed suddenly ponderous, tolling her doom.

"I wasn't drunk that night, or any other night," she insisted, her words dropping like heavy footfalls into the stillness. "Your Honor, I—I don't know what happened." On the verge of blurting, *I'm almost positive I was drugged,* she thought better of it and said, "All I know is I fainted, and when I woke up the next morning, my daughter was gone. *He* took her. Not because he cares about her welfare but because I'd told him I wanted a divorce. Can't you see what he's doing? He set me up. But *none* of it's true. Not one word."

"So you didn't show up at your husband's house—pardon me, the, ah, marital residence—the afternoon of Tuesday the seventeenth and attempt to force entry?" Ripley stared pointedly at her injured foot, still wrapped in its somewhat grubby Ace bandage.

Noelle's face burned. A rivulet of sweat worked its way out from under her bra strap to trickle down her spine. "I never said that."

"This is outrageous." Lacey twitched in her seat. "My client isn't on trial here!"

"No, and that's exactly what I was attempting to avoid." The judge spoke sharply, and for the first time Noelle became aware of a nasty edge to his voice. Like a merry elf who wasn't an elf at all, but a mean little gnome. "However, it appears we're getting nowhere with all this. For the time being, I'm going to rule that the minor in question remain with her father until *both* parents have been evaluated by a court-appointed psychologist."

"*No!*" Noelle reared up on legs that suddenly felt elastic, as if they might stretch on and on forever. "You can't do this! Please, you don't understand. She's only five!" Tears slipped down her cheeks, but she didn't bother to wipe them away. "I'm the only one who knows

181

she likes her juice in a *cup,* not a glass, and that she won't go to sleep if the blinds aren't all the way drawn. She loves graham crackers but won't eat the cinnamon-flavored kind. She—" Noelle stopped, suddenly aware that everyone in the room was staring at her, aghast. Even Lacey.

Then the judge's eyes cut away, and his fey tone dissolved into one of crisp authority. "I'll allow supervised visits three times a week: Monday, Wednesday, and Friday, from one to four. Under the guidance of Child Protective Services down the hall. See my secretary on the way out for instructions."

The hearing, if that was what this was, had ended. Noelle sank back in stunned disbelief. The strength had gone out of her legs, and she was only dimly aware of Lacey patting her arm. Like a rabbit's to a snake, her gaze was inexorably drawn to Robert, who was already making his way toward the door. He glanced back at her with an expression just shy of a smirk.

White-hot rage billowed up inside her, eclipsing everything else.

Suddenly she couldn't breathe.

The room blurred and faded, like a badly scratched print of an old movie. Just then she remembered something else about *Treasure Island:* that Ben Gunn wasn't just a harmless eccentric. In his solitude, deprived of all he'd once held dear, his mind had become unhinged.

That was exactly what she felt happening to

her. As Noelle sat trembling in her chair, sick with fury and despair, the thought that jumped into her mind was like a rat scuttling after Ben Gunn's cheese: *What I really need right now is a drink.*

At twelve forty-five on Friday, Noelle pulled up in front of the courthouse for the first of her scheduled visits with Emma. She'd spent a bad night, pacing the floor and berating herself endlessly. But what could she have said or done that would have made things turn out differently? Any fool could see the judge was on Robert's side. Had she sat back and let Lacey do all the talking, the outcome would have been the same. In the end, too, Robert would win, just as he always did. She grew so despondent that at one point, in the early hours of the morning, she went as far as to pour herself a shot of brandy from the cut glass decanter in Nana's china closet. Just to help her get to sleep, she told herself. They all thought she'd fallen off the wagon anyway; she might as well enjoy the benefit of it. For several long minutes she'd stared as if hypnotized at the glass trembling in her hand, its familiar vapors rising up to soothe her like a murmured promise. Then, with a low cry, she'd dashed into the kitchen to hurl its contents down the drain.

Morning had brought a renewed sense of hope. The memory of her close call the night before had left her with an uneasiness that was hard to shake, but she took comfort in the fact that she *hadn't* slipped. Not because she was so virtuous but because in a life where booze had once reigned supreme there was now something even more important: her child. She had to stay strong and sober—as much for Emma as for herself.

Now, as she once more climbed the court-house steps, a new fear rose to tighten its fingers about her throat. Robert would have told their daughter that she was sick or crazy...or both. Admittedly, her own actions the other day had done nothing to prove him wrong. Suppose he'd brainwashed Emma to such a degree that she *wanted* to stay with him. The possibility left Noelle momentarily paralyzed, one hand clutching the ornate wrought-iron rail, the slight tenderness in her right foot, from which she had removed the bandage, entirely forgotten.

But to give in to that kind of thinking was exactly what Robert wanted. Once, during an argument, he'd claimed to know her better than she knew herself, and for an awful instant she'd wondered if it was true. But she knew now that it wasn't. For one thing she was stronger than he imagined. No match in terms of clout, true, but if there was one thing she had learned how to do, it was to endure. She had weathered a childhood of waiting for her mother, lying in bed each night, listening for the turn of her key in the lock. She'd navigated the turbulent seas to sobriety. For years she'd put up with Robert's cold silences and criticism and the lifestyle to which she was no more suited than a school horse to the racetrack. The storybook character she'd most identified with as a child was the resourceful pig in "The Three Little Pigs." Now she would have to do the same: build a house the Big Bad Wolf couldn't blow down.

Robert would have been surprised to learn that she had already begun laying the bricks. Her father was investigating some shady business dealings Robert might or might not have been involved in. Though she doubted Dad would be able to find much—Robert was in a class by himself when it came to covering his ass—she'd spent enough time around newspaper reporters to learn to expect the unexpected.

In AA there was a saying: *More will be revealed.* And maybe something would be revealed about Robert.

Inside, as she climbed the stairs to the second floor, Noelle was flooded by a new determination. She remembered when Emma was born, twenty-eight hours of labor that had ended in a cesarean. But the moment her tiny daughter was placed in her arms any lingering discomfort she might have felt vanished as if by the wave of a magic wand. She would never forget the utter trust with which Emma had gazed up at her, as if comprehending that this was her mother, who loved her and would protect her always.

Noelle blinked back tears as she turned down a corridor that ended in a glass-partitioned door on which was stenciled SCHOHARIE COUNTY CHILD PROTECTIVE SERVICES. Her heart was beating high in her throat. In her right hand she clutched a shopping bag that held a new Barbie, a roll of stickers, and a dozen of the miniature iridescent butterfly clips Emma was currently enamored with. She was early; it was only a few minutes to one. Would Robert be on time? Or show up late just to spite her?

She walked in to find her daughter kneeling on a chair at one of the desks, absorbed in the crayons and coloring book some thoughtful employee had provided. Noelle felt her heart take flight.

Emma looked up. Her face flooded with joy as if a light had come on. "Mommy!"

She wore a ruffled yellow sundress with a heart-shaped bib, and her dark hair was plaited in two neat braids tied with lengths of fat pink yarn, a familiar touch, courtesy of Grandma Van Doren. In her rush to scramble off the chair, the buckle on one of her sandals caught on the lacy hem of her dress, and Emma nearly went tumbling headlong to the floor. Noelle lunged forward, catching her just in time.

She hugged her daughter tightly. "Oh, sweetie. Do you know how much Mommy missed you?"

Emma wriggled from her grasp and spread her arms wide. "*This* much," she crowed.

An older heavyset woman with poodle-permed hair wearing a kelly green pantsuit rose from behind a desk to introduce herself as Mrs.

Scheffert. Noelle had to resist the urge to wring the woman's hand in gratitude when, instead of merely standing guard, she ushered them into an empty office, leaving the door discreetly ajar. Her gratitude would seem disproportionate, and she didn't dare risk Mrs. Scheffert's reporting that her actions had been in any way unusual.

The moment they were alone, Emma pounced on the shopping bag. "What did you get for me, Mommy?"

"Snips and snails and puppy dog tails." It was her standard line, but Emma giggled nonetheless.

Noelle sat down cross-legged on the carpeted floor, and Emma immediately plunked down in her lap, so forcefully Noelle was left breathless. But she didn't mind. Watching her five-year-old rustle through the shopping bag, delighting in each gift, she'd never felt more content.

Impossibly Emma seemed untouched by her ordeal. It was more than Noelle could have hoped for. It was more than she'd imagined the heavens would allow. She found herself wanting to speak in whispers so as not to break the spell.

An hour and a half later, Emma had tired of playing old maid and go fish with the cards Noelle had brought and was now absorbed in styling Barbie's long blond hair. The doll, her head sprouting every last one of the butterfly clips, resembled a patient being prepped for a CAT scan.

"Mommy, when are we going home to Nana's?" Emma asked.

Noelle felt her throat catch. "Oh, sweetie. I'm afraid you can't come with me. Not today."

Emma looked up, her clear, trusting blue eyes clouding over. "How come?"

*Because your monster of a father won't allow it.* Noelle blinked hard and forced a smile that felt as if it had been carved into her face with broken glass. "You remember when we first went to stay at Nana's, right after she got home from the hospital?"

Emma nodded vigorously. "We has to take care of her 'cause she went to the doctor and got a op...*opraisin.*"

"That's right. An operation. But there was another reason, too. Remember when I told you that daddy and I couldn't live together anymore?"

"Uh-huh." Emma seemed to take it for granted that mommies and daddies didn't always live together. A sign of the time, Noelle supposed. In her daughter's Montessori class, at least a third of the kids' parents were divorced. "Daddy said that was before and that things are different now."

Noelle swallowed hard. "What else did Daddy tell you?" It was an effort to speak normally.

"That I'm s'posed to stay with him till you come home." Emma's pinched little face was almost more than Noelle could bear. "Mommy, when *are* you coming home?"

188

"Oh, sweetie." With a low, choked cry, Noelle pulled her daughter to her, hugging her tightly. "You remember when Nana had trouble getting to the bathroom by herself, and I had to help her?"

"Like when you used to wipe me?"

Noelle smoothed her hair. "Not exactly, but sort of. Right now, Nana needs me to take care of her."

"I know how to help. *I'll* wipe Nana."

"You're a *big* help," Noelle agreed, her heart breaking.

"That time I found Nana's medicine under the bed? She gave me a whole dollar and said I was the bestest finder in the world."

"You're not just the best finder. You're the best *everything*." Noelle's voice wobbled. "And I'll still see you. Every chance I get."

"I know." Emma crawled off her lap and went back to arranging Barbie's hair, humming contentedly under her breath. But no sooner had Noelle breathed a sigh of relief—dear God, what a weight off her mind to know that, at the very least, her daughter's fears had been put to rest—than Emma once more asked, "Can we go now, Mommy?"

"You mean back to Daddy's?"

Emma shook her head vehemently. "I want to go with *you*." A petulant note crept into her voice.

"I'm sorry, sweetie, but you can't. As soon as Nana's better, I promise I'll come get you."

Noelle recalled Lacey's warning. At the

time, she'd thought nothing could be harder than resisting the urge to run after her daughter. Now she knew better. Leaving her was the hardest thing she'd ever had to do.

"I want to come *now*." Emma started to cry.

It began with sniffles and quickly escalated to full-blown sobs. As she held her daughter's small heaving body in her arms, rocking from side to side in a useless effort to calm her, Noelle felt certain her fractured heart would break.

*H*ours later she sat motionless on a bench in the town square. Somehow the entire afternoon had slipped by unnoticed. She had a vague memory of leaving the courthouse and of feeling the need to rest a bit before driving home, knowing that if she didn't, she might not make it in one piece. Now she saw that all the children scampering over the jungle gym had gone home. Shadows were beginning to creep out from under ladders and slides to slither over the churned-up sand below. Even the surrounding benches were mostly empty.

Noting the clerks and secretaries making their way down the steps of the courthouse, she glanced at her watch and saw that it was a few minutes past five.

*Do they know?* she wondered with a dull ache. *All the forms they staple and punch and stamp, all the duplicates and triplicates stuffed into files and envelopes—do any of them have the slightest notion of the impact it can have on someone's life?*

Probably not. The men and women hurrying past were concerned with little else besides beating the quickest path possible to home. No one cared about a little girl named Emma. While they thought about what they were going to have for supper or if their favorite TV show was going to be a new episode or a rerun, Noelle sat dying a slow death at the prospect of each visit with her daughter ending like this last one—with Emma having to be pried from her arms. Mrs. Scheffert, the old biddy who'd seemed so nice at first, had shot her a reproving look over Emma's head, as if it all were Noelle's fault somehow.

It felt as if something vital had been torn from her. What she wanted was so natural its very simplicity was a cruel irony, like a trick mirror fooling you into thinking there was a doorway where there wasn't. She wanted her daughter. Nothing more, nothing less. She wanted to be among the mothers who'd stood calling to their children through cupped hands that it was time to go. She wanted to walk along the sidewalk with her daughter's small hand in hers. She—

"Mind if I join you?"

Startled, Noelle glanced up. A man stood before her, the sun at his back throwing his face into shadow. It was an instant before she recognized him. In chinos and a short-sleeved shirt, minus his doctor's coat, Hank Reynolds might have been just another passerby, a man of medium height, with light brown hair, whose muscled arms and shoulders suggested regular workouts at the gym.

Except for his eyes, which caught the sun as he lowered himself onto the bench—eyes the dark amber of tea laced with brandy.

"I'm afraid I'm not very good company right now," she warned.

Hank smiled warmly. "I'll take my chances."

He had a newspaper tucked under one arm and a grocery sack balanced in the crook of his elbow. He lowered the sack onto the grass at his feet. "I usually take the short way home, but it's such a beautiful day I decided to walk through the square instead." He nodded in the direction of her foot. "Looks a lot better than the last time I saw it. How does it feel?"

Noelle shrugged. "All I can say is, it's the least of my worries."

Hank was silent for a moment, looking out over the lawn where a couple of teenage boys were tossing a Frisbee. "If you feel like telling me about it, fine," he said at last. "If not, we can just sit. I'm in no particular hurry."

"As you can see, neither am I." Her voice cracked, and she abruptly found herself on the verge of tears.

He glanced at her in concern. "That bad, huh?"

"You don't want to know."

Hank touched her arm. "Try me."

*He's just being nice,* she told herself. *Nice Dr. Hank, beloved of children and old ladies alike.* "I'm afraid it's a bit out of your bailiwick," she said with an attempt at an airy laugh that fell far short of its mark.

"You'd be surprised. In my line of work I'm

192

exposed to pretty much everything—even the stuff that isn't catching." A rueful smile tugged at one corner of his mouth.

In the old days, she would have said, *Thank you, I appreciate the offer, but I'll be fine.* But that was the Noelle of before. The dutiful daughter who from age ten through eighteen had smiled her way through the rounds of parties, openings, and premieres her mother had dragged her to. The company wife who'd found refuge amid the bright clamor of cocktail parties, in the wineglass that was never empty and never quite full. At this moment, the woman emerging from the too-tight skin of her former self didn't seem to have any such reservations. Without further ado, Noelle burst into tears.

"I'm sorry." She gulped when she could at last trust herself to speak. "I'm making a fool of myself. You should go home. Your ice cream will melt." She gestured toward the pint of rocky road poking from his grocery sack.

"I can always buy more."

To her profound gratitude, Hank didn't pat her on the back or murmur false reassurances. He merely handed her his handkerchief, a neat pressed square that smelled faintly of fabric softener.

They sat together in silence while Noelle mopped her face and struggled to regain her composure. Finally she said, "It's a long story."

"I'm a good listener."

She studied him out of the corner of her eye.

He might not be the kind of man who inspired strange women to slip him their business cards—home numbers scribbled on the back—as regularly happened with Robert. Hank's appeal wasn't so overt. But it was undeniable nonetheless. Even the slight overbite that reminded her of Pete Caswell, an altar boy at St. Vincent's whom she'd had the biggest crush on back in the fifth grade. Despite her mood, she felt her heart quicken.

"Maybe another time," she told him.

"In that case, I'll treat you to a cold drink instead." He reached into the sack, pulled out a Seven-Up, and thoughtfully popped the tab before handing it to her.

"Thanks." She tilted her head back and drank deeply. She thought she'd never tasted anything so delicious.

Long brushstrokes of orange and purple tinted the horizon, where rooftops twinkled in the golden rays of the setting sun. From where she and Hank sat, as companionable as an old married couple, the distant slamming of car doors had dwindled to an occasional thunk. A breeze had kicked up, stirring the stagnant air and rustling the leaves overhead. Noelle became aware of Hank's hand, curled loosely on his knee. Against the tan fabric of his slacks, it looked large and capable. Unexpectedly she felt a stab of longing—for what exactly, she couldn't have said.

She pointed toward the fountain at the center of the square, featured on postcards sold at Gleason's Pharmacy, a graceful Art Noveau nymph ringed with spouts in the shape of lily pads. "If that girl could talk, think of the stories *she'd* tell."

Hank smiled, the creases at the corners of his tea brown eyes flaring. "Maybe that's why she spends her days weeping instead."

She shot him a sharp glance. "Crying isn't always the answer."

"No, but it sometimes helps."

She looked into Hank's kind face and saw something she hadn't seen before: a quiet strength that seemed to rise from a place deep within. He reminded her of her father, of that look Dad sometimes got: of an immovable object meeting an irresistible force.

"My husband has temporary custody of our daughter," she began, the words coming easily now, rising like the water bubbling to the surface of the fountain. "I have supervised visitation three times a week. Today we sat in a room with the door open so a social worker could keep an eye on me, to make sure—" She broke off, staring down at the grass and imagining the look of pity she was certain Hank wore—pity mixed with wariness perhaps. Suddenly she didn't want his sympathy. What she wanted, *needed,* was simply for this nightmare to end. "It's all so unbelievable, the very idea that I would ever neglect my little girl...." She cleared her throat. "When she was a baby, I made all her food from scratch. I wouldn't have dreamed of feeding her from a jar. It might sound paranoid, but I even kept the cleaning supplies on a high shelf. I didn't trust those safety latches."

"I see plenty of kids who'd have been spared a trip to the hospital if their mothers had been as paranoid," Hank observed mildly.

"The worst of it is that I can't protect her *now*. She's suffering, and I can't do a thing to prevent it." Noelle paused to blow her nose into Hank's wonderfully voluminous white handkerchief. When she lifted her head, she felt cleansed somehow, the soggy gray weight of her sorrow drained away and in its place a gleaming blade of anger. "I'm sure you hear a lot of women say their husbands are evil, but mine really is. I used to believe he loved his daughter, but now I'm not so sure. He's using her to crush me, and the awful thing is, it's working."

"From where I sit, that's not how it looks." Meeting his gaze, she saw that Hank didn't pity her. His expression was coolly assessing, even admiring.

"What—what are you saying?" she stammered.

"That the woman I see is perfectly capable of kicking down any door that stands in her way."

Noelle smiled reluctantly at the image of herself as Xena, Warrior Princess. "Emma's five," she said softly, "that age when every other sentence is a question. I just wish I had all the answers."

"Then you'd be like that guy over there. They'd erect a statue of you in some park."

He gestured toward the one of Luther Burbank, a gray squirrel perched like a miniature aide-de-camp on one bronze shoulder.

Noelle laughed, watching the squirrel scamper back down to retrieve an acorn from the grass below. With the toe of one sneaker she nudged a wet spot on Hank's grocery sack. "Looks like you're too late to save that rocky road."

"Story of my life." He shrugged and stood up. He hoisted the groceries under one arm before offering her the other. "Will you allow a fellow wayfarer to walk you to your car?"

This time, when Noelle rose to her feet, her legs didn't threaten to collapse. She found she could walk quite steadily, one arm resting lightly in the crook of Hank's elbow. Her fingertips brushed the fine hairs along his muscled forearm, and she was acutely aware of the heat of his skin against hers. Nana and her mother would be wondering what was keeping her, she thought. They'd be worried. But at that moment, for the first time in days, Noelle felt safe and strong.

# Chapter Seven

Even after all these years, Mary could have found her way to the Lundquists' in her sleep. The old farmhouse, with its deep porch and kitchen garden out back, stood at the junction of Blossom Road and Route 30A. As she pulled into the driveway behind a fire engine red Ford Bronco that could belong to none other than Jordy Lundquist, the youngest of Corinne's three brothers, who from the time he was old enough to drive had favored flashy cars in lipstick shades, she felt a low bittersweet ache. She'd heard that Jordy was married with two kids and was struck anew by the tragedy of Corinne's not having had a chance to do the same: grow up and get married, have children. Memories hovered like the butterflies flitting in and out of the tall grass on either side of the drive.

Stepping from her Lexus onto the dusty drive, Mary could almost see her best friend perched on the shady top step of the porch, elbows propped on her knees, her head sprouting a dozen fat curlers. She could almost hear her yell out, *Hey, Ma-ary Ca-a-a-ther-ine!* Corinne, who'd loathed nick-names—due to years of being teased by her three brothers, otherwise known as the Triassic Trio—had been the only one besides her parents to call her by her full name.

Mary lingered a moment, inhaling the sweet scent of alfalfa and fresh mown hay. A big chocolate lab unfolded itself from the shade of a slippery elm and ambled over to greet her. He looked like a grown-up version of the puppy she'd gotten for Noelle when they first moved to Manhattan, a sweet-natured dog no more cut out for city life than her daughter, which after a few months and several hundred dollars worth of damage she'd been forced to give away. Luckily, the Lundquists had been only too happy to take him, saying a farm could never have too many dogs. Mary bent to pet his head, releasing a cloud of dust that made her sneeze.

"Hey, fella, you by any chance related to Boomer?"

Son of Boomer, as she already thought of him, woofed in reply, his vigorously wagging tail stirring up even more dust. Mary smiled. It had been twenty years since her last visit, but from the way Corinne's mother had acted over the phone you'd have thought it was yesterday. "Don't bother knocking," Nora had warned. "My hearing's so bad I wouldn't know to answer. I'll leave the front door unlocked—you just come right on in."

They'd settled on Friday afternoon. Nora would be away until then visiting her eldest son, Everett, and his wife, Cathy, who'd recently given birth to their fourth child. The garden had a whole mess of tomatoes coming in, she said. She'd be busy putting them up and could use the company.

Mounting the porch steps, Mary wondered if she ought to have been straight with Nora about her real reason for coming. How would Nora feel when she learned this wasn't exactly a social call? It had been a long time, yes, but some things you never get over, and losing your only daughter had to be one. Dredging up memories about Corinne was sure to be painful.

But as Mary stepped into the house, as familiar as the one she'd grown up in, it was she who felt as if she'd gone back in time. There was the doorway to the living room with its ascending notches marking the heights of the Lundquist children at various ages. And the stain on the hooked runner where Everett had once spilled a pitcher of grape Kool-Aid. Even the lamp with its cracked shade from when Corinne had gotten a little carried away twirling her baton was exactly as it had been.

In the kitchen she found Corinne's mother elbow deep in a sink full of suds. As Nora turned to greet her, Mary was struck by how little she, too, had changed. Her beautiful flaxen hair had merely faded to the color of parchment. The fine wrinkles around her eyes were scarcely noticeable against their deep cerulean, the exact shade of the Blue Willow china lining the shelves of the old pine cupboard against the wall. Only her hands, lumpy and twisted with arthritis, betrayed her age.

"My heavens, you startled me!" she exclaimed, wiping her hands on the dish towel tucked into the waistband of her denim skirt.

She stepped forward to envelop Mary in a hug. "I thought you were Jordy, sneaking up on me that way. I sent him out back for more tomatoes."

She gestured toward the window, where all that was visible of Corinne's brother was a broad back rising and falling amid the vines that twisted up stakes and spilled over the ground. "Lord bless him," she went on, "he stops by at least once a day to see how I'm getting on. It's a real comfort, but between you and me that boy sure can eat. You'd never guess he has a wife at home who feeds him." Nora glowed nonetheless, as if reveling in the fact that she hadn't outlived her usefulness.

Mary glanced about the spacious kitchen with its chipped cabinets in need of painting, thinking how different it was from her mother's Formica shrine to tidiness. A bowl of freshly poached tomatoes sat cooling on the counter; beside it, rows of sparkling Mason jars waiting to be filled. Atop the old-fashioned enamel oven were two loaves of homemade bread, still in their pans, their aroma bringing back memories of Corinne and her tramping in after school, hungry enough to eat a bear.

"It's incredible. Nothing's changed," she marveled, slowly shaking her head.

"I could say the same of you." Nora stood back to scrutinize her. "Goodness, Mary Quinn, don't tell me you went and got your face lifted."

Mary laughed. "Even if I wanted to, I don't know when I'd fit it into my schedule."

Nora shot her a queer look. Softly, she said, "You ought to slow down, Mary. Life comes along but once, and if you don't grab hold, it'll slip right through your fingers."

Nora's admonition had an unsettling effect that Mary was quick to brush away. She replied airily, "I'll keep that in mind...though at the moment it seems I have my hands plenty full."

Nora pulled the dish towel from her waistband, folding it neatly over the drainer on the counter. "Come, let's you and I sit and have some lemonade while Jordy's out scaring off the mealybugs. You still like yours with enough sugar to stand a spoon up in?"

Mary smiled. "I'm afraid my sweet tooth isn't what it used to be. I'll save it for one of your gingersnaps."

She sank into a chair at the table, slipping off her espadrilles to cool her feet against the tile floor polished to glassy smoothness by decades of scuffling shoes. Watching Corinne's mother bustle about, setting out glasses and a plate of cookies, Mary once again felt a stab of misgiving for having misled Nora about the purpose of her visit. Maybe she should forget the whole idea. What was the point? After all this time the chances of Corinne's mother remembering anything new were slim to none.

*Her daughter is dead, but yours isn't. You owe it to Noelle to at least try,* whispered a stern voice in reply.

Mary waited until Nora sat down before

asking, "How many grandchildren is it now? I've lost count."

Nora beamed as she poured lemonade from a big glass pitcher. "Eight, and still counting. Quint and Louise are expecting their third in November. Wouldn't you know every one of my boys waited until I'd practically given up hope before getting married? Fortunately they all found wives young enough to bear lots of children." Her gaze dropped. "What about you, Mary? Why is it I don't see a wedding ring on *your* finger?"

"Once was enough, I guess." She kept her tone light.

Nora nodded knowingly. "Well, I can see why you'd have trouble finding someone to replace Charlie." She reached for a gingersnap, her knotted fingers scrabbling briefly over the plate before managing to capture one. "I remember when you were kids, crazy in love. Can't say it came as much of a surprise when I noticed you growing feet for stockings."

Mary blinked in amazement. "You guessed I was pregnant?"

"I have sharp eyes." Nora tapped her temple with a finger bent and twisted like a tree root.

Mary sipped her lemonade, feeling flustered and all of a sudden much too warm. She found herself remembering the night she and Charlie had gone skinny-dipping in the lake. He'd told her she was the most beautiful thing he'd ever seen. Right then and there she'd decided there would never be anyone but him.

And there hadn't been, not really.

"Corinne took it hard when you ran off and got married." Nora went on. "I think she saw it as the end of something you and she had shared."

Mary nodded slowly. "I sensed it at the time, but I think we were both afraid to admit it." A brief silence fell and she became uncomfortably aware of Nora's bright blue gaze. "The truth is, I've always felt a little guilty. I should have been there for Corinne. And— and I wasn't."

"None of us were." The shimmering intensity of Nora's eyes was almost blinding. "Poor Ira, it near broke his heart that she hadn't felt she could come to us."

Mary remembered Corinne's father as stern but loving. As strong as her own father had been weak. Corinne *had* been more than a little intimidated by him, come to think of it. "So you never found out what made her—what was troubling her?"

"Why, no. That's what made it so hard, that she didn't leave so much as a note."

Mary felt foolishly disappointed. She'd known it was a long shot, but she'd nonetheless hoped for a thread, however slender, that would provide some sort of lead. Now what?

"I'm sorry for raking all this up," she apologized.

"Don't be." Nora wiped a tear from her eye and reached over to pat Mary's hand. "It's good to remember, even when the remembering is hard."

Mary took a deep breath and confessed. "I'm afraid I haven't been very honest with you, Nora. I didn't come just for old time's sake. I'm here because of my own daughter." She paused, laying her hands flat against the table. "I don't know if you'd heard, but Noelle has a little girl of her own."

"I know—read the announcement in the paper when she got married. I remember thinking the poor child didn't know what she was getting herself into." Nora shook her head in disgust. "Of all the men to choose from."

"Well, she finally wised up. Now Robert's trying to take their little girl away from her." Mary felt a little burst of anger, remembering how smug he'd looked in court.

"Nothing that man did would surprise me."

"What makes you say that?"

Nora pushed aside her glass as if she'd suddenly had too much. "I never met anyone colder. Even as a boy, there was something...not quite right about him. At the funeral he acted like he'd barely known Corinne." Her hand shot out to close about Mary's wrist. Her eyes were like twin flames burning in the pale oval of her face. "Keep an eye out for that girl of yours, Mary Quinn. That's all I'm saying."

"I'll do my best." Mary shuddered, suddenly repelled by the twisted knots of flesh pressing into her hand. She drew away as soon as she could do so without its seeming rude, asking, "Nora, is there anything else you remember about that time, anything at all?"

The older woman thought for a moment, then shook her head. "Corinne didn't confide in me much, especially about Robert. It should've been my first clue that something was wrong. She didn't act like you did with Charlie. It was like he had a hold over her...only I wouldn't call it love."

"Do you think he had anything to do with"— Mary hesitated to plant an idea that would haunt Nora to her own grave—"with Corinne's being so distraught?"

Nora drew a hand over her face as if wiping fog from a windowpane. "I know they argued. The last time they were out together, she came home looking upset. She'd been crying. When I asked her what happened, though, she wouldn't say."

"Is that all?"

Nora shook her head. "I'm sorry I couldn't be more help."

"It was a long time ago. *I'm* sorry for dredging all this up." Mary reached for her lemonade, which was too sweet even without the extra sugar, and finished it just to be polite. Then she rose to her feet. "I should be going. I've kept you long enough."

Corinne's mother stood up, too, absently patting the pockets of her skirt as if looking for something she'd misplaced. The troubled look was gone from her face, replaced by a warm smile. "Nonsense, I enjoyed the company. Here, let me give you some of these cookies to take home. You haven't eaten a single one."

She was seeing Mary to the front door when she stopped short. "Wait. I have something else for you. Meant to give it to you years ago, but with one thing or another I never got around to it. Stay put. I'll go get it."

Nora started up the stairs, her hand gripped tightly about the banister. The wall to the second floor was a gallery of framed photos, and a portrait of Corinne with one front tooth missing, grinning like a jack-o'-lantern, jumped out at Mary. She remembered vividly the day it was taken. They'd been in the fifth grade, and Corinne had just been appointed a captain of the girls' volleyball team. Even though Mary was the worst player by far, Corinne had chosen her first. From that day on, there'd been no separating them.

*Corinne, if you're up there, watch over my daughter. She's the one who needs you now,* Mary pleaded silently.

Minutes later Nora returned holding something small and square wrapped in a flowered scarf. She handed it to Mary with the grave dignity of a priest offering a chalice. "It's Corinne's diary. She'd have wanted you to have it."

Mary's heart quickened. She'd forgotten Corinne kept a diary. "Are you sure?"

"I'm sure."

"Then I'll treasure it always. Thank you, Nora...for everything." Mary hugged her good-bye.

She was walking to her car when a man in dusty jeans carrying a bucket of ripe tomatoes came trotting around the side of the house. Jordy Lundquist was the image of Nora, the same blue eyes and baby-fine blond hair, the same sturdy build. Only taller, by at least a foot. He was waving at her as if she hadn't seen him, as if she could possibly *miss* seeing him. Mary smiled, remembering when Corinne's chubby kid brother used to tag after Corinne and her the same way.

He was panting when he caught up to her. "Mary! Why didn't you call out the window and let me know you were here?"

"Your mother and I got talking, and before I knew it, it was time to go. I'm sorry, Jordy. Another time?" She put out her hand.

He pumped it vigorously. "Next time you're in the neighborhood stop by the house. I'd love you to meet my wife and kids. I have two, you know—two girls, Jessie and Jillian."

She smiled at his obvious pride in his family. "Thanks, I'd like that. It was wonderful seeing your mother again." She hesitated, then said, "I hope I didn't upset her too much."

Jordy carefully set the bucket down at his feet, eyeing her curiously. "Upset her? Heck, Mary, she's been looking forward to your visit all day."

"We talked about Corinne."

A cloud passed over the sun just then, and Jordy's eyes seemed to darken as well. She'd expected him to pass it off as perfectly normal—why *wouldn't* they have talked about Corinne?—but he was looking at her with a sudden wariness that struck a jarring note here in

208

the drowsy summer sunshine with the smell of fresh-picked tomatoes drifting up around them.

"What about Corinne?"

"Oh, you know. The old days."

Jordy seemed to relax. "The old days," he echoed. A slow smile spread across his broad face, catching in the creases that radiated like sunbursts from the corners of his bright blue eyes. "Heck, I could tell a few stories of my own. I didn't tag after you and Rinny all those years for nothing."

"I don't doubt it for a minute." Mary tossed a smile over her shoulder as she climbed into her car. She rolled the window down to wave good-bye. "Bye, Jordy. It was nice seeing you."

Driving home, she thought, *Something happened back there.* Jordy had acted funny when she mentioned Corinne. Why? Because he still hadn't gotten over her death...or was there something more? She puzzled over it for several minutes before reluctantly pushing it from her mind. No use speculating. When the time was right, she'd pay Jordy a visit, find out what, if anything, he knew. In the meantime, she had Corinne's diary....

Mary was less than a mile from home when she remembered her cell phone. It rang so often these days she hadn't dared leave it on while at the Lundquists'. Usually her assistant, calling with updates, occasionally a client to whom she'd given her direct number. No sooner had she switched it on when she heard its familiar trill.

"Mary, thank God you're there. Something's come up." Brittany sounded uncharacteristically out of breath. "It's Leo. Apparently he's having some sort of nervous breakdown. He's holed up in his apartment, and his sous chef is on the verge of mutiny."

Mary felt herself break into a sweat. *Oh, Lord, what next?* Leo LeGras had been hired to cater the Rene's Room banquet, for which she'd already plunked down a hefty deposit. For a function this size, it wouldn't be easy finding another caterer of his caliber on such short notice.

"Can you get him on the phone?" she asked.

"I've only left about eighty-five messages. No luck getting past the doorman either. Mary, I can't handle this alone. You've got to *do* something." Her normally capable assistant was clearly at wit's end.

"I'll drive down next week," Mary told her. "I don't know which day yet. Can you can hold it together until then?"

There was a short pause. Then Brittany answered direly, "I didn't tell you the worst of it. Mr. Lazarus got wind of your being out of town, and he isn't too happy about it. When he hears about *this*, I wouldn't want to be in your shoes."

"Between you and me, Lazarus is a horse's ass." Mary had never liked the man. Rene's Room aside, he wasn't shy about capitalizing on his wife's death.

"Yeah, but he was married to one of the most beloved stars of all time." Brittany didn't have to tell her it would be bad PR for them to piss off a man with Lazarus's connections.

"Anything else I should know?" Mary asked, more brusquely than usual. Her assistant's calls never failed to remind her of how far out on the proverbial limb she'd crawled.

"Just the usual." Some of the tension went out of Brittany's voice. "We struck out with *Regis and Kathie Lee* on Merriman's book, but we're still working on Oprah. Oh, and Lucianne Penrose's manager called from Miami to scream bloody murder. Apparently the local TV crew that was supposed to cover her shoot never showed."

Mary groaned. Whenever Lucianne was shooting an outdoor commercial for her diet centers, she always tried to have it covered by the local press—double the bang for the buck. "Whose screwup was it?"

"No one's, far as I can tell." Brittany's voice was beginning to break up amid the static. "It was all set to go with WPLG. Something more important must've come up."

"More important than Lucianne? It'd have to be a presidential assassination attempt." Mary indulged in a dry laugh, which did nothing to dispel her sinking sense of despair. Or the debt of gratitude she owed her staff. "Hey, Brit, in case I don't tell you enough, thanks for holding the fort down."

"My pleasure. Mark sends his love, too." Her voice grew even choppier. "We're breaking up.... I'd better sign off."

Mary thumbed the end button and shoved

the phone back in her purse. She couldn't deal with one more headache right now. Not with everything she'd worked so hard to build going to—

Glancing out the corner of her eye, she was distracted from her thoughts by the sight of Corinne's diary on the seat beside hers. Did it hold any stunning revelations about her death? Doubtful. If the Lundquists had had reason to suspect foul play, they'd have long since gone to the police. No, if there was anything to be revealed, it was between the lines. And who better to decipher it than the friend Corinne had trusted above anyone else? Mary's pulse quickened at the prospect.

*I should show it to Charlie. For better or for worse, we're in this together.* She smiled ruefully at the thought even as she turned sharply onto the road leading to town.

"*Y*ou didn't honestly think we'd find anything, did you?"

Charlie spoke softly, gazing out at the lake from his back porch, where he and Mary sat comfortably ensconced in a pair of Adirondack chairs. Hours had passed since they'd arrived at the cabin, driven here by the frenzy of the newsroom. Poring over the diary with Charlie, followed by a surprisingly good supper his daughter had helped prepare, she'd lost all track of time. Now, with dusk falling, Mary was startled to realize how late it had gotten. The lake had darkened to the hue of tarnished silver, and the silhouettes of trees stood out against the purpling sky, where the first stars were faintly sketched.

"I don't know what I expected." She sighed. "Sylvia Plath, I suppose." The notion of her friend as a manic-depressive poet brought a faint smile to her lips.

In reality, Corinne's diary had revealed nothing more than the hopes and dreams of a perfectly average sixteen-year-old girl. The last entry, dated three months before Corinne's death, was almost heartbreakingly banal. *Went to Laura's party with R. We fought the whole way there. At the party he didn't talk to me once. I was so mad! I pretended I didn't care when he left without me, but it was all I could do to keep from crying. J. gave me a ride home. He's nice. More about that later.* Whoever "J" was.

"Maybe you're thinking of what it was like for us."

Charlie spoke lightly, but she caught a note of tamped pain in his voice. Mary turned to regard him solemnly. In the amber glow of the porch light, his sharply etched profile made her think of those on ancient Roman coins. Yet he would have laughed at the idea that there was anything noble about him. Here, at his cabin on the lake, he was merely a man in his natural habitat, as relaxed as she'd ever seen him. He'd changed out of his work clothes into faded jeans and a worn chambray shirt. On his sockless feet he wore a pair of ancient, scuffed Dock-Siders.

Mary wondered what he'd have thought if

he'd known how often she'd fantasized over the years about summer evenings like this: sitting on a porch with Charlie somewhere, moths flickering overhead, and a whippoorwill calling in the distance.

With an effort she pulled her thoughts back to Corinne. "And maybe we're missing something," she said. "Maybe it's not about what's there, but what *isn't* there. If Corinne had any thoughts of suicide, I see absolutely no indication of it."

Charlie turned to smile at her. "Anyone ever tell you you'd make a good reporter?"

"Seriously, Charlie. Is it so farfetched to imagine she might have been"—a cool breeze had kicked up. Mary broke off, crossing her arms over her chest—"murdered?" she finished softly, almost as if wondering aloud.

"Anything is possible," he said thoughtfully. "But we have to stick to the facts. Whatever we might suppose, there isn't a shred of evidence to support that theory."

"But if Robert *did* have something to do with it, he's even more dangerous than we thought."

Silence fell. She could hear the faint plink of feeding trout and night birds calling to one another from the stands of speckled alder and white birch that grew thick along the shore. Mary listened to the hollow lap of water against the dock, where a small skiff was tied. It did nothing to lull her fears.

She wished Noelle were with them now, but she'd begged off Charlie's invitation to supper, saying she had a headache. Apparently today's visit with Emma hadn't gone well. And Mary had a feeling things were going to get a lot worse. Frustration rose in her. She felt as helpless now as she had all those years ago when Noelle was desperately ill and she hadn't known what to do.

"Either way you're right to worry." She saw a muscle flicker in his jaw. "You want to know something? When I saw him walk into the courtroom the other day I was a heartbeat away from smashing his face in. If Bron hadn't been with me, I'm not at all sure I wouldn't have done just that."

As if on cue, from inside came the clatter of Charlie's daughter dropping something in the midst of washing up, a pot or a pan from the sound of it. There was a muffled cry of "Shit!" Through the screen door Mary was afforded a view past the living room into the kitchen beyond, where a shadowy figure bent to retrieve it from the floor.

"From what I can see, it sounds as if she'd have cheered you on."

"Bron acts tough, but she's a lot more fragile than she seems." Charlie shook his head in fond exasperation. "With Noelle, it's the other way around—she's tougher than she realizes."

"Were they close growing up?"

Noelle had been fourteen when Bronwyn was born. Yet Mary knew little about the Christmas and summer vacations she'd spent with Charlie and his second wife and their daughter. At times she'd had the oddest feeling Noelle was hoarding those memories, as if she feared that in sharing them they'd be tainted somehow.

Charlie gave a low chuckle. "Thick as thieves. There were times, I swear, I could have walked out the door for good and it would've been weeks before they'd have noticed I was gone." He lowered his voice. "It's funny, though, how two sisters can be such complete opposites. Noelle, bless her, never gave me a moment's worry, but Bron, well, there's a wild streak in her. Maybe it's from growing up motherless, I don't know."

He looked so bewildered at that moment she longed to reach out and take his hand. The words slipped out before she could stop them. "What was your wife like?"

His smile of fond remembrance cut deep. "Vicky? Funny and bright. A little absent-minded. She was always misplacing things, like keys and umbrellas. She'd make shopping lists, then lose them. It became a family joke. But the one who always laughed loudest was Vicky." Softly he added, "You'd have liked her."

"I'm sorry I didn't have the chance to know her." She'd met Vicky only once, at Noelle's wedding, and had been struck by how nice she was. Pretty, too. But that didn't stop Mary from withering a little inside at the thought of Charlie and her together. "From what you've told me, I'm sure she'd be proud of the job you've done raising Bronwyn. She's a good kid, Charlie. Anyway, sometimes one good parent is better than two not so good ones."

"You have a point there."

"I envy you actually."

"How so?"

"I would have loved another child," she confessed, staring down at her hands. Her nail polish had begun to chip, but she hadn't noticed until now. Little by little her old habits were falling away. "I always wondered what it would be like to feel happy about being pregnant or to hold a newborn in my arms without being scared to death."

When Charlie didn't respond right away, she felt a moment of panic. Had she revealed too much? Perhaps she'd reminded him of a time he'd just as soon forget.

"Some things just aren't in the cards, I guess," he remarked mildly. She glanced up at him. His expression was flat, unreadable, and she felt her heart wither a little more. When he reached over to flick something casually from her arm, she flinched. "We should go inside. You'll be eaten alive by the mosquitoes."

He started to get up, but Mary put out a hand to stop him. "I'm fine, really. Would you mind if we took a walk instead?"

Charlie searched her face before nodding slowly. When he rose, the creak of his chair was like an exhaled breath. He called, "Bron! Mary and I are going down to the lake. We won't be long."

A second later Charlie's teenage daughter materialized as if out of nowhere, silhouetted against the screen like an exclamation point. "You don't have to shout, Dad. I'm not deaf, you know." The screen squealed open, and the girl stepped out onto the porch.

Mary, poised on the top step, smiled in an attempt to ease the tension that had been building all evening. "Thanks again for dinner, Bronwyn. It was delicious."

Bronwyn shot her a cool look. "All I did was the salad."

Mary tried not to take the girl's dislike of her personally. Hadn't Noelle been prickly at that age? Having her father to herself all these years surely hadn't helped either. Bronwyn's jealousy was palpable. Charlie was right about one thing: His younger daughter was a handful.

*If she were mine, I'd worry, too,* she thought. But he ought to save his concern for the boys who would fall under the spell of this teenage siren of his. Even in shorts and a rumpled Red Sox T-shirt, she looked the part of a temptress, her long legs brown and supple as a pearl diver's, her heavy jet black hair swaying at her slender waist.

"Well, anyway, it's such a lovely evening, I thought it'd be nice to take a stroll." Mary was quick to add, "You're welcome to join us if you like."

Ignoring her, Bronwyn turned to Charlie. "Dad, why don't you take Rufus? He's been cooped up in the house all day. He could use the exercise."

"Not this time, pumpkin," Charlie said. "He'll be chasing after every field mouse, and I don't feel like plowing through the bushes at night. I'll take him out when we get back."

Bronwyn gave him a long, measured look. Mary began to feel uncomfortable, even a tiny bit irritated. *It's just a* walk, *for heaven's sake. What on earth does she think is going to happen?*

They were strolling along the dirt path that sloped down to the lake when the girl called out plaintively, "Okay if I take the car, Dad? I told Maxie I'd come over after dinner."

Mary glanced back over her shoulder. In the yellow glow of the porch light, Bronwyn suddenly looked awkward and self-conscious, a bundle of emotions she didn't know what to do with. Unexpectedly Mary's heart went out to her, this wild, motherless girl who was the spitting image of her father.

Charlie appeared to hesitate. Mary heard the reluctance in his voice when he called back, "All right. But I want you home by midnight. And no side trips, okay?"

"Thanks, Dad!" Bronwyn sounded light-hearted as she bounded back into the cabin, the screen door smacking shut behind her.

Mary and Charlie walked in silence for the first few minutes. The path was fairly well traveled, and the moon that had risen over the tree-tops bright enough to see by. Its reflection glided over the tarnished surface of the lake as they strolled along beside it. This was when she liked it best, when it was too dark to see more than the distant lights of the condos that had sprung up like toadstools along the opposite shore; when the limitlessness of the starry sky overhead made her forget the smallness of her home place.

After they'd gone a short distance Charlie turned to her and said, "I apologize for the way Bronwyn acted. She can be a little overprotective at times."

"Understandable. She's had you all to herself all these years."

He sighed. "It's not easy raising a teenager on your own. Whatever I say or do, it seems like the wrong thing."

Mary thought of Noelle. "Maybe it's enough that you're trying," she said. "Maybe that's all that really counts."

The path wound in a narrow ribbon along the shore, except where occasionally swallowed up by dense woods. Charlie walked as if he'd know his way blindfolded, but Mary had to pick her way more slowly over the rocks and fallen branches. At one point, when she tripped and nearly fell, he grabbed her arm. Afterward, it seemed safer merely to hang on, though she was acutely aware of every awkward step that brought her bumping up against him.

When the path brought them nearly to the edge of the lake, they stopped for a moment to catch their breaths. Charlie pointed out the condos glimmering along the opposite shore, a raw gash of cleared land faintly visible beside it. "Last summer alone Van Doren & Sons slapped up fifty new units. And apparently there's no end in sight." His voice was filled with disgust. "They even got a variance to divert the creek that used to run through there. Of course it doesn't hurt that practically everyone on the town council is a crony of our son-in-law. "

"Can't something be done to stop it?"

"There's nothing illegal about it—nothing anyone can prove, at any rate." In the moonlight Charlie's face might have been carved of granite. "But I'm working on it, believe me. Starting next week, I'm running a series of editorials that are bound to get people talking."

"Sounds risky. Aren't you afraid of getting sued?"

He shrugged. "I won't be making any accusations. Just asking some questions that are sure to ruffle a few feathers."

"How is that going to help Noelle?"

Charlie gazed out over the lake, where moonlight rippled in narrow, glinting bands. Idly he said, "You know how they dredge for bodies? They throw a stick of dynamite in the water and see what floats to the surface."

Mary shivered in the cool breeze that had kicked up. "Let's hope it doesn't end up doing more harm than good."

Charlie wrapped an arm about her shoulders, which only made her shiver harder. "Want to head back?"

"In a few minutes. Let's walk a little farther." She didn't want the magic of this evening to end.

Clearly Charlie felt the same way. His arm remained tucked about her shoulders, kindling a warmth that even the rapidly descending chill of night did nothing to dispel. She leaned into his shoulder, truly contented for the first time in days. Had he dreamed of this, too? Lain awake nights, listening to the sound of his heartbeat and wondering if somewhere out there she was doing the same? It was wrong to indulge in such feelings, she knew. Wrong and dangerous.

Nevertheless, the pull was too strong. Somewhere, at the core of it all, she and Charlie were connected in a fundamental way. She'd known it since they were teenagers, and nothing in all the years since had weakened that sense of belonging. Walking beside him, her head nestled against his shoulder, she felt as if the blood that coursed through his veins were flowing directly into hers.

Charlie kissed the top of her head. A brush of lips, a whisper of breath, that traveled straight down through her like something warm that had been spilled. There was no longer any doubt where this was leading. A voice deep inside Mary urged her to turn back, but she ignored it. The tug toward Charlie was far greater, as elemental as the moon itself.

The path meandered inland, and they paused again to rest in a small clearing ringed with birch trees that glowed pale as limbs against the surrounding underbrush. Dandelions dotted the tall grass like tiny stars. The chirping of crickets sounded unnaturally loud in the stillness.

Mary found a boulder wide enough for the

two of them to sit on. Her pulse was racing, but not from exertion. She felt excited and at the same time terrified of what waited not around the next bend but right here in this meadow, with its soft grass and perfect ring of trees like God's thumbprint pressed into the landscape.

Looking around her, she marveled softly, "Why don't I remember this place? I'm sure I must have walked through it a hundred times."

"Things always look different in the dark."

Charlie brushed a stray pine needle from her hair, his fingertips grazing her temple. He was like a fever, inflaming her, causing her to grow weak. Filling her head with delirious imaginings. How could she ever have believed, even for one minute, that she'd found a substitute in those other men? There was no one like Charlie. There never had been, and there never would be.

Sitting down, she was even more acutely aware of his height for some reason. His lanky frame folded beside her. The shadow pooled at his feet. When he turned to take her in his arms, it felt as natural as breathing, as inevitable as the distant lapping of water in the stillness.

"Mary," he said softly. Just that, her name. Like a prayer.

He cupped her face gently in his hands and kissed her. His mouth was warm, with a trace of sweet smokiness from supper. Mary yielded to it as she'd known all along she would, deep down, from the minute she'd laid eyes on Charlie, seated at her mother's kitchen table. They would make love; that was part of God's plan, too. Here on the grass, under the moon, with the crickets singing.

The feeling was so strong she had the sense of actually dissolving into him, like candy on the tongue or snowflakes falling against warm cheeks. In a rush it all came flooding back: how it had felt with him in the beginning, when they were sixteen, how not even the threat of hell, or her mother's wrath (synonymous in her mind), could have kept her from Charlie's arms.

Mary clung to him now, feeling long-dead senses awaken one by one. The brush of his fingers against her neck that brought an answering tug low in her belly. His mouth, which kissed with just the right combination of tenderness and urgency. When he gently lowered her onto the grass, she thought that if he were to stop right now, she would die. He might as well stop her from taking another breath.

But Charlie wasn't stopping.

He undressed her slowly and with such care the act alone caused her to cry out, shivering with pleasure. "Mary, Mary," he whispered over and over. He kissed every patch of skin as it was laid bare. Only when she was naked did he pause to take off his own clothes.

"Hurry," she whispered. Then: "No, don't. Oh, God, Charlie, I want this to last forever."

He spread his shirt over the ground. As she lay on it, Mary could feel spears of grass poking up though the soft, worn fabric.

Kneeling over her, Charlie gazed down, tracing with his fingertips the curve of her belly and soft mound below.

"You're beautiful," he told her, as if seeing her for the very first time, as in a way he was. He dipped his head and brought his tongue to one nipple, a delicious shock that flooded her with warmth.

As he explored further, she moaned softly, stroking the back of his head. Then he was lowering himself onto her. The boy she'd known so intimately was now a mature man whose body she ached to explore: each clearly defined muscle and fascinating fold, each thrust that spoke of the control he'd mastered through the years.

"Am I going too fast?" he murmured at one point.

"No, no, please, whatever you're doing, keep doing it," she whispered back. It felt wrong and at the same time gloriously right. No rules, no inhibitions. Just the moon...the sweet sigh of the wind in the trees...and Charlie.

When it was over, he rolled over onto his back, and they lay side by side, letting the breeze dry their sweaty limbs, barely noticing the mosquitoes that hovered as if over a banquet. For a long while neither of them said anything. Mary was the first to speak.

"Did we really think we were going to get away with it? Look but don't touch?" She laughed breathlessly at the idiocy of it.

She turned her head and found him gazing

at her calmly, as if only one of them had been fooled, and it wasn't Charlie. Even so, she knew it was crazy. This was exactly what had gotten them into so much trouble in the first place. Only now, thirty-one years later, they faced a different kind of challenge.

Charlie rolled onto his side, propping himself on an elbow. "I, for one, was under no such illusion." He smiled down at her, his head cradled against his palm.

"Either way, we're asking for trouble. I'm not going to stick around forever, you know."

"Call it a trip down memory lane then—if it makes you feel better."

"That's safer at least."

He plucked a blade of grass from beside her ear and chewed it thoughtfully. "There's just one problem." He grinned, a flash of white teeth in the darkness, then gathered her in his arms and kissed her deeply. When he pulled back, he asked teasingly, "Does *that* feel like a thing of the past?"

She hesitated, her mouth inches from his. It wasn't the past, or even the present, that was troubling her. With Charlie, it was the future that could do real harm. Soon, in a matter of days or weeks or months, the time would come to say good-bye. Once again it would be some other woman picking up the pieces when she was gone.

But that day would come soon enough, she decided. Tonight she would think only of this. Of Charlie. Of the lake glinting darkly through the trees and the grass beneath them, stubbornly pushing its way up through the ground.

She owed them both that much.

So Mary said nothing. She merely kissed him back, opening her mouth to him in a silent plea for forgiveness, all the longing in her heart rushing up to meet him.

# Chapter Eight

Bronwyn finished washing the last pot and placed it in the drainer. She'd saved a scrap of chicken for Rufus, sprawled like a matted orange rug at her feet, but when she tossed it to him, he only licked it as if to show his appreciation, then flopped back onto the scuffed linoleum. Poor old Rufus. She'd been a baby when they'd gotten him. That would make him—what? A hundred and five in dog years? She supposed that if she lived that long, she'd be picky about what she ate, too.

She bent down to scratch behind one of his raggedy ears. "Holding out for a bigger bribe? Sorry, Ruf, this is as good as it gets. But I'm counting on you anyway not to rat me out."

At the thought of her daring plan Bronwyn's heart began to race. It had been taking shape in her mind for days, ever since Noelle's court date. Now the time had come to put it into action.

Oh, she knew what they thought: that she was too young to be much help, that she'd just get in the way. As if they had accomplished so much! If they were so smart, how come Noelle still hadn't gotten Emma back? They all acted as if that creep Robert were practically invincible. But that was just what he *wanted* them to think.

Bronwyn knew better. Last summer her sister had gotten her a job at Van Doren & Sons, and she'd seen a thing or two. Like the safe where Robert kept a second set of books, which she was sure the IRS would be interested in knowing about. A safe to which she just so happened to have the combination. But that was another story.

Right now her main problem was that her dad, much as she hated to admit it, was clueless. These days it wasn't *she* he saw but a collection of parts: her three earrings in each ear, pierced belly button, and wardrobe that in his words showed too much skin and not enough practicality. He'd be surprised to know, for instance, that she was still a virgin. And that yesterday, at Scoops, she'd been made Employee of the Month. And when you got right down to it, which of them was going to end up walking Rufus tonight? Personally, she wouldn't bet on the tall man in jeans who was so blinded by love he couldn't see straight.

Did he think she hadn't noticed? Jeez. He might as well be wearing a flashing neon sign, it was that obvious. Even when Mummy was alive, she'd noticed that Dad never talked about his first wife unless the subject just happened to come up—almost as if he were afraid to. Then he'd get this funny faraway look on his face, as if whatever he was remembering were too private to share. Mummy had noticed it, too. But the great thing about her was that she'd somehow understood. Bronwyn thought maybe it was one of the reasons Dad had married her...because she accepted him the way he was, leftover heartaches and all.

But things were different now. For one thing Mummy wasn't around, and Mary *was*. Also, you'd have to be blind not to see she was just as crazy about Dad as he was about her. Bronwyn didn't know where all this was leading; all she knew was that she wanted no part of it. As Maxie would say, *Ixnay onay— that's pig Latin for no fucking way.* Her best friend had a saying for practically everything, usually with a four-letter word worked in. When Bronwyn had confided in her, Maxie, true to form, had given the most accurate assessment of the situation to date: that it was shaping up to be one big *Melrose Place* rat-fuck.

What Bronwyn hadn't admitted to her friend was just how scared she felt. This thing with Noelle could drastically change *all* their lives, not just her sister's. *And I, for one, am not going to sit back and wait for some stupid judge to make up his mind.* Maxie had an aunt and uncle who'd been going at it for *years*. In the

229

meantime, *anything* could happen. Noelle, who already looked like death warmed over, could get sick, *really* sick...like Mummy. Robert could permanently brainwash poor little Emma. And Dad...

*He could end up getting married again.* She shuddered at the thought.

But there was a problem with her plan: She couldn't carry it out alone. And there was only one person she could count on to help her.

Nevertheless, as she was reaching for the phone on the wall, the thought of what she was about to ask of Dante caused her hand to freeze in midair. *If you get caught, you could both wind up in jail.* As for her boyfriend, it wouldn't be the first offense. Six months ago a DUI had earned him a night behind bars and a suspended sentence, which, oddly enough, was how they'd met.

Bronwyn would never forget the day Dante Lo Presti had walked into her life. She volunteered twice a week for One Voice, an organization that provided readers for the blind. And guess where you-know-who wound up doing his hundred hours of community service? Dante had been assigned to take her place with old Mr. Goodman, who in addition to being blind had Alzheimer's and occasionally got this idea people were stealing from him. The week before, he'd accused her of making off with his toothbrush, of all things. She wasn't alone. Bernie Goodman had fired two other volunteers before her.

So there she was waiting for her replacement

to arrive, and in walked this guy, who on a scale of ten had to be at least an eleven and a half. With his leather jacket and motorcycle boots, his bad boy smile and bedroom eyes, looking like a fasten-your-seat-belt Disney World ride. When Dante asked offhandedly if she'd like to hook up with him later on down at Murphy's, she hadn't hesitated to climb on board.

The trouble was, Dante wasn't exactly PG-rated. For one thing, he was eighteen, though just barely. As far as her father was concerned, that made him some kind of sex-crazed pervert. It didn't help either that Dante looked at least three years older, with permanent five o'clock shadow and grease under his fingernails from working at Stan's Auto. If only Dad would get to know him, he'd discover that underneath it all Dante was really sweet. But how was that going to happen when Dad had forbidden her to see him?

So she sneaked out with Dante every chance she got. She felt terrible about lying to her father, but he'd left her no choice. And in a sense he *had* gotten his way. Between school and both their jobs and all the stupid gyrations she had to go through, pretending she'd made plans with one of her friends when she was really meeting Dante, they hardly saw each other.

They made up for it by talking on the phone, sometimes long into the night when Dad was working late. She'd lie on her bed in the dark with the receiver pressed to her ear and a pillow squashed against her belly to keep it from tumbling at the sound of his deep, throaty voice. She'd never felt this way with another boy: hot one minute, cold the next. Scared of where her own body seemed to be taking her.

She knew Dante felt the same way. Why else would he put up with their not being able to see each other more often? But liking her was one thing, commiting a crime on her behalf something else altogether. He might get angry when she asked. He might even break up with her.

Her heart crumpled at the thought. She didn't know what she'd do if that happened. Curl up and die probably. Or join the army, as Maxie planned on doing after graduation.

Quickly, before she could weaken, Bronwyn dialed Dante's number. He shared an apartment with two guys famous for ignoring call waiting—Maxie's theory was that Troy and Mike were heavy into phone sex—and now she prayed for someone to pick up.

Finally the line clicked. "Yo."

It was Dante. She'd recognize that voice coming at her from under a jacked-up car with the air compressor blasting. Her heart began to pound, a reflex as automatic as a dog wagging its tail. It was an effort to speak normally.

"Hey. It's me, Bron. I was just wondering, you doing anything tomorrow after work?"

"You got something in mind?" Oh, that throaty rumble. Maxie had groaned that she must be made of asbestos to have resisted going all the way with a guy that sexy. And

Bronwyn couldn't think of a single good reason why she shouldn't. *Just because* didn't count as an excuse, according to Maxie.

"I thought maybe we could go for a drive or something," she answered lightly. Her heart was banging so hard it might have been the thump of Rufus's tail against the floor.

There was a pause. She could hear the TV muttering in the background. Then Dante said, "I'll see if I can get off a little early. The usual spot?" It was a sore point that they couldn't meet out in the open, but so far he'd been cool about it.

"Yeah, sure. Around four, okay?"

It wasn't until she hung up that Bronwyn let out her breath. She felt cold, too, though it had to be eighty degrees in here. Minutes later, driving over to Maxie's in her father's beat-up Chevy Blazer, she was still shivering.

The following afternoon she didn't get off work until nearly a quarter past four, thanks to an elderly woman who couldn't make up her mind between cherry vanilla and toffee crunch. Letting herself out the door, Bronwyn prayed that Dante would still be waiting when she got there.

He was. Right where they always met, in the little alley behind the movie theater. Slouched up against the brick wall, smoking a cigarette. Six feet of tanned muscle clad in tight Levi's and an even tighter tank top. A pair of Ray-Bans was pushed up into his dark curls, and on the chiseled biceps of one arm a tattoo stood out, the Chinese symbol for *chai*. Life.

As in *real* life, not the ridiculously sheltered existence she led.

As always, there was that little beat before he spotted her in which she wondered, *What does he see in me?* Dante had been on his own since he was sixteen. He drank (though no longer got wasted). He smoked. And though he'd only alluded to it, she was sure he'd slept with *lots* of women. She, on the other hand, drank nothing stronger than root beer, and the closest she'd gotten to having sex was the one time she'd let her old boyfriend, Chris Bartolo, sort of accidentally on purpose rub up against her until he came.

"Sorry I'm late." Bronwyn was out of breath from running the whole way. "There was this stupid woman—oh, never mind. You been waiting long?"

Dante tossed his cigarette to the ground, pulling away from the wall with a fluid movement that made her think of a cat burglar. "Ten minutes or so, no big deal." He shrugged, crushing the smoldering butt with the heel of his motorcycle boot. "Stan the Man let me off early, like I asked."

"That was nice of him."

Dante's full mouth curled in a sneer. "Yeah? Well, he owes me, the prick. I still haven't gotten paid for last month's overtime. Serve him right if I quit."

"Why don't you?"

"Yeah, and what would I do for money?" Dante was looking at her in a way she didn't like. Sort of squinting at her, half amused, as if it were just the sort of suggestion a girl like her *would* make. "This town, every high school dropout with two semesters of shop under his belt would be lining up to take my place."

"You're right. Forget I said anything." What a jerk she was! Not everyone scooped ice cream to earn extra money for college; some people had to work for a *living*.

Dante arched his back, working a hand down the front pocket of his jeans, where his cigarettes were stuffed. As he did so, his tank top pulled free, and Bronwyn caught a glimpse of his flat brown belly with its trail of dark hair that disappeared down into his waistband. She felt a sudden queer lightness in her stomach, as if she were on a roller coaster climbing that first hill.

He lit a cigarette and took a hard pull. As they made their way out of the alley, careful to check both ways before exiting onto North Main, he said, "I still might quit one of these days, who knows? Maybe it's time to move on, get out of this two-bit cowshit town."

She clamped down on a flutter of panic, asking casually, "So what's keeping you?"

He flashed her a cocky grin that went right through her like a warm scoop through ice cream. "Nothing. Not a thing." But his tone of voice, and the way he was looking at her, made it sound like a caress. "Anywhere special you want to go?" She followed his gaze to the dragonfly green Camaro parked behind Hook, Line & Sinker.

Usually they headed out to the creek, or the

trails along Windy Ridge, where you could hike for miles without running into anyone. But those spots were risky in another way, so secluded that one thing usually led to another. Before they knew it, they'd be lying on a sand spit, or in a bed of pine needles, with half their clothes off. Today she didn't want that. Today was for taking care of important business.

"How about the cemetery? We haven't been there in a while."

The one she was referring to was the old Lutheran cemetery, eight or nine miles outside town. The church had been washed away in a flood some years back and hardly anyone went there anymore, dead or alive. With its deserted paths and huge old shade trees, it was the perfect place to walk about undisturbed.

Or to talk of things you didn't want overheard.

The queer lightness in her stomach intensified. *It's not too late to back out,* a voice whispered. *Nobody's got a gun to your head.* Then she thought of her sister...and of Noelle's mother. No, she couldn't afford to chicken out. It was like that poster on the wall of Mr. Melnick's classroom: *Carpe diem.* Seize the day. *Before it seizes you,* she added silently as she ducked into the Camaro.

Minutes later they were cruising down Route 30 with the windows rolled down and her long hair fluttering like a banner in the breeze. She sneaked a glance at Dante, who was concentrating on the road, twin sparks of sunlight reflected in the curved lenses of his

Ray-Bans. Smoke drifted sideways from the cigarette tucked between the first two fingers of his hand. If he were to get caught breaking into Robert's office, she thought, who would believe it hadn't been his idea? Dante would wind up behind bars while *she* got off with a suspended sentence.

But without him she'd be screwed. The kind of stuff she knew about only from watching TV, Dante was familiar with firsthand. Like how to hot-wire a car...or pick a lock. With no burglar alarm to trip them up, an office closed for the night would be a piece of cake for someone like him.

A short while later he pulled to a stop where the dirt road to the cemetery ended in shady turnabout. A few dozen yards to their left stood a tumbledown wooden shed chained shut with a rusty padlock, all that was left of the old church grounds. Beyond, an overgrown path sloped up to the cluster of headstones on the hill.

She started to get out of the car, but Dante stopped her. "Wait."

He pulled off his sunglasses and tossed them onto the dashboard. Then he leaned over to kiss her. Slow and sweet and thrilling. She felt herself plunge down the roller coaster's first hill. When Dante kissed, it wasn't like other guys, as if he were somehow asking for permission. He simply took what he wanted...in a way that made her want it, too.

His lips parted, the tip of his tongue lazily exploring her mouth. He smelled faintly of nicotine, and though she minded that he smoked, for some reason the scent of it excited her when they were kissing. Maybe because it made him seem more dangerous somehow. She shuddered with pleasure as he smoothed a hand up the back of her neck, pushing his fingers up under her hair to knead her scalp gently. When he began to circle her jaw lightly with his thumb, she felt herself grow faint.

Tentatively at first, then with growing boldness, Bronwyn opened her mouth to let her tongue meet his, working a hand up under his tank top to stroke his back where his spine ran in a crease between the thick slabs of muscle on either side. Her palm stuck to his moist skin. He smelled of sweat and grease and the pink soap in a jar on the grubby sink at Stan's Auto. She imagined him stripped naked, rinsing off in the shower, and the queer sensation in her belly grew stronger, leaving her barely able to breathe.

The hand resting on her thigh reminded her of the time Dante had unzipped her jeans and pushed his hand down inside her panties. She'd been embarrassed by how wet she was. When he slid a finger into her, she'd grown rigid, afraid to move, to wriggle even, feeling herself on the verge of something truly embarrassing, like at night, when she stroked herself to climax under the covers.

Now he was reaching under her T-shirt instead, unhooking her bra. Bronwyn moaned softly, not self-conscious about her small breasts as she'd been with other boys. Dante cupped them reverently, his calloused fingertips tingling against her sunburned flesh.

"Your skin feels hot," he murmured into her hair.

"I fell asleep sunbathing on the dock."

"Too bad I wasn't there to wake you up."

"Oh, yeah? I'd have been risking something a lot worse than a sunburn, believe me," she said with a low laugh, nibbling on his ear.

Nevertheless, the thought of her father left her uneasy. *What Dad doesn't know won't hurt him*, she told herself. But this time it wasn't working; the guilt wasn't going away. Because *she* knew. And in a strange way it *was* hurting him. They weren't as close as they used to be, for one thing. Once upon a time she could tell her father anything. Now they only talked about stupid everyday stuff.

Bronwyn abruptly drew back. "Mind if we take a walk?" she asked. "It's getting a little warm in here. I could use some air."

Dante let go of her at once, but she sensed his frustration. Once, when she asked why he never gave her a hard time like other guys, he just shrugged and said that was the difference between men and boys. Now, though, she thought she saw a faint look of disgust cross his face. Was he getting tired of this? However patient, a *man* assumes you'll eventually sleep with him.

"Whatever." His voice was tight.

He leaned across her to flip open her door,

239

and she was suddenly seized with panic, fearing he would take off with a squeal of tires the instant she stepped outside. When he climbed out after her, she felt almost light-headed with relief.

Side by side they picked their way up the weed-choked path toward the graveyard. The trees formed a ragged canopy overhead, and the grass beneath was littered with twigs and acorns that crackled and skittered away under their feet. The only sound was the chirping of birds accompanied by the far-off rustle of the creek.

Farther up the hill, headstones began to appear. Many of them were moss-grown and tilted askew, their inscriptions barely legible. Bending to run her thumb over a lichen-crusted marker, Bronwyn felt a strange peace settle over her. She loved cemeteries, especially old ones. Did that make her weird? Probably. But there was such a sense of connectedness to it all. Of belonging. Even the names on the headstones were as familiar as those of people she might pass in the street. Adolfo Terrazini, 1934–1978: He had to be related to her art teacher, Mr. Terrazini. And over there, the one that read: *Patience Whittaker 1920–1921, She Trod Lightly on This Earth Who Walks with Angels Now.* That could be none other than the firstborn child of Maxie's great-grandmother, who'd died when she was just a baby.

Bronwyn came to a stop before a simple granite headstone she hadn't noticed during her earlier wanderings. Its inscription was less worn than the others, making it easier to read.

CORINNE ANNE LUNDQUIST
1952–1969
BELOVED DAUGHTER AND SISTER

A light chill shimmied up her spine. "My father went to school with her," she remarked softly. "She was only two years older than me when she died."

"How did she die?" Dante asked.

"She killed herself. Can you imagine?"

"Yeah, I can."

Something in his voice made her turn toward him sharply. Dante was staring off into the distance, wearing a strange look. He glanced back at her, defiantly almost. In the dappled shade his storm gray eyes looked almost black. "Just because I've thought about it," he said, "doesn't mean I'd ever go through with it."

Bronwyn thought of her mother, buried in the Catholic cemetery on the other side of town. What she wished more than anything was that she'd had a chance to say good-bye. She'd been nine when Mummy died, and in those days kids weren't allowed into hospital rooms. That's what she remembered most about her mother's death: feeling angry and cheated. Angry at the doctors and nurses. Angry at Dad. Angry at Mummy even.

"Not everyone sees it as a choice." Her hands tightened into fists, her arms stiff and unbending at her sides. "My mother, for instance. She fought hard to the very end."

Dante was silent for a long moment, staring out over the valley below, where the creek wound in a dark gold ribbon through clumps of weeping willow. When he spoke, she hardly recognized his voice. It was soft, bruised almost. "I don't remember my mother," he said. "She died when I was two. From a drug over-dose." He shrugged, but she could see the pain on his face. "My stepmother—she was no bargain, either. She never let me forget, not for one instant, that I wasn't her own flesh and blood."

The thought of Mary intruded once more. As they turned and began making their way back down the hill, Bronwyn reached for his hand. "Dante? There's something I need to ask of you. It's a pretty big favor, so I'll understand if you say no."

He smiled. "You want me to talk to your dad about us, right?" He sounded as if he were only half kidding.

"It's not about us. It's for my sister. Well, mostly." She dropped her gaze, suddenly unable to meet his eyes.

"The sister you told me about...with the kid?"

She nodded. "Noelle's in a tough spot right now. She could lose her little girl for good if—if something drastic isn't done."

He glanced at her uncertainly. "What exactly did you have in mind?"

Bronwyn took a deep breath. Her heart was pounding so hard she could feel it in her face. This was it—now or never. "I need you to help me break into my brother-in-law's office," she said in a rush. "There's a safe where he keeps an extra set of books. If it was suddenly missing, I'll bet he'd do just about anything to get it back. Even...even drop this stupid custody suit."

Her words seemed to hang in the air like the smell of ozone after a thunderclap. Dante didn't say anything at first, just pulled his hand away to fold his arms over his chest. In the hot stillness, there was only the whirring of insects and drone of a car engine somewhere off in the distance. When he spoke at last, it was with such force that she jumped a little.

"Are you *nuts?* Do you know what would happen if we got caught?"

"I know it's risky. That's why I need your help."

"Jesus, what do you take me for? I repair car engines for a living. I don't go around busting into people's offices. The trouble with you is you watch too much TV." He shook his head in disgust. "Even if we *could* break in without getting caught, you think cracking a safe is so easy?"

"It is if you have the combination."

His eyes narrowed. "You've thought of everything, I see."

"It's printed on a card he keeps locked inside his desk. But I memorized it."

Dante rolled his eyes. "Don't tell me. The one time he wasn't paying attention, you just happened to glance over his shoulder. Then, of course, knowing you, you *had* to see what was inside that safe."

She grinned. "How did you know?"

"Because I'm a genius," he shot back angrily. "A genius who should have his head examined."

"Does that mean you'll do it?"

Dante held out a hand, traffic cop style. "Whoa. I didn't say that."

She felt a tremor of excitement nonetheless. "But you'll think about it at least?"

"I don't suppose you snitched a key to the office while you were at it."

She shook her head, wishing now that she had.

"Either way, you're on your own," he growled.

Maybe it was the nervous glance he flicked her or the way he abruptly darted ahead, stalking off in the direction of his car, but Bronwyn suddenly sensed there was more to his anger than met the eye. She scurried to catch up with him.

"Dante." She grabbed hold of his arm. "What is it? Is there something you're not telling me?"

He shrugged her off and kept on walking. "Let's just forget it, okay?"

"If there's something I should know, please, tell me."

"You don't get it." He swung around to face her, eyes flashing. The tattoo on his tightly clenched arm flickered like something alive. "I work for the guy, okay?"

She gasped and took a step back. The air felt

suddenly thick, like hot soup that would choke her if she tried to breathe it in. "You...*what?*"

Dante dropped his gaze, digging into his pocket for a cigarette. "Look, it's nothing illegal. Just errands, deliveries...that kind of stuff. A few hours a week at most."

Bronwyn licked her lips, which suddenly felt parched. "What kind of errands?"

He hesitated, his gaze flicking up at her over the hand cupped about his cigarette. "Last time, it was an envelope I delivered to...to some guy."

He thumbed his lighter and the tip of his cigarette flared like a red eye blinking open. In that instant, with his face cast in its devilish glow, Dante's furtive expression said it all. She didn't have to ask if the envelope had been stuffed with cash.

Her face stung as if slapped. Of all the scenarios that had run through her mind, she never in a million years could have imagined this one. *I don't know this person,* she thought. Just a little while ago he'd had his tongue in her mouth and his hands on her breasts, but she didn't know him. Not really.

Maybe her dad was right about Dante.

At the same time, she found herself thinking, *He didn't have to tell me. Maybe this is his way of warning me.* But of what?

Suddenly, for no particular reason, Bronwyn felt as if unseen eyes were watching them. She could almost *feel* them, the ghosts of all those people buried up on the hill, rustling like the leaves overhead. Goose bumps scuttled up her arms.

But before she could pump her boyfriend for answers, the car engine droning in the distance grew suddenly louder. A shiny white boat of a Cadillac was pulling into the parking area below. A woman in dark glasses with a scarf tied over her head climbed out, wearing slacks and a long-sleeved blouse on what had to be the hottest day of the year. She walked slowly, the way an invalid might, clutching a vase of flowers. White roses, Bronwyn saw as she drew closer. How strange that anyone would leave such expensive flowers to wither on a grave. A grave out in the middle of nowhere, where no one had been buried in more than twenty years.

She didn't know why, but some instinct made her duck behind a tree, pulling Dante with her so they wouldn't be seen.

# Chapter Nine

The Monday after Noelle's court hearing, an editorial bearing Charlie's by-line appeared on page two of the *Register,* one that sent shock waves throughout the community. By late morning it was the talk of town.

# CONFLICT OF INTEREST
## AT TOWN HALL?

In days of old, when a grateful citizen threw an extra chicken or two a town councilman's way, no one thought twice. What was a jug of homemade cider or a bushel of potatoes among friends? These days the issue isn't so clear-cut. What do you call it, for instance, when a real estate developer shells out sizable consulting fees to an attorney who just so happens to be the Public Commissioner for Land Use? Illegal? Unfortunately, no. But there are many who would argue that unethical doesn't even begin to cover it.

From 1992 to 1995, when Frank Perault, a local tax and real estate attorney, served in public office, he was also on the books at Van Doren & Sons. "Consulting fees" totaling nearly $70,000 were paid out at regular intervals. The folks at Van Doren & Sons would have us believe it was all strictly aboveboard. Perault was an attorney hired, among other things, to "facilitate transactions." In plain English, he made it easier for his developer friends to rape and pillage virgin tracts of precious lakeside land. It was Perault's job as Public Commissioner to protect said resources. But let's take a look at the facts. During his three-year reign an unprecedented number of variances were voted through. They include permission to clear 25 acres of land along the north shore (1994), and the same year, the removal of several species of fish and fowl from the list of our region's protected wildlife. The diversion of Mohawk Creek (1993) and the allocation of funds for a public road to access the Mohawk Village development (1995) mark the nadir of Perault's tenure.

The result is that the land passed down from our forefathers now bears such fancy real estate monikers as Heritage Park and Trout Basin and Mohawk Village. Litter dots a shoreline once unspoiled, and water that once teemed with trout and striped bass is now stocked by hand, like a supermarket's shelves.

Who profited? Not the townspeople. Not even the owners of those brand-new condos, who paid through the nose for a tranquil spot that no longer exists. So in all fairness, I propose a vote. Is it fair for one greedy developer and his fair-weather friends to line his pockets at our town's expense? The ayes have it.

Shortly before noon, when Charlie showed up at Halpern's for his weekly shave and haircut, Gus Halpern greeted him with wary good humor. "Don't know that I can risk going anywhere near *you* with a razor," the barber joked. "You might put it in your paper that I nicked you."

"'Bloodthirsty Barber Seeks Revenge,'" Charlie quipped in return. "If I've been shorting you on the tip, Gus, just say so."

He settled into the barber chair. It was nearly lunchtime, and he was the only customer in the shop. The timing wasn't accidental. After a morning of nonstop calls, the last thing he needed was a running commentary from the peanut gallery of regulars that usually lined the bench along the wall.

Gus fastened the drape about his neck, the same beige nylon drape that had been in use since the Eisenhower administration. That's what Charlie liked about this place, why he hadn't switched over to one of the newer unisex salons springing up like crabgrass in the strip malls just outside town; it was predictable. The barbershop itself might have been the model for Norman Rockwell's famous *Saturday Evening Post* cover, minus the *Sports Illustrated* swimsuit calendar on the wall, and you could practically set your clock by Gus Halpern. As soon as he was done here, he would flip over the sign in the window, lock up, then stroll across the street to Murphy's, where he'd order a ham sandwich and a Dr Pepper.

Charlie let out a deep sigh of exhaled breath as the chair was tilted back. "What's the word, Gus? They getting ready to tar and feather me down at town hall?"

The barber ruminated for a minute or two, the crease in his meaty brow deep enough to have tucked a penny into. A big man in his mid-sixties, with a face like an English bulldog, he'd learned his trade working alongside his father, Pete, who'd recently passed on at the ripe old age of eighty-nine. Charlie relied on Gus as the town's unofficial ear as well. There was something about lying back in a barber chair with a hot towel about your face, Gus had once shared with him, that softened more than a man's follicles. He'd heard stories that only priests and bartenders were normally privy to. And though discretion was half the secret to his success, Gus provided a useful overview. A sort of one-man Gallup poll, as it were.

"Let's just say there's a few who wouldn't mind seeing you take a spill off the old soapbox," he confided. "Most folks are behind you, though. Just don't ask for a show of hands. That's some pretty powerful mojo to piss on."

"Is there any other kind worth pissing on?"

"Easy for you to say. But a lot of folks around here owe their living to those bastards." Fortunately Gus was among those who didn't count on Van Doren & Sons to pay the rent.

"I'm beginning to get the idea. So far I've had three businesses yank their ads." Charlie gave a rueful laugh. "And let's not even get into the slew of canceled subscriptions."

In truth, he wasn't terribly worried about loss of revenue. The paper had weathered such storms in the past. Even if it was to fold altogether, what was that compared with his family? No, what troubled him was the degree of influence Robert yielded in this town. It was certainly no secret to Charlie that his former classmate was slick—for years he'd longed to expose the man, holding back only out of deference to his daughter—but others had been surprised to learn of the town council's incestuous relationship with Van Doren & Sons. If he was lucky, another stick or two of dynamite would succeed in blowing the bastard right out of the water.

Charlie closed his eyes, soothed by the shaving brush gliding in tight circles over his jaw. Wheels within wheels, he thought. At the center was his elder daughter, fighting for her child. A wheel that had set into motion those around it. Like this unfinished business—he didn't dare give it a name—with Mary. He felt a sudden tightening in his rib cage, thinking of what they'd done the other night and what he *should* have done thirty years ago.

An old memory surfaced. His eighteenth birthday, celebrated with a jug of cheap wine passed among his housemates. By then he'd been living in a ramshackle Victorian with five other kids, three guys and two girls. It'd been months since Mary had moved back in with her parents, but he'd nevertheless clung to the hope that she would one day return. Hope that was shattered, as hope often is, not by a momentous epiphany but by a single careless remark. His roommates and he had been seated cross-legged in a circle on the living room floor, well into their down payment on tomorrow morning's hangover, when Sally Garon (a girl he later bedded), lifted her paper cup of Gallo red to proclaim with bleary-eyed profundity, "Here's to Charlie's bride...for cutting him loose."

That's when it finally sank in. Mary wasn't coming back.

The years that followed had been marked not by the usual milestones of birthdays and anniversaries but by hard work. Gradually Charlie was promoted from office boy to copy editor to managing editor, then at long last editor in chief. His only solace, however bittersweet, was watching Noelle grow from a baby into a solemn little girl with his raven black hair and her mother's gray-blue eyes. The day she left for the city, his carefully balanced world once again slipped its cogs. After kissing his ten-year-old daughter good-bye, and receiving a solemn (and somewhat reproachful) peck on the cheek in return, he'd gotten in his car and started driving, no particular destination in mind. He'd been headed north, that was all he knew, for that was the extent of his awareness. All night and well into the next day he'd driven without stopping except to refuel. Until he was turned back at the Canadian border. Apparently he hadn't thought to bring his passport, which was just as well. Otherwise, he might have ended up in Saskatchewan.

Instead, he'd taken the long route home, following the rocky, windswept New England coastline. Just north of Cape Cod, near the town of Ellisville, a brutal nor'easter and bonenumbing exhaustion descended with equal force, and he checked into the first inn he happened across, a charming bed-and-breakfast run by an even more charming Welsh girl named Victoria. He slept for twenty-four hours straight, and when he woke up, Vicky fed him an enormous breakfast of bacon and eggs and waffles. He stayed for three days.

Wheels within wheels. If Mary hadn't left him, setting into motion a series of events over which he'd had no control, he wouldn't have met Vicky or had Bronwyn. And how could he be anything but grateful for that? Yet somehow it had all come full circle. The other night with Mary—Christ, it was just like before, when they were a couple of horny teenagers who couldn't keep their hands off each other. Only better...maybe because they were old enough to appreciate the gift they'd been given. Each touch that had once stood alone, unchallenged, now colored by the loving, and not so loving, embraces they'd known. Each whispered endearment made more precious by the knowledge of how easily the things and people you love can be snatched away.

*Face it, Charlie boy, you're on borrowed time.* When all this was over, she'd go back to her life in the city: business, friends, maybe even a lover. He couldn't ask her to give all that up; it wouldn't work even if she tried. Any more than he could cash in everything he'd toiled so hard to build. No, the smart thing would be to quit while he was ahead.

Didn't he have enough on his plate as it was? Not just Noelle but his younger daughter as well. Lately Bronwyn had been moody and distant. He didn't have to be hit over the head to know why: that boy who'd been sniffing around, Dante Lo Presti. Charlie had had him checked out, and though concluding the kid wasn't much of a threat, despite his tattoo and tough guy swagger, he'd begun to feel uneasy on the nights he worked late. Who knew what his headstrong daughter might get up to? He'd forbidden her to have anything more to do with Dante, but had Noelle listened to him when he warned her about Robert?

Charlie recalled with bile rising in his throat the day his elder daughter told him she was in love. He'd wanted to be happy for her, his solemn child who so often did only what was expected of her. But he'd known what was in store: a man who would break her heart, and possibly break *her*, too. He'd hoped that Robert's charm would eventually wear thin— Christ, the man was *his* age—but it hadn't happened. When Noelle told him they were getting married, he'd sat her down and tried gently to dissuade her—to no avail. Six months later Charlie was walking her down the aisle. On that occasion, too, he'd chosen his words with care. Embracing her, he'd murmured, "I hope he makes you as happy as you deserve, honey."

For a while it seemed she *was*.

Gus tilted the chair upright, jolting Charlie from his reverie. The barber had exchanged his razor for a pair of shears, and snippets of hair began to drift down around Charlie's ears. Looking at his reflection in the mirror, he was startled to find his father's face staring back at him: Frank's knotted jaw and deeply grooved cheeks, his beleaguered eyes. Pop couldn't control Mom's drinking, but Charlie wasn't about to go down without a fight. Not while he drew breath on this earth, not with his family at risk.

The town council's monthly meeting was tonight, he recalled, the highlight of which would be the debate over the proposed Sandy Creek development. It would be interesting to see how many people turned out and even more interesting to see who, if anyone, had the guts to stand up to Robert. The local environmentalists, a small but fiercely active group headed by Mary's sister, would no doubt do battle on behalf of the threatened bird. But Robert was sure to make an equally strong case in favor of unrestricted building's being the lifeblood of the town's economy.

*Just don't get* too *smug, you bastard,* he warned silently. In light of his daughter's predicament, Charlie wasn't going to lose much sleep over the orange-crowned warbler. But tonight's forum, if nothing else, might provide useful in exposing Robert for the bully he was. When tomorrow morning's edition of the *Register* hit the stands, Charlie vowed, its volley would echo from the hilltops.

Thirty years ago he had hesitated at a major crossroads. He'd failed to fight for what was rightfully his. He wouldn't make that mistake a second time.

$\mathcal{E}$arly that evening when he arrived at the meeting, even Charlie was amazed by the turnout. Burns Lake's town council wasn't particularly known for its drawing power, and the advantages and disadvantages of various proposed budget cuts, municipal funding, and waste disposal alternatives were not exactly edge-of-the-seat theatrics. But tonight the gray metal folding chairs lining the council chamber on the ground floor of the Justus R. Wright Building were filled to capacity. He'd be lucky to find an empty seat.

Slipping into a chair in the back row, he spotted Mary near the front, seated beside her sister. He wasn't surprised to find her here, but his pulse quickened nonetheless. Watching her lean over to whisper something in Trish's ear, Charlie couldn't help being amazed anew by how different the two sisters were. Trish, plain and earnest, with her tentative smile that flickered like a faulty light bulb...and Mary, slender and stylish, looking as poised as a seasoned politician on the firing line.

*Christ,* he marveled, *she's even more beautiful now than at seventeen.* Dressed simply, in pale yellow slacks and a sleeveless white cotton sweater, and wearing sandals that consisted of four narrow straps and probably cost more than her sister cleared in a week. The sun had put some color into her pale cheeks, he was pleased to note. Or was it the residual glow of their lovemaking?

Once more their interlude in the woods flashed through his mind. Lying with Mary in the grass, her hips arching to meet his, her readiness alone telling him everything his stupid male ego longed to believe: that it had been months, maybe even years, since she'd been properly made love to.

For Charlie, it had been a door opening to provide a glimpse of the yearning heart that beat inside this confident, sophisticated businesswoman. He'd nearly cried at the waste of it all. The lost years. The years ahead without her. Knowing he was helpless either to stop loving her...or to stop her from leaving. The hardest part was not knowing when, or even if, they would make love again. The other night the magic had begun to fade and reality to set in even before they'd reached the cabin. Mary had told him she wanted to slow down, think things over. They weren't kids anymore; they couldn't just barrel ahead without considering the consequences.

*Kids,* he'd thought dourly, *who'd have managed just fine had we listened to our hearts instead of our elders.* But he'd said nothing. What was there to say? Proceed with caution? No, if he'd learned anything from past experience, it was that decisions involving others couldn't be forced. Mary would have to come to it on her own.

At five past eight the mayor called the meeting to order. A retired insurance broker with a ruddy face polished by too many expense account meals, Grant Iverson reminded Charlie of an old possum fat off feeding out of garbage pails. Charlie saw him glance anxiously at Robert, seated in the front row. *Strange bedfellows,* he thought.

He was gripped by a sudden violent urge to do some serious damage. Was the pen truly mightier than the sword? Maybe, but at times there was no substitute for simply plowing your fist into your enemy's face. Charlie was almost glad when the first order of business turned out to be the debate over whether or not to install parking meters along York Avenue. Its dullness served to blunt the sharp edge of his fury. Flipping open his notepad, he scribbled a few words. He'd have Anne Marie Daugherty, his lifestyles editor, follow up with a piece on the shopkeepers and what it would mean to them.

The next two items on the agenda were dispensed with quickly, the council voting unanimously to increase the budget for the fire department and to replace the litter baskets in town square. It was only a quarter past nine when the mayor cleared his throat into the microphone to announce, "As for the last item—this, ah, business about the bird—I'd like to remind all you good people that tomorrow is a workday, so let's not drag it out." He was looking straight at Trish, who'd shot out of her seat so abruptly the stack of flyers on her lap spilled to the floor. Cheeks burning, she bent to retrieve them.

Robert was quick to seize the advantage, stepping up to the dais as smoothly as a shotgun's oiled hammer sliding home. Every eye in the room turned toward him as he leaned into the microphone.

"Thanks, Grant. If we're lucky, we might even catch the last inning of the Red Sox game." He grinned and, like any polished performer, waited for the ensuing chuckles to abate before continuing. "In the interest of making this easier on everyone, I've taken the liberty of running off copies of the report provided by Professor Farnsworth, head of ornithology at Northwestern University." He signaled to one of his flunkies in back, a skinny crew-cut kid who immediately started making the rounds with a stack of the impressive-looking spiral-bound reports. "What it boils down to, in a nutshell, is that the orange-crowned warbler is a migratory bird that just so happens to have temporarily migrated into our little neck of the woods. You might think of it as a Boy Scout troop that's lost its way in the woods." More chuckles, and this time even a few loud guffaws. "Not that I don't have some sympathy for the little guys. All I'm asking is that we don't make a mountain out of a molehill."

His folksy delivery, the equivalent of a broad wink, elicited a chorus of murmured approval. Even Charlie felt a grudging admiration. He'd known Robert was good, but not *this* good. While he went on shoveling the shit about the various lengths to which Van Doren & Sons had gone to ensure the safety of *all* manner of flora and fauna, Charlie watched in horrified fascination as the audience was slowly but inexorably reeled in.

But not everyone was hanging on Robert's every word. Trish and Mary, along with a faithful corps of Green Earth and Audubon Society tub-thumpers, eyed him with cold disdain. When it came time for Trish to speak, she rose to the occasion.

"Remember the days when we used to be able to swim in the lake without worrying about runoff from septic tanks?" Her eyes were shining, her voice steady and clear. "Or walk in woods that are underwater now, thanks to the diversion of Mohawk Creek? Just a few months ago, before the land for Cranberry Mall was cleared, you could go there to pick wild raspberries and gooseberries." She paused to look about the room, which had fallen unusually silent. "Don't get me wrong. I'm not opposed to *all* progress. Where would this town be without its roads and buildings, its parks and monuments? But we have to draw the line somewhere. We have to know when to stand up and say enough is enough. A small brown bird that's not much to look at"—she turned to cast a wry glance at her sister—"may not seem worth fighting for. But did you know that bulldozing Sandy Creek would destroy more than just their nests? Fledglings that haven't yet learned to fly would be slaughtered by the dozens. The sanctuary of a species rarely seen outside its native California would be wiped out in a single stroke. Not by an act of God or by town fathers putting the welfare of its citizens first. But by a company whose only motive is greed."

She pointed a finger at Robert, who no longer wore the patina of easy victory. He was frowning openly now, and a tic had started up in his right eye. "It's not just the orange-crowned warbler that's endangered." Trish went on. "We *all* are. Our whole way of life. If we don't fight this, what will we tell our children when they ask what it was like to catch minnows in the creek or pick wildflowers in the meadows? How will we *face* them?"

Silence fell over the room. Meaningful glances were exchanged. Mary looked amazed, as if the sister she thought she'd known had been replaced by someone she hardly recognized. A woman with the power to sway an audience, whose impassioned words had touched off a murmuring that quickly grew to a roar. Hands shot into the air. People who just a few minutes before had been too timid to speak were now eager to share their opinions.

The debate soon swelled to such a clamor that Herb Pelzer, the land use commissioner, a portly man with a fringe of light brown about his shiny dome, moved for a referendum. The public works commissioner, Donald Richter, quickly seconded the motion, and the council voted unanimously that a special ballot be drafted, to be cast in six weeks' time.

Moments later, Charlie caught up with Mary and Trish on the steps outside. Mary glowed with sisterly pride. "Oh, Charlie, wasn't she wonderful?" Turning to Trish, she added, "I swear, if it'd been an election you'd have won by a landslide."

Charlie smiled easily at Trish. "Actually, it's not a bad idea. *Have* you ever considered running for public office?"

"Heavens, no. I'd be hopeless." Color rose in her cheeks, and in the blink of an eye, like Cinderella at the stroke of midnight, the impassioned zealot was transformed back into Mary's self-effacing younger sister.

"That's not how it sounded back there."

"Oh, that was different. When I really care about something, I tend to get a little carried away." Trish beamed at the small crowd gathering about to congratulate her.

Charlie felt a moment of anxiety when she drifted off into the huddle of supporters, leaving him alone with Mary. Would she tell him she'd thought it over and decided it would be best if they remained at arm's length? Worse, would she say nothing at all?

"I'll be quoting your sister heavily in tomorrow's edition." He flashed the mini recorder in his hand.

"Well, if it's anything like today's editorial I'm sure the town will be buzzing. According to Elaine Richards down at the post office, it's been the main topic of conversation since early this morning."

"Being an overnight celebrity isn't all it's cracked up to be."

"What do you mean?"

"This afternoon I got a call from Robert's attorney—not Beale but his corporate flunky, Brett Jordan." Charlie lowered his voice. "Let's just say I was warned...and not too subtly."

Mary looked mildly alarmed. "He threatened to sue?"

"That, and worse. He hinted the fire department could shut me down for violations."

"What violations?"

"In an old building like mine, believe me, they'd find some," he said. "But that'd be more of a nuisance than anything. What I find most interesting is that Robert didn't waste any time in lashing back, which makes me wonder if we're sitting on an even bigger powder keg than we thought." They started down the steps, Mary maintaining a decorous foot or so of space that felt more like a mile. "How about Jordy Lundquist? Did you get anywhere with him?" He'd spotted Corinne's brother at the meeting and recalled her mentioning having run into Jordy the other day at Nora's. Jordy, she said, had seemed a little nervous when the subject of Corinne came up. Mary had planned on doing some further investigating.

Mary shot him a rueful look. "I stopped by his house yesterday. He and his wife couldn't have been nicer, but if he's hiding anything about Corinne I didn't get to first base," she confessed. "I was hoping he could at least shed some light on who the mysterious J was— you know, that guy Corinne mentioned in her diary. But he didn't have a clue."

"If you feel like kicking around any more ideas, stop by the newsroom tomorrow. I'll be around all day." Charlie kept his voice casual, arranging his face in a pleasantly neutral expression.

She stepped back to avoid being jostled by a boisterous group making its way down the steps, inadvertently brushing up against him. Charlie caught a trace of her scent: no perfume, just soap and clean clothes, the delicate kind you wash by hand and hang on the shower rod to dry. He could see a faint band of moisture glistening on her collarbone, and the memory of how she'd felt, naked in his arms, rose up to taunt him. He remembered the countless nights of his youth, drifting to sleep with something of hers clutched to his chest—a dress or a slip, once an old sweatshirt he'd found stuffed in the back of a drawer. Even her hairbrush, tangled with auburn strands, had been an instrument of sweet torture.

But if she was aware of the effect she was having on him now, she showed no sign of it. She paused on the bottom step to flash him her best PR woman's smile. "Tomorrow? I have to make a run into the city. If I get back at a reasonable hour, I'll give you a call."

Charlie shrugged agreeably. "You have my number."

Mary glanced up at Trish, who stood chatting with her supporters, oblivious of the fact that she was keeping her sister waiting. "Too bad her so-called fiancé couldn't make it tonight. I wonder if he has any idea what a terrific performance he passed up."

Charlie detected a note of irony in her voice and wondered if it came from personal experience. He felt a stab of jealousy at the thought of a lover, however feckless. "Probably not," was all he said. He saw no reason to mention Gary Schmidt's reputation for catting around. Carefully, he ventured, "She could be a while. It doesn't look as if her fan club is in any hurry to let her go. Can I give you a lift?"

Mary hesitated before replying, "No, better not." He might have gone home believing it was out of loyalty to Trish—if not for the meaningful look she shot him from under lowered eyelids. He was grateful for that much at least. "We'd just end up doing something I'd wish we hadn't. Not"—she touched his arm—"that the other night wasn't wonderful. It's just that I need time to think this over before we go jumping into the deep end."

Charlie didn't need to think it over. Like it or not, he was already in up to his ears. "Take all the time you need," he told her, his words sounding false and fatuous to his ears.

She studied him for a moment. "You got your hair cut."

"Today, as a matter of fact. It shows, huh?"

"Only if you look close." There was a beat in which he caught a flicker of regret in her eyes. Then she stood on tiptoe to kiss his cheek, a brush of lips so soft it might have been a whisper. A second later she was trotting over to retrieve Trish.

For a brief moment he indulged in a favorite fantasy, imagining what it would be like had they remained together all these years. Would they be like the couples strolling home through the park, arms linked, two shadows blending into one? The kind of couple about whom people were fond of remarking, *Aren't they cute? Still crazy about each other after all these years.* His heart caught as if on something sharp.

In the parking lot it wasn't hard to spot his Blazer. The lot, which had been full when he arrived, was nearly empty now. Shadows stretched in long furrows between the sparsely planted streetlights. Charlie was fumbling with his car keys when he felt something slam into him. The air left his lungs, and the pavement abruptly slid out from under him. He landed hard, breaking the fall with his right shoulder, a bright burst of pain that left him gasping.

A dark figure loomed over him.

Charlie sucked in a breath coppery with the taste of blood. "Christ, man. Why don't you look where you're—"

He was cut off by a throaty voice rasping, "Next time, Mr. Newspaperman, you better think twice about what you print."

Charlie struggled to make out his face, but it was too dark. He caught only the faint glimmer of an earring, the outline of a jaw that could have been a prizefighter's. In that first disjointed moment his only thought was: *Damn, you'd think those idiot councilmen could*

266

*have voted in a few more streetlights.* Then the loose connection in his brain ratcheted back into place, and he thought, *Robert. This is Robert's doing.*

He opened his mouth to croak, "You can tell that son of a bitch—"

But the shadowy figure had vanished.

Charlie dragged himself to his feet. His shoulder hurt, sending hot, pulsing waves down his arm. His elbow stung where it had been scraped raw. But the pain was muffled, like something sharp poking him through several layers of clothing. Adrenaline had taken over, downloading through his system in a sizzling rush.

He squinted in the direction the guy had run. Maybe he could still catch him. It didn't occur to Charlie that he was in no shape to run, much less tackle a man who outweighed him by at least fifty pounds. Fury had eclipsed good sense. He'd run several dozen yards when incredibly he caught up with his attacker, a big blond man climbing into a red Bronco.

Charlie was pulling back to take a swing when the man turned, his stunned face flaring into view.

"Jesus, Charlie."

Not his attacker but Jordy. Big, sweet Jordy Lundquist, who faithfully chauffeured his widowed mother to the Shop 'n' Save every Wednesday afternoon; who coached his daughter's hockey team, and served as a deacon at their Lutheran church. Jordy's mouth hung slack, and in an odd high-pitched voice he repeated, "Jesus, Charlie, you scared me."

"Not half as much as *you* scared me," Charlie wheezed.

It hit him then, like an aftershock. Rocked by a wave of dizziness, he swayed on his feet. He might have collapsed if Jordy hadn't reached out to grasp his elbow firmly.

"Hey, Charlie, you don't look so good." Jordy's concerned voice seemed to float down from somewhere above his left ear. "What happened to you?"

"I just got blindsided," Charlie managed to gasp.

"Big guy? Navy windbreaker?" Jordy frowned. "I saw him run past just a minute ago. Looked like he was in a hurry."

"Did you see his face?"

Jordy shook his head. "I didn't get a good look."

Charlie sagged against the Bronco, letting out a ragged breath. "Neither did I. Sorry, Jordy, I didn't mean to come after you like that. I thought you were him." He gingerly probed his shoulder, assessing the damage.

"You okay?" Jordy asked.

"A little bruised, but I'll live."

Satisfied, Jordy relaxed. "Hey, you know something, it's really weird running into you like this. I was looking for you at the meeting."

"I was all the way in back. The guy with the fake mustache," Charlie joked feebly in reference to his new notoriety. Right now the last thing he needed was to have his ear bent with some well-meaning but useless offer of support. Nevertheless, he found himself asking, "What did you want to see me about?"

Jordy reached inside his denim jacket and withdrew a manila envelope. "It was Mary's stopping by the other day that made me think twice. Dad didn't want my mom to know about this; he gave it to me just before he died. But when Mary told me about your daughter, I figured the secret had been kept long enough." He handed the envelope to Charlie.

"What's in it?" Charlie straightened with sudden interest, his pain forgotten.

"A copy of the coroner's report." In the harsh glare of the Bronco's interior light, the big flaxen-haired man looked troubled. "You'll understand once you've read it."

Initially the thought was just a vague, shifting grayness in the back of Charlie's head; then it burst into full, living Technicolor. Jesus, what if it was true? What if Corinne *had* met with foul play? That would explain why Robert was so hell-bent on shutting him up.

He stared at the envelope in his hands. Whatever it held, he thought, one thing was for sure: Compared with the can of worms he'd pried open already, this was going to look like a nest of rattlesnakes.

# Chapter Ten

July was drawing to a close, but Noelle scarcely noticed. She'd taken to avoiding calendars. She couldn't bear looking at all those neat little squares, each one as empty as the next. Better to do as she'd been taught in AA: Take it one day at a time. She could manage that, couldn't she? Yes, if she didn't think too hard about what might lie ahead. If she refused to let herself imagine, *even for one minute,* the possibility of losing her daughter for good.

Instead, she focused on their precious time together, on putting up a good front for Emma. It worked...most of the time. But Emma had started to come unglued as well. Yesterday she'd begged for an ice cream cone, then wept disconsolately when it became apparent that Noelle was going without her. "I want to come *with* you, Mommy. I don't *like* Mrs. Scheffert," she'd wailed. "I want to see Bronnie. I want to pick my *own* ice cream!" In Scoops, watching her sister sprinkle chocolate jimmies over Emma's mint chip cone, Noelle had broken down herself.

Bronwyn had had to take her in the back room, where she'd dried her eyes on a paper towel that felt like sandpaper. Her little sister was the only one besides Hank who hadn't offered false assurances. She'd said the exact right thing: "I don't know how you stand it, El. I'd go crazy. I swear I would."

Noelle found her honesty oddly refreshing. With Bronwyn she didn't have to smile and make show of bucking up, as she did with others. It was a relief, frankly, to admit openly that *she* didn't know how she stood it either, and yes, she *was* going a little crazy. At times she felt as wobbly as one of Emma's preschool projects, Popsicle sticks glued together precariously and stuck with bits of colored yarn.

Today she would have to apply extra glue. For today was Tuesday, and the court-appointed psychologist, a woman by the name of Linda Hawkins, was coming to evaluate her. After a sleepless night she'd awoken with a cold heaviness inside, like an iron weight pinning her to the mattress. "Just be yourself," Dad had advised. But Noelle had lost sight of what that was. These days a stranger, someone who jumped like a spooked horse at every loud noise and burst into tears at the slightest provocation, lived inside her skin. A person who occasionally had to hide out in the bathroom when it all became simply too much. What if she was deemed unfit? What then?

She was dragging herself out of bed at half past seven when her mother poked her head into the room. Mary, on her way into the city, was already dressed to the nines in a beautiful fawn-colored suit and cream silk blouse. Yesterday, when Lacey called with the news that a date had been set for the home visit, Mary had insisted on changing her plans.

Noelle had been equally adamant that she not. Now she wondered if she'd spoken out of habit more than anything else. After all, when *had* she been able to count on her mother? Perhaps she'd learned too well that the best way to avoid being disappointed was not to expect too much in the first place.

"I just wanted to wish you luck." Mary crossed the room to give her a perfume-scented hug. "Are you sure you don't want me to stay? I feel terrible about leaving you."

"I'm sure." Noelle spoke abruptly, for once not bothering to hide her displeasure. Why did it have to be *her* decision? A normal mother wouldn't have had to ask.

"It's not too late for me to call and reschedule my appointments." Mary faltered a bit, fingering the pretty silver pin on her lapel. "Nothing is more important than you, honey. You know that, don't you?"

"Do I?" Noelle turned away, tugging a robe over her nightgown. "When did I ever come first, Mom? *When?* Oh, sure, you were there when it *counted*—school plays and parents' night and graduations—but did it ever occur to you I might need a mother the rest of the time as well?" She couldn't believe she was speaking to Mary this way; the old Noelle wouldn't have dared. At the same time it felt long overdue.

"I did the best I could. It wasn't easy for me, living here with Nana." Mary's voice was soft.

"It wasn't easy for me either. I love Nana,

but I wanted *you*, Mom, not your understudy. Even after we moved to the city, I saw more of the baby-sitter than I did of you." Noelle was close to tears. She marched over and flung open the closet, knowing that no matter what she put on, she'd never come close to looking as fashionable as her mother. Staring at the clothes drooping dejectedly from their hangers, she said in a low, fierce voice, "Did you think coming here would change all that? Did you think I'd just fall into your arms with gratitude like the last thirty years never happened?"

"Oh, honey, I'm not sure *what* I expected." Mary let out a deep sigh of pent-up breath, but in place of her usual contriteness there was only calm resignation. "All I know is I've run out of excuses. I don't expect forgiveness. I just want—I want things to be different from now on."

Noelle turned slowly to face her, longing desperately to believe her but unwilling to risk yet another disappointment. Cautiously she said, "It isn't something you can just stick out your hand for. You have to *earn* it."

"I'm trying, honey."

Unexpectedly Noelle's heart went out to her. "I know you are, Mom," she said softly, blinking back her tears. "Look, you'd better hit the road before you get caught up in a lot of traffic. I'll be fine. I'll call you later to let you know how it went."

Mary seemed satisfied with that. "Promise? I won't be able to concentrate on anything else all day. Not," she was quick to add, "that I have the slightest doubt you'll make a good impression."

Noelle laughed uneasily. "Better keep your fingers crossed just the same. I might end up with the Wicked Witch of the East."

"If that's the case, you can always drop a house on her."

Thankfully Mary didn't offer any further advice. She looked at Noelle with the respect of a peer instead, as if confident that she was perfectly capable of managing on her own. For a fleeting instant Noelle believed it, too.

She spent the rest of the morning cleaning the house, top to bottom. She doubted it would be submitted to a white-glove test, but as Nana always said, it didn't hurt to put your best foot forward. Besides, sitting still wasn't an option. She was too antsy. If she didn't keep moving, she'd go stir crazy. As she pushed her grandmother's ancient Hoover over the living room carpet, a single thought beat in her head like a pulse: *Please, let Linda Hawkins like me.*

By a quarter to one she was showered and made up, her hair blown dry. The psychologist wasn't due to arrive until one-thirty, but Noelle wanted to be prepared in case she showed up early. Dr. Hawkins might very well try to catch her with her guard down, and if Noelle had learned one thing from this ordeal, it was *not* to trust in the kindness of strangers.

She slipped out of the dress she'd just put

on—a light cotton shift the color of marigolds that hung on her too-thin frame—and pulled another, more sober one from the closet. Standing before the full-length mirror, she held up her dark blue linen coatdress, then firmly shook her head. No, this wasn't a job interview. She didn't want to look like a supplicant. If she couldn't *be* her normal self, she at least had to look the part.

Noelle settled on a pale green sleeveless sweater and a pair of off-white slacks that were stylish without being too dressy, the sort of outfit she might have worn to a committee meeting or a field trip with Emma's preschool. After twisting her springy hair into a knot in back and slipping on a pair of gold earrings, she stepped back to view the effect.

*Would Hank approve?*

The thought sneaked in out of nowhere. She turned away from the mirror, frowning. How could she be thinking of Hank at a time like this?

*Maybe because he sees you differently from the way you see yourself: as strong, even admirable. Someone fit to tackle the battle ahead,* a voice whispered in reply. *Besides, let's be honest, you* like *being with him. He makes you feel good in a way Robert never did.*

Never mind that they'd met at the worst possible time. Even if she cared to find out where friendship with Hank Reynolds might lead, right now it simply wasn't possible. Not without Robert's getting wind of it somehow. And anything that might make her look bad in court was a risk she couldn't take.

Emma was her sole concern right now. No more false moves; she had to think like Robert in order to be as cunning. Starting today. She had to convince the psychologist that Emma belonged with *her*. How hard could that be? Dr. Hawkins was a woman. Maybe even a mother. She wouldn't be entirely unsympathetic.

Noelle squared her shoulders and stepped out into the hall. She paused only to look in on her grandmother, fast asleep in bed, as she headed for the stairs. Lately Nana's naps had been getting longer, sometimes stretching far into the afternoon. A sign that she was getting better or merely slipping farther away? Noelle felt a twinge of anxiety and made a mental note to have a word with Hank at her grandmother's next appointment.

In the kitchen, freshly scrubbed, its speckled green linoleum gleaming with a coat of wax, she poured herself a glass of lemonade. She couldn't recall a moment since Emma had been kidnapped (yes, *kidnapped*) when she hadn't felt parched, but however much she drank it never seemed to quench her thirst. The lemonade only made it worse. She followed it with a glass of water, which she immediately regretted. What if she had to pee in the middle of the interview? She could always excuse herself, of course. But might Linda Hawkins wonder if she was catching a nip from a bottle tucked in the pantry?

Noelle began to sweat. In the living room

she switched on the ancient rotary fan, which reminded her of when she was a little girl, practicing piano scales with one hand anchoring the fluttering pages of her exercise book. Now, as she sank down on the bench, she recalled how her small fingers had stumbled over the difficult chords. She hadn't played in years, but at Hazelden, as she sat through those endless groups, craving a drink and going quietly out of her mind, oddly enough it had been the one memory that kept her sane. In her mind she'd practice those scales over and over until they became a sort of mantra. She would feel the satiny coolness of the Baldwin's yellowing keys and hear the resonating plunk of each note. After a while the ache in her gut would ease.

Now it was as if she'd been plunged back into that dark period of her life. A time when she would reach for a familiar crutch, only to come up empty-handed. AA had helped, though as soon as she'd felt able to handle things on her own, she'd stopped going. Then she got pregnant, and there was no question of her drinking. Still, she should have kept up with the meetings. Maybe things wouldn't be so bad now. She'd have had her fellow members to draw strength from and her sponsor to provide guidance and moral support: Gwen Nolan, with her twenty years in the program, who knew a thing or two about the rocky road to sobriety. And if the impulse to drink surfaced again, as it had just the other day, she'd have had a safe place to—

The chiming of the doorbell broke the stillness, causing her to jump to her feet. She glanced at her watch. Quarter past one—damn, the woman *was* early. As Noelle made her way to the front door, each step was accompanied by the heavy thud of her heart. She felt faintly queasy as well, the sweetness of the lemonade turning to bile in her throat. *Please God, let her like me,* she prayed once more.

The door swung open to reveal a slender, not unattractive middle-aged woman in a dowdy tan suit and thick-heeled shoes, with a slim maroon briefcase tucked under one arm. Not the Wicked Witch of the East, but there was something odd about her nonetheless. It was a moment before Noelle realized what it was: Linda Hawkins was utterly hairless. No eyelashes, and only thin penciled lines above hazel eyes that seemed to fix on Noelle with disturbing intensity. On her head was a shoulder-length wig the lustrous brown of a mink coat.

Noelle tried not to stare.

"Dr. Hawkins? Hi, I'm Noelle." She fought the impulse to slide her sweaty palm down her pants leg. "Please, come in. My grandmother's taking a nap, so we have the place pretty much to ourselves."

The psychologist gripped her hand firmly, one quick squeeze, before stepping inside. "Please, call me Linda." She smiled warmly, alleviating some of Noelle's anxiety. "I'm told your grandmother is recuperating from surgery. She's feeling better, I hope?"

Noelle smiled back. Her mouth might have been strip of elastic stitched onto her face. "Oh, yes. Much."

"I'm glad to hear it."

In the living room Noelle gestured toward the sofa. Linda chose one of the chairs instead, propping her briefcase on the floor beside it.

"Can I offer you a drink? Some cold lemonade?" Noelle asked.

"No, thank you." Linda primly smoothed her skirt over her knees.

Noelle noticed a tiny run in her panty hose and was secretly reassured. It made this odd hairless woman seem more human somehow, someone with an elderly parent of her own perhaps, who had a fondness for cats and See's chocolates.

*See? there's nothing to be afraid of,* she told herself. Yet for some reason she *was* afraid. Cold panic sheeted through her like rain across a windshield. It was those stark lashless eyes, like those of a department store mannequin; they gave her the creeps. How on earth was she supposed to concentrate with the woman staring at her like that?

Sinking down on the sofa, she nevertheless forced herself to meet Linda's gaze. "I don't suppose you'd take my word for it that I'm a nice person?" she asked in a lame attempt at breaking the ice.

The woman surprised her with a chuckle. "You have the wrong idea about me, Noelle. May I call you Noelle? My job is simply to observe and make a recommendation to the court. I don't have a final say in any of this. And I don't bite, I promise." With a wry twist of her thin red mouth, she lifted her briefcase onto her lap. "Now then...let's start with a few questions, shall we?"

"Sure, go ahead. I have nothing to hide."

Noelle knew immediately that she'd phrased it the wrong way when Linda flicked her a curious glance, as if wondering whether or not she might indeed have something to hide. Sweat flooded her armpits, making her sweater stick to her skin. She pictured a thermostat like the one in the hallway and imagined thumbing the dial. *Stay cool...you've got to stay cool....*

"Do you have any interests, Noelle?"

"What?"

"Hobbies, that sort of thing."

Noelle's mind raced. She'd been prepared for an inquisition, but this felt more like a college interview. Clearing her throat, she replied, "I write."

"You keep a journal, you mean?"

"Well, yes, that, too. Mostly short stories and articles, though. I've even had a few published."

"Any I might have read?"

Noelle indulged in a dry laugh. "Not unless you subscribe to the *Baroid News Bulletin* or the *California Highway Patrolman*." She shrugged. "When you're starting out, you take what you can get."

"So it's not just a hobby. You're pretty serious about it."

Sensing a possible trap, Noelle backed off

at once. "Someday I'd like to write full-time. But for now..." Thinking of Emma, she flashed the woman a smile that was genuine this time. "Look, I know it's sort of old-fashioned to admit it these days, but there's nothing more important to me right now than being a mom."

Linda's only response was to scribble on her notepad. When she looked up, her face was expressionless. "While we're on the subject, let's talk a bit about child care. Who watches your little girl when you need to run an errand or if you should happen to feel, ah, indisposed?"

Noelle tensed. Was that a reference to her allegedly haven fallen off the wagon? There was nothing in Linda's tone to suggest it. Even so, she sensed she would have to tread very, very carefully.

"My grandmother, when she's up to it," she replied. "There's my aunt Trish, too. She baby-sits in the evening sometimes. Oh, and I have a teenage sister, Bronwyn. Emma absolutely worships her."

"It sounds as if you have a very close-knit family."

"We look out for each other."

"Even so, you must have had your hands full, taking care of a sick grandmother as well as a five-year-old child."

Noelle felt the first flicker of real alarm. It wasn't her imagination; this *was* a trap. Cautiously she said, "It's only for a little while. Like I said, Nana is much better. She'll be her old self in no time at all."

The woman directed her lashless gaze at the somewhat lurid painting over the sofa of Christ's crucifixion. "Well, yes, but let's suppose, just for the sake of argument, that her health *doesn't* continue to improve. Do you see yourself bringing in outside help?"

Noelle tried to picture her grandmother agreeing to such a thing. A stranger rattling around in her kitchen, sorting through her laundry? Someone in a white uniform and thick waffle-soled shoes carting trays up and down the stairs? No, Nana would never stand for it.

"I guess I'll just have to cross that bridge when I get to it," she said, hedging.

"Is that your general outlook on life?"

"Honestly, I don't see what this has to do with—" Noelle paused, glancing down at the sofa, at a loose thread begging to be plucked. Taking a deep breath, she said, "Look, Dr.— I mean, Linda—I pay my bills in advance. Twice a year I have my teeth cleaned and my car tuned. But as far as major life crises go, I believe that no matter what you do, you can never be fully prepared." *If I could have foreseen* this, *believe me, I wouldn't be sitting here now.*

Linda bent to jot something on her pad, her glossy brown wig bobbing with each vigorous stroke of her pen. Noelle could only imagine what she was writing. *Lack of impulse control. Displays signs of inability to cope under pressure.* She felt a sudden reckless urge to jump up and rip the offending notebook from Linda's hands. If she was going to be damned anyway, she might as well have the satisfaction.

"Tell me about your husband." Linda looked up at her with mild interest.

"What do you want to know?"

"Before all this, how would you describe your relationship?"

Noelle swallowed a cynical laugh. "We hardly ever fought, if that's what you mean. If we had a difference of opinion...well, let's just say Robert usually ended up getting his way."

"You sound resentful."

Noelle thought for a moment. "The strangest part is, I *wasn't*...until now. Now it seems odd that I didn't fight back. Maybe if I had, none of this would be happening now."

"How so?"

"I would have left him sooner, I suppose."

"Do you believe that's what contributed to your drinking?"

Noelle forced a grim smile. "I see you've done your homework. But the answer is no. I'm an alcoholic, thankfully sober now. I don't blame my drinking on anyone but me. All I'm saying is that my husband has a way of"—she paused, choosing her words carefully—"dealing with people who cross him."

Linda's thin penciled brow formed a perfect arch. "So you view this as a form of punishment?"

Noelle stared at the pen poised above the yellow legal pad. An ordinary ballpoint pen, forest green, with "Crossroads Realty" stamped in gold along the barrel. Most of Robert's properties were listed with Crossroads. Could there be a connection? She felt the muscles in her stomach clench.

"Yes and no. My husband loves his daughter, no question. He also likes being in control. When I told him I wanted a divorce"—she began to tremble at the memory and fixed her gaze on the rosy-cheeked Hummel figurines appearing to cavort with one another on the knickknack shelf over the TV—"well, he wasn't too happy about it. He became quite angry, in fact. Two days later I woke up to find my daughter gone."

"I'm sure you're aware of the fact that your husband's version of what happened is quite a bit different from your own." The woman's pale, rubbery face seemed to float, disembodied, in the dim light.

"Whatever he told you, it's a lie."

"I see." Linda tapped her pen against the notepad, waiting.

Noelle squeezed her eyes shut. "We'd had dinner together the night before. Just to talk, that's all. We hadn't even ordered yet when I began to feel...unwell. Like I was going to pass out. Then I *did*. Pass out." She opened her eyes to glare at no one in particular. "Now suddenly I'm being portrayed as the town drunk."

"*Had* you been drinking?" Linda flashed her a faintly apologetic smile. "You understand I have to ask."

"No." Noelle didn't elaborate. What was the point? The woman's mind was clearly made up on that score. The knowledge left her weightless almost, buoyed by a queer sense of abandon. "Do you mind if I ask *you* a question?"

"Not at all." Linda smiled pleasantly.

"Do you believe there's always two sides to every story?"

"In most instances, yes."

"But there *are* exceptions?"

"Occasionally."

Noelle leaned forward, hands tightly clasped. "Linda, there's something you have to know about me. If I believed I was a threat to my child, *in any way whatsoever,* I'd be the first to agree to some sort of—of temporary arrangement. However much it might pain me. But the truth is, *I'm* not the one who's hurting Emma."

"Are you suggesting your husband is?"

Seeing a flicker of uncertainty in the woman's eyes, Noelle pressed on. "All I'm asking is that you give me the benefit of the doubt. Don't jump to any conclusions until you have all the facts. Will you do that, please? For my daughter's sake?"

*"Noelle, honey, who's that you're talking to?"*

Noelle looked up to find her grandmother slowly making her way down the stairs. Her heart sank. Nana looked a fright, wearing the rumpled housecoat she'd slept in, her hair sticking up all over her head in a blizzard of yellow-white tufts. There was that cranky edge to her voice, too. Nana was never at her best when just up from her nap. *Please God,* Noelle prayed, *don't let her make this any worse than it already is.*

As Nana shuffled into the living room, Noelle quickly stood to introduce her. "Linda, this is my grandmother. Nana, remember I told you about Dr. Hawkins, that she was coming to interview me?"

"What for? Do you need a job?" Nana cocked her head, peering at the woman suspiciously. She had no use for what she called headshrinkers; in her opinion, they only confused matters.

"I'll be making a recommendation to the court regarding your granddaughter." Linda stood to shake Nana's hand. "I'm glad you could join us, Mrs. Quinn."

"Hmmph," Nana grunted.

*Don't say anything, please,* Noelle pleaded silently.

But there was no mistaking the glint in her grandmother's eye. "Well, I'll tell you what, Dr. Hodgkin, you can write in your report that Noelle here is the best mother around. Why, she'd lay down her life for that child."

"I don't doubt it," Linda replied smoothly, not bothering to correct the mispronunciation of her name.

Nana jabbed a crooked finger at the notepad. "Go on. Write it down."

"Nana, please..." Noelle pleaded.

But there was no stopping her. "It's a crying shame when a court that's supposed to uphold justice lets an innocent person get dragged through the mud instead. Why, I knew Calvin Ripley when we were in school together. He was a bootlicking worm back then, too. Which just goes to show, a black robe without a spine to hold it up isn't worth the fabric it's stitched from."

Linda's queer lashless eyes narrowed.

*I'm sorry,* Noelle mouthed in apology. She gently took hold of her grandmother's arm, but Nana brushed her aside impatiently.

"I'm not finished!" she snapped.

"Why don't I come back another time?" Linda suggested, casting a meaningful look at Noelle.

For a moment Noelle just stood there, trembling, too stricken to move. She couldn't believe this was happening. It was like some awful dream. *I've got to stop her. I've got to salvage whatever shred of credibility I have left.* Again, as she had that day with Robert, Noelle felt something stir to life inside her. Like a strong wind, pushing her forward. She stepped squarely in front of her grandmother, placing a hand on each shoulder. But Nana stubbornly twisted from her grasp. Noelle watched her teeter and reached to steady her. Then suddenly, to her horror, they *both* were tumbling to the floor. She landed with a jarring thud, her grandmother sprawled atop her.

"Awwkkkk!" Nana screeched. Her large soft weight pressed down on Noelle, suffocating her.

There was a stunned, motionless instant. Then they began struggling in unison to get up, somehow leaving them even more tangled. It wasn't until Linda seized Noelle's hand that she was able to free herself. Together they hauled Nana to her feet and into the nearest chair.

Nana clapped a hand to her heaving bosom. "Lord Almighty God! I thought I'd killed you!"

*I might as well be dead,* Noelle thought with a leaden sense of despair. If Robert had orchestrated this, it couldn't have gone any worse. God only knew what Linda Hawkins would write in her report now. *She probably sees this as some kind of insane asylum...with Nana and me as its chief inmates.*

But however misguided her actions, Nana hadn't meant any harm. Noelle would be damned if she'd apologize for her.

The psychologist hesitated at the door nonetheless, as if waiting for some sort of explanation. "Your grandmother certainly has some strong opinions," she observed dryly.

"I won't argue with that." It was on the tip of Noelle's tongue to make some placating remark, smooth over a situation that any fool could see was beyond salvaging. But when she opened her mouth, it was as if someone else were speaking, someone who'd been mostly silent until now. "I just wish I hadn't waited so long to have the courage of *my* convictions."

The number was written on a strip of masking tape stuck to the bottom of the phone. Days ago she'd put it there...just as a precaution. Now, still somewhat dazed from her bout with the psychologist, she found herself punching it in. She didn't know whether or not her sponsor was still at the same address. Or what excuse she'd give for having waited so long to call. All she knew was that it was time she stopped waiting for God, or Judge Ripley, to decide her fate.

Miraculously the line was picked up almost at once. "Hello?"

"Gwen?" Noelle clutched the receiver tightly. "Gwen, it's Noelle Van Doren.... I know it's been awhile."

Gwen Nolan gave a throaty laugh, and Noelle could picture her sitting back in her chair to light a cigarette: a heavyset woman with weary eyes that had seen too much and a smile as infectious as a child's. "Gawd, it *has* been a while, hasn't it? How the hell you been?"

"Staying sober," Noelle said with a rueful laugh to suggest what didn't need to be spoken aloud to a fellow AAer: that the road had its share of bumps. "Actually, Gwen, that's why I'm calling...."

By the time she got off the phone an hour later, with a promise to attend tomorrow night's meeting at the First Baptist Church, Noelle felt both stronger and lighter somehow. Why had she waited so long? What had she been so afraid of?

*That's not all you've been avoiding,* a voice whispered.

There was someone else she needed to talk to. Someone in a unique position to shed some light on her predicament. Who would know more about what went on at 36 Ramsey Terrace than her former neighbor, Judy Patterson?

Minutes later Noelle was in her Volvo on her way to Ramsey Terrace. *Judy has children of her own,* she thought; *she'll have some appreciation of what I'm going through.* They weren't particularly close, but regardless of her cowardice the other day, Judy had always been a good neighbor. Last winter, when Noelle had been laid up with that nasty flu, it was Judy who'd brought over a container of chicken soup and offered to look after Emma until she was better. Wouldn't she want to help now?

But when Noelle pulled up in front of the Pattersons' sprawling ranch house shortly past three-thirty, it looked deserted. She felt her heart sink, then remembered that it *always* looked as if no one were home. Judy kept the front yard immaculate: no bikes or Hot Wheels, no basketball hoop in the driveway. Her husband, Blake, owned a chain of discount drugstores and was on the road several months out of the year. Judy spent her mornings playing tennis at the club and working out at the gym. Her boys, when they weren't at day camp or in summer school, played out back or swam in the pool.

Judy, immaculate as always in Bermuda shorts and a crisp white blouse, wearing an apron that read, "The World's Greatest Chef," answered the door as promptly as if she'd been expecting company. Clearly not Noelle, though. Her mouth fell open in astonishment. "Noelle! What are you—gosh, this *is* a surprise."

"Sorry to just drop in on you like this," Noelle said. "Is it a bad time?"

Judy hesitated, then stepped aside to let her in. "I'm up to my elbows in cupcakes for the Little League team's bake sale. Don't ask! I'm such a pushover. But come on in. You can help me frost." She gave a little flutter of a laugh that didn't quite hide her nervousness.

Noelle's former neighbor was thin and blond. If Judy were ever to place an ad in a personals column (though the idea was ludicrous) that was how she'd describe herself, Noelle thought. Thin and blond. As if that were enough, even without being pretty. She had nice eyes, though. Turquoise blue, with thick dark lashes.

"What are they raising money for this time?" Noelle asked.

"New uniforms, what else? They wear them out faster than they can grow out of them."

"Boys will be boys," Noelle murmured politely as she followed Judy down the hallway into the kitchen.

"Amen to that. Honestly, the way my two go through their clothes, it's a wonder they have a stitch left to wear. Be thankful yours is a girl; they're so much easier." Judy abruptly swung around, wearing a stricken look. "Oh, Noelle, I'm sorry. Me and my big mouth."

Noelle was surprised by the newfound ease with which she was able to reply, "It's okay, Judy. And yes, I *am* grateful for Emma."

The kitchen, with its pickled oak cabinets and cheery Mexican tiles, was awash in mixing bowls and muffin tins. On the butcher-block island, racks of cupcakes had been set out to cool. As Noelle sat down at the table, a to-do list stuck to the refrigerator with a ladybug magnet caught her eye.

*This was the life I walked away from,* she thought. A life of endless busyness that had kept her from having to face the emptiness at its core. She didn't know if Judy ever felt the same way—probably not—but there had been times in the kitchen, separating eggs, when she'd been tempted to hurl them at the wall instead. Once, noticing a hole in one of her sheets, she'd wiggled a finger into it and, before she realized what she was doing, had ripped it right down the middle. Afterward, worried her housekeeper would think she'd gone nuts, she'd stuffed it into a garbage bag where Carmela wouldn't see it.

What had made it worthwhile was Emma. Her little girl. Her baby.

"Judy, I need your help." Noelle spoke quietly, but it might have been a shout from the way Judy looked up, startled, from the tin of cupcakes she was sliding from the oven.

She tacked on a bright smile nonetheless, placing the cupcakes atop the stove to cool. "Sure. Anything."

"You know what Robert's been saying about me. You know none of it is true." Noelle spoke firmly, allowing no room for disagreement. "If anyone can vouch for me, *you* can."

Judy had started lining another tin and now stood nervously fidgeting with a paper cupcake holder, her big marmalade cat, Tom-Tom, crouched at her feet as if expecting to be fed. From outside came the sounds of her sons splashing in the pool.

"What exactly did you have in mind?" she asked hesitantly.

"Would you be willing to testify on my behalf?"

Her friend stared down at the fluted pink holder in her hands. She'd managed to iron out most of its pleats and was now nervously shredding it. "Oh, Noelle." She glanced up, her pale cheeks stamped with color. "I'd like to. Really, I would. But...I can't." There was a loud splash outside, and she turned to yell out the open window, "Danny, remember what I said: Keep an eye on Junior!" When she looked back at Noelle, her eyes were shimmering with tears. "I'm sorry. Truly, I am."

Noelle began to tremble with outrage. *Wasn't I trustworthy enough to leave your boys with? To drive Junior home from school?* Only the slenderest tether of restraint kept her from walking over there and slapping the thin blond woman in the World's Greatest Chef apron, slapping her hard enough to knock her back against the wall.

Quietly she said, "I think you owe me an explanation at least."

Judy's expression hardened. "Look, I'm sorry for your troubles, but *we* still live here. Robert is our next-door neighbor. He and

Blake play golf together at the club. You don't know what you're asking."

Judy sounded angry, but there was something in her eyes.

Suddenly Noelle understood. "You're scared of him, aren't you?"

Her friend tossed aside the mangled cupcake holder. In the sunlight pouring through the sliding glass door, Noelle noticed for the first time that the hair on her upper lip was bleached. It stood out in a faint orangy fuzz.

"I think you'd better leave," Judy said in a low, shaken voice. "The boys will be in any minute, and—and I have to get these cupcakes frosted."

But it was more than fear of what Robert might do to her. Judy was acting downright furtive.

Full comprehension came swooping down like a bat from a chimney.

"It was you, wasn't it?" Noelle rose to her feet. "It wasn't much of a stretch to guess Jeanine's part in it, but I couldn't imagine who else would be rotten enough to say those awful things about me to the judge. Now I know. *You're* the one who backed up his lies."

Judy's eyes cut away. "I don't know what you're talking about."

"Yes, you do. He got to you, didn't he? Threatened you somehow."

Her friend abruptly burst into tears. Snatching a paper towel from its spindled holder, she pressed it to her face. "I don't have to listen to this," she whined childishly. "I could call the police and have you thrown out."

"But you won't."

Judy raised a tear-streaked face. Her eyes pleaded for mercy. But what mercy had Judy shown *her*? "Please, Noelle, just leave. Now. Before the boys see you. If Blake knew you were here, he'd—"

"What's Blake got to do with it?"

"Nothing. It's just—"

"He and Robert must be thick as thieves, all that time out on the golf course." Noelle advanced, both sickened and a tiny bit gratified to see Judy cower.

"It wasn't Blake's fault. He didn't want anything to do with it at first." Judy was sobbing openly now, holding the crumpled towel to her streaming eyes. "H-he just got a little overextended, that's all. Everything was going to be fine, though. He'd talked to the bank about renegotiating his loan. They were going to take it up at their next board meeting. Just a formality, they said. Then—then suddenly everything wasn't so fine."

Noelle didn't have to ask which bank. Robert sat on the board of Mercantile Trust. He'd have seen to it that they put the squeeze on Blake. She stared at the unfrosted cupcakes on the table, pale and spongy. Anger was seeping into her like icy seawater into porous rock. She could feel it swelling her veins, trickling down into her bones.

"I see," she said.

"You do?" Judy eyed her with timid hopefulness.

"I see exactly what I have to do."

Noelle watched the blood drain from her neighbor's face. *Good. Let her be afraid. It's time I stopped playing the timid rabbit and let someone else take that role.* She thought of that line from *Godfather II: Keep your friends close…and your enemies closer.*

"I'm going to phone my lawyer and tell her to expect a call from you." She went on in a cool voice of authority. Marching over to the refrigerator, she scribbled Lacey's number across the top of the to-do list. "You're going to tell her everything you just told me. Then you're going to give an affidavit refuting any earlier statements you've made."

Judy, her eyes wide with panic, began edging away. Bumping up against a tin of cupcakes perched too close to the edge of the counter, she scarcely seemed to notice when it tipped to the floor. There was a hollow clatter, and cupcakes scattered like billiard balls across the pale orange tiles. One plopped into the cat's water dish, which Tom-Tom darted over to investigate. Another was squashed under Judy's heel as she took a jerky step back.

"I can't do that!" Her voice was a hoarse rasp. "We'd lose everything! Blake's business…this house…*everything.*"

"You'll still have your children."

Noelle bent to retrieve a cupcake and tossed it to her neighbor, who fumbled before catching it. She was amazed by her utter lack of sympathy.

"Go ahead, call your lawyer!" Judy shrieked. "You can't force me to do anything I don't want to."

"Oh, can't I?" Noelle remembered something from months ago: driving past Danny's karate school late one night and seeing Judy's dark green Suburban parked in the alley alongside it. It had struck her as odd, and now she took a wild stab. "Speaking of husbands, maybe *yours* would be interested to know you're cheating on him."

Judy went pale. "How did you—" She caught herself, finishing weakly, "That's a vicious lie. Blake would know it wasn't true. Besides, you have no proof."

"Neither did you when you accused me of being drunk." Noelle was quick to remind her. "That's the funny thing about rumors, isn't it? They have a life of their own."

Judy made her think of a tennis racket that had come unstrung: eyes wild and her neat blond hair in disarray where she'd raked her hands through it. A clump of squashed cupcake clung to her sneaker. "Robert was right about you," she hissed. "You *are* a bitch."

Noelle gave her a long, level look. For the first time she saw clearly where she'd gone wrong. Not so much in trusting her neighbor as in having done no more than scratch the surface of her own life. She'd had no real friends in Ramsey Terrace. She'd *never* belonged here.

"You don't know the half of it." Noelle spun on her heel, tossing back over her shoulder, "I'll tell my lawyer to expect your call."

*N*oelle didn't know what made her stop at Hank's office on the way home. There was a time she'd have been too timid, too worried about bothering a busy doctor in the middle of the afternoon. But the person emerging from her old skin didn't hesitate to walk in unannounced. And as luck would have it, she caught Hank just as he was leaving. An artist buddy in Schenectady had invited him to a gallery opening. When he asked if she'd like to come along, she didn't hesitate to accept.

Minutes later they were winding their way up the ridge in his Toyota. For a long while Noelle didn't speak. She merely stared out the window at the green hills rolling away on her right, the scrub trees blending into tall pines as they climbed in altitude. Wisely Hank didn't attempt to engage her in conversation. He waited until she was ready.

"I met with the court-appointed psychologist today," she said at last.

"How did it go?"

"Awful." She told him about Linda Hawkins' visit, shuddering anew as she recounted the scene with Nana.

Hank absorbed it all with his usual unflappability. "Under the circumstances, I'd say you're holding up extremely well." He looked concerned nonetheless.

"Believe it or not, I'm beginning to feel as if I can cope." She didn't mention her showdown with Judy. He'd been told just enough to be warned: *any further contact with this woman could be hazardous to your health.*

"That doesn't surprise me."

*You hardly know me,* she wanted to protest. But that was the weird thing: she felt as if she'd known Hank Reynolds her whole life. "Tell me about *your* family," she said, suddenly eager to talk about anything *but* her own. "All I know is that you grew up in Kansas."

He gave a wry chuckle, shaking his head with what appeared to be a mixture of fondness and regret. "As a kid I used to think the line 'purple mountain's majesty' was something made up, like the Emerald City. In Baxter Springs, when you looked up, it was at grain silos." They'd climbed high enough now to see the valley spread out below, with its cluster of toy buildings and shimmering lake nestled between two hills. "My folks still own the farm, but they lease it out now that Dad's retired. Last time I visited, they were talking about selling it."

"Do you visit often?"

"Not as often as I should," he said. "I get out there every Christmas, though." Casually he reached over and took her hand. In the late-afternoon sunlight that washed over them in dappled waves, he appeared as wholesome and straightforward as Kansas itself. "I'd love to take you there sometime. You'd like it. When it snows, it's like a Currier and Ives Christmas card. You can almost hear the sleigh bells ringing."

Noelle was acutely conscious of his warm fingers wrapped about hers. "I'd like that," she told him. *Someday...but not now.* She thought of Christmases when she was growing up, of the artificial tree Nana had erected every year with its sorry little pile of presents underneath. Her mother had always done her best to make it cheerful, but even she couldn't make up for Noelle being an only child, or Nana being too old (or so she claimed) to bake fruitcakes no one would eat and pick up after a tree that shed. "Are you anything like your parents?"

"I take after my dad, I guess," Hank said after a moment's consideration. "He's stubborn like me. Knows how to dig his heels in." He flashed her his naughty choirboy's grin. "Except for one thing. Dad never really understood about my wanting to become a doctor."

"I thought it was the dream of every parent."

He shrugged. "I think he saw it more as my rejecting his whole way of life." His hands tightened about the steering wheel. "For my twelfth birthday, my folks gave me a rifle, a twenty-two caliber Browning. I spent the whole summer learning to shoot tin cans off the fence."

"Were you a lousy shot?"

"No, that was the trouble," he said. "I was actually pretty good at it. Dad must have thought so, too. He took me hunting come deer season. The day I shot my first and only buck, I hung the Browning up for good. I still have it, as a matter of fact. I keep it around as a reminder that some things are best left alone."

He slowed as they passed a scenic overlook, where a bronze plaque had been erected in honor of the Revolutionary War hero General Louis W. Church, victorious over the British troops in the Battle of Sandy Creek. Wistfully he added, "I figured if I ever had kids of my own, I'd teach them a different way."

"I can see now why you were so unhappy about your wife's not wanting kids." Suddenly curious, she asked, "Was that why you got divorced?"

"Mainly, but there were other reasons." He hesitated before confiding, "I found out she was having an affair. With one of her grad students."

"Was she in love with him?"

"The answer is yes." He shot her a glance. "And it wasn't a he; it was a she."

"Oh, Hank." Noelle was momentarily speechless. All she could think of to say was, "It must have been quite a shock."

Hank surprised her with a deep laugh. "It *was* a shock—to my male pride. It was quite a while before I could summon the courage to date again. I was sure it was something lacking in me, personally...not just the fact that I was a man."

"From what I've heard, it doesn't work that way."

"Oh, I knew. Intellectually, that is. But it's hard to be intellectual when your wife is sleeping with another woman."

"Would it have been any easier if her lover had been a man?"

"I suppose not," he said. "The truth is, I hardly ever think about Kathryn anymore. If anything, I wish her well. She got what she wanted. We both did in a sense."

They rounded a blind curve and a sweeping view of the valley beyond unfurled before her, one that was all too familiar yet somehow drastically altered. Her heart lurched. "Pull over!" she cried.

Hank slowed at once and veered onto the graveled shoulder. Scrambling out of the car, Noelle gazed bleakly at the ravaged woodland below. The site for Cranberry Mall, stripped of its trees and leveled, looked even vaster than when she'd last seen it. A great raw gash amid the surrounding greenery. A year from now, if all went according to schedule, a minimetropolis would stand where deer had once roamed. High-end chain stores, food courts, sports and theater complexes. She recalled Robert's arguing with her father that the mall would bring sorely needed jobs and tax revenue. To which Dad had responded that the increased traffic, inflated property values, and unwelcome tourists would more than make up for it.

She scarcely noticed when Hank slipped up alongside her and tucked an arm about her shoulders. "Mea culpa," he apologized. "I guess I wasn't thinking when I chose this route."

"My father used to take me picnicking here when I was little," she recalled mournfully. "When Robert first started talking about

302

developing it, I guess it didn't seem real to me. It was just a lot of brainstorming sessions and blueprints and three-martini lunches with Grant Iverson." She felt a wrench of loss, as if the scarred earth, once thick with trees, now dotted with trucks and graders and bulldozers, represented everything she herself stood to lose.

Hank's arm tightened about her shoulders. "I'd heard about the mall, but I had no idea of the scale it was on." He whistled softly between his teeth. "It must be fifteen or twenty acres."

"Something like that."

"Who's the lucky guy getting chewed out?"

Her gaze instantly picked out Robert amid a cluster of tiny figures in hardhats. He was giving hell to one of the workers and had adopted what she thought of as his alpha-male pose—head thrust forward, gesticulating with an upraised fist. Though the guy was at least a head taller, he cowered in response.

"That's his foreman, Mike Henshaw." Even from this distance she recognized Mike from the thick slab of belly slung over his belt. "He's been with the company over thirty years, so he must be used to it by now. From what I've heard, Robert's dad was even tougher on his crews."

"I take it the old man's retired."

"More or less. Cole still goes into the office for an hour or two every day, but he's basically out of the loop. There's no question who runs things now. I sometimes wonder what would have happened if Robert's brother—"

Noelle broke off, her attention drawn to a white newer-model Cadillac making its way along the dirt access road that linked the site to the highway just east of it. She recognized it at once as her mother-in-law's and drew in a sharp breath. What was *she* doing here? Wasn't Gertrude supposed to be home watching Emma? She watched the Caddy pull to a stop in front of the trailer that served as Robert's field office. An elderly woman climbed out, remarkably trim for her age, with a bulletproof bouffant an indeterminate shade between beige and blond. She wore a suit and high heels and carried a shopping bag.

A moment later the door to the passenger side flew open, and a small dark-haired figure bounded out. Noelle watched helplessly, invisible to her daughter, as Emma dashed toward her father. She felt as if the solid ground beneath her had suddenly given way.

Oh, God, it was too much. The last straw.

Yet somehow, incredibly, it was galvanizing her. Like a blowtorch burning away the excess layers of dead skin, leaving her newly minted. *If I had a gun, I would kill him,* she thought.

The epiphany was so strong and so unnerving that it caused her to sag, with a low cry, into Hank's arms. Her head was filled with a high white noise, like the sound of the wind finding its way through a cracked casement. She was aware of his hands—his fine healing hands— stroking her back, smoothing away the sharp edges of her pain. His breath was warm against her temple. When he kissed her, it was as if this were part of her journey, too, tied in with Emma somehow. As if the woman she'd first glimpsed in Hank's eyes, a woman with a mind of her own and heart that wasn't going to be put on hold, had at last emerged from the shadows into full sunlight.

# Chapter Eleven

It was dark by the time Mary passed through the tollbooth at I-87. All the way up the FDR and onto the Third Avenue Bridge, the traffic had been bumper to bumper. And she still had two hours to go. God, what a perfectly awful day. Starting with her morning staff meeting, at which Brittany had given her the litany of bad news: the clients who had been growing restless, the bookkeeper suspected of dipping into petty cash, the daily barrage of calls from Howard Lazarus concerning the Rene's Room banquet.

Her come-to-Jesus with Leo Le Gras had been the day's low point. Tracking him down at his SoHo loft, she'd found the soused caterer nearly incoherent. When a crisp reminder of his responsibility to her failed, she'd been forced to make a decision. Mentally writing off the sizable deposit she'd forked over, Mary had informed Leo nicely, but firmly, that he was fired.

Fortunately she'd come prepared. Armed with a short list of names from her Rolodex, she'd set out to find a replacement. The first candidate, Private Reserve on East Sixty-fourth, had been a near miss. She'd found the *pâté brisée* a trifle less than flaky, the *haricot vert* a tad overcooked. The chef had been accommodating, a bit *too* accommodating; he left her wondering if his availability had been such a miracle after all.

The chef at Mais Oui, in TriBeca, was the polar opposite, an overbearing primadonna who'd expected her to grovel at his feet. The sample dishes served to her on small Herend saucers had been divine, of course, but reluctantly she'd had to pass. After the near disaster with Leo, she didn't need any more temperamental caterers in her life.

By the time she arrived at Madame Gregoire's West End Avenue penthouse, Mary had nearly run out of hope. But one look at the stout French *maman* with her large work-reddened hands and gray hair twisted into a bun had been enough. Madame was as unaffected as her cuisine proved superb. Mary, stuffed from her two previous samplings, nonetheless found herself inhaling the tidbits of delicate lobster and shitake mushroom salad, the artichoke terrine and venison cubes marinated in peppercorn sauce. She'd made out a check on the spot.

Yet as she set out for home, Mary felt none of her usual sense of accomplishment, only a gnawing emptiness. What was a banquet compared with her daughter? She should have obeyed her instincts and stayed home. Apparently the interview hadn't gone well. Noelle had neglected to phone and wasn't home when Mary called. It was Doris who had given her the fill, muttering something about the woman being a horse's ass—strong language, coming from her mother.

*Poor Noelle,* she thought. *I should have been there.*

Mary flashed back on this morning's outburst. Noelle's words had stung, but she had to acknowledge there was some truth to them. What was also true was that she loved her daughter. How could she make Noelle *see* that? Had it been foolish to imagine that temporarily moving back home would make a difference?

*Home.* Even the word had lost its meaning. Where *was* home these days? Not Burns Lake, not anymore, though it wasn't without its share of pleasures. Sitting out on the porch in the evening, lulled by the creak of the swing. Sacks of homegrown produce left at the back door. Waking up to the sound of birds and the wick-wick-wick of sprinklers up and down the street. Every season, too, had its timeworn traditions. The annual Fourth of July parade, featuring the newly crowned Silver Beauty Corn Queen in a Cadillac convertible cruising down Main Street. The outdoor Nativity play at Christmas, followed by hot buttered rum and candlelight caroling. In October there was the Pumpkin Festival sponsored by the Daughters of the American Revolution, the highlight of which was a reenactment of the Battle of Sandy Creek, complete with muskets and cannon.

Yes, there was much to value about Burns Lake. The best it had to offer, though, was time. Precious time with her daughter and with Trish. On a much lesser scale her mother, too, who wouldn't be around forever.

*And let's not forget Charlie.*

Mary's hands tensed about the steering wheel. *Charlie.* Memories rose, warm as the air blowing in through the vents. Being with him was like going back to a house she'd once lived in and finding it virtually unchanged. Except her name was no longer on the mailbox. She was welcome to visit for as long as she liked, but sooner or later she'd have to go. The thought brought a pang of loss. She wished now that she hadn't stepped through the door. In the end, it would only make her leave-taking that much harder.

Remembering her promise to call him, she considered putting it off until tomorrow. Wanting Charlie from a distance, she thought ruefully, was a whole lot easier than resisting him in person. An hour and a half later, as she was turning into the exit for Burns Lake, Mary nonetheless found herself reaching for her phone. She tried the cabin first, and when there was no answer punched in his work number.

The line was picked up at once. A voice barked, "Newsroom."

She recognized it as Charlie's, though its gruffness took her by surprise. This was a side of him she'd never seen, and she was secretly intrigued. "It's me," she said. "I took a chance you'd still be at your desk. I hope you didn't think I forgot."

"What time *is* it anyway?" He sounded hoarse. She pictured him glancing at the clock on his wall, then scrubbing his face with an open hand—an old habit.

"Crazy day?"

"I'll tell you about it over dinner. You haven't eaten, have you?"

Mary hesitated before replying. Still full from her tastings, she'd planned to skip dinner. But an hour at the Curlycue Café wouldn't kill her, she thought. And frankly a strategy session was in order. As far as Corinne was concerned, she'd run out of leads. If Charlie had any ideas, she needed to hear them.

"I'm just now heading into town," she told him. "Meet you at the Curlycue in fifteen minutes?"

There was a pause. Then Charlie answered guardedly, "Let's make it somewhere more private. Something's come up, and I wouldn't want us to be overheard."

She felt her heart quicken. "Anything important?"

"Meet me at the cabin, okay? We can talk there."

Mary was suddenly aware of how close

she'd crept to the brown Escort in front of her; their bumpers were practically touching. Immediately she eased her foot off the accelerator. "What about Bronwyn?"

"She's staying over at a friend's." Mary heard a desk drawer slam, followed by the jingle of keys. "I'll pick up something at the Curlycue on my way home. You like shepherd's pie?"

She groaned inwardly at the thought. "A salad will do me just fine."

"You got it." There was a short intake of breath at the other end. "Listen, Mary, I'm glad you called. Last night..." Charlie let the sentence trail off. Clearing his throat, he finished lightly, "I'll keep the pie in the oven. You might change your mind."

She thumbed the end button and let out a sigh. She'd been thinking about last night, too. Bumping into Charlie after the meeting, she hadn't been prepared for the rush of emotion it brought, a strange and heady mix of longing and regret. Their interlude at the lake...dear God, had they really believed they could get away with it? Fall in love a little, but not too much. They were playing with fire, just like when they were teenagers. If they didn't watch out, they'd get burned.

Mary was so caught up in her thoughts she scarcely noticed how far she'd driven until she was turning onto the narrow tree-lined road where Charlie lived. Moments later she was pulling up in front of his cabin and making her way up the path of cedar rounds that meandered through the dense shrubbery of the yard—flower beds wouldn't have survived the deer, Charlie had told her. She was mounting the steps to the front door when it opened, spilling yellow light onto the porch. Her ex-husband stepped out to greet her, his big yellow dog at his heels.

Silhouetted in the amber glow, the two figures might have been a commercial for the joys of country life. Charlie, barefoot, in off-white chinos and blue-checked shirt rolled up over his elbows. The golden retriever with its plumed tail fanning back and forth. When Charlie bent to lightly kiss her cheek, she caught the faint menthol scent of his shaving cream. Resisting the urge to run her hand along his jaw, Mary bent to pat Rufus instead.

"You made good time," he commented.

"The last half hour was easy. It was the first two I could've done without." Mary laughed, feeling uncharacteristically nervous. *Why did he have to get better-looking with age?* she cursed inwardly. *Why couldn't he have had the decency to go fat and bald like other men?*

"Luckily the perils of commuting is one thing I've never had to deal with." He flashed her a wry smile as he held the door open for her. "On the other hand, I doubt I'll ever be awarded the Pulitzer Prize."

Mary stepped inside, once again admiring the cabin's rustic charm that somehow managed to avoid crossing the line into homespun kitsch. The hooked rugs and scuffed leather sofa, the comfortable chairs grouped about the large stone fireplace. On its mantel stood a silver-framed photo of Charlie's second wife, a pretty dark-haired woman with delicate features and a smile that lit up her whole face. The photo had been taken out on the dock, with the lake shimmering at her back. Her short hair was blowing up around her face. She looked happy.

Mary felt something twist inside her chest. She thought of Charlie and his wife sleeping together, snuggled under the covers of their big rough-hewn bed. Joking with each other across the table in their sunny kitchen. It was wrong of her to feel this way, she knew, wrong and petty and meanspirited. But she couldn't seem to help it. She was jealous of Vicky. Jealous enough to want to snatch that photo off the mantel and hurl it to the floor.

As quickly as it had come over her, the impulse passed. Shaken, Mary sank down in a chair, heavy with more than just weariness. *Dear God,* she thought, *have I really sunk so low? To be resentful of a dead woman? If Charlie only knew...*

Charlie must have seen how rattled she was. He shot her a curious glance and immediately fetched her a cold beer from the kitchen. Mary, sunk to her armpits in the huge old Papa Bear chair, sipped it gratefully. He even remembered that she liked Heineken. *You're not making this any easier, you know,* she wanted to cry in protest.

"It must be rough, all this running back and forth." Charlie sank down on the sofa, leaning

312

toward her with his elbows resting on his knees and his beer bottle loosely clasped in his hands.

"I'm managing," she said with a little shrug.

Charlie tipped his bottle in a silent toast. "You always do." His gaze moved over her, coolly admiring. "You look good, Mary. You've got some sun in your cheeks. And I like that color; it suits you."

She had to look down to see what she was wearing: her Armani suit, yes. "What's that old expression? I clean up good." She smiled, her gaze drawn to the painting over the fireplace, a surprisingly good oil of horses grazing in a pasture. "Frankly," she confessed, "it's gotten to be a real chore, dressing up to go into the city. I've become spoiled, bumming around all day in shorts and T-shirts. I'm convinced it was a man who came up with the idea for panty hose; no one who had to wear it would invent something so uncomfortable."

Charlie laughed. "I'll take your word for it." He set his beer down on the table in front of him, a thick slab of oak supported by wrought-iron legs. "Speaking of supper, you must be hungry. Give me a minute, and I'll throw a salad together."

He started to get up, but Mary leaned over to touch his knee. "Charlie? Would you mind if we just sat and talked a bit?" At the moment she doubted she could have managed more than a bite, not with Charlie looking at her like that, like a man with something other than food on his mind. She watched him settle back, eyeing

313

her guardedly. Before she knew it, the words were out of her mouth. "Do you remember our second date? Pretending we hadn't spent the first one madly making out?"

He smiled at the memory, fondly, if not misty-eyed. Had he come to the same conclusion as she? That any further intimacy would ultimately cause more harm than good. She'd hoped he would see it her way, but the thought nonetheless brought a sharp nip of regret.

"As I recall, we more than made up for it on the way home." Charlie chuckled.

"How could I forget?" The Jefferses' Oldsmobile had been so steamed up they'd had to crank all the windows down and drive around the block several times before daring to pull up in front of her house.

Nor had she forgotten the nights that followed. The evenings spent parked out at the lake, kissing for hours, until her mouth was swollen and her body ached with longing. Charlie hadn't pressured her then either. She'd *wanted* what came next. With all the willfulness of a heart yearning for the love it had been deprived of. It shouldn't have come as a surprise when not long afterward she discovered she was pregnant.

"And look where it's taken us." Charlie's smile was full of irony. "Did you ever think we'd be sitting here, two middle-aged parents discussing what's best for our grown daughter?"

"Never in my wildest dreams." It struck her that some things people were better off not knowing. Back then, had she been afforded a glimpse into the future, it would only have depressed her. "Speaking of Noelle, did you hear from her today?"

Charlie nodded. "I gather the interview didn't go so well. Something to do with Doris putting her two cents in. You know how opinionated she can get."

"Do I ever!" Mary groaned, feeling a fresh stab of guilt for not being there.

"It wasn't just the interview," Charlie told her. "Apparently, Noelle paid a visit to her former neighbor. You remember the Pattersons? They were at the christening." He stared grimly into the blackened fireplace. "It turns out Judy Patterson was the one who corroborated Robert's story. He was putting pressure on her husband, and she caved. Some friend, huh?"

Mary shivered, as if caught in a cold draft. What, precisely were they up against here? No ordinary opponent it was becoming increasingly evident. Who in this town *wasn't* in Robert's pocket?

"You said something had come up," she reminded him. "Was that what you wanted to tell me?"

"Partly." Charlie took another long pull off his beer. "But that's not all. There's something even Noelle doesn't know about."

Mary's heart was suddenly beating very fast. She watched as he wordlessly got up to retrieve his briefcase from the hall table by the door.

"See for yourself." He pulled a manila envelope from inside and handed it to her.

Mary didn't know why, but all at once she was afraid. Goose bumps skimmed up her arms like the brush of cold fingertips. For no reason that made any sense, she didn't *want* to know what the envelope contained.

Sensing her reluctance, Charlie said softly, "It's Corinne's autopsy report." His grave tone suggested there'd been more to her friend's long-ago suicide than met the eye.

Mary's chilled fingers fumbled with the envelope's clasp. So it was true, Corinne *had* been murdered. Dear God, all these years...

Charlie seemed to read her mind, his next words putting an end to any hope of being able to pin something on Robert. "There's no evidence of foul play," he said. "They tested for drugs and alcohol as well. Nothing."

"That still doesn't prove anything," she stubbornly insisted.

"Not conclusively," he said.

"So why do I need to see this?"

"There *was* something." Charlie walked over to perch on the arm of her chair, placing a hand on her shoulder. She could feel it through her jacket, heavy and warm, anchoring her somehow. "Corrine was pregnant."

She looked up with a sharp intake of breath. Even seated next to her, Charlie appeared far away, as if poised at the top of a steep staircase. "My God. Why didn't she—" Mary clapped a hand over her mouth. Corinne *had* tried to tell her. In a hoarse whisper, she asked, "How far along was she?"

"About six weeks. She must have just found out."

Mary brought a fist to her stomach, pressing against the yawning pit that had opened up there. "She *called* me, Charlie. About a week or so before—" she paused to gulp in air. "I was busy. I told her I'd call her back, but somehow I never got around to it. Maybe if I *had,* I could have stopped her from—"

He pulled her to him, muffling her words. As she buried her face in the soft folds of his shirt, it was as if time had stood still. As if the years in between now and that terrible winter day had never happened. She was seventeen again, clinging to her young husband while the fragile life they'd built dissolved around her like snowflakes.

"It wasn't your fault," he soothed. "She was scared and desperate." He didn't need to add, *Just like us.*

She drew back, tilting her head to peer up at him. "Assuming she really *did* kill herself. As far as I'm concerned, this still doesn't let Robert off the hook. If anything, it provides something that's been missing until now: a motive."

"How do we know she even told him she was pregnant?"

"Just for the sake of argument, let's suppose she did. Can you see Robert offering to marry her? With four months to go until graduation and Stanford practically within sight?" Mary thought for a moment, trying to put herself in Corinne's shoes. "I don't think she'd have agreed to an abortion, either. She was pretty religious."

"So she refuses to have an abortion and he kills her in a fit of rage? Then makes it look like suicide?" Charlie shook his head. "Sorry, much as I'd like to, I don't buy it. Like I said, there were no marks or bruises, no sign of a struggle even."

Mary slumped back in her chair. Charlie was right about one thing: Whichever way you looked at it, they'd come up empty-handed. "Poor Corinne. If only she could have told us what happened." The entries in her diary had abruptly stopped—six weeks? Yes, that would be about right—around the time she'd have gotten pregnant. Even so, Mary knew all too well the agonies her friend must have suffered. *If it hadn't been for Charlie....*

"At the very least," she went on, "he might have browbeaten her so mercilessly she saw no other choice. He's guilty of *something.* I just know it." Frustration rose in her. "What about that rape case he was involved in back in college?"

Charlie rose abruptly and paced over to the window. He stood staring out at the darkly glinting lake, where a night bird skimmed in search of prey. Was he thinking what she was, that this was the same man who'd fathered their grandchild?

"Another dead end, I'm afraid," he answered. "I had a colleague in California do a little digging. Apparently there's not much more to the story than what we already know. Except for one minor detail. It turns out that the accused rapist, young Justin McPhail, was on full scholarship."

"I don't see the significance."

She caught his ghostly reflection in the glass as he turned to face her. His expression was thoughtful, considering. "It just struck me as odd, that's all. The investigation, as it turns out, was dropped when the girl decided not to press charges. Which leads me to wonder if someone got to her. Someone with money, which McPhail's parents were clearly short of."

"What about the Larrabies?" she asked, remembering that Robert's college chum turned state senator, King Larrabie, had been involved as well. "They're richer than God."

"As rich as the Van Dorens at least." Charlie picked up an object off the table by the window, a pretty handblown paperweight, turning it over in his hand. Another of his wife's touches? "The girl could have been bought off by either boy's family, or maybe she really *did* change her mind."

"Do you believe that?"

"No. But again we don't have a shred of proof."

"Which leaves us back at square one."

"Yes and no. I have a hunch we may be on to something and just not know it." Charlie rubbed his chin, staring sightlessly at a point just past her head. She thought again of how he'd sounded earlier over the phone, like a dogged reporter racing to meet his deadline. Then his gaze shifted, and he was looking straight at her. "Last night, after I left you, someone jumped me in the parking lot. I didn't see his face, but I'm sure it was one of Robert's flunkies. The guy warned me that if I didn't stop sticking my nose in where it didn't belong, I'd be in for a lot worse."

Mary shot to her feet. "Charlie! My God, why didn't you call me?"

"I didn't want to worry you."

"Worried? I'm terrified! What if he meant it?"

"I'm sure he does." Charlie idly hefted the paperweight, making her think of a pitcher on the mound getting ready to throw. "But there's another way to look at it. I find it strange that a man with nothing to hide is going to so much trouble to prove it, don't you?"

"You think he's protecting something other than his reputation?"

"Everything I've printed so far is a matter of public record. All I did was put the pieces together to form a clear picture." His shook his head slowly. "No, my gut tells me there's more to it than that. I think he really *is* hiding something."

"The question is *what*?"

Mary felt as wired as if she'd just downed half a gallon of coffee on an empty stomach. Even Rufus could sense it; he stirred from his prone position on the rug at her feet to cast her an anxious glance. Carefully, as if it were something fragile that might shatter, she placed the envelope on the table in front of her. Later, she might be able to look at what was inside. But not now. And maybe not for a long while.

"Let's hope more will come to light." Charlie didn't have to add, *Before someone gets hurt.*

"Oh, Charlie." He looked so miserable: a man, a father, with his hands tied. It was exactly how he'd looked that long-ago winter day, just before he turned and walked away.

It struck her then that she hadn't been loved by either of her parents half as much as she had been by Charlie. If she hadn't been so young and scared, if she hadn't had a baby to think of, she might have realized it at the time. She might have made a different choice. Now it was too late to undo.

But not too late to take back some of what they'd been robbed of.

Like something long submerged floating to the surface, Mary rose and walked over to where he stood. Charlie didn't move. He just stood there, motionless, his pale reflection etched in the dark glass at his back. Scarcely realizing what she was doing, she brought her arms up, twining them about his neck. She felt him resist at first. Then, with a low, choked cry, he wrapped his arms about her. She could feel the paperweight, warmed by his hand, pressing into the small of her back.

Mary tipped her head back and felt his mouth close over hers. Why was it no man but Charlie had ever kissed her this way? With no beginning or end. *Like falling,* she thought, *falling off a dock into water so deep you can't see the bottom.* She heard the paperweight hit the floor with a hollow thud. Then he was cradling her face with both hands, drawing her to him as greedily as someone deprived of air might gulp in deep breaths. For an instant, she felt it, too: the same sense of urgency, of violent need. What would she do without this? How would she survive?

At the same time, it was all so right, so familiar: his taste, his scent—soap and shaving cream and the special smell that was Charlie alone. There was a spot on his chin, just under his lower lip, that he'd missed with his razor. She ran her tongue over it, catlike, hearing him moan deep in his throat. She could hardly breathe, he was holding her so tightly, but she didn't want him to let go. Not yet. Not ever.

"Stay the night," he whispered into her hair.

Mary had never wanted anything more in her life. Even so, she stiffened, drawing back. "Oh, Charlie, what would I tell Noelle? Not to mention my mother."

He aimed for a jaunty grin that came out lopsided. "In case you've forgotten, we're over eighteen."

"Really? I hadn't noticed."

The smile dropped from his face. His eyes regarded her solemnly. "I'm not going to try to talk you into anything, Mary. Because right now I'd say whatever it took, and that wouldn't be fair to either of us."

"Okay." Mary stepped back on wobbly legs. Her stomach followed a second later, floating lazily to meet her.

"Okay what?"

"I'll stay," she told him, placing a finger against his mouth before he could open it. "Not because you want me to. Because *I* want to. Just promise me one thing."

"What?"

"That we won't be having shepherd's pie for breakfast." She managed a smile as unsteady as her knees. "I don't think I could face that."

"It's a deal." Charlie smiled and tucked her arm through his, somewhat self-consciously, like an old-fashioned suitor taking her for an evening stroll. Even Rufus rolled eagerly to his feet, as if hoping to be invited along.

There was a moment just then, no more than the space of a heartbeat, when she could have walked away. But when he reached up to brush a strand of hair from her cheek, she knew there was no turning back.

In the bedroom with its picture window that overlooked the lake, Mary sat down gingerly on the bed. It was covered with a faded quilt that looked as if it had been in someone's family for years. His wife's? Charlie and Vicky had slept together on that quilt, she thought with a stab of jealousy. Their daughter had probably been conceived on this bed.

Charlie sat down next to her, the old pine frame creaking with his weight. "Having second thoughts?"

323

"No." She turned to him, suddenly certain of what she wanted—for the moment at least. "Just hold me, Charlie."

Whatever lingering doubts she might have felt, *this* felt right. Just like in the beginning. The crook of his shoulder where her head nestled in a perfect fit. The hair behind his ear that tickled the bridge of her nose. The only difference between now and then was in how tightly he held her, like a man who'd once been forced to let go.

"You know what I missed the most? Your smell." He smoothed a hand along her neck, speaking in a low husky voice. "After you left, it was almost a month before I could bring myself to change the sheets. Everywhere I turned there was a little piece of you. A strand of hair on the bathroom sink. A note you'd scribbled to yourself. But your scent"— his voice caught—"it was everywhere. Those first weeks after I moved out, I kept thinking I'd misplaced something. But I hadn't. It was just that I couldn't smell you anymore."

His confession released something from deep inside her, something wrapped in layers like a keepsake. She smiled into the warm curve of his neck. "I used to lie awake at night, thinking of you and wondering if you were doing the same," she confessed. "I would have called if I'd thought I could get away with it. But my mother would have listened in."

He sighed. "She didn't make it any easier, that's for sure."

Mary waited for the sharp prick of resentment she always felt, but it didn't come. Somewhere along the line, without realizing it, she must have found a way to forgive her mother. "It wasn't all her fault," she acknowledged. "I *should* have picked up the phone. I should have told you..." She let the sentence trail off. Some things were just too hard to admit.

"Told me what?"

She lifted her head. Through the prism of her tears his face was a blur. "That I was wrong."

"I've waited a long time to hear you say that." He touched the corner of her eye, releasing a tear that trickled down her cheek.

Slowly Charlie undressed her, then himself. Naked, they stretched out on the bed. She felt as she had the other night: a little scared, but not as scared as she ought to have been. Then she'd acted on impulse; it was something neither of them had intended. This, though, was very much considered. There would be consequences. One or both of them would very likely get hurt. Others might get hurt as well.

At the moment, however, none of that seemed to matter. Nothing else existed. It was just the two of them, face-to-face, the heat of their bodies warming them as evening cooled into night.

*He's all shank and bone,* she thought. That's what Charlie's mother used to say. Even his feet were long, with toes like fingers. She smoothed her palm along the bony ridge of his flank. She loved it all. The leanness of him, the beveled planes of his muscles like facets of a gem. She loved that he didn't shy from being touched in odd places—the back of his knee, the silky dampness of his armpit. He didn't find it strange. He didn't think her peculiar. He seemed to love it as much as she.

Mary arched as he brought his mouth to her breasts, taking first one nipple in his mouth, then the other. Teasing her exquisitely. She wanted to cry out that she was ready. She'd been ready for minutes, hours...years. The memory of the other night, when he'd taken her in the grass, was like a delicious dream from which she'd woken to find herself once more wrapped in Charlie's arms. She cried out softly as he moved lower, tasting her, exploring her with his tongue. An eternity of delicious sensations that lapped over her, one by one.

Then he was kneeling over her, straddling her. His face above hers sketched in shadow. "Am I going too fast?" he whispered.

She shook her head. She couldn't speak. She was having trouble catching her breath. Charlie seemed to understand and didn't rush. She felt him glide into her, filling her, wholly and perfectly. Mary shut her eyes, as if to seal the moment. They'd begun to sweat, sticking to each other and pulling away with soft sucking sounds. She knew that if she were to tilt her hips just so, she would come in an instant. And she didn't want to, not yet. She wanted to prolong the sensations, stretch this moment to cover a lifetime.

"Charlie," she whispered, pushing her fingers into his hair, gripping the back of his skull. She didn't quite know what she wanted to say. The thought teetered, half formed, on the outermost edge of her mind. Had she been able to voice it, she might have asked, *Why didn't you take me with you that day? Pick me up and carry me if you had to?*

Charlie moved inside her carefully, seeming to savor each stroke that brought them closer to the midnight that would break this lovely enchantment. The moon, caught in a windowpane, gazed down at them like a serene unblinking eye. Even the lake was quiet. No birds calling, no leaves whispering. It was as if the entire world were holding its breath.

She came in a burst, like an exquisite exhalation.

Charlie followed an instant later, crying out through clenched teeth, "Jesus." He shuddered, his head rearing back, droplets of sweat splashing like warm rain against her cheeks and forehead.

Afterward they lay together without moving, hearts racing, their bodies deliciously joined. She didn't know where she ended and he began. That was the way it had always been with Charlie.

At last he rolled onto his side. "You're awfully quiet." He smoothed her hair back where it had stuck to her temple.

"I was just thinking…"

"About what?"

"Apples." She smiled up at the ceiling.

"Remember that little orchard down by the paddock? How the branches nearest the fence were always bare?"

Out of the corner of her eye she caught the flash of his smile. "Yeah, I remember. The horses couldn't get enough of those apples."

She stretched, hearing her joints pop. Even that was blissful.

They lay beside each other, holding hands in the darkness, not speaking, neither of them wanting to break the spell. Reality would intrude soon enough. In a minute or two she'd have to get up, call home. Charlie would pad into the kitchen and turn off the oven, from which the smell of overcooked shepherd's pie was currently wafting. But for now the moment hung suspended, like the moon caught in the window pane overhead.

Mary thought instead about biting into one of those apples. She could almost taste its sweet, gingery flesh, feel its clear, sweet juice running down her chin. She remembered the air, cidery with the scent of windfall. And Charlie, most of all Charlie, standing beside her, tall and lean, his cheeks scrubbed with cold, straining up to reach the tallest branches.

Arriving home the following morning around ten, Mary was surprised to find her mother just getting out of bed—with the help of Noelle, who was struggling, without much success, to pull her nightgown over her head. Doris wasn't cooperating in the least. She just sat there, arms slack. Like a doll, one of the dried-apple dolls in the window of The Basket Case.

"Nana, if you don't help me, I'll never get this off." Noelle had managed to free one arm and was holding the other aloft while she fought to peel off its sleeve.

"Well, for heaven's sake, you don't have to shout! There's nothing wrong with my hearing." Doris's voice was muffled by the folds of nightgown covering her face.

"I'm not shouting," Noelle said calmly. "I'm just trying to—"

Mary darted forward. "Here, let me help."

Together, they managed to wrestle the nightgown off.

Noelle cast her a grateful look over the head emerging in a flurry of snowy tufts, like goose down from a ruptured pillow. "Okay, Nana, we're going to help you into the bathroom now. There's a nice hot bath waiting for you. Can you stand on your own? There, that's it. Good, you're doing just fine."

"I'm *not* an invalid," Doris snapped as Mary took one arm and Noelle the other. "Just a little sore from yesterday. If it hadn't been for that dreadful woman..." She glowered darkly at no one in particular. "Who did you say she was? Emma's teacher? Schools these days—every Tom, Dick, and Harry thinks he has a degree in child psychology."

"It was the psychologist sent by the court, remember, Nana?" Noelle said patiently, as if for the umpteenth time. She looked tired and a bit pale, but seemed steadier somehow, more focused, like a boat that had been listing that was now back on course.

"What happened?" Mary asked.

"She lost her balance and fell. Yesterday, when Dr. Hawkins was here." Noelle's mouth tightened, but she offered no further explanation.

"Hawkins? Who's that? My doctor is Hank Reynolds. You can look it up." Doris jabbed a finger at the desk in the corner, on which a worn red leatherette address book sat.

Mary's heart sank. Was her mother losing her marbles along with everything else? She could hardly bear to think of it. Doris seemed so frail in her nakedness, with her wrinkled skin and flattened breasts drooping like a pair of old socks. Mary realized suddenly that her mother was only a few years younger than the old ladies from church that Doris used to look after, shut-ins whom she'd dutifully visited twice a week, helping out with small chores and seeing that they had enough to eat. To Mary, a child at the time, they'd seemed impossibly ancient. Now her mother was one of them. The thought left her feeling strangely displaced, as if a familiar landmark by which she'd always navigated had abruptly vanished.

"A hot bath will do you a world of good, Mama." She aimed for a cheerful, upbeat tone, hoping she wouldn't be questioned about last night's whereabouts, as they lowered Doris into the steaming tub.

She watched her daughter gently scrub Doris's back with a soapy washcloth, and experienced a dizzying wave of déjà vu. In her mind, she was seeing a similar picture in which the roles were reversed: Doris holding the dripping cloth instead, with the infant Noelle naked and gleaming before her. The memory clutched at Mary's heart.

As if Noelle had somehow picked up on her thoughts, she smiled down at her grandmother, recalling, "This reminds me of when I was little and you used to give *me* baths."

"You were like a little fish, slippery as one, too," Doris clucked.

"You used to threaten to take away my rubber ducky if I didn't stop wiggling." She giggled, and incredibly Doris chuckled in return.

Noelle was relaxed with her mother in a way that Mary couldn't imagine being. She felt suddenly envious of their relationship, wishing she'd known that kind of closeness...not only with her daughter but with Doris as well. *Maybe it's not too late,* a voice whispered.

When they'd finished bathing her, Mary and Noelle hoisted Doris from the tub and toweled her dry. She leaned on them heavily, as if fearful that she might fall. At one point Mary's shoe slipped on the wet tiles and she nearly lost her balance. She could see Noelle struggling to stay afoot as well. But together they managed to get her into a clean nightgown and back onto the bed, where Doris collapsed with an exhausted sigh.

"I didn't know you could feel this tired from doing nothing," she croaked.

"Would you like me to bring you a tray?" Noelle offered. "Some tea and toast maybe?"

Doris shook her head. "No. I believe I'll close my eyes and rest a bit." The pink curve of her skull, visible through her wet hair, made her seem even more vulnerable somehow.

Noelle hesitated before stepping out into the hall. Mary was about to follow her when she heard her mother call out softly, "Mary Catherine? Would you mind reading to me a bit?"

Mary froze, her hand on the beveled glass doorknob. Outside their showdown over Noelle, she couldn't remember the last time her mother had asked anything of her, except to please pass the salt or to pick up a carton of milk at the store. Slowly she turned around and walked back over to the bed. Settling into the chair beside it, she asked tentatively, "What would you like me to read?"

"Bible's on the nightstand."

*Of course,* Mary thought. *What else would she want read to her:* Lady Chatterley's Lover? She reached for the worn leather-bound Bible. In her mother's room, once her father's, too—a hodgepodge of leftover furniture from other parts of the house and porcelain knickknacks that had overflowed the shelves downstairs—she nonetheless felt an odd peace steal over her. The sunlight filtering in through venetian blinds fell in long slats over the worn blue carpet and quilted floral bedspread. Downstairs she could hear the faint clattering of Noelle fixing breakfast.

The Bible fell open to the page marked by a faded red ribbon but before she could begin reading her mother announced out of the blue, "You didn't fool me a bit, you know—calling last night to say you were staying over in the city. I know where you were. With Charlie."

Mary was too stunned to deny it. "How did you know?"

"I've seen the way you two look at each other. Besides," Doris added slyly, "you're wearing the same clothes."

Mary felt angry at being caught in a lie, one she never should have been forced to tell in the first place. She took a deep breath. "Charlie and I are grown-ups, Mama. We don't need anyone telling us what to do."

"Is that what you think I'm doing? Oh, honey..." Doris reached out to grip her hand. Her skin felt loose under Mary's fingers, like a glove that was too big. "At my age I'm past all that."

For a moment Mary was too stunned to reply. When had this change of heart occurred? For that matter, when had her mother last called her *honey*? So long ago she could hardly remember. Once again she felt as if her bearings had been snatched away. Their old way of relating to each other hadn't been good, but it *had* been familiar. What now?

"I didn't know it was that obvious," she ventured at last.

"A person would have to be blind not to notice." Her mother gave a grunt that fell just short of a laugh. "Is it serious?"

"I don't know."

"Would you tell me if it were?"

"Probably not."

An awkward silence fell. Then Doris surprised her again by confessing, "I wasn't always easy on you and your sister, was I?"

*Not my sister, just me,* Mary retorted silently. Her gaze shifted to the window, where a squirrel was skittering up the yew tree outside. She'd slept barely four hours the night before, begrudging even that much time away from Charlie's embrace, and could dearly use a nap herself. She didn't need this baring of conscience, which smacked of the confessional. Another of the myriad of ways by which her mother was made to feel that much more superior to everyone else.

"We survived, didn't we?" was all she could trust herself to say.

"I suppose that's one way of putting it. I just wish..." Doris paused, wearing an expression Mary had never before seen. Regret? Was her mother capable of such an emotion? Then it was gone, and she said with her usual tartness, "Never mind. One way or another, I'm sure you and Charlie will figure it out." Her eyes drifted shut, and her head seemed to sink deeper into the faded pink pillowcase. Gradually she relaxed her grip on Mary's hand.

Mary opened the Bible. *This is what grown-*

*up daughters must do,* she thought. *Let go of the past. Forgive.* With a lump in her throat, she began to read, "'For He shall give His angels charge over you, to keep you in all your ways....'"

Within minutes Doris was fast asleep. Mary tiptoed from the room and followed the aroma of freshly brewed coffee downstairs to the kitchen. A place had been set for her at the table, she saw, and she sank down gratefully in front of it.

Noelle plunked a steaming plate before her: two fried eggs neatly arranged alongside triangles of buttered wheat toast. "It looks delicious," Mary said, suddenly starving.

"Nana asleep?" Noelle poured mugs of coffee, then brought her own plate to the table and sat down.

Mary nodded, sipping her coffee. "I read the verse about Sodom and Gomorrah, just to make sure. Not a peep." She met her daughter's eyes over the rim of her mug. "Now, tell me about yesterday. I want to hear *everything.*"

Noelle sighed wearily. "It's a long story. Can we save it for later?" The light pouring in through the window fell over her curly dark head, igniting it with reddish sparks.

Mary sat back, faintly stung. "Of course."

Noelle reached out to touch her hand. "What I meant was, can't we just *be*?"

Mary felt something warm slip from the clenched fist in her chest and float upward. She thought of what had just taken place

335

upstairs and wondered what it would have been like, years ago, had she been able to do the same: simply relax with her mother.

"I don't see why not," she said lightly.

They talked of other things while they ate: Mrs. Inklepaugh's garden next door and the new curtains Noelle was planning to sew for the kitchen; Alice Henshaw's litter of kittens and the sale on mulch down at Orchard Supply—ordinary things that demanded nothing in return. Before long the conversation turned to more important matters, and by the time they finished eating, Noelle *was* telling her about yesterday. Even the part about Judy Patterson.

Mary shook her head in disbelief. "You let her off easy, if you ask me. I'd have throttled her."

"It's funny, but in a weird way Judy helped me see something. I realized that things have got to change. *I've* got to change. I can't play the victim anymore." Even without Mary's help, it was obvious Noelle had found the strength to cope.

"So what happens now?"

"We wait for Dr. Hawkins to submit her report."

"How long will that take?"

"Lacey says it could be a couple of weeks, hopefully not more than that. Meanwhile, I'll still see Emma. It's something at least."

Mary was struck once again by the subtle difference in her, a quiet resolve evident in every gesture and word.

She glanced at the clock on the wall. It was only eleven-thirty, yet a whole day seemed to have passed since she'd slipped from the warmth of Charlie's bed.

"Are you doing anything special this afternoon?" she asked on impulse.

"No, not really," Noelle said. "Why?"

"There's someone I want to visit. An old friend. I'd love for you to come along."

"Anyone I know?"

Mary shook her head, smiling sadly at the memories that rushed at her like wind-driven snow. "No, but you'd have liked her."


The Lutheran cemetery where Corinne was buried was the oldest in Burns Lake, dating back to the late 1600s, when the earliest Dutch and German immigrants had first settled the region. The original church had long since washed away in a flood, replaced by a more modern one conveniently located in town. But the cemetery remained. It occupied a hill overlooking Schoharie Creek. Huge old trees fed by runoff grew so thick in places they formed a bower over the headstones below, headstones rounded with time and the elements, their inscriptions worn in places so as to be almost unreadable. To Mary, they had the look of old people huddled together in mutual comfort.

The rusted gate at the entrance gave a squeal of protest as they pushed their way inside. It was just after one, and there wasn't a soul in sight. Mary wondered if Corinne was the last person to be buried here. Even back then the cemetery had seemed ancient and unused. She remembered that Corinne's parents had chosen it only because their family plot was here.

She looked about, at the sunlight spangling the unkempt grass, the granite headstones dulled by layers of dirt and moss. Some graves looked more neglected than others. But surprisingly a few were adorned with flowers. On one, which bore the inscription, "Beloved in Life, Mourned in Death," was a coffee can filled with wildflowers long since withered to stalks.

"I can't believe it's been thirty years," Mary marveled softly as they strolled among the thicket of headstones. "I remember Corinne's funeral like it was yesterday."

"I asked Robert about her once, back when we were first married," Noelle volunteered. "I remembered your telling me they used to date back in high school. But he claimed to barely remember her. I suppose it had something to do with his brother's getting killed not long after." She turned to Mary. "Did you know that Buck was their mother's favorite?"

Mary wasn't surprised. "*Everyone* liked him better," she said. "He was nicer than Robert, for one thing. Though I'll admit I didn't know him all that well."

"Gertrude has photos of him all over the house. It's creepy, really. Sort of like a shrine." Noelle pushed aside a low-hanging branch. "I didn't know her back then, of course, but I always got the feeling that something went out of her when he died."

"It's a horrible way to lose a child."

"She still puts flowers on his grave every year on the anniversary of his death," Noelle said, hugging herself as she walked. "A dozen white roses, tied with a red ribbon. It must have some kind of significance, though I'm not sure what."

"I don't think Corinne's mother has been here since the funeral," Mary said. "From talking to her, I get the feeling she'd rather not be reminded of the *way* Corinne died."

"I thought about killing myself once." Noelle paused at a marker nearly hidden by thick clumps of grass. "Every day I'd promise myself I was going to stop drinking, but I *couldn't*. Dying seemed the easy way out."

"Oh, honey..." Mary felt as if she ought to have known somehow.

But when Noelle looked up, her expression was calm. "Everything changed when I had Emma," she said. "I'd gotten sober by then, sure, but from the very first moment I held her in my arms, I knew that nothing in my life was ever going to be as important."

Mary thought of Corinne's unborn baby and shuddered.

They resumed walking. "I think I see it over there." Mary pointed up ahead, where a nearly life-size statue of an angel with one wing broken off at the tip marked the grave next to Corinne's.

But Noelle wasn't looking at the angel. She was staring in bewilderment at the flowers just beginning to wither on Corinne's grave: a vase of white roses adorned with a bright red ribbon.

# Chapter Twelve

That same day, an op-ed piece detailing the long-established ties between Robert Van Doren and Senator Larrabie appeared in the *Register*. As Mary and Noelle were making their way home from the cemetery, puzzling over the mysterious roses on Corinne's grave, on the other side of town Charlie was juggling a slew of angry phone calls. Several more businesses, including a major auto dealership, Gideon Ford, yanked their ads. Dozens of irate Van Doren supporters weighed in. There was at least one death threat, as well as a stern warning from Larrabie's attorney in Albany.

By the following day, the furor had died down somewhat, or so it seemed. Friday morning at half past five Charlie was woken by a call from his janitor, who'd arrived at the *Register* to find every single ground floor window smashed. By the time he arrived on the scene, a suspect was already in custody: a young man with a prior misdemeanor by the name of Dante Lo Presti.

When Bronwyn heard the news her initial reaction was one of outrage. Dante would never do such a thing! She was as certain of his innocence as she was that her rotten brother-in-law was the *real* culprit behind all this. But it wasn't long before doubts began to creep in. Dante *had* talked about quitting his job and moving out of town, she recalled. For that he'd need money. Also, she had to admit there was an air of danger to Dante. Wasn't that what made him so attractive? That feeling when she was with him of always being on the verge of something thrilling.

And then there were the odd jobs he'd done for Robert, many of them questionable, if not downright illegal.

Either way, she wouldn't rest until she'd gotten to the bottom of this.

By two o'clock of the same day, within an hour of learning he'd been released on bail, Bronwyn was bicycling over to his apartment on Sashmill Road, across the street from the wrecking yard.

Dante appeared at the door looking weary and disheveled, his eyes bloodshot and his jaw shadowed with beard growth. For the longest moment he just stood there staring at her, until she began to grow nervous. She hadn't seen him since that day at the cemetery. They'd spoken on the phone a few times, but neither was willing to admit being wrong—Bronwyn for trying to rope him into her scheme, and

Dante for not telling her earlier about his connection to Robert. Each time she'd hung up feeling angry and confused and hurt all at once. Yet one thing stood clear in her mind: she wasn't going to condemn him on hearsay alone.

"You heard, I guess." Dante stepped back to let her in. He was barefoot, wearing a rumpled gray tank top and navy sweat pants.

"Yeah, I heard."

Bronwyn flicked a glance about the dimly lit living room, its curtains still drawn from last night. It was a mess, as usual. Magazines scattered everywhere, beer cans and an overflowing ashtray on the coffee table. The rubber tree by the phone adorned with messages on Post-Its.

Dante walked straight past her, not kissing her, not even looking at her. A lump formed in her throat, as if she'd just dry-swallowed an aspirin.

"Want a beer?" he called from the kitchen.

"No, thanks. I don't drink, remember?"

He emerged holding a Coors in one hand, a Coke in the other. "Sorry, I forgot. Wouldn't want to get in trouble with the old man, would you? It's bad enough you're sneaking around behind his back with the scum of the earth." There was a sneering edge to his voice that she didn't like.

She bristled. "That's not fair. *I'm* not the one who called the cops on you. My father had nothing to do with it either." Bronwyn marched over to snatch the Coke from his hand.

"Yeah? So it's nothing more than a coincidence that the lowlife Daddy's little girl is hanging out with just happens to get busted?" In the grainy gray light Dante's eyes looked almost black. His forehead gleamed with sweat. From the wrecking yard across the way came the jarring sound of steel being crushed, a sound like a herd of dinosaurs munching on tinfoil.

"Look, don't beat me up. I'm on *your* side, remember?" She popped the Coke's tab, sinking down on the arm of the sofa. "If you say you didn't do it, I'll take your word for it."

"I didn't do it." His tone was surly.

Bronwyn eyed him closely. Even with all the evidence against him, a voice in her head whispered, *He's telling the truth.* She didn't know how she knew; she just did. She sipped her Coke, slowly, so she wouldn't spoil the moment by burping.

"Okay, let's back up. You work for Robert, so you must have some idea of who *is* responsible."

"I don't know shit. All I know is, I'm minding my own business and that asshole Wade Jewett picks me up for questioning. Then wham, I'm booked, fingerprinted, the whole nine yards." Dante tipped his beer back with the violence of someone being punched in the mouth.

"Who put up bail?"

"My boss. Do you believe it? The little prick actually came through."

"That was decent of him."

"Like hell. I'll be kissing his ass for the next ten years at least. With Stan the Man, there ain't no such thing as free lunches."

"Are you always this cynical?" she asked.

"Only when I've spent the morning in jail watching some drunk barf his guts up." Dante's gaze slid over her like cool water. "But you wouldn't know about shit like that, would you? The worst thing that's ever happened to you, I'll bet, was being kept after school."

"Dante, why are you doing this?" Bronwyn was close to tears. On the blank TV screen across from her, she caught her distorted reflection, a tiny face atop an elongated body. Her hands, clenched into fists at her sides, looked enormous, like in cartoons.

Dante's shoulders slumped, and he let out a breath halfway between a sigh and a grunt. Walking over to the sofa, he sank down next to her, dropping his head into his hands. Thick tufts of brown hair stuck up between his fingers. "I'm sorry," he muttered. "I have no right taking it out on you."

Tentatively she reached over to stroke his back, its muscles so tight she might have been caressing a suit of armor. In the muted light the tattoo on his arm seemed to glower darkly. "It's okay," she told him. "I know you didn't mean it."

There was a long silence filled only with the chittering whirr of an ancient fan and the Jurassic munching from across the way. Then Dante lifted his head to fix a weary gaze on her.

"The fact is, I *don't* know who did it. That's what I told the cops, and that's what I'll tell the judge. But between you and me it's not the whole truth."

Her stomach lurched. "What do you mean?"

He appeared to wrestle with himself. Then, at last, he spoke. "You didn't hear it from me, okay? Because I don't mind admitting the guy scares the shit out of me. I mean, jump me in a dark alley and I'll fight back. But this guy...he scares me, okay?"

Bronwyn licked lips that had gone dry as toast. "Are we talking about who I *think* we're talking about?"

He nodded, taking another hit off his beer. "One of his guys runs it by me the other day. Mr. V wants me to do this thing. Nobody gets hurt, he says. Nobody'll even know it was me. And I tell the guy, no way. No fucking way. I'll deliver packages, but trashing private property ain't what I'm about. So he gets right up in my face and says, 'Don't fuck with the boss. You fuck with him, man, your ass is grass and he's the lawn mower.'"

"What did you say back?" The words emerged as a breathless squeak.

"Nothing. The next thing I know, I'm under arrest." Dante shook his head in disgust.

*So I wasn't just imagining it,* she thought. *Robert really* is *more than just your everyday garden-variety creep.* Something truly terrifying occurred to her just then. What if her sister was in danger of losing more than her child? What if Noelle's *life* was at stake? She shuddered, gripping her Coke can hard enough to dent it.

"But if you're innocent, what proof did the cops have?"

"Proof?" Dante's mouth curled in disdain. "The only proof they need to go after a guy like me is somebody pointing the finger. Everybody knows that numb-nuts Jewett is in up to his eyeballs with the Man. It doesn't take a genius to figure it out."

"The deputy sheriff is in with Robert?" It struck her suddenly as melodramatic, like an episode of *Diagnosis Murder*. She started to smile, but her boyfriend's next words quickly wiped the smile off her face.

"He'd shoot you and call it an accident, if the Man told him to." Dante's tone was flatly matter-of-fact. "The other day, when you asked for my help? It wasn't getting busted I was scared of. It was what he'd do to us if we got caught." He twisted around to grip her elbow. "Promise me you won't go anywhere near that office. *Swear* it, Bron."

"All right, I swear." She felt a secret little thrill at his concern. But reluctantly she'd already come to the same conclusion: that breaking into Robert's office was far too dangerous an enterprise to embark on solo.

"I'm serious. You could get hurt."

She cocked her head, eyeing him narrowly. "You know something, don't you? Something he's done that's more than slipping money under the table or sending goons to trash my dad's building." Bronwyn felt a glimmer of excitement. This could be even better than cracking his safe.

Dante let go of her elbow, which throbbed where his fingers had dug into it. "Believe me, I wish I did. But whatever he's up to, he's not about to get caught. You can be damn sure that last night he, personally, was nowhere near your dad's building."

"So what makes you think the sheriff was in on it?"

"Timing, for one thing." Dante reached for his cigarettes on the coffee table. As he lit one, she saw that his hand was trembling. "The cops were called at five A.M. They didn't show up until five-thirty. How come it took them half an hour to get there?"

"According to Dad, they were all the way across town."

"Five deputies on duty and they're all conveniently in the same place? Yeah, right." With a snort of derision Dante blew a jet of smoke from the corner of his mouth. "It didn't take that long to pin it on me, you can be sure of that."

"But if what you're saying is true," she argued, not entirely convinced, "if the sheriff really *is* turning a blind eye, that would mean Robert could literally get away with..."

"Murder." Dante finished for her.

Bronwyn felt the blood drain from her face. A chill swept over her, scattering goose bumps like fine sand down her arms and back. "Oh, my God. You're serious, aren't you?"

"As a heart attack."

"What about my sister? What if he—he hurts her in some way?" Bronwyn began to shiver, hugging her arms to her chest. "Oh, God, Dante...now I really *am* scared."

When he slipped an arm about her waist, pulling her down beside him, she didn't resist. He smelled sweaty, as if he hadn't showered. But she didn't mind. Oddly, despite the fact that he'd spent the morning in jail, she trusted him. Bronwyn leaned into him. His nearness excited her: a low, loose sensation in her belly like the one she got when skinny-dipping in the lake at night.

He crushed out his cigarette in the ashtray with a sizzle of red sparks, and suddenly he was kissing her. Hard, with his tongue. Hard enough to feel the edge of his teeth. Dante had never kissed her quite so...urgently, as if everything up until now had been just the warm-up leading to *this*.

Before she knew it, she was on her back with Dante practically on top of her. They lay like that for several more minutes, kissing until the skin around her mouth began to sting from his beard stubble. Between her legs she throbbed as if a warm hand were pressing her there. *Stop this*, she told herself. If her father found out...well, let's just say a few broken windows would be the least of his concerns. For Dante, it would be straight back to jail, Do Not Pass Go, Do Not Collect $200. If not for vandalism, then for sex with a minor.

But she couldn't seem to stop. She didn't *want* to stop.

It wasn't until Dante was tugging her T-shirt over her breasts that she was jolted into wriggling out from under him. "What about your roommates?" she asked breathlessly, yanking her shirt down as she sat up.

"What about them?" Dante rolled over, placing his head in her lap.

"One of them could walk in any minute."

"No problem. We'll just take this into the bedroom."

"If we do that, we'll just end up—"

"Fucking?" He flashed her a wicked grin.

"Is that how you think of it? Just...fucking." She felt angry and cheap and exhilarated all at once.

"You say it like there's something wrong with it." Dante's gray eyes slanting up at her in the dim light made her feel as if she were teetering on the edge of something steep. "Face it, Bron, you're not one of those girls who give a shit about going to the prom or having a guy to spend money on you. You're different. You just don't know it yet. Any guy lucky enough to fuck you, and God, I hope it's me, will be getting more than just that, believe me. And so will you, trust me on that one, so will you."

She eyed him narrowly. "How do I know you're not making all this up just to get me into bed?"

"Relax, and I'll show you."

Dante reached up to run a grease-stained fingertip over one nipple, sending a cascade of delicious shudders through her. She looked down at him, his full mouth curled in a knowing little smile, his dark hair spilling over her lap. The words were out of her mouth before she knew she'd spoken them.

"Okay. Let's do it. I guess now is as good a time as any."

Dante grinned lazily and in a single fluid motion rolled to his feet, pulling her with him. As he led the way down the hall, Bronwyn thought of the nights she'd lain awake, unable to sleep, yet resisting the urge to reach under the covers and relieve the pressure between her legs, thinking there must be something wrong with her for doing it as much as she did, something truly sick. Then finally giving in, because after all, no one had to know, right? Not even Maxie.

She felt that way now. As if it weren't a choice, as if she *had* to do this...or she wouldn't be able to get through the rest of the day.

Stepping into his bedroom, Bronwyn was pleasantly surprised to find it neater than the rest of the apartment. Its simple bed and dresser were the kind you buy unassembled and put together yourself. An autographed photo of a race car driver hung on the wall, and the shelf over the stereo was lined with CDs. Dante popped one into the changer, and Sarah McLachhlin's sweet, plaintive wail filled the room.

"Will it hurt?" she asked, suddenly nervous as she sank down on the bed.

"A little. But don't worry, I know what to do."

Dante sat down next to her, gently pushing her onto her back. Unexpectedly he ran the tip of his tongue lightly over her temple, right up to the corner of her eye. She shivered. It was as if all her body's heat had collected between her legs, leaving none to warm the rest of her.

They kissed awhile longer. Then he slowly undressed her. Only when she was completely naked did he peel off his own clothes. As Bronwyn lay on her back, her knees pressed so tightly together they quivered, he murmured, "Relax." He pried her legs apart, just enough to allow his hand access. Then carefully, oh-so-carefully, he inserted two fingers, wriggling them far up inside her. She felt a sharp twinge, followed by a trickle of warm wetness. She looked down, startled to find the inside of her thigh smeared with blood.

"Oh," she exclaimed softly.

Losing your virginity had always seemed like such a big deal. She'd imagined it to be like in the movies, lots of moaning and thrashing about, culminated by a painful, bloodletting thrust. But this...it had been like a loose tooth being wiggled free.

"Now for the fun part," Dante whispered.

He kissed and stroked her some more, until the uncomfortable throbbing between her legs was lost in the waves of pleasure that rippled through her. Dante must have done this with other girls, she thought, *lots* of girls, but the idea didn't bother her as it once might have. Instead, it relaxed her, knowing that he was in charge, that he knew what to do. With Dante, there would be no embarrassing fumbles leading to awkward moments of indecision. No need to explain why her body seemed to know, from the nights spent practicing on her own, exactly what it needed.

She was amazed, in fact, by her boldness. Touching him as intimately as she touched herself when alone. Before this, she'd seen him naked only from the waist up, and even that had thrilled her—the thick, hard muscles in his arms and chest, the brown plank of his belly—but she now knew what lay at the end of that dark little trail of hair disappearing down into the waistband of his jeans. At last she'd seen what it looked like: a penis, fully aroused. Dante's, she marveled, was really quite amazing. Long and thick and marbled with veins that pulsed beneath her fingertips. She stroked it until Dante pulled her hand away.

"Don't," he groaned. "I'll come."

"Go ahead," she said, suddenly curious about that, too. "I don't mind."

"No, you first."

He fumbled in the drawer of his night table for a condom, letting her watch as he tore open the packet and expertly rolled it on. By the time he gently pushed her onto her back, spreading her legs even farther this time, she was more than ready. She was practically on the verge of coming herself. It stung a little when he eased into her. Then the waves of pleasure once more took over, obscuring everything else. Dante moved slowly, careful not to hurt her. Looking up into his face, she saw his concern. If she could have found her voice just then, she would have told him how it felt. Incredible. A million times better than when she stroked herself. If he didn't stop moving, she would—

Then she *was* coming. Like a roller coaster ride barreling down that last steep hill, the warm wind rushing at her. Bronwyn gasped with the unbelievable high of it. "Oh, God...oh, Dante." She clung to him. *So this is what it's like,* came the thought, clear and distinct. If she'd known, if only she'd known...

Moments later he came, too, with a great warrior's yell. She watched his face contort, savoring the sense of power it gave her, knowing *she* was responsible. *She* could do this to a man, make him quiver and pant and cry out with desire. She smiled, thinking this was how Cleopatra must have felt.

"That was nice," she said when it was all over.

"Just nice?" Dante rolled onto his side, eyeing her curiously.

"If I say any more, you'll get a swelled head. And I don't mean just down there." She cast a meaningful glance at the condom drooping from his penis. "But you're right about one thing: It beats the prom, hands down."

Dante grinned, his gaze traveling over her naked body, sprawled indolently across the rumpled bedspread. "Yeah, well, I'd have gotten you a corsage, only I wouldn't know where to pin it."

She rolled over, lifting herself onto her elbows, her chin propped on the heels of her hands. "Would you call what we just did fucking or making love?"

"Both," he said.

"Isn't that like a chapter with two headings?"

"More like a book you have to read to see how it ends."

*How will this one end?* she wondered.

Her mind drifted back to Noelle, and she felt a stab of guilt. Here she was, wallowing naked in bed, while her sister was out there, in mortal danger for all she knew. She had to do something, warn Noelle. But how? If she repeated what Dante had told her, her sister would want to know where she'd heard it. That would put Dante at risk. Not to mention that her dad would find out, and she'd be grounded for the rest of her life.

"I've got to go," she announced suddenly.

"Go where?"

"I need to see my sister."

"Now?"

"It's important." She jumped up and grabbed her jeans off the floor.

Dante looked as if he might to try to talk her out of it. His penis, incredibly beginning to stir to life once more, was particularly eloquent on the subject. Then he shrugged and sat up, reaching for his car keys on the nightstand. "Come on," he said. "I'll take you."

They'd fallen into a routine. Noelle would arrive to find Emma waiting stoically in the reception area, her stuffed dog, Bowwie,

354

clutched to her chest and her pink Barbie backpack strapped to her bravely squared little shoulders. Yet as soon as she laid eyes on Noelle, her small face would light up as if it were Christmas morning, and she would race to the door to hurl herself into Noelle's arms. Then, in the lunchroom that afforded them some privacy, at least five to ten minutes had to be allotted for snuggle time. Emma would burrow into her lap, clinging to Noelle the way she had as a baby, occasionally reverting to sucking her thumb. She would insist, too, on being read the most babyish of the books Noelle had brought. Dr. Seuss's *Green Eggs and Ham* was the current favorite.

"'I do not *like* green eggs and ham,'" she'd parrot emphatically. "'I do not like them, Sam-I-Am!'"

When Emma felt secure enough to crawl down off her lap, they would either sit or lie on their stomachs on the carpet and for the precious time that remained simply play. Pretend games mostly, with the dolls in Emma's backpack (Barbie always had the featured role, of course, the gaudier the wardrobe the better). When she grew tired of dolls, there was the tote bag of books and toys thoughtfully provided by Trish. Last but not least, the ritual of the ice cream. Near the end of their visit Noelle would pull out the list of flavors from Scoops, and Emma would spend several minutes elaborately pondering which to choose before settling on her all-time favorite, mint chip.

As soon as the ice-cream cones were consumed, the tears and whining would start. This was the part Noelle dreaded, more than the tears she herself would shed on the way home. More than the sleepless night ahead. Today, for some reason, it was worse. Emma, who until a few minutes ago had been happily sorting through a box of PlaySkool farm animals, had gone from tears to sobbing and was now quickly approaching meltdown.

"I w-whu-want to go with *you*," she wailed. "I don't whu-whu-want to w-wait here for D-Daddy."

"Oh, sweetie, I wish I *could* take you," said Noelle, close to the breaking point herself. She sat with Emma on her lap, drinking in her smell, the unmistakable scent of her child that only *she* would know blindfolded. "But the judge won't let me, not just yet."

During their last visit she'd spelled it out for Emma, in terms simple enough for her to grasp. She'd explained that there were people, including Daddy, who thought that Nana's might not be the best place for her to live and that first Mommy had to show them it was okay. No amount of reasoning, though, could change the fact that Emma missed her.

"I hate Daddy! He's m-muh-mean!" she sobbed.

Noelle felt a sharp prick of alarm. "How is Daddy mean?"

"He won't l-luh-let me c-call you! I *told* him. I can do it all by myself. I know the number and *everything*. But he g-got mad and yelled at me." Emma lifted a face swollen and blotchy from crying. It was all Noelle could do to keep from scooping her up and carrying her outside, damn the judge, damn that stupid woman out there with her piggy little eyes and well-meaning chatter.

"What about Grandma Gertie? She's nice to you, isn't she?" It took a supreme effort to sound normal.

"She takes me to the playground sometimes." Her daughter's sobs began to subside.

"Does she take you other places, too?" In her mind Noelle was seeing her mother-in-law's big white Caddy winding its way toward the site for Cranberry Mall.

Emma nodded, one stockinged foot swinging back and forth. "I didn't like it when we went to the cement-tary, though."

Noelle grew suddenly alert. "She took you to the cemetery?"

Her daughter's dark head bobbed up and down, pigtails dancing. "The one where Uncle Buck went. Grandma says it's where dead people go before they get to go to heaven."

A chill settled over Noelle. She thought about the withered roses on Corinne's grave. Only one person could have left them: Gertrude. But why? Corinne couldn't have been more than a distant name from the past, a girl Robert himself claimed to hardly remember.

Her mother had shed some light on it the other day, on their way home from the cemetery, telling her about the autopsy report that revealed Corinne to have been pregnant. Yes, that might explain why Gertrude, sentimental about her own flesh and blood, would mourn the loss of a grandchild, even an unborn one. But why *white* roses, like those for Buck?

"Did Grandma bring flowers?" she asked.

"Uh-huh."

"Roses?"

"Uh-huh." Emma lay quietly with her head against Noelle's shoulder. Her tantrum was over, with only a few hitching breaths here and there. "Daddy says I can have a turtle."

Noelle smiled at the suddenness with which a five-year-old's mood could shift, like a summer thundershower that's over almost before it's begun. "A turtle? Won't that be nice."

Emma's foot stopped swinging. "Mommy, what's a all-ca-colic?"

Noelle stiffened. Clearly her husband, probably his parents, too, had been discussing her in front of Emma. "You mean an alcoholic," she replied as calmly as she could. "It's a disease, Em. Kind of like an allergy. Alcohol makes certain people sick." She took a deep breath. "Mommy's an alcoholic. That's why Daddy drinks wine with dinner and I don't."

"Grandpa says you're too sick to take care of me." She gazed up at Noelle, wide-eyed. "Is it true, Mommy?"

Noelle brought her cheek to rest against the crooked part in Emma's hair, her voice catching only a little as she murmured, "No, sweetie. Nothing in the world could ever keep me from taking care of you. It won't be much longer. Then we'll be together *all* the time. Cross my heart."

She cupped a hand over Emma's smaller one, guiding it to form an invisible X on her chest. It reminded her of making the sign of the cross, all those endless Sunday masses when she was squeezed into the pew next to Nana. It would have been incomprehensible to her as a child that she would one day have a little girl of her own, as unimaginable as God himself. Now she thought, *I know there's a God because otherwise I couldn't stand it. I'd have fallen apart long before this.*

At the door she somehow managed to smile and wave good-bye. Emma, her small hand tucked into the social worker's, waved back. A little girl with shiny brown pigtails and a crooked part, looking to Noelle like the world's smallest soldier caught in the crossfire of a battle she didn't quite understand.

Trudging down the courthouse steps with her head tucked low, Noelle didn't see her sister at first. It wasn't until Bronwyn called out that she looked up, startled, to find her standing on the sun-dappled sidewalk below, peering up with a hand cupped over her eyes.

"Wow, I'm glad I caught you. I was afraid you'd left." Bronwyn bounded over, a golden-limbed gazelle in baggy jeans and a Tommy Hilfinger T-shirt.

"What's up?" Noelle asked, keeping her voice light.

"I need to talk to you about something. Are you in a hurry?"

"In a hurry to do what, run home and floss my teeth?" Noelle gave a hollow laugh. A sisterly chat was the last thing she felt in the mood for. On the other hand, what good would it do to wallow in her misery? The AA meeting she'd attended the other night had reminded her of something important that she'd lost sight of: that sometimes the best way to help yourself is by helping someone else. "We could sit in the park," she suggested.

"Uh, well, I was thinking of someplace a little more private." Bronwyn cast a furtive glance over her shoulder, as if scouting for shadowy men in trench coats who might be stalking her.

Noelle fought to keep a straight face. It was a family joke that Bronwyn could turn the opening of a letter into high drama. Maybe it was all those Nancy Drew mysteries she'd devoured as a kid. At the time, Noelle hadn't seen the harm in passing her somewhat antiquated (even then) collection onto her sister, but now she wondered if it hadn't in some way contributed to Bronwyn's tendency toward melodrama.

"Nobody will bother us," Noelle said, slipping an arm through her sister's.

Bronwyn darted another look over her shoulder before reluctantly giving in. "Well...I guess that would be okay."

Together, they crossed the street. This time of day, with the temperature in the low eighties, the park was pretty much deserted—just a few hardy old-timers seated on benches and strolling about in the shade. Later, when it cooled down, mothers would bring their children to play, and young lovers would lie on the grass, whispering to one another between stolen kisses.

Noelle thought of Hank. This morning when she brought Nana in for her appointment, she'd been certain everyone in the waiting room could see right through her, that they knew exactly what she was feeling. How was she supposed to act normal when all she could think of was him kissing her?

Noelle sank down gratefully on a deserted bench by the fountain, under a huge old linden tree. The heat had sapped what was left of her energy; even in her sundress and sandals she was sweating. She eyed the bronze nymph fountain, from which a fine mist floated to sprinkle the stones at their feet, thinking how nice it would be to slip out of her sandals and wade barefoot in the cool water.

The two sisters remained silent for a minute or two, each lost in her own private and not so dissimilar thoughts. At last Noelle said, "I missed you at Scoops." Today was her sister's day off. "I had to *ask* for extra jimmies on Emma's ice cream cone."

Bronwyn turned to smile at her. "Don't tell me...mint chip, right?"

Noelle smiled back. It was the one little joke they'd managed to wring from all this, the fact that Emma always ordered the exact same thing. Reaching into her purse, she withdrew a folded square of paper, a crayon picture Emma had drawn. She spread it over her knees. "That's me." She pointed to a stick figure with a head topped by black squiggles, flanked by two other figures. "See, there's Nana...my mother, too. I told her Grandma Mary is staying with us."

Bronwyn tilted her head for a better look, holding her long hair back with one hand. "The one of you looks a little like Pamela Anderson Lee. Where did those boobs come from?"

"Certainly not from me." Noelle was surprised to find herself laughing. "Emma is heavy into Barbie these days. Coming from her, this is the highest form of praise." With a sigh she folded the drawing and tucked it back into her purse. "So, what is it you wanted to talk to me about?"

"I'll tell you in a minute." Bronwyn toyed nervously with her hair, twirling it around her finger. "First, you have to promise not to say anything to Daddy."

"I can't promise that until I know what it is."

"God, you're so predictable." Bronwyn rolled her eyes, knowing better than to argue. Noelle, because she was so much older, had always been more second mother than sister. "Okay, there's this guy. His name's Dante."

Noelle looked at her, startled. "The same Dante who smashed the windows in Dad's building?"

Her sister frowned. "What happened to innocent until proven guilty?"

"Uh-oh, I smell trouble already. This is the same guy Dad told you to keep away from, isn't it?" Noelle shook her head in disbelief. "Lord, Bron. Only *you* would be in hot water like this. Does Dad know?"

"That's the whole point. He *doesn't*. And I'd like to keep it that way. You won't tell, will you?"

Noelle studied her sister's anxious face. Dad would be angry, all right. But mostly worried. *She* was a little worried, too. What on earth did Bronwyn think she was doing, hanging out with some tattooed biker type? Their father's reaction could end up being the least of her troubles. What if this guy did something to hurt her, or ruin her life?

Then she remembered that she'd made the so-called safe match, marrying Robert. An older, successful man with a sizeable 401K who'd tooled to work in a shiny new black Mercedes. The truth was, other than what Dad had told her, she knew next to nothing about this Dante character. So who was she to judge?

"I won't say anything...for now," she said. "Just promise *me* you'll be careful. This guy sounds like trouble."

"He's not the one you should be worrying about." Bronwyn glanced furtively about before bringing her dark-eyed gaze back to Noelle. "El, what do you know about Robert's business dealings?"

"Other than what I picked up working in his office, you mean? Truthfully it was so long ago I don't remember much."

"What would you say if I told you Robert was the real culprit behind Daddy's windows getting smashed?" Bronwyn dropped her voice to a whisper, though there wasn't anyone remotely within earshot.

"I wouldn't exactly be shocked, if that's what you're driving at." Noelle had already come to the same conclusion; the timing was simply too coincidental.

"Well, suppose that's not all he's guilty of."

Noelle began to grow a little impatient. "What exactly are you getting at?"

Bronwyn looked down at their shadows stretching over the worn paving stones, linked like the cut-out figures Noelle used to fashion for her with scissors when she was little. Hesitantly, she began, "Well, you see, the thing is, Dante sort of works for Robert." She glanced up sharply. "It's not what you think. Just odd jobs and deliveries, that kind of thing. But he, like, *knows* stuff, stuff you'd pick up from just hanging around."

"What kind of stuff?"

"Nothing concrete. All I know is that he's scared of Robert." Bronwyn had her hair twisted so tightly about her finger its tip had begun to swell and redden. "If *he's* scared, then you should be, too. Scared for your *life.*"

Noelle wanted to take her sister seriously. God knew she had reason enough to believe the worst of Robert. But this...well, it was simply too much. Her husband was a monster, all right. He'd drugged her. He'd stolen her child. But murder? No, she didn't think even Robert would go that far.

"Bron, don't you think you're getting a little carried away here?" Noelle spoke gently. She was thinking of the time she'd taken Bronwyn camping. She'd been in her early twenties, her sister just nine or ten, the age when spooky stories about one-armed escaped convicts and serial murderers on the loose were trotted out at every slumber party. Bronwyn, though, had taken it a step further, spinning an elaborate fantasy about the ranger—an admittedly spooky-looking fellow— being a vampire that roamed the woods at night. When the time came to turn in, her sister was so frightened she couldn't sleep.

"El, I'm not kidding." A desperate note crept into Bronwyn's voice. "I know you think I exaggerate sometimes, and maybe I do. But this isn't one of those times."

"Okay, let say you're right. What am I supposed to do about it?"

"Don't go off alone with him or anything."

Noelle gave a short dry laugh. "There's about as much chance of that as there is of my getting kidnapped by terrorists."

"Well, then don't go anywhere alone *period*."

"I promise, Scout's honor." She held up two fingers. "No dark alleys, and no blind dates. Maybe I should get myself a Doberman pinscher, just to be on the safe side. What do you think?" When Bronwyn didn't crack a smile, Noelle slipped an arm about her shoulders. "Look, Bron, I appreciate your concern, really I do. And I *will* be careful."

She remembered when Bronwyn was born.

She'd been fourteen and had secretly resented her stepmother. Yet the moment she laid eyes on her tiny sister, wrapped in a fuzzy yellow blanket, everything changed. She forgave Vicky on the spot. Dad had done the right thing marrying her, she'd thought, for how else could he have given her this wonderful gift?

"Not to change the subject, or anything," Noelle said, "but just how serious is it with you and this Dante character?"

Bronwyn shrugged nonchalantly, perhaps a bit *too* nonchalantly. "We hang out, that's all. No big deal."

"Are you sleeping with him?"

Her sister gave a startled laugh, a dark flush rising in her cheeks. "What makes you ask *that*?"

"Your expression just now."

"Oh, God—is it that obvious?"

"Only to someone who knows you as well as I do." Noelle gave her sister's shoulders an affectionate squeeze. "I just hope you're using birth control."

"Actually, we've only done it once," she confessed.

"Once is enough, believe me. I should know. That's how *I* was conceived."

The fact that her parents had been only a year older than Bronwyn hit home with new impact. She'd known they were young; she just hadn't been able to picture *how* young. Suddenly, she felt a new appreciation for what her mother had to have gone through.

"Don't worry, we were careful," Bronwyn assured her.

Noelle thought of Hank and of how careful they would have to be. Tonight, she was having dinner with him at his apartment. And why not? They were friends, weren't they? As long as they didn't take it any further than that kiss up on the ridge, what was the harm? Still, she couldn't help feeling more than a little apprehensive.

"Was it as good as you hoped it would be?" she asked.

Bronwyn ducked her head, the color in her cheeks deepening. "Let's just say there are some things you don't learn from books."

"My first time was with Robert," Noelle confided.

"Was it awful?"

"No, not at all. It was—" she'd blocked out the memory so effectively she now had to struggle to recall what it had been like—"efficient. That's how I remember it. As if he were performing some kind of magic trick."

"Did it get better the more times you did it?"

"I suppose so, in a way. The trouble was, as I fell more and more out of love, I grew less and less interested. So, you see, the real trick was the one I'd played on myself."

"I don't know if I love Dante," Bronwyn said. "I'm crazy about him, of course, but that isn't the same thing, is it?"

"No, not quite." Noelle smiled to herself, once more thinking of Hank.

Was she falling in love with him? Maybe, but given her present state of mind, she wouldn't have trusted her heart to know the difference between love and simple gratitude for Hank's kindness. She *was* looking forward to this evening, though; that much she knew.

She wouldn't think about the way he'd kissed her, or where it might lead. Nor would she think about her legal woes. She owed herself, and Hank, an evening free of *sturm und drang*. That wasn't so much to ask, was it?

"*I*'m actually a pretty decent cook." Hank spoke with the air of a novice marveling over the fact. "You like pasta, I hope?"

They stood elbow to elbow in his tiny but surprisingly well-equipped bachelor's kitchen— Noelle at the counter chopping cucumbers for the salad and Hank at the stove tending a boiling pot with enough spaghetti in it to feed a small army. She turned to smile at him.

"Love it."

"Good, because it's the only thing I know how to make."

"Just pasta?"

"Pasta with marinara sauce. Pasta with pesto. Pasta with mushrooms and garlic. Pasta with—"

"I get the picture." Noelle laughed, and the sound of her laughter seemed magical somehow, not at all wrong—like water springing up from cracked dry ground.

Hank regarded her with tender amusement.

368

His face was ruddy from the rising steam, his light brown hair curled about his temples. He wore a butcher's apron over khakis and a blue oxford shirt, making her think of a chef on TV. Someone putting on a show. She felt unexpectedly touched by his desire to impress her.

"Everyone likes pasta," he went on, "so it's a safe bet when you're having company, not to mention a necessary survival skill."

"There's always Murphy's Diner," she reminded him.

"Oh, I've been that route, believe me." He fished a strand of spaghetti from the pot and nibbled on the end, pronouncing, "Not quite. Another minute or two." He turned to give her a rueful look. "A single guy, eating alone at Murphy's every night. I might as well have taken out an ad in the paper."

Noelle caught his meaning. "Let me guess. Every unmarried woman in Burns Lake between the ages of twenty-five and fifty suddenly had an overwhelming urge to cook for you."

Hank rolled his eyes. "My first year they were leaving casseroles on the doorstep. I ran out of room in my freezer. After a while it started to seem morbid, like someone had died."

"Maybe they were just being neighborly," she said teasingly.

"Either way, it was giving me a complex. I began to wonder if there was something about me in particular. You know, like was I unconsciously sending out signals that I was looking

369

for a wife?" Hank hoisted the pot from the stove and poured its contents in a great roiling gush into the colander in the sink.

"Those poor women. I hope you let them down easy at least."

"I didn't have to. I just stopped eating out every night and started grocery shopping," he said. "Eventually they got the message and the casseroles stopped coming." He cranked on the tap, running cold water over the steaming colander.

"What a relief." Noelle carried the salad to the table, thinking, *Is he trying to tell me something?*

Certainly there was nothing about this apartment, the converted parlor floor of a white elephant Victorian, to suggest a floundering bachelor existence. Though sparsely furnished, the parlor that served as both living and dining room—with an open kitchen off to one side—was warmly inviting. Handsome oriental rugs were scattered over polished floorboards. An oak sideboard stacked with papers and books faced the matching oak table at which she stood. There was even a fireplace, with a cane-back rocking chair in front of it.

Hank clearly wasn't shopping for a wife, unconsciously or otherwise. The only question was why it should matter to her. *She* certainly wasn't in any position to apply for the position. Noelle caught her reflection in the mirror over the sideboard: a woman who'd taken the time to pin her hair up and put on a nice dress; a woman with flushed cheeks holding a wooden salad bowl with the same air of eager self-consciousness as had, she imagined, the bearers of all those unwanted casseroles.

*It's just dinner,* she told herself. *Nothing more.*

At the table she kept the conversation light. Hank told her about the difficulties of taking over from a figure as beloved as old Doc Matthews. Noelle confided that she'd begun writing again. It had started with her journal, but lately, to take her mind off things, she'd even written a few short stories. Hank said he'd be interested in reading one, and she promised to show him the story she was working on now.

They'd nearly finished eating when Hank cleared his throat and said, "I don't mean to bring up an unpleasant subject. On the other hand, it seems rude *not* to ask. Anything new with your case?"

"Not really. We're sort of at a stalemate, thanks to my husband. He sets up a date to meet with the psychologist, then reschedules at the last minute. Meanwhile, my lawyer can't make a move until we get our hands on that report." She made an effort not to sound gloomy. Hadn't she cried on Hank's shoulder enough? "This is delicious, by the way. You weren't kidding—you really *are* a good cook."

"Thanks. The zucchini is courtesy of my landlady. There's enough of it in her garden out back to end world hunger." Hank poured himself another glass of wine and thoughtfully remembered to replenish her tumbler of Perrier. "Speaking of Lacey, I saw her just the other day. She stopped in to get her prescription renewed."

Noelle remembered that Lacey suffered from hayfever. "You didn't tell her about us, did you?" The question popped out unbidden, like a spring from an overwound clock. Heat rose in her cheeks. *For heaven's sake,* she thought, *what is there to tell?*

But Hank didn't seem put off. "No, as a matter of fact, I didn't," he said mildly. "It would have been unprofessional, don't you think?"

She carefully folded her napkin and set it alongside her plate. "Hank, there's something you should know. In case you…well, if things should reach a point when we—" She stopped, bringing a hand to her painfully warm face. "This is so embarrassing. You probably have no idea what I'm trying to say."

"I think I get the picture," he told her. His face was aglow in the candlelight, his gaze steady and calm. "You're worried about our getting too deeply involved. You're thinking it wouldn't be wise. Not while you're still technically married; it might look bad in court." He reached across the table to take her hand. "How am I doing so far?"

She nodded, lacing her fingers through his, taking in their nurturing warmth as she would have a medicine he'd prescribed. "Oh, Hank, I wish we could have met five years from now."

"In my opinion, there's never a wrong time for meeting the right person."

He brought her hand to his mouth, turning it to kiss her palm. A kiss tender and courtly, yet with the promise of passion. No words could have reassured her more. Noelle felt something tightly knotted inside her suddenly loosen. It was going to be okay. He would wait.

Reluctantly Hank let go of her hand and got up to clear the table. "How about dessert? I'm afraid my culinary skills don't extend to baking, but on my way home I picked up a quart of peach ice cream from Scoops."

"Sounds wonderful," she said, relieved that he knew when to let go of a sensitive subject.

Part of her wanted nothing more than to make love to Hank, now, this instant...to feel his arms about her, his naked body pressing up against hers; to know the kind of intimacy that hadn't been possible with Robert. But this was nice, too: a rest from all that surging emotion, a chance to catch her breath and simply *be*.

In the meantime, Noelle would keep her eyes open, not just for the real and potential dangers ahead but for the possibility of something or someone good in her life. Someone very much like the man in chinos and blue oxford shirt standing before her now.

# Chapter Thirteen

"What makes you think they arrested the wrong guy?" Mary glanced at Charlie, hunched over the wheel of his Blazer as he negotiated the twisting mountain road in the pouring rain.

"God knows I'd like nothing more than to pin the blame on that punk." Charlie frowned as he struggled to peer through the rain sheeting across the windshield. "But whatever his crimes—and I have a feeling Bronwyn knows more on *that* subject than she's letting on—Dante Lo Presti wasn't the one who trashed my building."

"How can you be certain?"

"His shoe size, for one thing. Lo Presti wears a ten—I checked with his boss—and the boot prints in the dirt outside had to be twelve or thirteen, at least."

"I thought you said the police didn't find any evidence."

"Not by the time they finished trampling all over it." Charlie flicked on the radio and dialed it to a local station that gave a twice-hourly update on road conditions.

When they'd made plans to a visit Corinne's eldest brother, Everett, up near Albany, the weather had been the least of their worries. Now, if they were to arrive in one piece, they'd have to take it slow and easy. Mary thought of all those broken windows Charlie had spent most of yesterday boarding up. *It could have been worse,* she thought. *What if it had been raining?*

"Are you saying it was on purpose, that Wade made *sure* there'd be nothing to trace it back to Robert?" Judging from her chance encounter with Wade Jewett on the street, Mary wouldn't have put it past him.

Charlie took it a step further. "I wouldn't be surprised if old Wade himself was the culprit. God knows his feet are big enough."

"With a mean streak to match." Mary peered out her window at a wet smear of green, all that was visible of the valley below. Just a few more miles and they'd be at the junction for the interstate, where the going would be a little easier.

Still, she wondered if the trip had been such a good idea. It wasn't just her growing anxiety about the situation; it was all this time alone with Charlie. She'd have had to be blind not to see that he was in love with her. And utterly self-deluded not to realize she was on the same rocky road to ruin. With one minor difference: In all these years she'd never really fallen *out* of love with her exhusband.

"Either way," Charlie said, "Wade's nothing more than a hired gun. And I don't see much likelihood of Robert getting arrested. Which again begs the question, What is he so afraid of our finding out?"

"Maybe Everett will be able to shed some

light on it," Mary said with more optimism than she felt. "He's the eldest. He'd remember more than Jordy."

"Assuming this has anything to do with Corinne. There could be some other body buried out in the north forty that we don't even know about," Charlie speculated aloud. He glanced at her, quick to add, "Just a figure of speech, of course. More likely it has to do with some moneymaking scheme of his—kickbacks, bribery, you name it. I wouldn't be at all surprised to find out there was an account in the Cayman Islands with Robert's name on it."

"So you think this is a waste of time?"

He hesitated before replying. "Speaking as a newsman, no. I think any lead, however slim, is worth following up on. As your lover, though, I'm just shameless enough to admit that any excuse to be with you has merits on that basis alone."

Mary lightly socked his shoulder. "You really *are* shameless."

"Want me to prove it? I could pull over until this rain lets up. I'm sure we could find a way to entertain ourselves in the meantime." He flashed her a devilish grin.

Secretly Mary would have liked nothing more. Since the night at the cabin she'd thought of little else. Why is it, she wondered, that your own bed is never as warm after you've been in your lover's? Simon had called last night from Seattle, and she'd found she couldn't wait to get off the phone. The whole time she'd been thinking about Charlie. His habit of delivering a line utterly straight-faced, so it was a moment or two before you realized he was joking. How he looked first thing in the morning: the hair that after all these years still stuck up in a cowlick, his stubbled chin now peppered with gray. Even how he liked his eggs: sunny-side up.

When she started to make the bed, he'd gently pushed her away, saying, "No, leave it." And she'd understood from his tone that he hadn't wanted this evidence of their love-making to be so quickly erased. That little gesture alone had touched her more than any words.

"Never mind the free show we'd be putting on for anyone who might happen along," she replied with mock primness. Glancing at her watch, she saw that it was just past eleven. "Besides, Ev and his wife are expecting us for lunch."

Charlie winked. "In that case we'll just have to let the sun come out on its own...without any help from us."

Forty minutes later they were pulling into the driveway of a neat two-story Cape Cod in a brand-new development just north of Albany. Everett's wife, a youthful dark-haired woman far too slim to have just given birth, greeted them at the door with a newborn infant nestled in the crook of her arm.

"Oh, you poor things, you must be half drowned," she declared, hustling them inside as quickly as they could peel off their slickers.

"Come on in, make yourselves comfortable. I'll tell Ev you're here. He's down in the basement with his birdhouses."

"Birdhouses?" Mary looked up from the sodden shoes she was tugging off.

The younger woman laughed, shaking her head in fond exasperation. "Didn't Nora tell you? It's his hobby. Ev makes birdhouses and sells them at a local craft shop." She stuck out her hand. "I'm Cathy, by the way. I feel funny introducing myself. Ev's told me so much about you it's like I already know you." She turned to smile at Charlie. "And you must be Mary's husband."

The heat that flooded her cheeks made Mary forget the dampness of her hair and clothes. She was on the verge of correcting Cathy when Charlie shook her hand, replying simply, "Charlie Jeffers, nice to meet you. And who's this pretty young lady?" He leaned forward to peer at the baby swaddled in pink.

Cathy followed his gaze, wearing the smitten look of any new mother. "Cory. Short for Corinne."

Mary started in surprise, and was grateful when Charlie slipped an arm about her shoulders. A moment later they stepped into the toy-scattered living room to find themselves knee-deep in the Lundquists' three older children, ranging in age from seven to two. Charlie immediately knelt down to help the middle child, a pretty dark-haired girl, untangle a lamp cord from the wheel of her Fisher-Price grocery cart. Watching him, Mary was struck by his easy manner with the girl. What would it have been like had they raised Noelle together? Would their daughter's life have turned out differently? Would she herself have been a better mother? The thought brought a faint, bittersweet ache.

Moments later Cathy returned with Everett in tow. He was big and squarely built, like Jordy, but with their father's dark red hair and long, somewhat mournful face. In truth, Ev was anything but mournful. It merely took strangers a while to realize that what they'd mistaken for dour was really just Scandinavian imperturbability.

He greeted them warmly nonetheless. "Mary...Charlie...good to see you. Good of you to come all this way, too, especially in this weather." He turned to peer out the window, where the downpour had tapered off to a steady drizzle. "Before you go, Charlie, I could use a hand hauling the ladder up the basement stairs. There's a leak in the roof over the laundry porch I want to have a look at."

"Be happy to do more than that," Charlie was quick to volunteer. "If you've got some tar and a brush, between the two of us we could patch it up in no time."

Ev nodded. "If it's dry enough by then, I just may take you up on that offer, Charlie."

They retired to the kitchen, where between dodging toys and bribing the children with graham crackers Cathy managed to get lunch on the table. Mary held the baby while Ev's wife put out bowls of hearty-looking soup and a loaf of crusty bread, an enormous Niçoise salad, and dishes of homemade pickles. Clearly Cathy Lundquist was a woman after her mother-in-law's heart.

As for Mary, she gazed in wonder at the infant asleep in her arms—the baby named after her best friend. Little Cory even looked a bit like her namesake, the same blond hair and upturned nose, the same dimple just north of her chin. If Corinne had had a daughter, she couldn't have looked more like this child.

She thought of Noelle, how at times she'd despaired of them ever being close. Now suddenly, she saw it in a whole new light. *We're still in the fight at least. And where there's life, there's hope...*

Over lunch, which was as delicious as it looked, they talked about Ev's thriving career as an engineering consultant and his minor avocation as a maker of birdhouses. How he and Cathy had met: at a trade show, back when Cathy had held the unlikely title of regional vice-president for a tool and die manufacturer. And what a joy their children were, terrible twos, tantrums, two A.M. feedings and all.

When the kids were down for their naps, the adults retired to the living room, where Mary and Charlie at last got down to the real reason for their visit. They brought Ev and Cathy up to date on Noelle's situation as well as their suspicions concerning Robert. Mary was careful to avoid airing her suspicion that Corinne might have been murdered, and was pleasantly surprised when she found Ev as open on the subject of his sister as Jordy had been closed.

"I wish I could be more help." Seated on the sofa with his large work-worn hands folded in his lap, Ev shook his head. "Truth is I don't remember much—I was away at college then—except that toward the end Corinne and Robert didn't seem to be getting along. She was pretty miserable, in fact." Absently he plucked free a tiny sock stuck to the throw cushion at his elbow and smoothed it between his large blunt fingers. "The last time I saw her alive, though, I remember like it was yesterday. It was Saturday night and I was home for the weekend. She and her boyfriend had gone to the movies. They must've had a real blowout because she came home upset. I mean *really* upset, like...like someone had died. 'Course I didn't know then that she was..." He paused, chewing his lip.

"Pregnant," Cathy, nursing her newborn in the rocking chair by the fireplace, spoke gently. "It's okay, Ev. You can say it. They don't paint a scarlet letter on your chest these days."

"So you didn't find out until afterward?" Charlie, gazing thoughtfully at the bookcase lined with family photos, turned to look at Ev.

"That's right." Corinne's brother shook his head regretfully. "I wish she *had* come to me, though. I'd have...well, I'm not sure *what* I would have done, but she wouldn't have had to suffer all alone, that's for sure."

"Do you think she told Robert?" Mary wondered aloud. "I mean, he *was* the father."

"Most likely, though I wouldn't swear to it." Ev wore a troubled look. "I can only tell you that whatever they'd been arguing about, it was serious. Corrine looked like something the cat had dragged in. Her face was all swollen and red as if she'd been beat up. At first I thought he'd hurt her in some way. I almost wish he had. If that'd been the case, believe me, Robert Van Doren would be the one pushing up daisies, not my sister." His face darkened. "But it was only because she'd been crying so hard."

"Did she say what the fight was about?" Charlie's eyes narrowed, his blunt tone that of the seasoned newsman Mary had only recently come to know and respect.

"No, except..." Ev dropped his voice as if he didn't want the children to hear. "I remember her saying, over and over, 'He'll never forgive this.'"

So he *had* known. "Meaning Robert," Mary assumed aloud.

"I thought so at the time," Ev said. "Looking back, though, I wonder if it was Dad she was most afraid of. It would've been a bitter pill for him to swallow. But he'd have come around in time, I'm sure of it. He wasn't a bad man...just hard."

Mary thought of something else. "Do you know if she was seeing someone else at the time?" she asked.

Ev looked startled. "Someone Robert didn't know about?" He didn't have to add that if

Robert *had* known such a thing the guy would've been beaten to a pulp.

"That's right," she said.

He thought for a moment, then shook his head. "Anything's possible, I suppose. Like I said, I wasn't around much. But I don't think so. What makes you ask?"

"Something in her diary. She mentioned getting a ride home from a party—a boy who was referred to only as J."

Ev sat back, rubbing his chin. "The only one I know with that initial is my brother Jordy. And he was barely fourteen at the time, not even old enough to drive."

"Well, whoever he was, they were probably just friends." Despite her words Mary remained unconvinced. There was no real evidence that Corinne had been sneaking around behind Robert's back, yet Mary had a gut feeling they were missing something here—a key element without which none of the rest of it made sense. With a sigh she rose to her feet. "Ev...Cathy. We've kept you long enough. Lunch was delicious, and you've been more of a help than you know."

"Offer's still open to give you a hand with that roof," Charlie said with a glance out the window. The rain had stopped, and Mary could see a rainbow glimmering faintly in the rapidly clearing sky.

"Thanks, Charlie, but I'd better wait...give the shingles a chance to dry out."

"Let me give you a hand with the ladder at least."

Ev shook his head. "I'll get to it later. To tell the truth, I'm suddenly feeling a little tired. All that talk about the past." He lapsed into a pensive silence, then brightened suddenly. "If you'll wait right here, though, I have something for you."

He disappeared into the next room, and she could hear the clomping of his boots on the basement stairs. A minute later he reappeared carrying a beautifully crafted birdhouse fashioned from birch. "It's for the two of you," he said. "Just nail it to a pole, and come spring you'll have hours of home entertainment."

Mary felt herself flush, but Charlie seemed unfazed. He reached to accept it with a graciousness she found as touching as the gift itself. "Why, thank you, Ev. I know just the spot for it."

For a blissful moment Mary indulged in the fantasy that come next spring, she would be around to see the birds build their nest, to watch as their babies learned to fly. Then, just like the rainbow evaporating from the sky, the fantasy ended, and reality set in: She would be long gone by then. The knowledge left her with an ache that remained with her throughout the long drive back to Burns Lake.

If Mary's sister had had any say in the matter, the orange-crowned warbler would be the first to take up residence in Charlie's new birdhouse. The referendum on the proposed Sandy Creek development was scheduled for a vote in just three weeks' time, and Trish Quinn was putting good use to every minute of it. She'd mobilized a small army of volunteers to distribute flyers door to door. A rally that took place in front of town hall ended in a crowd of supporters trooping back to her store for coffee and dessert. Professor Lars Thorsen, a renowned ornithologist who'd written a book on the subject, had been invited to lecture. The result was a town far more divided in its loyalties than anyone would have imagined. Contrary to popular belief, it appeared that not everyone in Burns Lake depended on Van Doren & Sons for his or her livelihood.

Late Saturday afternoon, just back from her visit with Ev and Cathy Lundquist, Mary strolled into The Dog-eared Page to find her sister transformed once more from small-town shopkeeper into a shiny-eyed, pink-cheeked zealot. Trish broke away from a huddle of supporters to greet her.

"Did you bring it?" she asked eagerly. In place of her usual jumper Trish wore a cream-colored silk blouse and fitted blue skirt. Her hair was different, too, swept back over her ears with a pair of mother-of-pearl combs. The overall effect was becoming.

Mary held out a manila envelope containing the videotape she'd promised her sister, a yet-to-be-aired documentary about the effects of rampant development on local wildlife in a small North Carolina town. Through her connections at WNET she'd managed to snag a copy, for which Trish had arranged a special screening this evening at the Unitarian Church of the Divine Apostles. Its minister, according to Trish, was a fervent apostle as well...of tough conservation measures.

"It wasn't easy," Mary confided. "I practically had to get down on my hands and knees and beg. But the producer's a friend who owes me, so she caved in pretty quick."

"Thanks. Now I owe *you*. Big time." Trish beamed up at her. "You're coming tonight, aren't you?"

"After all the trouble I went to? I wouldn't miss it for the world."

What Mary didn't tell her sister was that the fate of the orange-crowned warbler was the least of her concerns. Trish would only feel bad for pouring her heart into this cause as opposed to wringing her hands over Noelle. Not that Trish wasn't concerned about her niece. It was just that this was how Trish coped. When faced with insurmountable odds, she headed for the nearest brick wall that *could* be scaled.

"We rented extra chairs," Trish prattled on excitedly, "and Reverend Joe—oh, Mary, I can't wait for you to meet him, he's so *committed*— Joe arranged for the choir to sing afterward. Something, oh, I don't know, really *stirring*, like Faure's *Requiem*."

"How about 'This Land Is Our Land' instead? You wouldn't want to seem elitist." Mary spoke from a publicist's point of view, not meaning to sound critical, which was exactly the effect it had.

"Oh. Well. Yes. I'm sure you're right. I never thought of it that way." The light in her sister's face abruptly dimmed, and a familiar look of hesitation crept in.

Mary, feeling a stab of regret, was quick to change the subject. "Do you need a ride, or is Gary picking you up?"

Again it was the wrong thing to have said. Trish smiled bravely. "He's not sure he can make it, so I made other arrangements." Her sister began to fuss with a display of gardening books, her small, plump hands fluttering over the basket of artificial African violets beside it. "He's been so busy lately, you know, with Little League and all." She pushed the basket closer to the center of the table. "There. What do you think?"

"Lovely." Mary smiled. This was her sister in a nutshell: She'd bend over backward to make the world beautiful while ignoring what was ugly or out of place in her own life.

She was turning to go when Trish dropped her voice to ask, "How's Noelle holding up? I haven't heard from her in days."

"Better," Mary told her. "It's really amazing how she manages to keep it together. She's a lot stronger than any of us gave her credit for. But I think the one who's most amazed is Noelle herself."

Privately she thought it had something to do with a certain Dr. Reynolds. Her daughter had arrived home late last night looking flushed, with a new spring in her step, though she insisted that Hank and she were just friends.

"Well, give her my love," Trish told her as Mary was heading for the door.

*She'll need more than that,* Mary thought as she strolled along the sidewalk. Though Noelle had become better at hiding it, each visit with Emma tore her apart as much as it bolstered her. Worse was the endless waiting with no guarantee of a positive outcome. Robert continued to drag his heels while they were no closer to digging up any new evidence against him than in the beginning.

The roses on Corinne's grave, for instance. What did they mean? Noelle's theory was that it was somehow linked to Corinne's unborn child.

"Gertrude's not like you," she had said that day at the cemetery. "All she's ever wanted out of life is to be a wife and mother." They'd been sitting on a stone bench overlooking flowerbeds long since withered to dust. Noelle hadn't meant any insult, but Mary winced inwardly nonetheless. "She expected to have lots of grandchildren. You should see the album of photos devoted to Emma. It's practically heavy enough to crack the glass on her coffee table. If she'd known Corinne was carrying Robert's child..."

"She'd have mourned it as if it had been her own?"

"Exactly."

"Even after thirty years?"

"She's funny that way. You wouldn't know it to look at her, but there's a real sentimental streak under all that ice. Every year on our anniversary Gertrude used to send us a flower arrangement that was an exact replica of my bridal bouquet."

"She must be very popular with her florist," Mary observed dryly.

"Can't you just see it? She's ordering the bouquet for Buck's grave and thinks, 'While I'm at it, why not kill two birds with one stone?'" Noelle conjectured.

"It sounds more practical than sentimental," Mary said.

If Gertrude was still mourning the loss of her grandchild, she thought now, either something wasn't quite nailed down in her rafters or there was more to it than met the eye.

That evening at seven-thirty sharp, Mary arrived at the Unitarian Church of the Divine Apostles to find its basement social hall jammed nearly to capacity. Reverend Joe Wilcox, a short thick-set man with curly graying hair and an infectious smile that revealed a gap between his front teeth, greeted her warmly at the door.

"I'd have known you anywhere. You're exactly as Trish described you," he said, clasping her hand in both of his, his gray eyes twinkling.

"I take it that's a compliment." Mary gave a self-effacing little laugh.

"You really have no idea, do you?" The reverend tilted his head to one side, regarding her intently. "To hear your sister tell it, the sun rises and sets by you."

Mary grimaced. "I haven't always walked the straight and narrow."

"Maybe that's what she admires, that you took risks."

She eyed him more closely. There was clearly more to Reverend Joe than his dog collar might imply. "I'll keep that in mind," she said, giving his hand a quick squeeze before moving off to find a seat.

Slipping into a chair in back, she looked around. Most of the faces were unfamiliar, but she recognized at least half a dozen, kids she'd gone to school with whose features seemed to peep mischievously from behind sagging jowls and chins, crow's feet and wrinkles. Helen Haggerty, a former cheerleader and homecoming queen, now quite plump, spotted her and waved, but Helen's smile didn't quite reach her small, coldly curious eyes.

To the right of Mary sat Cara Townsend. When they both were sophomores at Lafayette, Cara had been her partner in biology. Now a henna-haired mother with bad teeth and a smoker's cough, Cara nonetheless hadn't lost her soft spot for animals. Remembering her partner's squeamishness at dissecting a frog, Mary wasn't surprised to hear her remark, "Susie, my fourteen-year-old, hasn't slept a wink since reading those articles in the paper. The idea of all those innocent baby birds being slaughtered—" Cara broke off to deliver a rattling cough into her handkerchief.

Betty Pinkerton, owner of the Sweet Stuff Bakery on Front Street, heaved her bulk into the empty chair next to Cara. A huge woman who claimed to be a walking advertisement for her wares, she exuded equal amounts of warmth and goodwill.

"Why, if it isn't Mary Quinn!" she exclaimed. "I'd heard you were back in town. And Lord, just look at you: skinny as ever. I remember when you and your sister used to stop by the bakery on your way home from school, just beggin' to be fattened up." Betty sat back to fan herself with one of the programs that had been handed out at the door, sprigs of curly white hair fluttering about her face.

Mary smiled at the memory. "I still remember your sugar cookies. You used to give us kids all the broken ones."

"Still do...when I can get away with it." Betty rolled her eyes. "Parents these days, you don't want to know. Why, to hear them tell it, you'd think sugar was the Antichrist."

Mary winked. "Next time I'm in the mood for sin, I'll stop by."

Betty's hearty laugh caused her chins to quiver and sent ripples down her ample bosom. "Your daughter, now, she's not above giving her little girl a cookie to nibble on now and then." She leaned over Cara to whisper, "Poor thing. I heard what happened. If there's anything I can do, you be sure and let me know."

Mary was unexpectedly moved. "Thanks, Betty, I will."

At that moment the lights dimmed. On the

projection screen TV in front, the credits were now rolling. A bird's-eye view of a quaint rural town panned into view, and a man's voice began to narrate in deep, fulsome tones, "Progress. Our pioneer forefathers measured it by their livelihoods and sometimes their lives. They cleared forests and pushed boundaries, not out of greed but out of the simple need to claim their stake in a strange and often hostile new land...."

Mary glanced at the empty chair to her left. She'd saved it for Charlie, who was running late. Now, cloaked in darkness, she smiled ruefully at the ease with which she'd begun thinking like an old married for whom the world came in twos. After this how would she be able to return to her life of single servings and single beds, tickets for one and seats at the end? It was different with Simon. Unconsciously she must have chosen him for the very reason she found him so frustrating: He was seldom around. When Simon was away, he left no hole in the tightly woven fabric of her life.

She turned her attention back to the film and soon found herself absorbed in its intimate portrayal of ordinary people in a small town very much like this one, grappling with the effects of industrial pollution. So absorbed that when a familiar voice, not Charlie's, murmured "Excuse me, is this seat taken?" she was startled into dropping her program.

Robert. She glanced up in alarm, but before she could open her mouth to answer, he was settling in beside her. In the dim light he regarded her pleasantly...the way a cat might regard a mouse it was getting ready to make a meal out of.

Mary felt a surge of adrenaline, like when her car skidded on slick pavement or she just missed getting run over by a taxi.

"I'm sorry, this seat *is* saved," she informed him in an icy whisper.

Robert acted as if she hadn't spoken. "Mary, what a coincidence finding *you* here." His low voice was rich with sarcasm.

"I said—"

Strong fingers closed about her wrist. "I heard you the first time." Robert's tone, in contrast with his steely grip, was almost frighteningly affable. Just as it was beginning to hurt, he released his grip and sat back in his chair, a small smile of triumph on his lips. Out of the corner of his mouth, he murmured, "Have I missed much?"

Mary's mind flew back to their junior year in high school, the night Robert had made a drunken pass at her at a party. When she slapped his hand away, he'd become incensed. "Everybody knows what a little whore you are," he'd hissed. "I've heard your boyfriend isn't the only one slipping it to you." Then, with a grin like black ice on a deserted road late at night, he'd vanished into the crowd. She'd spotted him a few minutes later holding court with his jock friends, an arm draped about Corinne's shoulders while she gazed up at him adoringly.

She'd never told Corinne.

"You'll love the ending," she whispered back. "The town wins a two-hundred-million-dollar class-action suit against the developer."

She was gratified to see him stiffen ever so slightly. Yet Robert only chuckled softly, saying, "I always enjoy a good fight."

Mary, though, had no stomach for it. Not here, where she couldn't fight back. Abruptly she stood up and began making her way toward the door. She didn't need this. Robert was just trying to unnerve her. It wasn't enough that he'd threatened Charlie. Now it was *her* turn.

She pushed open the door and was climbing the steep flight of steps to the street when Robert's oh-so-pleasant voice floated toward her. "I'm curious about something, Mary. Was it your idea to come back? Because knowing how my wife feels about you, I find it hard to believe *she'd* have asked."

Mary swung around, her cheeks stinging as if slapped. "You *bastard*," she hissed. "How dare you?"

Standing at the bottom of the steps, pooled in shadow, Robert might have been an actor in an old black-and-white movie, his handsome features thrown into stark relief by the glare of a streetlamp, his teeth bared in a mirthless grin. A veteran Hollywood reporter had once told Mary that the true definition of a star is someone who can walk into a crowded room and have people turn around simply because they *feel* his or her presence. The same could be said of evil, she thought. Evil in its purest form was the flip side of stardom, the dark side of the moon, the tunnel at the end of the light.

"You're a long way from New York City, Mary," he said softly, a slight tic causing his right eyelid to flutter. "You have no idea what you're up against."

Her heart was pounding. They were alone, and it suddenly occurred to her how easy it would be for him to slip up behind her as she was walking away, to seize her by the throat. She wanted to run but didn't dare turn her back on him.

She forced herself to meet his gaze. "There's something *I'm* curious about," she said. "Why would someone with nothing to worry about go to so much trouble to protect his reputation? Or is there more to it than that? Is it going to jail that you're afraid of?"

He stared at her, his eyes flat and fixed as a cobra's. "Didn't your mother ever teach you not to stick your hand in where it doesn't belong? You might get bit." His voice was deceptively gentle, that of a father chiding a mischievous child.

But she'd dealt with men like him in the past. Fear was the commodity they traded in; if you withheld it they were powerless. "Are you threatening me, Robert?" she asked, as forthrightly as she could muster with her heart going a mile a minute. "Because if you are, let me warn *you* that I've been known to bite back."

Robert's face closed as suddenly as a fist, and his pale eyes glittered. He didn't lunge toward her, he didn't so much as *move,* yet she felt a rush of panic that sent her darting up the few remaining steps.

She was breathing as hard as if she'd climbed six flights.

Had he followed her? She glanced about to see if anyone would hear her if she screamed. But the aptly named Church Street was quiet, its buildings shuttered. A bicycle stand glimmered in the darkness a few yards away. Her eye fell on an old Schwinn that wasn't chained—as few bikes in Burns Lake were—and she thought about straddling it and pedaling as fast as she could to her car, parked two blocks away.

Then the moment of panic passed. She glanced at the key ring in her hand, feeling somewhat foolish. *He didn't threaten you, not really,* she told herself. What had shaken her so profoundly, she realized, was the ease with which he'd zeroed in on her deepest insecurity. What else did he know?

Mary didn't realize how shaken she was until she clipped the bumper of the car in front of her as she was pulling away from the curb. She gripped the steering wheel hard, as if her arms might float away otherwise. It occurred to her that Trish would wonder why she'd bolted without a word. She made a mental note to leave a message on her sister's answering machine when she got home.

She was approaching the intersection of Main and Bridge when a dark gray Volvo—

unmistakably Noelle's, with its dented front end—caught her eye. Her daughter had stayed home tonight to keep an eye on Doris, who wasn't feeling well, so hers was the last car Mary would have expected to see idling on the shoulder in front of the 7-Eleven with a sheriff's cruiser pulled up behind it.

Noelle, caught in the harsh glare of its headlights, stood arguing with the cop, a large, heavyset man with his back turned so Mary couldn't see his face.

She jammed on her brakes hard enough to skid the last few feet, screeching to a stop inches short of the cruiser's bumper. Not bothering to shut off her engine, she leaped out and dashed to her daughter's rescue.

"This is ridiculous. I was *under* the speed limit, and you know it." Noelle's exasperated voice floated toward her. "Now if you'll just excuse—" She spotted Mary and cried out, "Mom!"

The sheriff swung around clumsily, gravel skittering out from under his boot heels. Wade Jewett. She should have known. "Stay out of this, Mary. It's got nothing to do with you." He shot her a fierce glare before turning back to Noelle. "Ma'am, I'm afraid I'm going to have to ask you to take a breathalyzer test."

Noelle froze, clearly stunned. But she quickly regained her senses. "I'll do no such thing. I'm not drunk, and you know it." She started to brush past Wade, but his meaty hand closed over her arm.

"Wade Jewett, you take your hands off my

daughter!" Mary's voice, trained by years of having to shout in order to be heard at loud parties and press conferences, didn't fail her now. It rose over the hum of traffic, the roar of a mother bear rearing up to protect her cub.

Wade turned to sneer at her with almost buffoonish contempt. "A little late, aren't you, Mary? You should have been there when she was pouring the first drink."

In a weirdly elliptical moment that seemed to spin out and out, Mary had time to note the half-moons of sweat under his arms and a tuft of something that looked like Kleenex caught in the handcuffs swaying from his belt. She sensed his nervous excitement the way she knew to cut a wide berth around certain dogs. This wasn't a random ticketing, she thought. Wade Jewett had been lying in wait.

"You haven't changed a bit, have you? You've just expanded your repertoire." Mary eyed him with disdain. "Oh, yes, we knew it was *you*, back in ninth grade, making all those anonymous calls to me and my friends."

The sneering grin dropped from Wade's raw hamburger patty of a face. "You don't know shit."

"Your brother told us. Even *he* thought you were disgusting."

In the blink of an eye his mask shifted, and Wade Jewett, lumbering outcast of Lafayette High, stood revealed in all his naked adolescent priapism. "Skeeter? That little shithead wouldn't've had the balls to do that to m—" He stopped, realizing he'd put his foot in it.

"I didn't say anything at the time because I felt sorry for you." She pressed on coldly. "You were such a creep, and if that was the only way you could get a girl to talk to you...well, how pathetic was that. I had no idea, of course, how much lower you would sink."

"That's enough from you, lady. You just shut your mouth and step aside or I'll—I'll...arrest you for obstructing justice." Mary caught the furtive gleam in his eyes as he swung back to Noelle. "Ma'am, like I said, I'm going to have to ask you to—"

Something clicked in Mary's head, as distinct as a frozen twig snapping in two. Lunging forward, she swung at Wade with her purse, delivering a hard wallop to his back that sent him lurching forward, dust from his heels spinning up into the headlights' glare.

The next thing Mary knew she was being tackled and slammed against the cruiser, her arms rudely wrenched behind her back. She heard Noelle cry out, and an instant later there was the jingle of cool handcuffs snapping about her wrists.

"*Y*ou look as if you could use a friend. Either that or a hacksaw."

Mary looked up to find Charlie, a tall charcoal-haired man in jeans and a rumpled navy sport coat that had seen better days, walking along the fluorescent-lit corridor toward the jail cell where she'd been cooling her heels for the better part of an hour. He was smiling at her the way people do when humor is the only means by which to cope with an untenable situation. She didn't smile back.

"What took you so long?" She rose from the inch or so of hard bunk she'd deigned to occupy.

Charlie jerked a thumb over his shoulder. "Deputy out front gave me a hard time."

"Let me guess. Wade Jewett, right?" Mary cast a disgusted glance at the door to the squad room.

Charlie nodded, the tail end of his smile still tugging at a corner of his mouth. "I hear somebody finally gave that fat-assed bully the kick in the ass he deserved."

This time Mary *did* smile back. "I'd have done more than that if he hadn't handcuffed me." She looked past him. "Where's Noelle? I thought she was coming with you." By rights her daughter ought to be sharing this cell with her, but in all the confusion of her arrest Noelle had luckily managed to slip away. Apparently Wade Jewett had decided that one family member behind bars was enough; two might create a scandal.

"I told her it might be awhile, and she didn't want to leave Doris that long." Charlie paused, as if gauging how much Mary could stand to hear, then said, "There was some question as to whether or not you'd be allowed bail."

Mary shuddered at the thought of remaining locked up in here all night, listening to Avery Wilkinson, the town drunk, snoring wetly in the cell next to hers. "Well, are they letting me out or not?" she demanded fiercely.

"One of the deputies is signing off on the paperwork as we speak."

"How did you manage it?"

"I threatened to run a front-page piece on police harassment. Wade backed down pretty quick after that." Charlie flashed her a grin, then glanced at his watch, adding with his usual deadpan delivery, "Just in time to catch a drink down at the Red Crow."

At the mention of the Red Crow Tavern, Avery Wilkinson, in the cell next to hers, lifted his shaggy gray head to mutter blearily, "Have one for me, pal," before plopping back down on his bunk. Mary exchanged an amused glance with Charlie.

She didn't dare laugh. If she let herself laugh, she'd start to cry, and who knew where that would lead? This was beyond surreal. Like the bad acid trips her classmates in college used to talk about, something that she, an eighteen-year-old mom with baby food stains on her clothes and a permanent case of exhaustion, could barely relate to at the time.

"What I need more than a drink is a shower and a change of clothes." She stepped forward to wrap her hands about Charlie's knuckles, adding softly, "And, hey, in case I forgot to mention it—thanks. What would I do without you?"

Charlie shrugged. "You'd manage somehow. You always do." She caught a faint edge in his voice.

Minutes later they were being ushered out the door by a pimple-faced young deputy. Wade Jewett, seated at his paper-strewn desk, only glowered at them impotently as they passed.

In the parking lot behind the station Charlie turned to Mary, remarking dryly, "I seem to recall your once commenting that nothing ever happens in a small town."

"I stand corrected." Mary took the arm he offered, and they began walking toward his Blazer, their shadows stretching stilettolike in the pool of light cast by a lone streetlamp. "Did Noelle seem upset when you talked to her?"

"Some, but she was mostly irate, which I take to be a good sign." He touched her elbow. "Speaking of which, I think it made quite an impression on our little girl, your going to bat for her like that."

Mary felt a secret little thrill. Robert's taunt earlier this evening seemed distant now, like something from another lifetime. She hadn't yet gotten around to telling Charlie *that* part, but she knew that when she did, it wouldn't hurt quite so much. Smiling, she said, "I'll call her from the car to let her know I'm on my way."

When they reached his Blazer, Charlie didn't immediately reach for the door. He just stood there, looking at her, his long face pooled with shadow, his eyes glinting with words unspoken and emotions long submerged. They were alone, the only sound the distant barking of a dog.

"I don't know what I'd have done if anything had happened to you." He spoke with an intensity that hit her like something too hot gulped down on an empty stomach. "Promise me you'll never pull another stupid stunt like that."

Mary opened her mouth to protest that she'd done what *any* mother would when he abruptly pulled her into his arms. With a sigh she burrowed into the warm refuge of his embrace. Charlie smelled faintly of woodsmoke and the honest sweat of a man with a good deal invested in those he loved. She could feel his breath ruffling her hair and the hard muscles in the arms pressed to her back.

"I'm not going to make a promise I can't keep," she murmured into his collar. "I'd do it again in a heartbeat, and you know it."

"Yeah, I know. That's why I love you."

His words hung in the still night air. She turned them over in her mind, the way she'd once turned over in her hand a pretty blue stone he'd fished from the creek to give her. She could almost feel it in her palm, smooth and warm. Did she dare say it back? Did she dare venture that far out on a limb?

She drew back, holding her hands braced against his shoulders. Running a thumb along his jutting collarbone, she smiled to herself, thinking what a challenge he must present to the legions of women who'd like nothing better than to fatten him up. But she liked him just the way he was. What she'd have liked even more would be to lie down with him every night and wake up every morning with his lanky limbs draped over hers.

An inexpressible sorrow swept over her.

"Oh, Charlie. There are lots of promises I wish I could make."

"Yeah, I know that, too." He sounded sad. In the distance the dog barked on and on. Closer by a car engine rumbled to life. Finally, after what seemed an interminable silence, he cleared his throat. "Hop in. I'll drive you to your car."

Minutes later they were at the intersection of Main and Bridge, where Mary was relieved to find her car exactly as she'd left it, except for one thing: a slip of paper tucked under the windshield wiper. She'd been ticketed for illegal parking.

# Chapter Fourteen

"It isn't good *or* bad. In fact, it's pretty much what I expected." Lacey looked up from the psychologist's report on her desk.

Noelle felt her insides begin their familiar tumble. Lacey hadn't given any details over the phone; that was why she'd come dashing over in her shorts and T-shirt, hair still damp from the shower. Not quite recovered from last night's run-in with Wade Jewett, she now had this to contend with. Well, either way, it was better to *know*.

"What does it say?" she asked, nervously glancing about her lawyer's office—the top floor of a Victorian mansion housing the Emily T. Cates Memorial Library—as if the answer might somehow lie amid its cozy clutter and seat-sprung plush chairs smelling faintly of cat.

Lacey peered at the report through the dainty half-rim glasses perched on the end of her upturned nose. "It is Dr. Hawkins's assessment that you appeared anxious and somewhat high-strung, yet showed extreme concern for the well-being of your daughter. She has reservations, however, about your ability to cope with the demands of a young child in addition to the burden of caring for your grandmother. In short, though you don't qualify for Mother of the Year, you're not a menace to society." She looked up, frowning. "It's what she wrote about your husband that worries me."

Noelle felt her tumbling insides lurch to a standstill. Had Robert done something to Emma? Harmed her in some way? *Maybe I had to believe he was a good father because the alternative was unthinkable.*

"My daughter is all right, isn't she?"

Lacey looked momentarily confused. "What? Oh, yes. I just meant that...well, let me put it this way, if it were up to her, Robert would be canonized. He clearly had this Hawkins woman eating out of his hand." She made no attempt to hide her disgust.

Oddly, Noelle felt her tension ebb. It was strange, she thought, how a thing you've been dreading, when it finally hits you, can come as almost a relief. She felt as if a rope to which she'd been tethered, chafing and pulling, had snapped, leaving her to drift weightlessly.

An instant later, she plummeted to earth with a hard smack.

"Where do we go from here?" Her voice sounded peculiar to her own ears, hollow and tinny like the recorded message on her answering machine.

"The report's been submitted to the judge. Now it's just a matter of setting a date for the final hearing." Lacey set the document aside, leaning forward to fix Noelle with a concerned gaze. "Hey, kiddo, are you okay? You don't look so good."

"I'm fine." Noelle spoke tersely. She was tired of being treated like an invalid. Feeling sorry for herself wasn't going to help either. "Look, let's be honest. We both know Robert has this town wired. Why should it come as a shock that Linda Hawkins is in on it, too?"

"Let's not go off the deep end here." Lacey regarded her sternly, hands clasped in front of her like a schoolmarm. "I won't deny your husband has a great deal of influence in this town, but I see no evidence of any mass conspiracy. And frankly any talk of that outside this office will make it even worse for you."

"Worse than it already is? I don't see how that's possible."

Didn't Lacey see the connection? Her dad's windows getting smashed. Being targeted by Wade Jewett. If it wasn't a conspiracy, someone up there truly didn't like her.

"Relax. I didn't say anything about giving up, did I?" Noelle's lawyer, reaching up to pinch a dead leaf from the philodendron in the window, flashed her famous take-no-prisoners grin. "I'm not out of ammunition either. That's the other thing I wanted to talk to you about. Yesterday I got a call from your former neighbor Judy Patterson. Frankly, after what you'd told me, I was surprised to hear from her."

"I'm surprised, too." For all her threats Noelle hadn't really expected Judy to come through. When two or three days passed without word, she'd pretty much decided to let the matter drop. Now a seed of hope cracked open in her, sending up a pale shoot. Was this the lucky break she'd been praying for?

Lacey's next words crushed that hope. "She wasn't very helpful, I'm afraid. She told me she felt bad about what had happened and wanted to know if there was anything she could do to help...short of sticking her own neck out, that is."

"How noble of her." Noelle gave a scornful laugh.

"We could always subpoena her." Lacey had suggested it once before, but Noelle had vetoed the idea. They could force Judy to testify, sure, but to what end? A woman who'd make false allegations in an affidavit wouldn't stop at perjury.

"No," she reiterated. "Judy would just cry and act pathetic, making it look like we were picking on her." The crisp authority with which she spoke surprised Noelle. In the beginning she wouldn't have dreamed of speaking her mind so assertively. But times had changed, and she'd changed, too. Wade Jewett had been the final straw. "I have a better idea," she said, a thought taking shape in her mind.

Last night, when her mother had gone after Wade, there had been a wild look in her eyes...as if, given the chance, she would have killed him. A surprising truth had been brought home to Noelle in that instant: she and her mother were more alike than she'd realized. The instinct to protect her offspring was as strong in Mary as it was in her.

Was her mother-in-law any different? Gertrude would surely go to almost any lengths to protect her son. Cover for him. Lie to the police.

*Maybe even murder a pregnant girl who would have ruined his life.*

Noelle reeled at the thought. Maybe she'd been looking at this the wrong way. Suppose it wasn't her unborn grandchild Gertrude was mourning. Suppose the roses on Corinne's grave had been the guilt offering of a woman assuaging her conscience.

"There's someone besides Judy we could subpoena." She spoke cautiously, her mind not quite willing to grasp this astounding new theory. Not until she explored a little further.

"Who?" Lacey looked dubious.

"My mother-in-law. She wouldn't say anything that would hurt her son, of course, but it might raise some questions with the judge. Also, I have a feeling Gertrude Van Doren knows more about all this than she's letting on."

Lacey pondered the idea, absently toying with the top button on her demure white blouse. "I'm not sure the judge would allow it. Let me give some thought as to how we would present it, okay? In the meantime, don't do anything without checking in with me first."

"Like confront Gertrude on my own?" Noelle was surprised by the coolness with which she met Lacey's gaze.

"Don't even think it," the diminutive lawyer warned in her best longshoreman's growl. "Have you forgotten what happened the last time you decided to play Deputy Dawg?"

"Yeah, I broke my foot instead of Robert's head."

"Lucky for you."

"Are you saying you wouldn't have done the exact same thing in my place?" Noelle once more surprised herself by speaking out. "Come on, Lacey, you'd have charged over there like a rhino if it'd been your *dog*."

Her lawyer laughed. "Okay, you have a point, but let me remind you that from here on we have to tread very, very carefully. I think it's fairly obvious which direction the wind is blowing, but if and when we file an appeal, which I'm warning you right now looks likely, I want this case airtight."

Noelle felt her stomach twist. An appeal? She'd known from the beginning it was a possibility, maybe even a probability. But she still wasn't prepared for the numbing sense of letdown. She'd waited so long already. How could she possibly go another week or month...or more?

Facing Lacey squarely, she said with an honesty that had become easier with each layer of her old self that was stripped away, "It's ironic, really, because that's how I've lived my life until now: carefully. Going by somebody else's rules, afraid if I did what *I* wanted, it would somehow blow up in my face. But my life blew up *because* I was too careful. And now I have to live with the fact that I lost my little girl by doing the so-called right thing...by trusting the one man I should have bolted my door against."

Lacey rose and walked around to perch on the fat arm of the chair next to Noelle's. In her white blouse and pleated skirt she looked like a sly Catholic schoolgirl contemplating some sort of mischief. But her voice was gentle and knowing.

"I don't blame you for being frustrated, kiddo. The wheels of justice grind slowly, all right, and, yeah, sometimes it feels like you're caught in them, being slowly crushed. But trust me, you don't want to go flying off half cocked.

It could backfire and end up making things worse."

"And if I sit nicely with my hands folded in my lap, what then?"

"I won't insult your intelligence with a lot of false assurances." Lacey always dished it out straight; that's what Noelle liked best about her. "But we've got to face facts. *You're* the one on trial here, not Robert. You have a prior history of drinking. Plus, he's already established himself to be a more than fit parent." She ticked them off on her fingers, one by one, each indisputable fact a cold spike in Noelle's heart. "Anything you say to Robert or to any member of his family can and *will* be used against you."

"You think I don't know that already? That I'd have tried kicking his door down if I'd felt I had a choice?" Noelle thought of Hank tenderly bandaging her sprained ankle, and for some reason it gave her the strength to go on. "Somebody has to fight for my daughter. If *I* don't, who will?"

Lacey stood up, folding her arms over her chest. "I can't offer any flashy alternatives, I'll admit. And not being a mother myself, I can only imagine what you must be going through. But, Noelle, I'm confident that in the end, if we tough it out, you *will* get your daughter back. Hard as it is, you just have to be patient."

"Patience," Noelle said in a hard voice so unlike her own that her mind's eye blinked open in surprise, "may be a luxury I can't afford."

Lacey cocked an eyebrow. "Can you afford the consequences?"

"I don't know." Noelle stood up and paced restlessly to the window that looked out on the lawn, where a harried-looking young mother was herding a gaggle of children up the front path.

The children's laughter and the hollow clomping of their feet as they scampered onto the porch echoed in the stillness of Lacey's office. Noelle ached for all the places she used to take her daughter: story hour at the library, the playground in the square, Ben Franklin's for flower seeds to plant in Nana's garden. Her throat was tight, but she wasn't going to let herself cry. The time for tears was past.

When she turned, she found her lawyer gazing at her not with exasperation but with a newfound respect. "Whatever the outcome of all this, kiddo, I want you to know you have more than just a lawyer in me. You have a friend."

Every other Tuesday afternoon, Gertrude Van Doren, as treasurer of the Burns Lake Historical society, conducted tours of the Elsbree House high up on Windy Ridge Road. It was a matter of civic pride, she'd declare loudly and often to anyone who would listen, that their town boasted one of the oldest homes in the country, dating back to the Revolutionary War. The mansion, a finely appointed three-story Federal graced with Ionic columns and an ornate fanlight, had been fully restored in the late 1970s, largely because of the efforts of the historical society. But a source of even greater pride was that its original owner, Justus C. Elsbree, a prosperous Tory merchant and town father, was Gertrude's great-great-grandfather.

As Noelle guided her Volvo up the steep, bumpy road to the Elsbree House, she recalled that her mother-in-law's passionate interest in its restoration had coincided roughly with the death of her elder son. Knowing now what it was like to lose a child, she wasn't surprised that Gertrude would throw herself into such a project. It must have been the only way she could cope with her loss.

A loss that made her surviving son that much more precious.

Noelle squinted against the sunlight reflecting off her dusty windshield, an anxious voice in her head fretting, *Just what do you expect to accomplish here? She'll have you thrown off the premises.*

Aloud she muttered firmly, "No, she won't." It would look bad in front of the tourists, and God knows Gertrude would do anything to avoid a scene.

Nevertheless, her heart bumped up into her throat with each lurch of her wheels over the potholed road. The best she could hope for, really, was that her mother-in-law would be surprised into blurting something she'd intended to keep secret.

In the parking area Noelle found a spot in

the shade that wasn't taken and climbed out of her car. The view was breathtaking. The Elsbree House, which occupied the highest point on the ridge, looked out on a vista of rolling green hills that gave way to fields of corn and patches of shorn earth dotted with bundles of hay. Climbing from her car, she was struck anew by the grandeur of it and felt a small burst of confidence. Emma's ancestors had forged their way up here to make a home; her daughter came from hardy pioneer stock. She would get through this. They *both* would.

Noelle started up the path, the house rising before her, imposing and grand—a bit spooky as well. It had been rumored among her friends when they were growing up that the house was haunted. But that was before it was restored, back when the pediment over the front door had been home to roosting pigeons, and the fanlight, with several of its wedge-shaped panes missing or broken, had seemed to leer like an upside-down jack-o'-lantern.

At first the pristine tourist attraction that had risen from the magnificent wreck had been like new shoes needing to be broken in. But it had been long enough now for the new bricks to have worn to the earthy patina of the old, and the Virginia creeper to have once more spread up around the shuttered windows to brush the pedimented eaves. Nevertheless, Noelle felt a chill as she stepped through the front door into the shadowed entry. *There's no such a thing as ghosts,* she thought, *but the past can haunt you all the same.* She wondered what ghosts were lurking in Gertrude's past.

At the foot of the stairs a pretty dark-haired teenager dressed in colonial garb sat at a table stacked with brochures. She looked up from filing her emphatically nineties nails—black, with a kaleidoscope pattern of pink and purple swirls—to cast a desultory glance at Noelle.

"Tour's almost over," she announced in a bored voice. "The next one's not till four-thirty. You can buy your ticket now and come back if you want."

"Actually I'm looking for Mrs. Van Doren," Noelle informed her crisply. "Is she giving the tour?"

She tensed, half expecting to be given the suspicious once-over, but the girl merely nodded. "She usually sticks around afterward to answer questions and stuff. You can wait over there." She gestured distractedly at the parson's bench along the wall.

Noelle lowered herself stiffly onto the bench. Several more minutes passed. She could hear floorboards creaking overhead as the tour group was herded from one room to the next, accompanied by the faint murmur of voices. Gertrude would be expertly reciting the history of each piece of furniture and objet d'art, weaving in tales of the twelve children borne by Lucy Elsbree. For an added bit of color there was the century-old scandal of Justus Elsbree II's taking a sixteen-year-old Iroquois girl as his wife. And lest any hasty conclusions be drawn about the purity of her lineage, Gertrude would be quick to add that the poor girl had died before bearing him a child and that Justus had married again, a woman of sterling pedigree who went on to become her great-grandmother.

At last the band of tourists began making their way down the stairs. A stout gray-haired couple, the man leaning heavily on his wife's arm, followed by a family of four: an overweight wife in pink shorts, her balding husband, and a pair of skulking adolescents who looked as if they couldn't wait to sneak out back for a smoke. Gertrude brought up the rear, wearing a coral linen jacket over a flowered silk dress. Her low pink heels matched her dress, and as usual every strand of her beige blond hair was perfectly in place.

She was in the midst of explaining why the ceilings were low and the windows small. "You must understand, there was no such thing as central heating in those days. My great-great-grandparents were fortunate enough to have their coal delivered weekly, but for those who couldn't afford it winters without proper insulation would have been unbearable."

Gertrude caught sight of Noelle and came to an abrupt halt, clutching the polished banister. The moment seemed frozen in time, like the vintage photographs on the wall: her mother-in-law's pale, astonished face, the diamond pin on her lapel flashing sepia in the muted glow from the fanlight. Then she recovered her composure, stepping down onto the hooked runner.

"Please feel free to wander about the grounds before you go. There's a lovely garden out back," she called to the departing tourists. When they turned to thank her, she mustered a gracious smile and gave her patented reply. "Believe me, the pleasure was all mine. History is such an important part of our lives. Where would we be without it?"

When they were alone except for the girl in the mobcap, Gertrude at last turned to acknowledge Noelle. "My goodness, this is a surprise," she exclaimed, forcing a smile and bringing her hands together in a noiseless little clap. "You're looking well, dear."

Noelle bit back the urge to retort that if she was, it was no thanks to her or her son. Every muscle in her body felt spring-loaded, ready to catapult her forward, arm extended to slap that stiff little smile off her mother-in-law's face. Instead she rose to her feet with as much dignity as possible.

"Hello, Gertrude. How have you been?"

"Oh, well, you know." Gertrude shrugged as if to indicate that she suffered from the usual aches and pains.

"And Cole?"

"Fine, just fine." Gertrude absently fingered her pin, which was in the shape of a flower basket. Noelle was once more reminded of the roses on Corinne's grave. "His knees have been giving him some trouble lately, but the doctor says it's nothing more than a touch of arthritis. And your grandmother, how is she doing these days?" Her expression was one of bright, fixed interest.

"Never better," Noelle lied.

"Well, that's just wonderful to hear. Please give her my best. Now, if you'll excuse me, I have to dash." Gertrude made a move to step past her, but Noelle was quick to block her path.

"I was hoping we could talk."

Color rose in Gertrude's cheeks, and her eyes—pale blue, like Robert's—widened in alarm. Her smile had the look of something hastily patted into place. "I'm afraid this isn't a good time. The next tour starts in an hour, and I have some errands to run before then." She cut a wide birth around Noelle and headed for the door.

"No problem. I'll just tag along." Noelle fell into step with her.

Gertrude waited until they were outside, discreetly out of earshot, before replying, "Please understand, dear, it's nothing personal. But someone might see us and...well, it would give the wrong impression."

"What? That I'm a concerned mother looking for answers?" An acid note crept into Noelle's voice. "Heaven forbid."

They were walking along the brick path bordered in snapdragons and delphiniums that nodded in the stiff breeze that had given Windy Ridge its name. Yesterday's rain had left the surrounding grass damp, and Gertrude seemed unaware of the dark stain seeping up from the soles of her pink pumps as she set out across the lawn in the direction of her Cadillac, parked in one of the slots reserved for staff. As she stepped onto the pavement, the measured click of her heels reminded Noelle of a line from a nursery rhyme, "Hickory dickory dock, the mouse ran up the clock..."

She caught up with her mother-in-law as she was unlocking her car door. When Gertrude turned to face her, Noelle was surprised by the look of genuine sympathy she wore.

"Whatever you might think, dear, I bear you no ill will," she said gently. "An aunt of mine had a—well, to put it delicately, she was a tippler. But she wasn't a bad person. Any more than you're a bad mother. If only you could think of this as being what's best for—"

Something in Noelle's expression caused her to halt in mid-sentence, a look of mild panic flitting across her face. Yet Noelle wasn't aware of anything other than feeling suddenly cold, as if a tap had been cranked open inside her, releasing freezing water into her veins.

"What's best for Emma? Come on, Gertrude, you don't honestly believe all that horseshit Robert's been dishing out." Even her voice was different, harsh and controlled.

Gertrude's mouth tightened. "He was right about one thing: You *have* changed. And not for better." She jerked around, reaching for the door handle.

This time Noelle didn't try to stop her. She simply walked around to the passenger side and calmly got in. Her mother-in-law froze with one foot inside the car and her rear end poised to drop into the driver's seat. She plopped down with an astonished cry.

"Why, of all the—" Her mouth snapped shut, then fell open again, like a fish gasping at the bottom of a boat. "This is private property, and you're—you're *trespassing*."

"I'll be out of your hair as soon as you give me some answers." Noelle spoke evenly, but her heart was pounding in great dull thuds. "Let's start with what you know about Corinne Lundquist."

*"Corinne?"* Gertrude gasped, bringing a hand to her chest. "What on earth has that poor girl got to do with any of this? Why, you were just a baby when she died." At the same time, Noelle noticed, she hadn't needed any reminding of who Corinne was.

"She was my mother's best friend, for one thing."

"Well, then, your mother must have told you it was nothing more than a senseless tragedy." Gertrude kept her voice light, but her hands, tightly clutching the boxy white purse in her lap, told a different story.

"I didn't ask how she died. But since you brought it up, why don't you tell me what you remember about it."

Gertrude's face went slack, and Noelle could see that her coral lipstick had crept up into the little pleats around her mouth. She suddenly looked old, as old as Nana. "It was a suicide, that's all I know."

"Are you absolutely certain of that?"

Gertrude shot her a peculiar look but gave no sign that she was guilty of anything other than leaving flowers on a dead girl's grave. "Well, I hardly see how it could have been an accident."

"There are other ways to die."

"Are you suggesting—?"

"I'm not suggesting anything. I'm *asking.* Did Robert have anything to do with her death?" She refrained from adding, *Or did you?*

"Of course not!"

"Do you know that for a fact?"

Gertrude put a hand out as if to ward her off, though Noelle hadn't moved so much as an inch in her direction. In a tremulous voice she answered, "You didn't know her. She was a deeply troubled girl. I believe her parents—her father, at least—were quite religious. It must have been terrible for her...when she learned she was expecting."

Something clicked in Noelle's head, like a tumbler falling into place. "How did you know Corinne was pregnant?"

An insistent tapping against the glass caused Gertrude to twist around, one eye rolling back to cast a panicked glance out the back window. But it was only a low-hanging branch blowing in the wind.

She slumped back in her seat. A fine mist of sweat had dampened her brow, causing the powder in its crevices to cake. "I—I must have heard it somewhere," she stammered. "At the funeral perhaps?"

"You weren't at the funeral. I asked my mother." Noelle leaned toward her, close enough to catch the cloying scent of her perfume. "What *really* happened, Gertrude? What are you hiding?"

"Nothing!" Frantically she struggled to insert the key into the ignition, but it took several attempts before she was able to jam it in. The engine roared to life.

"Was he really with you the night Corinne died? Or did you lie to protect him?" Noelle pressed on.

"I refuse to continue this—this outrageous discussion a moment longer." Gertrude leaned across her in a cool brush of silk to wrench open her door. "Get out. *Now.*"

Noelle ignored her. "You *know* something, don't you? Just like you know what he's doing to me. All the lies and innuendoes...making it look as if I'm not fit to care for my own child. How can you go along with it? How can you let him do that to Emma?"

Gertrude stared sightlessly ahead, her hands gripping the steering wheel. Her lips were pressed together so hard they were quivering. "No. Robert's a good man. A good *father.* He wouldn't do anything to hurt Emma."

"But he *is* hurting her."

"No, he's protecting her. There's a difference."

Noelle tried a different tack. "Did you know he was cheating on me?"

Gertrude blinked several times in rapid succession, clearly startled by the revelation.

But she quickly recovered. "That's between you and Robert," she replied primly.

"I just thought you should know, that's all. Your son isn't the upstanding family man he pretends to be."

"Get out," Gertrude ordered once more, but this time it came out sounding more like a plea.

"Just one more thing." Noelle had saved her best shot for last. "Why the flowers on Corinne's grave?"

Gertrude jerked around to gape at her.

"I saw them. White roses, tied with a red ribbon." Noelle watched a muscle in her mother-in-law's face twitch in response. "They were for the baby, weren't they? *Robert's* baby. Your grandchild."

Gertrude made a noise deep in her throat, a tiny, strangled squeak like a small animal that had been stepped on. She looked frantically about, as for a means to escape. Then, as if not knowing what else to do, she reached for her seat belt, moving in crabbed jerks as she strapped it over her chest and lap. But the buckle wouldn't snap into place, her hands were trembling so, and after several attempts she let it fall into her lap with a small cry of dismay.

"I have to go," she whispered. "Please."

"Was he was pressuring her to have an abortion? Is that why she killed herself?" Noelle forged on mercilessly. "Or was he angry enough to save her the trouble?"

Gertrude sagged back against the seat, closing her eyes as if the effort to keep them open was suddenly too much. When she spoke, it was in a strangely hollow voice.

"Robert *was* upset, but not for the reason you think. It was because—" she gulped in a shallow breath—"because the baby wasn't his."

Noelle sat back, stunned. This wasn't what she'd expected. But in a way, didn't it make even more sense? Robert, furious over Corinne's unfaithfulness, would have lashed out, yes…and perhaps gone even farther. Still, there was something that didn't quite fit…

She turned to Gertrude. "I don't understand. If the baby wasn't your grandchild, then why the roses?"

Her mother-in-law's arms fell to her sides like dead weights. In a voice equally dead, her lips barely moving, she said, "It *was* my grandchild. It was Buck's baby."

# Chapter Fifteen

That night the weather turned uncommonly brisk. Only two weeks into August, and already the summer nights had begun to grow shorter. Cool breezes drifted down from the mountains. For the last four nights in a row a low bayoulike mist had crept in over the lake, making the call of the loons sound lonelier than ever. At the cabin, where Mary sat huddled about the kitchen table with her ex-husband and daughter, she thought for the first time that it was perhaps *too* quiet. The piping of frogs and slap of water against the dock seemed unnaturally close. She thought she heard the dip of an oar as well, but maybe it was only her imagination. *When you're on edge,* she told herself, *it's easy to hear ghosts in everything that goes bump in the night.*

In another part of her mind, though, she marveled at the cozy tableau they made: she and Charlie and Noelle. How amazing that they could sit like this, sipping hot cocoa, bare toes curled over the rungs of their chairs, as though they'd done so on countless such evenings. Not just three disparate people washed ashore by circumstances, but what she'd always yearned for: a family.

"At least we know now who the mysterious J is." Mary gazed out the blackened window in which her reflection, distorted by the panes, looked strangely spectral. "James Buchanan Van Doren, Buck for short. God, why didn't I think of it? Corinne hated nicknames. She had a real thing about it."

"But why only that one mention in her diary?" Noelle wondered aloud.

"My guess is, it went something like this." Charlie weighed in. "In her last entry Corinne mentions getting into a fight with Robert on the way to a party. When he left her stranded, someone took pity on her and gave her a ride home—his brother, we now know. She and

425

Buck struck up a bond. They had something in common, after all. The next thing you know, they're lovers. She didn't dare write about it in her diary; someone might have found out."

"But someone *did* find out," Noelle reminded him.

"The question is, How could she have been sure the baby was Buck's, not Robert's?" Charlie absently rolled his mug between his palms.

"Simple," Mary told him. "She was a virgin until Buck." Charlie shot her a quizzical look, and she was quick to add, "Don't you see? It's the only thing that makes sense. Corinne and I knew *everything* about each other, until I got too caught up with my own life to see past my own nose. When you first told me she was pregnant, I thought it was strange. She'd been seeing Robert for over a year. She'd have *told* me if they were sleeping together. Besides, their relationship was always rocky. I think she was afraid of getting that close." She sipped her cocoa thoughtfully. "With Buck, it would have been different. He was older, after all. And quite good-looking, as I recall. A nicer version of Robert. If they were serious about each other, Robert would have found out eventually. I think the baby just brought things to a head."

"Let's take it a step further," Charlie said. "Suppose Robert *did* kill her in a fit of rage, then set it up to look like suicide. There's still no proof. Not unless we were to have the remains exhumed. It's possible—not likely, mind you, but *possible*—that with the advances in technology since the first autopsy, a forensic pathologist might turn up something that was missed."

The gruesome thought had occurred to Mary as well. Even so, she was quick to discard it. "Oh, God. I don't even want to *think* what it would do to Nora. Isn't there another alternative?"

The three fell silent, wisps of steam rising from their mugs in the cooling air. Mary was surprised by the intensity of her sadness after all these years. It was as if in some ways she'd put off grieving until now. Poor Corinne. The thought of her friend, alone and scared, was almost too much for her to bear. It was a place she knew intimately. She, too, had feared being cut off by her family and wondered how on earth she was going to manage without their support. In her case those fears had come to pass. And Corinne, dear, impressionable Corinne, had witnessed it all. No wonder she was desperate.

Mary glanced across the table at Charlie, who sat with his arms folded in front of him wearing a pensive look, a man who'd borne his own share of grief. Yet there was a streak of optimism in his face as well, a sense of life's glass being half filled in the lines that radiated like sunbursts from the corners of his eyes and in the upward curl of his mouth.

Noelle leaned forward on her elbows. "We don't need proof to stir up suspicion. What if we were to just rattle Robert's cage? Like you've been doing with your editorials, only the kind of stuff that would get people *really* talking."

Mary eyed her daughter, once again noting the difference in her. A new determination had put color in her cheeks and a bit more flesh on her bones. Again, as she had the night of her arrest, Mary felt an almost visceral pull toward her daughter, a desire to guard her at any cost. Yet it was clear that Noelle was perfectly capable of defending herself. Mary leaned sideways instead to slip an arm about her and was touched and a bit surprised when Noelle brought her head to rest against her shoulder.

Charlie looked dubious. "I already thought of that, but it could just as easily backfire. Robert's stock is still pretty high in this town. His supporters, not to mention his lawyers, are sure to take a dim view of any mudslinging that doesn't have a solid basis in fact. And believe me, with an election coming up in November, the weight of public opinion won't be over-looked by the honorable Judge Ripley."

"There's another reason to watch our step," Mary said, thinking of her run-in with Noelle's husband the other night. "We all know Robert isn't the type to take things lying down. If you back him into a corner, he might...well, I wouldn't want any of us to get hurt."

"He doesn't know yet what it's like to be backed into a corner. But *I* do." Noelle spoke with a fierceness that Mary had never heard in her. "The way I see it, I have nothing left to lose. If having Corinne's remains exhumed is the only way of finding out whether or not—"

She broke off at the scrape of footsteps on the back porch: Bronwyn, back from walking Rufus. The door banged open, and the big yellow dog charged in, tracking mud across the kitchen floor, followed closely by Charlie's younger daughter, bringing a draft of cool air and a sudden change in mood.

Bronwyn yanked open the refrigerator. "Anything to eat? I'm starved."

"Just some potato salad left over from supper," Noelle told her.

With a groan the girl pushed the fridge shut. "I'm not *that* hungry."

Charlie glanced up at her distractedly. "There's ice cream."

Bronwyn turned to glare at him. "Honestly, Daddy. If *you* had to spend all day staring at great big tubs of ice cream, you'd know better than to suggest such a thing."

Charlie appeared to take no notice of her bad temper. Maybe *he* was used to it, but Mary wasn't. She frowned. If one of her young interns had spoken to her that way, he or she would've been fired...or at the very least given a stern lecture. Noelle hadn't been like that as a teenager, had she? Mary remembered her as being quiet, perhaps *too* quiet. Maybe she *should* have talked back more. Maybe none of this would be happening now if she'd learned to stick up for herself when she was younger.

Bronwyn's foul mood lifted as quickly as it

had descended. She slipped up behind Noelle and twined her arms about her sister's neck. "I know. Why don't I make waffles?" she proposed sweetly. "With those blueberries we picked in the woods this morning."

"It's after ten," Noelle told her. "I should be getting home."

"There's no rush. Your aunt Trish said she'd stay over," Mary volunteered.

Bronwyn shot her a glance that seemed to say, *Don't get any ideas about being part of* this *family.* Yet the look she directed at Charlie was almost plaintive. "Daddy, how do you think it makes me feel when you stop talking the minute I walk in? I'm not stupid, you know. I *know* what's going on. And if you don't let me do *something,* even something as idiotic as making waffles, I—I don't know, I'll explode or something."

Charlie shot her a wry grimace. "Point taken. I didn't mean to leave you out, pumpkin. I just didn't think it was fair to involve you any more than was necessary." A slow smile spread across his face, and the kitchen—with its faded wallpaper and lacquered pine cabinets darkened to the color of cider—seemed to brighten. "Blueberry waffles? Well, now, that strikes me as a fine idea."

"Oh, Bron." With a sigh Noelle reached up to give her sister's arm an affectionate pat. "Just promise me you'll never have children with a man you don't trust."

"Who says I'm ever having kids?"

Bronwyn straightened and padded over to

the counter, where she began opening cupboards and pulling out mixing bowls and measuring cups. Reaching into the refrigerator for a carton of milk, she stood poised a moment, staring sightlessly ahead, the harsh glare casting a long blade of shadow over the scuffed linoleum. Then she shook her head as if to clear it and shut the door. The kitchen was soon filled with the clattering of spoons against bowls and the aroma of waffles sizzling in the iron.

Mary thought, *I could get used to this.* Late nights about the kitchen table, listening to the chirp of peepers and crickets outside. No ringing phones or blinking message lights. No frantic clients calling from tiny airports in the Midwest, shrieking that they'd missed their flights. No traffic sounds, even. Just this: the quiet of an evening in which, even with a crisis looming, there was time to sit back and enjoy life's smaller pleasures.

She surprised herself by devouring three waffles smothered in butter and drenched in maple syrup from a farm up the road. When everyone's plates had been scraped clean, Charlie and Noelle got up to wash the dishes, shooing Mary onto the porch. No sooner had she settled into a chair than the screen door creaked open behind her. She turned, a bit taken aback to see that it was Bronwyn.

The girl hesitated before crossing the porch and sinking down on the top step. For an instant, silhouetted against the silvery lake wreathed in mist, her long legs folded in against her chest and her waist-length hair spilling over her knees, she could have been Corinne.

"The waffles were delicious," Mary told her. "I ate too much, though."

"You can afford to. You're skinny enough." It didn't sound like a compliment.

After a moment of awkward silence Mary made another attempt. "I'm glad it's cooled down a bit. The breeze feels nice, doesn't it?"

Bronwyn shrugged. "Summer's almost over."

"That reminds me, your father tells me you'll be starting your senior year in the fall." Mary plowed on gamely. "You must be thinking about which colleges to apply to. I remember when Noelle was your age, she couldn't wait to be on her own."

Bronwyn shot her a look that seemed to say, *No wonder. If I were your daughter, I'd feel the same.* But the girl *wasn't* hers. And when you got right down to it, wasn't that the point? "My PSAT scores weren't so hot," she confessed. "I'll be lucky to get into *any* college."

Mary chuckled knowingly. "I felt the same way when I was applying. Who was going to take a single mom with a baby? But six years later there I was with my bachelor's degree."

"I know. Noelle told me all about it." In the moonlight that had found its way through the mist Bronwyn's olive skin gleamed pale gold. She brought a hank of hair to her mouth, brushing its ends over her lips. "She said you were gone a lot in those days."

Mary felt a familiar stab of guilt. But rather than leap in with justifications, she merely replied, "She's right. I was."

There was another lengthy pause; then out of the blue Bronwyn asked, "Did you know my mother?"

"I met her only once. She seemed very nice."

"She was. Pretty, too. People couldn't get over how pretty my mother was."

"You look a little like her, you know."

"Everyone says I look like my dad."

"Well, yes. But you have her eyes. She had lovely eyes, I remember."

Bronwyn studied her closely, as if searching for an answer Mary didn't have. Then her eyes cut away, and she slapped her arm, remarking idly, "The mosquitoes around here, boy, they'll eat you alive if you don't watch out."

"I know what you mean."

"Bet there aren't many where you live."

"We have other kinds of pests." Mary smiled. "Muggers, rapists, you name it. Summer is the worst, for some reason."

"Well, nothing like that ever happens around here. You must find Burns Lake pretty boring."

"Oh, it has its charms."

Under the cover of darkness Mary indulged a small smile. From inside came the sound of the tap being cranked off and Noelle's voice blending comfortably with Charlie's. When a mosquito landed on her leg, she gently brushed it away. Bronwyn, she saw, was eyeing her curiously.

"Don't you ever get homesick? I mean, for the city."

At the moment Mary didn't feel a bit homesick. But all she said was: "Sometimes. It isn't where you live necessarily; it's what's familiar. You get so used to a certain way of life you can't imagine it any other way. Then something comes along to upset the balance, and you realize there are lots of possibilities you just didn't see before."

Bronwyn went back to staring out at the darkened lake, with its pale fingers of mist trailing over the surface. "I guess," she acknowledged grudgingly. They lapsed once more into silence. Mary was about to get up and go inside when a girlish voice piped shyly, "Do you really think I look like her?"

"Come over here where I can see you." Mary waited for Bronwyn to unfold from the steps and walk over to where she sat. She regarded the girl for a moment, this leggy creature like a character out of *Midsummer Night's Dream,* tiny insects wheeling about her shining crown like fairy dust. She was Charlie's, through and through, right down to the frown line that curved like an apostrophe over her right eyebrow, but some burst of compassion made her say, "Oh, absolutely."

The faint clatter of plates drifted toward them. And a sound that might have been Rufus's tail thumping against the floor. The spell was broken. Bronwyn dropped her eyes as if embarrassed to have been caught begging like their old dog for approval. Abruptly she spun about and dashed inside, the screen door slapping shut behind her.

Two days passed without incident. On Wednesday Mary drove into the city to meet with her biggest client, diet guru Lucianne Penrose, who was being interviewed by the Ladies' Home Journal. Noelle, following her visit with Emma, spent the latter part of the afternoon exploring various options with her lawyer. And Charlie made a lightning trip to Albany to see if he could wrangle a quote from Senator Larrabie. Though the Register's broken windows had been replaced, the furor over its negative press on Robert and his cronies was still very much ongoing.

The following day brought a new outbreak of vandalism, though, this time an abandoned warehouse on the outskirts of town. Windows were smashed, and a fire was set. Fortunately the blaze was put out before any major damage was done. Charlie nonetheless sent two of his best and brightest, Trent Robeson and Gina Tomaselli, to cover it. When Gina returned with a statement from Robert, denying any involvement, Charlie ran an article on the front page of Friday's edition, under the headline:

*LOCAL BUSINESSMAN*
*QUESTIONED IN FIRE*

435

Two days later a deacon at First Baptist arrived early Sunday morning to find the church defaced with graffiti. Far more distressing was the damage to its adjacent cemetery. Several headstones had been toppled, and in a particularly cruel twist of irony a marble statue of John the Baptist was found decapitated, its lichen-furred head gazing blindly up at the sky from a nest of brambles.

Bronwyn heard about it over the local AM station as she bicycled to work, plugged into her Walkman. She shuddered, thinking of that old expression about a goose walking over your grave. No *real* damage was done, true, but she had a feeling this rash of vandalism was only the beginning of worse things to come. Arriving at Scoops, she rushed to call Dante.

"It's me." She kept her voice low and an eye on Mr. Norwood, bent over his adding machine in the back room. "Have you heard the latest? It looks like your boss is up to his old tricks."

She could hear the blatting of an air gun in the background. Then Dante growled, "Yeah, I heard. And just for the record I ain't workin' for Mr. V no more. I quit two weeks ago." She didn't have to ask if he'd been questioned in connection to these most recent crimes; his tone said it all. A solid alibi was presumably the only thing keeping him out of jail.

"There's something I don't get." She dropped her voice even lower, cupping a hand over the receiver. "Going after my father was one thing, but what does you know who have to gain from trashing a church?"

"Like I'm some kinda mind reader? How would I know?" Dante sounded irritated, though she sensed it wasn't directed at her. "Look, I can't talk about this over the phone. Can you get off work in an hour or so?"

"I'll tell Mr. Norwood I have cramps if I have to." It was the first excuse that popped into her head. Maybe because she was relieved to have her period. She'd heard too many stories about condoms breaking.

They'd been together three times since that first one, each better than the last. With Dante, she was finding out that all those sexy novels she'd devoured were mostly a load of crap. The real thing was a million times better. The thought sent a curl of warmth up her midsection.

"Meet me at my place around noon." Dante hung up.

The rest of the morning Bronwyn could hardly concentrate. She mixed up orders, giving a woman who'd asked for cinnamon swirl a scoop of coffee almond fudge instead, then forgot to put a filter in the coffee machine so that it filled with sludgy grounds. The last straw was a group of kids who paid for their cones with eight one-dollar bills and received a ten in change. Mr. Norwood, mistaking it for a case of teenage hormones run amok—he was more accurate than he could have known—practically shooed her out the door at lunchtime, claiming it was for *his* sake that he was giving her the rest of the day off.

She pedaled furiously down Main Street,

turning left at the American Legion Hall. A few blocks down, at the Agway, she turned left again and kept on going until she reached the wrecking yard, a quarter of a mile to the south. As she biked past it, Bronwyn caught a glimpse of a rust-eaten chassis dangling from the steel jaws of an enormous crane. She was mounting the rickety staircase to Dante's apartment when a loud, thudding crash from across the street caused it to sway slightly.

At the door, Dante greeted her with a kiss. His mind, though, was clearly elsewhere. Inside she watched him pace over to the window, where he stood staring out at the wrecking yard. He was wearing his overalls from work, light blue with his name stitched over the front pocket. Fresh grease marks overlapped the paler ones that hadn't quite washed out. With a jerky motion he reached for his cigarettes atop the TV.

"I shouldn't be talking to you about this," he said, lighting one and twisting his mouth to blow out a jet of smoke. "You know too much already."

Bronwyn advanced on him, frowning. "Dante, if you're keeping something from me...."

"Let's just say I've been tipped off."

"By one of Robert's goons?"

"No. By a friend." He flicked a nervous glance at her. "It doesn't matter who. All you need to know is that something's coming down. Something a lot bigger than the petty JD stuff that's come down so far."

Her stomach lurched. "Something involving Noelle?"

"Maybe I'm getting this second hand. Let's just say my friend is closer to the Man than yours truly, but there's a limit to what he knows."

Fear funneled through her like hot water through ice. You read about it in the papers all the time, she thought: Divorced dad goes berserk and murders his ex-wife. Oh, God. The day she'd tried to warn her sister, Bronwyn had begun to think that maybe Noelle was right: Maybe she *was* overreacting. It certainly wouldn't be the first time. But now she knew better.

"What am I supposed to tell my sister?" she demanded. "I can't go to her without some facts. She already thinks I'm blowing this way out of proportion."

"Just tell her to get the hell out of town."

Bronwyn sighed with frustration. "Dante, this isn't helping. I'd never be able to convince her to do that. Not without Emma. Anyway, it could be *months*." She stepped around behind him to circle his waist with her arms and press her cheek to his back. "If you know something more, tell me. Please."

She felt him tense. His muscles under the worn canvas overalls were as unyielding as a statue's. Dante was literally scared stiff, she realized with a jolt. Not for Noelle or Emma. For *her*.

"First," he growled, "you have to promise to stay away. *Far* away."

"From *what*?"

He spun around to grip her arms. His eyes were dark and hooded; his calloused fingers dug into her flesh. "Promise."

"Okay, okay." She pulled away, rubbing her arm. "I promise."

Dante hesitated, regarding her dubiously. Then he sighed—the sigh of a tough guy who'd just as soon it didn't get around that he had a thing for a certain dark-eyed girl with trouble written all over her innocent-looking face. "Tomorrow night, he's hitting another church," he said. "United Methodist out on Grandview."

She shook her head in confusion. "I don't get it. What, if anything, does Robert hope to accomplish by all this? Is he doing it just for kicks or is there some master plan?"

"I don't know. That's what scares me."

Bronwyn was scared, too. She stared at Dante while her mind raced. *My sister is in danger,* she thought. Real *danger. The kind that jumps out at you from a dark alley. The kind that means business. But what exactly does that creepy husband of hers have up his sleeve?*

One way or another, she was going to find out.

# Chapter Sixteen

At the other end of town Doris had just settled in for her afternoon nap. She was dozing, about to drop off, when the phone ringing down the hall jerked her back to consciousness. Groggily she wondered why no one was answering it before remembering that Mary was off on some business and Noelle next door taking Polly Inklepaugh up on her offer of zucchini from the garden. Polly always planted way too much, she thought. Now that the kids were grown and scattered to the four winds, it was just she and Harry, and honestly, how many jars of pickled beets can two people possibly eat? Polly ought to have done as she'd suggested and donated some of those pickles and preserves to the drive St. Vincent's held each year at Christmas. But the woman rarely listened to her, though you'd think, after forty-odd years of living next door to each other—

The phone rang on and on, mindless of Doris's infirmity and the fact that she'd just as soon not have to get up and shuffle down the hall only to have the person hang up before she could answer it. Maybe she should have given in to Noelle's insistence and bought an answering machine. She just hadn't seen the point, not with her being home all day with nothing better to do than pick up the phone herself. But that was before she'd begun spending more time on her back than up and about. Now it was the trials of Job just to haul her decrepit body out of bed. A body that had begun to seem alien and ill fitting somehow, like a wrong-size dress bought by mistake that she hadn't gotten around to returning. Lately she even needed help going to the bathroom.

*It's the one thing they never tell you about old age,* she thought, *that it isn't the aches and pains or even the loneliness that'll do you in. It's the humiliation of having to be lowered onto the toilet by someone whose diapers you once changed.*

If only that infernal phone would stop its ringing. Shouldn't Noelle be back by now? Polly was no doubt chewing her ear off, never mind that Noelle had problems on her own, *real* ones, and didn't need to hear a lot of yammering on and on about Polly's selfish son and his amnesia every year around her birthday or her daughter's so far fruitless attempts to bring more silly Inklepaughs into this world. Saints preserve us, she thought, that woman could talk the bark off a tree. A high price to pay for a load of zucchini that anyone with a garden couldn't give away fast enough this time of year.

Still, the phone rang on. Who could it be? That smarty-pants Buxton girl? The thought gave Doris a little jolt. Suppose it *was* Lacey, with good news about little Emma? My, wouldn't that be something. And how would it look that she'd been too lazy to walk twenty paces down the hall to take the message? *Shame on you,* a voice scolded.

Doris hauled herself out of bed, every bone in her body creaking with the effort. A wave of dizziness swept over her and she stood rocking on her feet, clinging to the bedpost for support. Oh, how she longed to climb back under the covers! These days she couldn't move without some part of her yipping in pain. She imagined a small animal—a gopher or a mouse, something beady-eyed with sharp yellow incisors—its teeth sunk to the bone. Clutching her left side, she shuffled out into the hall, biting her lip to keep from crying out.

The phone continued to ring. She could see it atop its little oak table on the landing at the end of the hall. A hall that stretched before her like the tunnels she'd traveled through as a child to visit Grandmother Cates in Boston. She recalled how panicky she used to feel plunged into sudden darkness with the train rocking to and fro, the clacking of its wheels a deafening roar. She felt almost as frightened now, not of being swallowed whole like Jonah but of falling and not being able to get up.

Doris placed a hand on the wall for support, just below the gallery of framed family photos that glinted in the dim light. There was Mary Catherine at three, bundled in her snowsuit, helping Daddy shovel the front walk. And Trish at eight, proudly showing off her brand-new front teeth. Ted had been so patient with the girls, far more patient than she. She'd tried—maybe not hard enough—before reluctantly coming to the conclusion that the Lord hadn't seen fit to bless her with a forbearing nature.

She winced at the pain in her side, her gaze straying to a more recent photo of her elder daughter and granddaughter, taken nine years ago at Noelle's wedding. She remembered suddenly that today was Noelle's anniversary, which they'd almost certainly go out of their way *not* to celebrate. Doris peered at the photo: Noelle, in her white gown and veil smiling too broadly, and Mary Catherine with one arm held stiffly about her waist looking a bit shell-shocked by it all. Yes, a difficult day—most of all for Charlie's wife, who couldn't have helped noticing the glances her husband kept stealing at Mary Catherine.

It struck Doris now that in the weeks since her daughter's return much had changed. Like trees that in reaching for the sun lean into one another, the two of them had grown closer. More relaxed with each other somehow and, perversely, quicker to be short when grouchy, the way family members do when not walking on eggshells. Mary Catherine had blossomed in other ways as well, not just as a mother, but as a woman, though credit for that was due almost exclusively to Charlie.

As she slowly shuffled along the hall, leaning heavily into the wall, Doris thought with genuine regret: *Forgive me, Lord. I know I didn't make it easy for them. They were young, yes, but so were Ted and I...only a few years older when we tied the knot. I should have been more under-standing. I should have—*

Sudden silence brought Doris to an abrupt halt. The phone had stopped ringing. *Hell's bells,* she cursed inwardly (the dirty little secret she kept from her children was that she often swore, though never out loud). What if it *had* been for Noelle?

Come to think of it, where was the girl? It seemed hours since she'd stepped out for what was supposed to have been only a few minutes. The sunlight filtering through the transom over the front door had slipped between the stair rails to cast a ladder of shadow over the steps below. On the radio in the kitchen, tuned to WMYY, a band was playing a song from Doris's girlhood, reminding her of when her husband and she were first married and Ted had surprised her with a romantic weekend in the city. They'd stayed at the Waldorf Hotel, where they'd waltzed to Eddie Duchin's orchestra. Doris allowed her gaze to alight on a photo of the two of them taken many years later on their silver anniversary. Both stout and gray, Ted's defeated eyes—he'd been diagnosed with emphysema shortly thereafter—showing no memory of that enchanted evening of dancing and champagne.

A line from a poem drifted into her head: *Allow not love to wither like summer bounty left unplucked.* If she'd been prone to such fanciful turns of phrase, she'd have told her daughters to heed that advice. Trish, with her silly pretensions about that selfish boob she was supposedly engaged to, who had as much intention of marrying her as of buying the gas station where he pumped his gas. And Mary Catherine—dear Lord, what would she have told her eldest?

*I was wrong about Charlie. He's a good man.*

When the phone began ringing again, Doris started, lurching unsteadily as she reached to answer it. "Hello?" Her voice was thin and querulous; the receiver huge and clumsy in her hand.

"Mrs. Quinn? Oh, thank goodness! I was about to give up." The girlish voice at the other end was high pitched with relief. "Did I wake you?"

"I was lying down. Just resting my eyes," Doris was quick to add. "Who is this?"

"Bronwyn. Bronwyn Jeffers." As if there could be another girl with such an unlikely name in all of Schoharie County.

Doris felt a stab of irritation that she'd been dragged out of bed for nothing. "If you're looking for Noelle, I'm afraid she's stepped out."

"Do you know when she'll be back?"

"Oh, anytime now, I should think. She's just next door. Why don't you call back in a few minutes?"

The girl hesitated. "I hate to put you to the trouble, Mrs. Quinn, but do you think you could get her for me? I wouldn't ask, except...well, it's important."

Just how important could it be? With sixteen-year-old girls there was only one thing important enough to drag some perfectly innocent person to the phone: boyfriend troubles. Doris grew even more irritated. "Like I said, she'll be back any moment. It can wait until then, can't it?"

"Actually it's more of an emergency." The girl really *did* sound desperate.

Doris straightened. "Well, for heaven's sake, why didn't you say so in the first place?"

"It could be life or death. Please, Mrs. Quinn," Bronwyn pleaded.

A picture of Noelle's half sister formed in Doris's mind: a honey-skinned girl, all legs and hair. Charlie's girl, through and through. No, of course she wouldn't be making this up. Doris brought a trembling hand to her throat.

"Hold on," she said. "I'll go get her..."

Doris, her heart beating much too fast, placed the receiver on the table and turned to grasp hold of the banister. She was halfway down the stairs when all at once they seemed to slide out from under her like a steep, pebbled incline giving way. She cried out, more in surprise than in fear, skidding the last half dozen steps on her backside before landing with a horrid thump on the floor below. There was a dull crunch, like a bone snapping. A searing pain flashed through her. She mewed weakly, unable to manage more than that. Waves of grayness lapped over her, and there was a high ringing in her ears, like when a TV station signed off for the night. Then she, too, slipped into oblivion.

The moment she stepped through the back door, Noelle sensed something amiss. The house was quiet, too quiet. Even the air seemed to swirl about her like dust motes in the wake of a sudden exit. "Nana?" she called out, lowering her grocery sack full of fresh-picked zucchini onto the kitchen counter.

No answer, just the radio playing softly.

*You're being paranoid,* she told herself. It couldn't have been more than half an hour at most since she'd gone next door. What could have happened in so short a time? Even so, she wished that she hadn't given in when Mrs. Inklepaugh plied her with coffee and cake, then insisted on loading her up with more squash than they could possibly eat in a month.

Noelle wondered idly if her grandmother still had that recipe for zucchini bread. She could make an extra loaf for Hank. He'd appreciate it, she thought. On the other hand, she wouldn't want him to be reminded of all those cakes and casseroles left on his doorstep by lonely ladies with marriage on their mi—

A sudden noise caused Noelle to freeze. "Nana?" she called again. Suppose it wasn't her grandmother? Suppose it was Robert lying in wait?

There it was again. It sounded like a moan. Noelle, heart in throat, dashed out into the hall. She was rounding the corner into the front entry when she spied her grandmother, crumpled at the foot of the stairs like a carelessly discarded coat.

Noelle collapsed onto knees gone suddenly boneless. Nana was unconscious, her face a waxy grayish white, but her eyelids were fluttering. She wasn't dead. A wave of relief swept through Noelle.

"Nana, don't move. I'm going to call Hank." The calmness with which she spoke surprised her; she was trembling so badly she didn't know how she was going to stand, much less climb the stairs to the phone.

But somehow she summoned the strength, only to find the phone on the landing mysteriously off the hook. Nana must have tried to reach her at the Inklepaughs', then forgotten to hang up; she was getting so forgetful these days. Noelle thumbed the switch hook and quickly punched in Hank's number.

His nurse receptionist, Diane Blaylock, blessedly wasted no time in putting him on. When Noelle told him why she was calling— once more surprised by the steadiness of her voice, which was in direct contrast with the hammering of her heart—he was quick to take charge.

"Don't try to move her," he cautioned. "She may have broken something. Just stay put until I get there."

Hank arrived minutes later accompanied by several firemen. Noelle had left the front door open, and when he dashed in, still in his white coat with his tie askew, she nearly wept with relief. He knelt at once to take her grandmother's pulse and gently probe for anything that might be broken.

"You're going to be all right, Doris," he murmured soothingly. "You've taken a bad tumble, that's all." Hank gestured at the strapping firemen standing by with a gurney.

Nana groaned, struggling toward consciousness. "No...hospital," she muttered thickly. "Got to find my grand—Noelle? Noelle, honey, where are you?"

"I'm right here, Nana," Noelle called from a few feet away.

"Emergency..." Nana's eyes rolled in fear, eyelids fluttering.

Hank patted her hand reassuringly. "Yes, we're taking you to the emergency room, Doris, but don't worry. I'll make sure they don't keep you any longer than absolutely necessary."

"No...please...have to tell Noelle..."

He produced a syringe. "I'm giving you a little something for the pain. Just relax. In a minute you won't feel a thing."

Noelle watched her grandmother's eyes drift shut. An immense gratitude welled up in her. It was as if all her adult life she'd been looking through the wrong end of a telescope and was now seeing the man she should have been married to all along. A man in wrinkled chinos and a plaid shirt missing a button who wasn't the least bit suave or fashionable but who was worth ten of any movie star you'd care to name. When he glanced up to fix her with his warm tea brown gaze, she thought with a pang of regret, *I'd have you in a minute,*

*Hank Reynolds...if my world would just hold still long enough for you to hop on.*

The irony was that today was her anniversary. She hadn't remembered until just this morning when it had occurred to her, in the midst of brushing her teeth, that nine years ago she'd been blissfully preparing for a wedding without the slightest notion of what she was getting into.

Hank insisted on driving her to the hospital in Schenectady. "Think of it as a favor to me," he said, gently but firmly pulling the car keys from her hand.

"What about your other patients?" she asked.

"Diane can hold the fort down until I get back."

Noelle was climbing into her Volvo when she heard the phone begin to ring inside the house. It had been ringing off and on for the past ten or fifteen minutes, but she hadn't bothered to answer it. And she wasn't going to now. Whoever it was would just have to call back. Putting it out of her mind, she closed her eyes and said a little prayer that her grandmother would be all right.

Before long Hank and she were racing north on the interstate as fast as the speed limit would allow. They arrived at the hospital just as Nana was being wheeled out of Radiology, still groggy and muttering something incoherent about Bronwyn, of all people. Noelle was relieved to note, though, that the color was back in her cheeks and even more relieved when the resident on call informed her that her grandmother was suffering from nothing worse than a slight concussion and a cracked rib.

Hank stayed until she was comfortably installed in a semiprivate room before reluctantly taking his leave. Monday evenings he made his rounds at the Sunshine Nursing Home, he explained, and if he didn't go now, he'd be late.

Noelle insisted he take her car. She'd catch a ride back with her mother, she said. But he wouldn't hear of it. When his cab arrived, Hank gave her a quick, hard squeeze, murmuring, "Call me when you get home, okay? No matter how late it is."

"You got it." She kissed him on the mouth. Here, where no one knew them from Adam, there was nothing to prevent her from doing so.

It was well after dark by the time her mother and aunt arrived at the hospital. Trish had spent the better part of the day at a book fair up in Saratoga Springs, and Mary had been out and about all afternoon, tracking down various friends of Buck Van Doren—to no avail apparently. Of course it was the one time her cell phone battery had chosen to die.

They walked in to find Nana fast asleep, with Noelle nodding off in a chair at her side. Yawning, she rose to greet them.

"She's fine. Just a little bruised and shook

up. The doctor said she could go home tomorrow." Noelle kept her voice low so as not to wake her grandmother.

"Go home and get some rest, honey," Mary told her. "We'll stay a while in case she wakes up."

Noelle glanced at her watch, surprised to see that it was close to ten. "I should wait. Nana was really worked up about something. She kept muttering that I had to call Bronwyn—that it was important."

"You know how confused she gets. I'm sure it was nothing." Aunt Trish took her arm and steered her toward the door. "If she wakes up, we'll explain that you had to leave. Your mother's right—you should get some rest, or *you'll* be the one in need of medical attention."

Noelle thought of Hank and wondered if that would be so terrible.

Mary accompanied her out into the corridor. The strain of the last few weeks was beginning to show on her as well. She looked drawn, her eyes faintly bloodshot. She brought a hand up to stroke Noelle's hair lightly. "Drive carefully, okay?"

She sounded just like Nana. *One day I'll be telling Emma the same thing.* Noelle felt a pang at the thought.

It was a quarter to eleven by the time she pulled into her grandmother's driveway. An accident on the interstate had left several lanes blocked, adding a good half hour to her trip. She was climbing the steps to the house, so wiped out all she could think of was getting out of her sweaty clothes and into bed, when a dark figure loomed from the shadows at the farthest end of the porch. Noelle let out a strangled cry.

"Relax. It's only me." Bronwyn stepped into the feeble glow of the porch light.

Noelle dropped into the wicker chair by the door, a hand pressed to her wildly bucking heart. "You scared me half to death!"

"Sorry. I didn't mean to spook you." Wearing a faintly sheepish look, Bronwyn sank into the chair beside hers. "I tried calling, but you weren't home. I've been trying for *hours*."

"My grandmother fell and hurt herself. I was at the hospital."

"Oh, my God." Her sister looked as stricken as if she'd caused it. "Is she—I mean, she's going to be all right, isn't she?"

"Luckily, it's just a cracked rib. She's coming home tomorrow." Noelle suddenly remembered the phone that had been ringing when she left, and Nana's incoherent muttering at the hospital. "What's so important it couldn't wait until morning?"

"Remember Dante, the guy I told you about? The one I'm seeing?" Bronwyn leaned forward in her urgency.

"The guy you're sneaking around with behind Dad's back, you mean," Noelle corrected.

"Don't be snotty," Bronwyn growled. "This is *serious*."

"You're not going to give me that cloak-and-dagger rap again, I hope." Noelle felt a chill edge up her spine nonetheless. It was easy to joke, but since finding out about Corinne and Buck it hadn't been so easy to dismiss her own growing fears. She could well imagine the teenage Robert attacking his girlfriend in a fit of jealous rage . . . just as she could imagine him coming after *her*.

"Dante knows things," Bronwyn persisted.

"What things?"

Bronwyn leaned close, her dark eyes pooled with shadow. "Whoever broke Dad's windows and trashed that church is planning something even worse for tonight."

"Why are you telling *me* all this? Why not go straight to Dad?"

Her sister's shoulders sagged. "If I did that, I'd have to tell him *everything*. Once the cat is out of the bag about Dante, I'll be grounded for the rest of my life."

"If what you're saying is true, don't you think it's worth the risk?"

"That's just the thing. I have no way of knowing if it *is* true."

"Well, what am *I* supposed to do about it?" There were times Noelle honestly couldn't believe the things that came out of her sister's mouth.

"We can't go to the police," Bronwyn said.

"That's for sure." Noelle rolled her eyes.

"I suppose the *safe* thing would be to bury our heads in the sand and hope nothing comes of it." Bronwyn began to chew on her thumbnail, an old childhood habit. The crafty expression she wore was equally familiar. "On the other hand, what if we could catch the guy in the act?"

"You mean Robert? He wouldn't be stupid enough to get his hands dirty," Noelle scoffed.

"One of his goons then."

"You've seen too many movies." Noelle reached over to give her hair a playful yank. "Anyway, let's say we manage to catch this goon in the act of—whatever. What proof would we have? It'd be our word against his."

"I thought of that, too." Bronwyn bent down to retrieve something from her backpack. Dad's video camera, Noelle saw. "We get the guy on tape, then show it to the state police in Albany. With this kind of evidence, they'd get a confession out of him in no time."

"Oh, great. Now we're Cagney and Lacey."

"Who?"

"Never mind. Where is all this supposedly taking place, anyway? Do you even know *that*?"

"The Methodist church out on Grand-view."

Noelle sat upright, suddenly interested. Robert's parents belonged to United Methodist. It was where she and Robert had gotten married. It was also where Buck was buried, in the Van Doren family plot.

Coincidence? Maybe, but if that was the case it was one coincidence too many. A good reporter, she knew, would see this as cause for investigation, if nothing more. Still, she hesitated. Something just didn't feel right.

"Did it ever occur to you that *we* might get caught?" she asked. "If this guy, whoever he is, works for Robert we could be putting ourselves into a dangerous situation."

"You want Emma back, don't you?"

Anger rose in Noelle, quick and hot. "I won't even dignify that with an answer."

"Look, I'm sorry, but don't you *see*? This could be your one opportunity to pin something on that creep. Think how you'll feel if you don't take advantage of it."

Bronwyn's words hit home. How *would* she feel?

Hugging herself, she stared out at the lighted windows up and down the street, standing out in the darkness like beacons of sanity. What would the neighbors think if they were to eavesdrop on this conversation? Nice, ordinary people who might cluck in sympathy at the faces of missing kids on milk cartons but otherwise give little thought to one of their own being taken from them. People who went to work and came home and ate supper in front of the TV, who joked about dryers that ate socks without the capacity to imagine how they'd feel if a whole chunk of their life were suddenly to vanish.

Abruptly she stood up, propelled to her feet by a sudden surge of adrenaline. She grabbed her sister's backpack and slung it over her shoulder. When Bronwyn didn't immediately jump up—too stunned no doubt— she barked, "Well, what are you waiting for?"

The United Methodist Church was all the way out on South Grandview, a mile and a half from where Grandview Avenue proper ended and the road began its meandering journey into the hills around Windy Ridge. Built in the late 1800s, it might have served as the model for the churches you saw scattered throughout New England: sturdy white clapboard with a steeple from which a bell tolled the hours on Sunday. Alongside a red-brick path flanked by neatly mown grass, a spotlit bulletin board encased in glass held an announcement of upcoming services and special events. As the two women approached on foot, having cautiously parked the Volvo a quarter of a mile or so down the road, Noelle's eye fell on the large block letters spelling out the spiritual message of the week: RUNNING ON EMPTY? STOP IN FOR A FILL-UP.

She indulged in a small, grim smile. *Well, Lord,* she thought with a certain macabre appreciation, *it looks like I've come to the right place.* Whatever came of tonight's expedition, she wouldn't walk away empty-handed.

She recalled the services she and Robert had attended with his parents. In her drinking years it was the only time she could sit and reflect in peace on the muddle she'd made of her life. Later, after she'd gotten sober, she was glad simply for the chance to rest her mind and spirit after the endless, numbing rounds of dinners and cocktail parties. Another, less comforting thought crept in. *Wasn't there a part of you that liked it, too? The rosy picture it made, you and your handsome, successful husband seated beside his socially prominent parents.*

Robert wasn't entirely to blame for the sham of their marriage, she thought. Hadn't she bought into the myth—lock, stock, and barrel? The quietly toiling office Cinderella plucked from obscurity by her handsome, much older boss. Transformed overnight from an ordinary young woman leading an ordinary life into a fairy princess.

But as long as she'd had Emma, none of it had been wasted. There could be no regrets. And if tonight's mission, however foolhardy, put her one step closer to her child, then the risk would have been worthwhile.

She glanced about, struck by how cinematic it was: the deserted church, the full moon, the low-lying mist courtesy of God's special effects department. Imagine Lacey finding out what she'd been up to tonight; her lawyer would think her certifiable. She wouldn't be too far off the mark, either.

A narrower path led alongside the church to the field out back. In the misty moonlight, amid pale spears of grass, the faint outline of the original church, which had burned down sometime in the mid-1800s, could still be seen. Golden yarrow and Queen Anne's lace had sprung up between the ancient moss-covered stones, and wild raspberries formed a tangled shroud over what was left of chimney.

The title of one of the Nancy Drew books she'd foolishly passed on to Bronwyn came to mind now: *The Clue in the Crumbling Wall.* Yes, that's what this was, she thought, something even sillier than a movie, a Nancy Drew novel. She suppressed a giggle. If she started to laugh, she wasn't sure she'd be able to stop.

Fifty feet or so beyond the ruins of the old church, a dirt path sloped up to a clearing enclosed by a low wrought-iron fence. The graveyard was well maintained and normally wouldn't have struck Noelle as spooky. But before this she'd only seen it in broad daylight. Now, in the moonlight, the shadows that had slipped out from under headstones and obelisks wreathed in mist made it look menacing somehow.

She shivered. A breeze smelling faintly of pine rattled the leaves of the densely packed trees overhead. She remembered that the church bordered on state forestland. Anyone who could have heard them shout for help was miles away.

Turning to Bronwyn, she whispered, "Suddenly this doesn't seem like such a great idea."

Her sister shrugged. "The best ones never do."

"I hope you remembered to put a tape in that thing." She tapped the video camera in Bronwyn's hand, thinking, *Great. A home movie of two women scared out of their wits.*

"Shh. They might hear us."

*Who* might hear them? This place was as silent as the—

Noelle thought better of completing the thought.

Bronwyn took her hand, gripping it tightly. Together they started up the path. Crickets chirped in the tall grass, and tiny night insects could be seen glimmering in the moonlight that fell in broad bands between clumps of barberry and low-growing shrubs. A picture flashed through Noelle's mind of her sister at nine, standing stiffly beside her mother's freshly dug grave: a skinny little thing with huge eyes, her small dark head drooping on the pale stalk of her neck.

Up close the graveyard seemed less creepy than it had from a distance. Maybe it was because she saw no evidence of Robert's dogsbodies...and frankly doubted they'd show. Or maybe it was just that part of her— the part that jumped at sudden noises and walked more quickly down darkened streets— had simply shut down like an engine on overload. The mind's version of an arm or leg falling asleep, when all that was left was the queer prickle signaling the return of feeling.

She looked about. At its farthest reaches the graveyard was steeped in shadow cast by the trees that crowded up against the fence, dense and black as a fortress. But the headstones that were visible were well kept, most adorned with flowers and wreaths. You could tell a lot about a dead person, Noelle thought, by how conscientiously his or her grave was tended. Especially if the date on the headstone was a recent one. The most lovingly looked after, and saddest, were those of young children. Briefly she played her flashlight over a polished granite plaque inscribed with:

DEAREST DAUGHTER THOU HAS LEFT US
AND THY LOSS WE DEEPLY FEEL
BUT GOD WHO HATH BEREFT US
CAN OUR SORROWS HEAL

The bedtime prayer Nana used to recite with her when she was a child came to mind now. *If I should die before I wake, I pray the Lord my soul to take.* Noelle shuddered. What a ghastly thing to teach a child: that you could go to sleep and not wake up. No wonder she'd had nightmares.

Beside her Bronwyn let out a strangled squeak. "Did you hear that?"

"Hear what?" Noelle clicked off the flashlight.

"It sounded like it was coming from over there." She pointed toward the dense thicket to their right. But Noelle saw nothing, and the only sound she heard was the hooting of an owl.

The tiny hairs on the back of her neck were standing up nonetheless. "I've seen enough," she hissed. "Unless your idea of fun is sticking around all night and getting eaten alive by mosquitoes."

Her sister had cried wolf once too often. Noelle knew it wasn't malicious. Bronwyn's imagination was like the book she'd read aloud to Emma so many times its binding had come loose, *Where the Wild Things Are*. A forest swarming with boogeymen and monsters.

"I *swear* I heard something." Bronwyn's eyes were black as the surrounding shadows. "Are you sure you didn't hear it?"

"The only thing I'm sure of is that we're acting like a couple of idiots." Noelle, more annoyed at herself than at her sister, started back the way they'd come.

The gate creaked loudly as she was letting herself out, making her think of the grange hall that every year on Halloween, as far back as she could remember, was made over into a haunted house. *There's nothing to be afraid of,* she used to tell herself. *It's all fake. Just a bunch of fake skeletons and fake blood and noises on a tape recorder.*

But there was nothing fake about this graveyard.

Just then a sudden movement by the fence caused her to jerk about. But it was only a tree limb swaying in the breeze, she saw. Something below it caught her eye: a mound of dirt half obscured by shadow that could have come only from a freshly dug grave. The prickling sensation in her head grew stronger, like circulation returning to a deadened limb. *They're all buried here,* she recalled. *Not just Buck. His whole family, going back generations. Over there, under those trees.*

When she opened her mouth to call to Bronwyn, only a dry croak emerged. She cast a panicked glance over her shoulder. But her sister, who a moment ago had been right behind her, was nowhere to be seen. There were only the headstones, staring back at her in blank disregard. Terror rose in Noelle like a solid thing rushing at her out of the darkness. She told herself, *The shadows are playing tricks on me. She's there; she's got to be there.*

Every instinct screamed at her to run, but she found herself moving like a sleepwalker instead, drawn in the direction of the Van Doren family plot. It was as if she were underwater, drifting amid the sunken remains of a lost civilization. In the dappled moonlight she floated past the plain, lichen-encrusted headstone of Jacob Van Doren, born 1775, died 1850. A stonemason, some distant part of her brain recalled. She noted the graves of Jacob's wife and children before pausing at a marble monument flanked by stone urns, far too grand for this simple graveyard, one that could belong only to Thomas Van Doren, Robert's great-grandfather. A cold-hearted man according to local legend, responsible for the deaths of six workers who'd been crushed when the substandard scaffolding on one of his buildings collapsed.

Then something wrong, something that jolted her. Here and there headstones had been cracked in two as if with a sledgehammer, leaving chunks of granite scattered amid the grass, their jagged edges gleaming white as bone. A stone figure lay toppled on its side, the statue of a little girl cuddling a dog: Robert's great-aunt Martha, who at thirteen had been run over by a drunken Fuller brush salesman driving a Packard, and whose beloved Scottie, MacPherson, died from a broken heart (or so it was told) not more than a month later.

Noelle came to a stop before the freshly dug grave she'd glimpsed from the path. Who in Robert's family had died recently? His ailing uncle Pete from Providence? His sickly cousin in New Haven?

Then her eyes fell on something protruding from the freshly turned earth: the rotting remains of a coffin. Her heart began a long slow-motion free fall. *God, dear God.* She didn't want to know whose coffin it was, oh, how she didn't want to, but she knew all the same. Her gaze was inexorably drawn to the headstone jutting at an angle alongside it, on which was carved:

JAMES BUCHANAN VAN DOREN
1948–1969

A cry lodged in her windpipe like something swallowed the wrong way. Suddenly she couldn't breathe. She felt as if she were choking.

Then she *did* hear something. It might have been the rustling of leaves overhead or a field mouse scampering among the dry twigs that littered the ground. "Bron?" she croaked. "Bron, is that you?"

A sudden movement out of the corner of her eye. A twig snapping that definitely was *not* a mouse. She spun about, her heart boomeranging in her chest. In the darkness her head smacked up against a low-hanging branch. A cracking blow that delivered a lightning flash of startled pain—anger, too, at her clumsiness—followed by a crimson-spotted darkness that skated lazily before her eyes. She was dimly aware of crumpling to the ground. Then the branch spoke.

Through the roaring in her ears, Noelle was surprised to hear a voice that sounded very much like Robert's say mildly, "Happy anniversary, darling."

# Chapter Seventeen

Five miles away, in the two-story building housing the *Register,* where several of the newly replaced ground-floor windows still bore strips of masking tape, Charlie Jeffers looked up from the article he'd been proofreading to note with surprise that it was nearly midnight. He glanced at the clock on the wall to see if the one on his desk was correct. How had it gotten to be so late? Bronwyn must be wondering what was keeping him. She might even have tried to reach him, but at this hour the switchboard took all incoming calls. He was picking up the phone when Tim Washburn, the new security guard, tapped on the door. Charlie looked up to find the retired county sheriff, a middle-aged man built square as a juggernaut, peering in through the glass partition.

"Sorry to bother you, Mr. Jeffers, but there's a young fella outside wanting to see you. I told him it was kinda late, but he was real insistent." Washburn's small mouth, bracketed by fleshy jowls, made no secret of his disapproval.

Charlie scrubbed his face with an open hand. He was tired. He was also accustomed to oddballs showing up at all hours, claiming to have spotted anything from an alien spaceship to some guy they swore was the spitting image of James Dean (never mind that Dean, were he alive, would be an old man by now). One of the jobs of the two-man skeleton crew that worked the nine to midnight shift was fielding such "hot" news tips. He'd have Freddy Slater handle this one. Freddy had been on staff nearly as long as Charlie had. He'd seen and heard it all.

"Did he say what it was about?" Charlie asked.

"No, just his name." The guard scratched the back of his neck, where a thick fold of flesh was covered in a fine, furlike stubble. "Dante Lo Presti. You know the guy?"

Charlie felt his exhaustion drop away, replaced by an odd, buzzing energy. "Yeah, I know him. It's okay, you can bring him on up, Tim."

He watched the blue-uniformed guard lumber off through the newsroom, which was deserted except for where Freddy's and Greg's computer screens glowed. His mind raced. When Dante Lo Presti was arrested, he'd sworn he was innocent...and Charlie believed him. Not, as he'd told Mary, because the kid was so squeaky clean, but because to his reporter's nose it had the smell of a frame-up.

What Dante *was* guilty of, though, was sniffing around his daughter.

Bronwyn had told him she wasn't seeing the boy, and Charlie had taken her at her word. But suppose she was lying? He'd be forced to take action. And that, he knew, would serve only to make Dante Lo Presti even more irresistible. Which could lead to...well, God knew what. The memory of what he and Mary had been up to at that age sent up a red emergency flare in his brain. No amount of punishment or restrictions, he thought grimly, could have kept them from one another.

A picture rose in his mind. Mary, at sixteen, her miserable expression telling him she was pregnant even before she said the words.

Jesus, was *that* what the kid wanted to see him about? Something Bronwyn couldn't bring herself to tell him? He found himself praying it had nothing to do with his daughter, that Dante was here on another matter entirely: to recant his earlier story or provide information about the real culprit behind the town's recent outbreak of vandalism. Even a holdup, Charlie thought grimly, would be preferable.

But the boy who was ushered into his office a few minutes later didn't look dangerous. Just nervous. No, more than that, *scared*. This muscle-bound eighteen-year-old who could have passed for at least three years older, wearing jeans that were too tight and a faded denim shirt with its sleeves torn off that showed his tattooed forearm. He glanced at Charlie, then away, his gaze flicking over the walls dotted with framed awards—Charlie's bronze plaque from the Lions Club alongside four years' worth of citations from the New York State Press Association—before coming to rest on a photo of Bronwyn on his desk. Charlie felt his chest tighten with a sudden, inexplicable rage.

"Have a seat," he said. It wasn't so much an offer as an order.

Clearly seeing no need for introductions, Dante dropped into the chair opposite Charlie's desk. "Mind if I smoke?"

Charlie was about to say no, but something about the boy's jitteriness made him change his mind. "Sure, go ahead."

Dante struck a match against the worn heel of a boot permanently creased at the toe. Briefly Charlie was reminded of someone he knew, but he couldn't think who. Then the kid abruptly leaned forward, bringing his forearms to rest against his knees. The cigarette tucked between the first and second fingers of his loosely cupped fist sent up a lazy curl of smoke.

"I guess you're wondering why I'm here," he said.

"The thought crossed my mind." It came out sounding more sarcastic than Charlie had intended, and he saw that it wasn't lost on the boy, whose eyes narrowed briefly.

But there was a hardened resignation in his face as well, as if Dante Lo Presti was used to being judged by men in Charlie's position. "Look, Mr. Jeffers, I wouldn't be here at all except..." He paused, dropping his head in a way that left its nape vulnerable and exposed. *Why, he's just a kid,* Charlie thought. When Dante lifted his head, Charlie noted with a small shock that his eyes were wet. "I think Bronwyn might be in trouble."

Charlie tensed. "What kind of trouble?"

"I don't know. All I know is that for the past few hours I haven't been able to reach her."

"She's home, where she always is this time of night."

Dante shook his head. "No. I even stopped by, just to be sure."

Charlie didn't ask what business it was of Dante's. He found himself volunteering instead, "She's probably at a friend's."

"Maybe, but I don't think so."

Charlie bristled at the boy's proprietary air. "Look here, mister," he said coldly, "if you have good reason to think my daughter is in any kind of trouble, you'd better spell it out right now."

Dante sat up, meeting his gaze squarely. Though Charlie caught a flicker of something he couldn't quite read, oddly, the kid

470

looked innocent of any wrongdoing. He took a hard pull off his cigarette.

"It's kind of a long story, but I'll make it short. I used to work part-time for Mr. Van Doren— odd jobs and stuff—but the thing is, I became friendly with some of his people. There's this one guy, he"— Dante broke off. "It's not important who he is. Just that he tipped me off about something going down tonight, over at the Methodist church on Grandview. Some heavy-duty shit that only the Man and one of his top people were in on."

"What does this have to do with Bronwyn?" Charlie growled.

"I let her in on it."

The tightness in Charlie's chest had become almost a cramp. So she *had* been seeing the boy, which meant she'd lied to him, god-dammit. He felt a burst of anger, and for the first time since she was little it occurred to him that his daughter might benefit from being shown the broad side of his hand.

But his sense of betrayal was quickly replaced by another, more sobering thought. What if Bronwyn *was* in some kind of danger? Lately, he'd been so caught up with Noelle he hadn't given a thought to the possibility that his younger daughter might be in jeopardy as well.

"I made her promise not to go anywhere near there," Dante went on nervously, "but, Jesus, she can be so stubborn."

The two men exchanged a knowing glance. Suddenly Charlie knew who Dante reminded him of: himself at that age. In the eyes of Mary's folks, he'd been nothing more than the kid from the wrong side of the tracks who had gotten their daughter pregnant. He thought of an expression his own mother had used often: *You can't judge a book by its cover.*

Charlie shot to his feet. "Come on, we'll take your car. You know the way, don't you?"

Dante nodded as he rose from his chair. "I towed a car once for Reverend Clifford. Brakes went out on him. Lucky bastard, he could've been killed." He followed Charlie out into the newsroom, where the staticky sizzle of the ham radio tuned to the police band seemed to carry an air of unspecified menace. Charlie felt a hand on his arm, and turned around to find Dante eyeing him quizzically. "Hey, it don't matter, but I was just wondering, why my car instead of yours?"

Charlie told him the truth. "Mine hasn't been tuned in a while. Engine's starting to knock."

No further explanation was required. Stan's Auto Repair wasn't the only shop in town, but it was the best. Dante didn't have to ask why Charlie had put off having it serviced. He merely nodded and said, "Bring it in next week. I'll have a look."

The drive out to South Grandview seemed maddeningly long but in reality took no more than fifteen minutes. Charlie was impressed by the way Dante drove, not recklessly or in any way showing off, but not purposefully cautious either. He steered his Camaro as if he'd been doing it half his life, which he probably had. Kids like Dante, he knew, were more often than not left to fend for themselves. An uncomfortable memory surfaced: He'd been fourteen, and his mother had taken him to Albany to buy school clothes. She stopped at a bar on the way home for "a quick one." Naturally she'd gotten shit-faced, and Charlie had been the one to drive them home. But the scariest part was that he'd known how.

Dante pulled to a stop in front of the church, and they got out. The night seemed very still except for the chirping of crickets and low, sibilant calls of night birds. Charlie glanced both ways down the sidewalk but saw no cars. Had Bronwyn ridden over on her bike? Unlikely. It would have been too far, especially at night. He felt stupid all of a sudden for pushing the panic button. Wouldn't it have made more sense to have phoned Maxie instead? High school best friends almost always knew where to find each other.

*Except Corinne. Mary hadn't known about Corinne.*

"Let's take a look around back," he suggested.

They cut across the lawn, the dampness of the grass seeping up through the soles of Charlie's battered bluchers. He'd had the good sense, at least, to bring a flashlight. In the field behind the church its beam caught the rusted handle of an old pump. The well must have belonged to the original church that had burned down. He'd learned what there was to know about the fire from back issues on microfiche in the newspaper's morgue. But this old place hadn't seen excitement like that in more than a century. The quiet here was so pervasive it felt like a natural element, as tangible and pure as the water once drawn from that well.

Then his gaze traveled to the small fenced-in churchyard several dozen yards up the path. He started toward it, feeling a bit foolish as he called out, "Bronwyn! Are you there? It's Daddy."

No reply. Charlie had started to turn back when he was brought to a halt by a sudden commotion up ahead, a violent rustling of leaves that made him think of a wounded deer crashing blindly through the underbrush. Then a dark figure burst from the shadows to come streaking toward him. Charlie was so startled he nearly dropped the flashlight.

In the split second before she emerged into full view, he recognized his daughter's slender build and the slight awkwardness of her gait, the result of her having been pigeon-toed as a baby. Her face glistened pale in the moonlight, and her bare arms were covered with bloody scratches. She didn't even glance at Dante. She headed straight for Charlie. Something hard inside the backpack slung over her shoulder jabbed him in the ribs as she threw herself into his arms, crying, "Daddy, oh Daddy!"

"Bron, honey, what the hell—"

She didn't let him finish. "I hid from him. In the woods. But there was no time to warn her." Her breath came in gulping bursts, her voice a high, nearly soundless shriek. "Daddy, you've got to find him. He's got Noelle!"

"Bron, what's this all about?" Charlie attempted to pry her upright, but she wouldn't let go. The same stubbornness that had brought her out here in the middle of the night was causing her to cling to him now like a terrified cat. He felt his own chest constrict with panic. "*Who's* got Noelle?"

It was Dante who answered in a flat, dead voice, "The Man."


Noelle woke to find herself lying on the ground, gazing up at the milky blind eye of the moon. On all sides was utter darkness. She groaned, rolling onto her stomach. The movement sent a spike of agony smashing through one temple and out the other. Nausea rolled up from her middle. She'd barely managed to raise herself onto all fours, wobbling like a newborn calf, when she threw up.

Lifting her head, she peered about in frightened confusion. She was in a rectangular pit as deep as a swimming pool that looked to be roughly twelve feet wide and about twice as long. But where *was* she?

Memory came sluicing back in an icy rush.

The image of Buck's violated grave rose in her mind: a horrid, gaping hole with whitish tendrils of root poking through the earth like the webbed fingers of some ghastly half-formed creature. And Robert's voice in the dark, taunting her...*Happy anniversary, darling.*

Somehow Noelle managed to struggle to her feet. With one hand braced against the damp wall of the pit, she waited until the ground beneath her had stopped swaying. She cocked her head, listening. But the only sound was the far-off whisper of the wind through the trees. If her husband was out there somewhere, he certainly wasn't making himself known.

Little by little, as her eyes adjusted to the darkness, she saw that the sides of the pit weren't entirely even. With a little luck and a lot of determination, she might be able to climb out. But what then? Was Robert up there, waiting to pounce?

Noelle broke out in a clammy sweat and felt as if she might throw up again. Her head throbbed with each tiny movement. She gingerly probed an egg-size lump on the back of her skull, wincing at its tenderness. It felt sticky. Pulling her hand away, she stared in horror at the blood smeared over her palm. In the darkness it looked black as India ink.

Reality hit home with the force of a blow. *This isn't just one of his mind-fuck games. He means business.* The thought propelled her into action. Kicking off her shoes, Noelle sought purchase in the slippery clay-like earth rising before her in what seemed an insurmountable wall and after several anxious moments at last gained a foothold on an inch or so of jutting rock. Reaching high overhead, she managed to grasp hold of a tuberous root that made her think of a thick, fleshy finger. She cringed and nearly let go but forced herself to hang on, pulling herself up, outstretched arms quivering, bare toes scrabbling for purchase, until her fingers closed over another root. Painstakingly she inched her way toward the top, the image of Buck's unearthed grave flickering behind her eyes all the while.

Was that what *this* was? A grave? *Oh, God, please no.* She was getting that grainy, loosey-goosey feeling again, as if she were going to pass out. Her head swam, and her arms and legs began to spasm uncontrollably.

With a final grunting heave, she hauled herself up over the edge and held herself braced with her elbows, feet dangling below, like a swimmer debating whether or not to climb out of the pool. Taking several deep breaths, she waited for her buzzing head to clear, then looked about to get her bearings.

In the silvery moonlight, a queer lunar landscape stretched on all sides, dotted with the huge hulking shapes of earthmovers. Gradually her eyes made out a pale stretch of dirt road and a dark line of trees in the distance. A billboard, its outline faintly illuminated, stood directly opposite the road, too far away to make out. But she didn't have to read it to know what it said:

PROJECTED SITE OF CRANBERRY MALL
OPENING NOVEMBER 2000

Other familiar landmarks began to materialize. The trailer serving as Robert's field office. A pair of Portosans. Her eyes began to pick out the individual shapes of the Cats as well. Excavators and track loaders. Bulldozers and backhoes. Graders with long-toothed blades that glittered in the moonlight.

Terror beat like a heart at the center of a vast numbness. *I'm not alone,* she thought. *He's out there somewhere.* She felt it in each of the tiny hairs prickling on the back of her neck and in her innermost belly, where the seat of all true knowledge lies. It didn't matter that she couldn't see him. That was the whole point, wasn't it? To trick her into believing she was alone, that all she had to do was walk to the highway and thumb a ride from the first good Samaritan to happen along.

*But you don't know that for* sure, a voice reasoned. *You've been wrong about other things. You could be wrong about this, too.*

It occurred to her then that there might be another means of escape.

Speculatively she eyed a Cat—a full-load track excavator—parked not more than a dozen yards away, beside the dune-size mound of dirt dug from the pit. Metal rungs led up to the cab that was perched on the flat box of its chassis like the glass lookout in a watchtower. Aeons ago, when she'd worked for Van Doren & Sons, one of her duties had been to fill out the order forms for replacement parts. She'd forgotten most of what she'd known, retaining random bits of information that were mostly useless. She knew, for instance, that the largest Cats weighed over three hundred tons and that the grease required to keep behemoths that size running made them prone to engine fires. (Robert had once likened the operating of such machinery to the handling of a very large incendiary device.) But she'd never actually operated one. Why would she have? Back then, if some fortune-teller had predicted that her life would one day depend on it, she'd have laughed at the absurdity.

But it was no laughing matter now.

Still, how difficult could it be? The keys were usually left in the ignition; who in his right mind would be stupid enough to imagine he could get away with stealing an earthmover? From Robert, of all people. As for which gears operated what, it wouldn't take a degree in engineering to figure out.

*You think it's as easy as flicking a few toggle switches? Honey, your little sister isn't the only one who's seen too many movies,* mocked a cynical voice in her head. A voice she recognized as her husband's. Robert, who'd spent nine years trying to cut her down to size, trying to make her believe her ambitions were less than worthless, laughable, really.

Anger rose in Noelle, momentarily eclipsing her fear. *I don't have to listen to him anymore,* she told herself. *I never had to. It was just that I didn't see it until—*

A shadow fell. And a voice from the darkness slid over her like icy water. "Tell me, darling. Did you *really* think you could get away

479

with it?" Robert's voice; only it was no longer in her head.

Noelle was so startled, her elbows collapsed under her like a rickety lawn chair, and in a hail of loose dirt she went sliding back down to land at the bottom of the pit with a jarring thud. She lay there a moment, struggling to catch her breath, too stunned to move.

*Get up,* a voice ordered. *Get up while you still can.*

Noelle scrambled to her feet, her head thumping painfully but her backside mercifully numb from the impact. Dizzy and disoriented, she peered up at the silhouette framed against the starry sky.

Fury seized her. A fury so great it didn't seem possible her flimsy frame could contain it. *"You fucking bastard!"* she screamed with such force that the tendons in her neck felt as though they might pop right through her skin like stays from a shirt collar.

Suddenly she understood. Why he'd let her climb to the top. Why he hadn't tied her up before she regained consciousness. Like a cat with a mouse, he'd wanted her to think escape was possible. It was all part of the game. Robert *enjoyed* tormenting her.

"Such language." His long shadow, angled over the edge of the pit, swayed from side to side as he shook his head in dismay. "But it shouldn't surprise me. I knew what you were when I married you. Trash, that's what you are. Irish lace curtain trash, just like the rest of your family."

Noelle felt very small all of a sudden, a tiny speck swallowed up by the deep pit and the star-strewn universe that arched overhead. "Why are you doing this?" she cried. "Isn't it enough that you've taken my child?"

"*Your* child?" She caught a flash of teeth, a hellish version of the charming, devil-may-care grin that had so captivated her as a naïve young woman. "I'm afraid that's not the issue here. As far as I'm concerned, all that's been settled."

"You think so? Well, you're wrong," she shot back, trembling so hard she could barely stand. "You might get away with it here in Burns Lake, but there are higher courts. I'll fight you, Robert. And I'll keep on fighting you. Even if it takes years."

"Well, then, maybe I can spare both of us that ordeal. Not to mention the legal bills," he added in a voice rich with amusement.

*He's going to kill me.* The thought sliced through her anger, clear and indisputable as something she'd known all along. Perhaps deep down she had.

She shuddered, gripped with terror, not so much for herself as for her daughter. *What will happen to Emma if I'm not around to protect her?* "You're crazy," she told him. She'd sensed it, sure, but its full scope hadn't struck her until now. Not just the controlling, unscrupulous kind. But crazy as in Son of Sam. The kind of crazy that would think nothing of murdering a girlfriend...or wife.

A low, disembodied chuckle. "I suppose

you'd be one to judge, wouldn't you, darling? You didn't spend six months in the nuthouse for nothing."

She could see where this was leading and refused to take the bait.

"What were you doing at the cemetery tonight?" Her voice quavered, and she hated herself for that. For letting him see how scared she was.

"I could ask the same of you."

"There are still a few people left in this town who aren't on your payroll," she informed him, not without a small degree of satisfaction. "One of them tipped me off."

"I could get you to tell me who, but it doesn't matter. Not anymore." Robert sounded distracted, almost as if talking to himself. "Tomorrow morning, when the good Reverend Clifford makes his rounds, he'll discover that the miscreants who've been causing such a ruckus around town, not to mention pushing up insurance rates, have left their mark on *his* hallowed ground as well. There'll be a police report, of course. And a sermon on Sunday about the sad decay of morality among today's youth. The good reverend should know. He has a special interest in little boys. One seventh-grade boy in particular, one of his choristers, Jeff Norword's kid." She caught another glimpse of his gloating grin and felt her stomach roll. "You'd be surprised how much I know, darling. Your doctor friend, for instance. I know all about you and him. I have just one question: are you fucking him?"

"Stop it! *Just stop it*!" She brought her fists to her ears, beating softly as if to drive his words from her head.

"My guess is you are." Robert continued in that horrid, disembodied voice. "You might've been fucking him all along, for all I know. All that sanctimonious crap about me and Jeanine, but you're no better than that trampy little sister of yours."

Noelle's head jerked up. "What have you done with Bronwyn?" she demanded in a shrill voice scarcely recognizable as her own. "If you've hurt her, I swear, I'll—"

"What? Have me arrested?" His laugh took on a mean, grating edge. "Don't worry. I have no interest in what she may or may not have seen. Who'd believe her anyway? They'd say she was just lying to protect her grease monkey boyfriend."

Hanging tightly to the frayed rope of her sanity, Noelle pointed out reasonably, "Then you don't have to worry about me either. I'm just another drunk who's fallen off the wagon, remember?"

Robert fell silent, and for a wild moment she imagined he was going to let her go, let her climb out of here and walk to the road. She pictured herself doing just that, hitching a ride, and if none came along, hoofing it to the nearest pay phone, where she would call Hank. His dear face floated into her mind; his kind brown eyes and the lines in his freckled cheeks that deepened into grooves when he smiled.

Then Robert spoke. "It's different. With you, it's personal." His voice was no longer bemused. He sounded not so much angry as...cold. The kind of cold that leaves hinges frozen shut and car engines unable to start.

Noelle instinctively began to back away, a shopworn line popping into her mind: *Well, it's been nice chatting with you, but I really must be going.* Weak laughter bubbled up her throat. Laughter that was knocked out of her when she bumped up against the solid wall of earth.

"You really *are* crazy," she told him.

This time he didn't disagree. "It's a shame, really," he said, regretfully almost. "It didn't have to be this way. I even had your anniversary present all picked out. A diamond pendant. Far too expensive, of course, but...nine years, I wanted you to have something special to remember it by."

"I have Emma."

At once she realized it was the wrong thing to have said. The shadow above her shifted, and Robert's face loomed suddenly, shockingly, into view. Noelle let out an involuntary little cry. She'd expected a monster, but it was only her husband. Smoothly expressionless and not without a measure of charm.

"You're wrong about that, too," he said.

In her desperation, Noelle took a wild gamble. "You might think you've won, Robert, but little girls grow up. She'll see you for who you are. Then *you'll* be left out in the cold."

She knew immediately that she'd struck a nerve. "You lying bitch. You don't know what you're talking about," he snarled. "Why couldn't you have left well enough alone? It wasn't enough you dragged your own family into it. You had to drag my mother in as well."

In her mind Noelle once again saw the rotting coffin beside his brother's open grave. "There's something I still don't understand," she ventured, desperate to keep him talking, to keep him from focusing on what he was going to do to *her*. "Why *Buck*?"

There was a beat, then Robert replied simply, "He deserved it."

She felt a moment of confusion. Then with a jolt the connection was made. Suddenly, horribly, it all made sense. *It wasn't Corinne he murdered. It was Buck.* That's why he'd dug up his brother's grave: to get rid of the evidence. And why he'd had his men trash the warehouse and that other graveyard—to make it look like just another random act of vandalism. Robert must have sensed they were closing in, that the inquiries her parents had made into Corinne's death, and possible exhumation, would eventually lead to Buck.

*His own brother.*

It must have been violent, she thought. Something so violent that even after all these years an autopsy would reveal it. She remembered her father's commenting just the other day, *They've made amazing strides in forensic medicine. Who knows what might turn up?* But he'd been talking about Corinne, not Buck. Without any of them realizing it, they'd stumbled on to the source of Robert's paranoia.

Noelle's mind processed all this calmly, like a prosecutor laying out facts for a jury. At the same time she recognized her mental detachment for what it was, the onset of hysteria. She thought: *A man who could murder his brother is capable of anything. Anything at all.* And something even worse: *I was married to this man. I bore his child.*

She glanced up to find that Robert had retreated from view. Was he gone for good? It seemed almost impossible to believe. But hope rose in her nonetheless, like crabgrass pushing its way up through a sidewalk.

With a cry she once more launched herself against the side of the pit. Wildly this time, roots breaking off in her hands, chunks of clayey earth dissolving under her blindly scrabbling feet. Incredibly, she'd nearly succeeded in scaling the wall—a good fifteen feet of crumbling dirt—when she heard the deep rumble of the Cat's engine firing to life.

Some instinct made her look down just then. A quick assessment of how far she'd climbed…or a sixth sense perhaps. That was when she saw it, half obscured by the shadows at one end of the pit: a skull.

It gaped up at her from atop a dirty tarp that had come unwrapped. Scattered alongside it were bones the color of old, rust-stained adobe. The dirt-clotted sickle of a mandible; a strip of rotted cloth, which she recognized with a sickening jolt as the remains of a necktie.

The hysteria glinting in the depths of her

mind rocketed to the surface. Noelle opened her mouth to let out a scream. But before any sound could emerge from her parched throat, the heavens opened up and a torrent of earth rained down.

$\mathcal{I}$t was shortly past midnight by the time Mary arrived home. She wasn't surprised to find the house dark. Noelle would be in bed by now, and to judge by how exhausted she'd looked, no doubt fast asleep. Letting herself in the front door, she flicked on the light, squinting at the sudden brightness. The long drive back had left her tired out as well. Naturally, Doris hadn't helped. Just as she and Trish were about to leave, their mother had put up a fuss with the nurse, and it was some time before they could get her settled down and back to sleep.

Mary was halfway up the stairs, shoes in hand so as not to wake Noelle, when she heard the knock at the front door.

She froze, her heart racing. Her first thought was that it had to be one of Robert's henchmen. She imagined a burly guy in a ski mask, wielding a gun or a knife, and she glanced about for a weapon of her own, something heavy enough to hit him over the head with.

Then came Charlie's voice, muffled by the door: "Mary, it's me. Open up."

She sagged with relief, her knees buckling slightly as she padded back down the stairs. Charlie, dear Charlie. Somehow he'd known she needed him. He must have been waiting outside in his car; she just hadn't seen him. Wasn't that just like him? Over the years, when embittered single friends griped that knights in shining armor were but a myth, she'd always suppressed a secret little smile. Because she'd known better, you see. Even with other men, she'd think of Charlie. How whenever they were caught in the rain, he'd take off his jacket and drape it over her...as unthinkingly as he might have popped open an umbrella. And how at night he always remembered to turn over on his stomach so she wouldn't be kept awake by his snoring. Little courtesies, sure. But they signified so much.

Yet when she threw open the door, Charlie's face—his dear face that could seem so serious, then lift suddenly in a smile of such brilliance it took your breath away—was haggard with worry. He wasn't alone either. Bronwyn hovered behind him, looking as distraught as she did bedraggled.

Charlie flicked a glance at the shoes in her hand. "You'd better put those on and come with us, Mary. Noelle's missing. We think Robert has taken her."

Mary had a very real sense just then of something rushing toward her, as real as if she'd been standing in the middle of a dark road with headlights bearing down on her.

The blood drained from her face, and she felt as if she might faint. Charlie must have seen it because he stepped up at once to slip an arm about her waist. It occurred to her in some distant, detached part of her brain that he was holding her the exact same way that *she* held her mother when assisting Doris up the stairs. In the muted yellow glow of the porch light, a moth fluttered close to his head. She watched it brush against a curly charcoal tendril before reeling back into the darkness.

"No," she said quite calmly. "It must be a mistake. Noelle's asleep upstairs."

But Charlie's face told a different story. "Mary, *think*. Think where he might have taken her."

Bronwyn stepped around her father and into the light. "We drove out to the Methodist church. A...friend tipped me off that Robert was up to something. We thought we could catch his guys in the act." Bits of leaf and twigs were snared in her long black hair, and bloody scratches stood out on her arms, in which a video camera was cradled as tenderly as a newborn infant. Though a bit muddy, it looked none the worse for the wear. "It's all here," she said, tapping the camera. "I hid in the bushes and got most of it on tape. Not his face—it was too dark—but what he was saying."

She flipped open the instant replay screen and pushed down on the play button. Darkness, then a blurry shape swam into view, followed by more fractured images as if the camera were being jostled. Sounds, too. The thrashing of leaves, the distant murmur of voices, the rush of panicked breathing. Then something heavy toppling to the ground, followed by a voice that caused her arms to tighten with gooseflesh.

*"Happy anniversary, darling."*

Mary drew away from Charlie to sink down on the staircase. "We were right all along. It wasn't just our imaginations or some wild-goose chase. He—oh, God."

She clapped a hand over her mouth, then just as abruptly as she'd sat down shot back to her feet. Her gaze locked on Charlie, standing before her with an arm about his daughter's shoulders like a man bearing up under a tremendous weight.

"You've been to his house, I assume." She was surprised by how calm she sounded.

"We just came from there. Not a soul in sight. His folks don't know where he is either. I think they're telling the truth, they looked pretty damn shook up," Charlie reported grimly.

"What about Emma?"

"She's fine. She's with them."

"Do they have any idea where he might have taken Noelle?"

Charlie shook his head.

"Dante...uh, my friend...is checking around," Bronwyn volunteered. "He's talking to some guys who work for the—for Robert."

Mary was slipping her shoes on when it hit her. "Wait. There *is* someone. It's a long shot, but he might be able to help." She dashed upstairs and was thumbing through the directory for Hank's number when something else occurred to her. "What about the sheriff's office?" she called down. "I don't suppose it would do any good to call them."

Charlie shook his head. "I did one better, got my security guard, Tim Washburn, to phone his buddies at state trooper headquarters in Albany. They're on their way."

Mary dialed Hank's number, and a foggy voice at the other end answered with the weary resignation of someone used to being awakened in the middle of the night, "'Lo?"

"Hank, it's Mary Quinn," she spoke urgently into the receiver. "Something's happened to Noelle. We think"—she hesitated, because the concept still felt so utterly preposterous, like something out of a B grade movie—"her husband's kidnapped her."

There was a beat of silence. Then Hank replied hoarsely, "Jesus, oh, shit. Let me throw some clothes on. I'll be right over."

"Can you think of anyplace he might have taken her?" she asked. "Somewhere Noelle might have mentioned?"

"Hold on. Let me think..." A rustling noise at the other end, as if he were throwing something on even as they spoke. She heard a heavy sound, like a shoe dropping to the floor. Hank was breathing hard. "Wait. Yes. Last week we were out for a drive and passed the site for Cranberry Mall. It struck me at the time..." He paused as if whatever he was thinking might be too farfetched.

"*What?*" Mary urged. "Hank, even if it's a wild-goose chase, tell me."

"Oh, Christ...I can't believe I'm even thinking

this, it's so macabre, but I remember thinking that if someone wanted to bury a—something they didn't want found, that would be the perfect place."

Mary was swamped by a terror so great that for an instant she couldn't catch her breath. Then she managed to say, "We'll meet you there. And Hank? If you own a gun, better bring it along."

Noelle's face and scalp stung from the dirt that rained down like shrapnel. A cloud of gritty dust enveloped her. Sprawled at the bottom of the pit, buried to her chest in a mound of loose earth and gravel, she coughed and spat, bringing up a mouthful of vile-tasting phlegm. She was getting that wobbly feeling in her head again of something loosely nailed down starting to slide out from under her.

*Don't you dare faint!* a voice screamed. *You'll never wake up.*

Clinging to consciousness, she shook herself free and crawled to the farthest corner of the pit, careful to maintain as much distance as possible from the bundled tarp with its gruesome contents. She struggled to her feet, peering up just in time to see the Cat's huge saw-toothed bucket poised overhead like the mouth of some ravenous mythical beast. Noelle cringed, expecting more dirt to come raining down, then saw that it was receding. She could hear the low whine of its hydraulic

492

boom, the hollow scrape of another load being scooped up. *Oh, sweet Jesus, he's going to bury me alive....*

Insane laughter clawed up her throat.

Noelle gave herself a hard mental slap. *Stop it. Stop thinking that way. You can't afford it.* She was afraid to die, yes, but even more afraid of what would happen to Emma.

She looked frantically about. But there was no escape. She was trapped. Within minutes she'd be suffocating under tons of dirt. No sooner had the thought entered her mind than a second torrent was unleashed on her. With a shriek Noelle dropped to her haunches, bringing her arms over her head in a futile attempt to shield herself. Fist-size clods broke against her back and head. Bright splinters of light flashed behind her tightly closed eyes. *He's won,* she thought. *He managed to beat me after all.* Even if she could climb out, he'd track her down and kill her. She began to weep with exhaustion and despair.

A memory from last summer flashed through her mind: taking her daughter for Red Cross swimming lessons. Poor Emma couldn't seem to stay afloat. Each time she flipped over onto her back, she'd start to panic. Even with the instructor, a nice, wholesome-looking girl named Stacey, holding a hand lightly pressed to the small of her back while coaxing encouragingly, "Relax. That's the trick. Just take a deep breath and let yourself go," Emma had remained stiff as a board. Afterward, swaddled in a towel, she'd sat shivering on Noelle's lap, sobbing, "M-m-mommy, I tried my very, very hardest, b-b-but it wasn't good enough!"

Now it was Noelle who spoke those words inside her head. *Emma, baby, I'm trying my very hardest, but sometimes even mommies can't stay afloat. It's not because I don't love you. No matter what happens, you've always got to remember that: that I loved you more than life itself....*

Dust swirled up around her, and she broke into a fit of coughing that made her retch. The mound at the bottom of the pit had doubled while above her the Cat's engine continued to rumble, a noise broken only by the ratcheting whine of its hoist.

Quite clearly she thought, *I don't want to die. Not like this.* If she'd been drowning, it wouldn't be so terrible. There was a kind of poetry in drowning, wasn't there? Like Ophelia. But to die like this, buried beneath a—a *shopping mall.* With an eternity of tired, swollen feet clopping overhead, giggling teenagers wearing too much makeup, mothers at the end of their rope tugging the arms of truculent children who whined, *"But, Mommy, you promised—"*

It was unthinkable. Worse, *ignoble* somehow.

The grinding overhead grew louder as it drew close to rain yet another heap of indignity on her. She pressed herself flat against the side of the pit. But there was no safe place, not really.

*Think,* a voice coaxed, *think...*

What came to her mind then was Aesop's fable about the clever monkey that tricks the

494

crocodile into carrying him across the river. She didn't know what made her think of it until she looked up and saw the underside of the Cat's inexorably lowering bucket, starkly outlined against the sky, a pale moon perched on its lip.

Nimble as the monkey in the fable, she scrambled to the top of the mound. It afforded her only a slight advantage, four or five feet at best, but maybe it was enough. As the bucket tipped and a fresh torrent began to rain down, she fought the urge to duck. Instead, she stretched up, reaching as high as she could, flinching only when a rock struck a stinging blow to her forehead. Gritting her teeth against the pain, she strained upward, holding her breath for what seemed an eternity until the bucket completed its groaning arc.

At the precise moment it had reached its lowest point, Noelle gave a little leap and grasped hold of the bucket's gritty, toothed lip. Her filthy hands slipped, and she nearly lost her grip. Then the boom began its jerky ascent and the bucket's angle shifted a crucial fraction of an inch. *Quick,* her mind shrieked, *before he sees you.* With a superhuman effort she heaved herself over the lip and into the bucket, which was as wide and deep as a bathtub—just enough for her to remain hidden from Robert's view.

Then she was airborne, rocking upward as if on a Ferris wheel, hunched low with one eye cocked on the great star-strewn bowl of sky overhead. She could feel the blood trickling from her forehead into her eye, but she ignored it. Later there would be time to attend to such things. Right now she had to concentrate merely on staying alive.

Moments later the boom began to descend. She could feel the bucket vibrate beneath her, hear the grinding of the Cat gears. Suddenly she was pitched onto the mound alongside the pit, half tumbling, half scuttling her way down its loose, slippery slope.

Noelle rolled to a stop on the hard ground, where she held herself as flat and still as possible. She hardly dared to breathe. Had he spotted her? *Please, oh, please, no.* Seconds ticked by, excruciating, interminable, while she listened to the harsh scrape of the bucket scooping up more earth little more than an arm's length away. Out of the corner of one eye she could see the treads on the Cat's huge belt tracks, a single groove of which was wide enough to have easily accommodated one of Emma's hands. Then, blessedly, the bucket swung up and out of sight.

She waited a beat longer until she was certain she was no longer in Robert's direct line of sight, before scrambling to her feet and breaking into a run. She didn't dare risk so much as a glance over her shoulder. Her eyes remained fixed on the acre or so of bare lunar expanse separating her from the road and dark line of trees just beyond.

A line she'd picked up from somewhere dropped like a nickel into its slot: *Feets, don't fail me now.*

Some deeper consciousness must have been

listening, because suddenly she was running faster than she ever had in her life, skimming over the ground as effortlessly as a leaf driven by a cruel autumn wind, scarcely registering the pain as a foot unaccustomed to being bare came down hard on a rock or sharp stick. She darted around a severed tree trunk jutting from the earth like a half-pulled tooth, then past a cement truck angled beside the freshly dug foundation of the mall's main concourse.

The road loomed ahead like a fabled city of yore.

She was gaining on it when the Cat's distant groan all at once seemed to grow louder. A surge of terror caused her to stumble and nearly fall. As she chased her shadow, bumping and swaying over the stark, moonlit earth like a creature even more terrified than she, Noelle could almost taste her fear, a taste very much like blood.

She tossed a panicked glance over her shoulder. The Cat, which resembled a huge mythical beast in the moonlight, wasn't more than a hundred yards behind her. She caught the wink of LCD gauges on its dash and, high up in the cab, a shadowy figure perched like a wrathful king on his throne.

*I tricked him, and he's not happy about it.*

Amid the roar of her terror, and the blood running in warm trickles down her cheek, the thought brought a cold smile of triumph to her lips.

Other than the moonlight stippling it in tiger stripes of shadow, the road to the site was dark as Charlie raced down it in his mile-weary Blazer. Mary rode shotgun, and Bronwyn sat in the rear, clinging to the seat in front of her as if to the pommel of a runaway horse. Gravel rattled in the undercarriage as they juddered over potholes, narrowly missing a raccoon that trundled across their path like a portly traveler hurrying to make a train.

Mary could see the chain-link gates up ahead—wide open, as if she and Charlie and Bronwyn weren't the first to arrive—and a trailer just beyond. Yet at first glance, in the narrow beam of the headlights, the site looked deserted.

"I don't see Hank," she fretted aloud.

Charlie reached over and groped for her hand, squeezing hard. "He'll be along any minute, I'm sure."

"I wonder if Dante will know where to find us." Bronwyn's voice was shrill.

Charlie pulled to a stop just inside the gates, and they tumbled out into the warmth of the summer night, in which the faint cool whisper of the surrounding woods could be felt.

That was when Mary heard it, the drone of an engine in the not-so-far-off distance, no doubt one of the earthmovers she saw scattered about like abandoned Brobdingnagian toys. But why was it being operated at night? As her eyes adjusted to the darkness, she scanned the scoured expanse before her, a good fifteen acres at least, mounded with dirt and criss-crossed with trenches. Several hundred yards away a bulldozer was rapidly approaching in a pale cloud of dust.

She saw something else, too, something that brought her heart swooping up from her rib cage to lodge in her throat: a small figure in its path, racing to outdistance it, racing as if for dear life. Noelle? Oh sweet Jesus, it *was* Noelle. The bulldozer at once became menacing in Mary's mind, a charging rhino of Jurassic proportions.

"Charlie, look!" She grabbed his arm.

Charlie saw it, too. His face went gray in the moonlight, and he made a low noise deep in his throat. Without a word he took off, sprinting faster than she'd have believed possible.

Before Mary could follow in pursuit, the sound of a car caused her to wheel about. She couldn't see its make but had no doubt it was Hank's. As it roared through the gates, skidding to a stop behind the Blazer, she dashed to meet it, leaning in through the open window. Hank's guileless midwesterner's face behind the wheel was drawn and hard, nearly unrecognizable.

"For God's sake, Hank, *hurry*!" She gestured wildly in the direction Charlie had gone, catching only a brief glimpse of the rifle glinting on the seat alongside Hank before he plowed into reverse. She leaped back. Sharp bits of gravel spun from his tires to nip at her calves, but she barely noticed. Because she, too, was running...running to meet her daughter.

*D*ust stinking of diesel filled Noelle's mouth and lungs, and a stitch in her side had turned to fiery agony. The monster's hot roar was all around her, a furnace in which she was being consumed. Yet, amazingly, her legs continued to churn beneath her.

Time, though, seemed to have wound down. It was as if she were viewing everything in slow-motion instant replay from a seat in a stadium high overhead. Her feet had grown heavy, but a queer lightness had overtaken her. As she ran, stumbling more often than not, her gaze was no longer on the horizon but on the miracle of her shadow, stubbornly lurching over the hard ground, propelled by the grace of God alone.

Quite calmly, she thought, *I'm going to die.*

As she ran, she prayed: *God, look after Emma...she's only five, and it's a hard world for a little girl without a mother. Nana's too old and sick, and, Daddy, if you'll pardon me for saying so, is a guy. My mother will give her what she needs....*

Noelle had always believed it an old wives' tale that in the final seconds before death your life flashes before your eyes. But now she knew it to be true. In a series of strobelike images, she saw herself at eight, on a summer camping trip at Lake George, clinging to her father as he carried her over a suspension bridge...and with her mother, at age twelve, shopping for her first bra...and, at sixteen, in the back seat of Gordon Hockstedder's Chevy Impala with her jeans scrunched down around her knees.

She saw Hank, too...

Noelle had a clear picture of him seated on the bench in the square, his large hands resting on his knees. Fleetingly she thought how lovely it would have been if they could have ended up like those old couples strolling hand in hand through the park, each hoping to be the first to go because life without the other would be intolerable. When she was gone, would Hank—

A new sound tunneled its way into her head: the high-pitched drone of a car engine. As she staggered along, bent nearly double from the stitch in her side, Noelle lifted her bleary eyes and saw what appeared to be a cloud of dust racing toward her. She blinked, and the cloud materialized into the shape of a car. Would it reach her in time? She risked another glance over her shoulder: a fleeting impression of a chrome grille twinkling dully in the moonlight like bared teeth—teeth that were going to eat her alive. All at once she was too numb and weary to care.

The car skidded to a stop several dozen feet ahead of her, throwing up a great swirling raft of dust. Through it she could make out the distant figures of a man and woman running toward her.

A gunshot rang out.

For a startled instant Noelle imagined it aimed at her. Her knees buckled, and she nearly fell. She almost *wanted* it to be over—for the sweet relief of being put out of her misery.

Then in rapid succession came two more shots, and she realized in some still-functioning part of her brain that they were being fired *over* her rather than *at* her. The realization was like a sharp instrument piercing the thick shell into which her mind had retreated. The panic she'd held at bay rose once more. But there was something else, too, a feeling she hadn't had in so long she almost didn't recognize it: hope.

The roar at her back seemed to diminish.

Glancing back over her shoulder, she saw to her astonishment that the Cat had abruptly veered off course and was now cutting east, toward the concourse where surveyor's stakes tied with red plastic tape marked the buildings that would one day rise there. Yet something was wrong. Its direction appeared aimless, that of a rudderless boat...

...headed straight for the dump truck in its path.

Instinctively she found herself croaking, *"Watch out!"*

In a trancelike state of almost exquisite horror, she watched the Cat plow broadside into the truck with a cracking boom, much like the noise their huge elm had made when it crashed through the roof of the garage during last winter's record-breaking storm. For a surreal instant, the two earthmovers appeared locked in an obscene embrace, like embattled lovers, groaning and bucking. Then the truck reeled onto its side, vanquished, while the Cat continued to butt at it, a track wedged against its crumpled bed, grinding fruitlessly.

The stink of diesel filled the air. There was a deafening whump, and suddenly the two were engulfed in a great orange-red rose of flame.

Noelle cried out again, watching it bloom up into the night sky, momentarily illuminating everything around her: the angled neck of a nearby crane, a stack of conduit pipe stacked alongside a trench. Shadows danced over the rosy-hued landscape like revelers about a bonfire.

*"Noelle!"* Somewhere in the midst of all the skirling madness a voice was calling to her.

For a terrified split second she imagined it to be her husband rising from the flames to complete his gruesome task. Then she saw that the figure racing toward her wasn't tall like her husband with Robert's long-legged stride. This man was several inches shorter, though equally athletic, and her heart soared as his dear face swam into view. *Hank...*

There was a moment when all the jumbled pieces fell into place—his idling car, the rifle in his hand, the flaming wreck spitting sparks up at the sky—before it was eclipsed by a relief so profound she sank to her knees in gratitude.

"Hank." She choked out his name.

Roughly almost, he pulled her into his arms, and she caught the clean laundry scent of his shirt mingled with the stink of sweat. With a low, strangled cry he buried his face in the crook of her neck while his hands set out to reassure him that she was still in one piece. They slid down over her arms and rib cage before reaching up to cradle her head. "You're bleeding...oh, Jesus..." When she began to cry, he clasped her to him, murmuring, "Shh, it's okay. It's just a little cut. Don't worry, I'll take care of it."

"Your sh-sh-shirt." She wept with her face pressed to his collar. "It'll be r-ruh-ruined."

"It's all right," Hank said soothingly, his own voice catching. "I'll buy a new one. You can help me pick it out."

For some reason that only made her weep harder.

"I c-couldn't r-run anymore," she sobbed.

Lovingly he caressed her cheek. "I know."

"He's d-d-dead, isn't he?"

"I'm afraid so."

"Okay. Okay then." She nodded, frowning with the fierce concentration of a slow pupil struggling to make sense of it all. Just over Hank's shoulder she caught sight of her parents with their arms tightly clasped about each other, which for some unfathomable reason made perfect sense.

"You're going to be just fine." Hank reassured her once more. "There's nothing to run from anymore."

Then he, too, began to sob.

Together they rocked as if in the palm of some great, unseen hand that was comforting them.

# Chapter Eighteen

For the remainder of August and well into September, it was the talk of Burns Lake. In Murphy's Diner old men swapped stories over thick white mugs of joe. Housewives getting their monthly perms at Lucille's Beauty Salon clucked to one another loudly over the drone of hair dryers. Parents of young children spoke of it when their little ones were safely out of earshot or fast asleep in their beds, keeping their voices lowered all the same. In shops all up and down Main Street business was brisker than usual for this time of year. And at Burns Lake Elementary, where Trish Quinn's longtime fiancé, Gary Schmidt, was winding up fall tryouts for the football team, he whispered about it in the locker room after hours to Amanda Wright, his current squeeze and mother of one of his team members.

The last time the town had seen anything even remotely as sensational had been in June 1985, when the postmistress, Alice Burns, ran off with a traveling aluminum siding salesman and was later found strangled to death in a ditch on the outskirts of Poughkeepsie. This was different, though; it made people distinctly uneasy that they could have allowed themselves to be so profoundly deceived. Many took it as a personal betrayal of sorts. For others it was a case of a good man's simply snapping beneath the weight of his conscience.

What no one was especially eager to face, much less look squarely in the eye, was the disquieting truth at the heart of it: that all those years they'd been harboring a cold-blooded killer. *Incubating* him, so to speak. The towheaded boy upon whom they'd smiled fondly, seeing him perched on his father's shoulders as Cole marched down Main Street as grand marshal of the Fourth of July parade. The fairhaired youth who had brought tears to many an eye when he'd spoken so eloquently as valedictorian of his high school class. Last but not least, the man whom many, though not all, had looked upon as a shining example of what one could achieve while remaining essentially decent. If Robert Van Doren had incited some whispering over the years, it was chalked up to the jealous husbands and boyfriends of women he'd bedded and the disgruntled employees he'd fired. No one was perfect after all. What man with a roving eye and a soft spot for the pretty ladies could resist when it was constantly thrown at him?

But there was no getting around certain facts that had come to light in the wake of the terrible occurrence out at Cranberry Mall. Months later, when the county sheriff's department had completed its investigation into the death of Robert Van Doren, as well as the far less recent ones of his brother and former girlfriend, it was concluded that Corinne Lundquist had been a victim of suicide as first recorded. Buck Van Doren, on the other hand, had expired from a crushing blow to the back of his skull, a fact that had been previously overlooked due to the extreme nature of the injuries that were presumed to have claimed his life.

Several arrests were made in the wake of those findings. Among them a fellow named Grady Foster, a pipe fitter formerly in Robert's employ who'd moonlighted as a bouncer at the Red Crow Tavern. A big man sporting an earring in one ear, with bleached blond hair sheared off at the top and tied into a ratty ponytail in back, he'd broken down and confessed to having vandalized the *Register* and Mackie Foods warehouse as well as the First Baptist Church. When questioned about the desecration of Buck's grave, though, he claimed to have been no more than a bit player. He'd dug down only as far as the coffin, he said, after which Mr. Van Doren had sent him home. His former boss must not have trusted him to complete the job, but neither was he alive now to corroborate Grady's story. Grady was consequently sentenced to eighteen months in the Schoharie County jail, the toughest sentence allowable by law.

The first week in September hundreds showed up for Robert's memorial service.

Some came out of curiosity, but most out of respect for his grieving parents, who, aside from occasional sightings of pale, shell-shocked faces glimpsed through the windows of the Cadillac (old beyond their years and bearing only a passing resemblance to those of Cole and Gertrude), had been in virtual seclusion since that fateful night.

Noelle Van Doren and her little girl, Emma, who, other than her dark coloring, bore a striking resemblance to her father, were among those who came to pay their respects. They were accompanied by Noelle's parents and teenage sister...and the town doctor, Hank Reynolds. It was noted, with raised eyebrow, that Mary Quinn and Charlie Jeffers, divorced lo these many years, appeared on the friendliest of terms nonetheless. But the lion's share of the gossip was reserved for Charlie's wild young daughter, arm in arm with that hoodlum boyfriend of hers, right out in the open with her father looking on. Elmira Cushing whispered to Shirley Hemstead, who repeated it to Sylvia Hochman at The Basket Case, that unless her eyes were deceiving her, Bronwyn Jeffers had a bun in the oven. Nothing could have been further from the truth, but that didn't stop tongues from wagging.

Among those *not* attending the service was Trish Quinn, who'd volunteered to care for her ailing mother instead. Trish had another reason for lying low, it turned out. Earlier that week she'd found out about Gary and Amanda, caught him, in fact, with his hand in the cookie jar, so to speak. She was handling it with as much dignity as a single woman in her forties could muster, but anyone who looked closely could see how fragile she was. She'd even gone so far as to seek spiritual solace from Joe Wilcox, pastor of the Unitarian Church of Divine Apostles.

The absence of two other people was noted as well. Wade Jewett, who'd been brought up on a raft of charges, primarily obstruction of justice. And Noelle's former neighbor Judy Patterson, who was rumored to be too grief-stricken. It seemed Noelle had been wrong about Judy's lover being her son's karate instructor. Gossip had it that the day the terrible news about Robert broke, Blake Patterson had arrived home late from a business trip to find his wife huddled on the floor of their bedroom, weeping hysterically. After some prodding, she'd confessed that Robert and she had been lovers. The following day Blake moved out, taking their two sons with him.

The second week in September Mary quietly packed up and moved back to New York. Though she continued to drive up on weekends and was often spotted out and about with her daughter and granddaughter or on the arm of that handsome ex-husband of hers, the visits became fewer over time.

In the beginning it had nonetheless seemed as though they just might pull it off. They were in love, after all. And, just like the first time, desperate to believe that love conquers all. If neither liked the idea of spending so much time apart, what could be done about it? Even Charlie agreed—albeit, reluctantly—that there was no way around it. Then, in November, Mary came down with a bad case of flu, from which she spent three weeks recuperating, one in bed and the other two catching up at work. Shortly after, Noelle and Emma came down with it, too, and Hank moved in temporarily to keep an eye on them, as well as on Doris, who'd grown quiet frail. Somehow he never moved out. Noelle protested often and vehemently—perhaps *too* vehemently—that it didn't change a thing as far as Mary was concerned. The house had more than enough room, and this way Hank and she could really get to know each other. But Mary stayed away for the most part, murmuring the usual polite excuses. Noelle and Hank needed time on their own, with Emma. Doris would be enough of a handful.

Certainly she could have stayed with Charlie. It was no secret that they were sleeping together. But on the two memorable occasions that she'd spent the night, somehow it hadn't felt right. For one thing, there was Bronwyn. Though Charlie's young daughter never came right out and said so, it was clear she didn't want Mary around. There was Charlie, too: the wistful expression on his face as he watched her go about her morning rituals—brushing her teeth, drying off after her shower, rooting about in the cupboard for a coffee mug—as if at the same time he were viewing the scenario in some future projected tense. A future in which every morning, not just here and there, they woke up and made love and had coffee and got dressed. The problem was, *she* could see it, too. So clearly at times, so maddeningly within reach, it became a permanent ache.

After a while it became easier to stay away.

Instead, she made weekend plans with friends, plans that would keep her in the city, keep her from weakening at the last minute. When Charlie made plans of his own, she was quick to hear about it. From Bronwyn, of course, who oh-so-innocently happened to drop that her father had taken a lady out to dinner. Mary didn't ask for an explanation, but Charlie gave it anyway. Paula Kent, that sharp new realtor who'd come up with the bright idea of applying for a federal grant to turn the Sandy Creek Development project (voted down ten to one in the referendum) into an official bird sanctuary, had asked *him* to dinner to discuss a series of ads she wanted to run. He hadn't elaborated beyond that, nor had Mary grilled him about any future dates he might have planned. She had no right, though she'd long since broken off with Simon Trager. If she'd wanted Charlie, he would have been hers for the taking. But to keep him dangling this way, no, it wasn't fair. She'd broken his heart once already. To do so twice would be worse than cruel. It would be—the thought of Doris had popped into her head just then—*un-Christian.*

Naturally the one weekend Charlie had

chosen to visit her it had rained nonstop, the phone never stopped ringing, and the restaurant to which she'd taken him for dinner, usually reliable, served terrible food at a near-glacial pace. He'd been a good sport about it, teasing that he didn't have to come all the way to the city for bad service and an overcooked meal; all he had to do was walk down the street to Murphy's Diner. They'd shared a good laugh, and when it turned out the movie they'd planned to see was sold out, had rented a video at Blockbuster instead. Yes, it had been a good weekend, after all. That's what she kept telling herself.

But for one reason or another Charlie hadn't been back.

The last she'd seen of him was in March when her mother passed away. Doris had been going steadily downhill for some time, and it came as a shock to no one—especially her daughters and granddaughter—when she went quietly in her sleep after a long and debilitating bout with pneumonia. Noelle and Trish grieved openly, and Mary in her own fashion. At the funeral, she placed a silver-framed photo on the coffin of her parents on their wedding day—presumably the happiest day of her mother's life—and said a little prayer that her mother, reunited with her father in heaven, would find the peace and contentment that had eluded her on earth.

Then spring arrived, melting the snow along with any lingering thoughts of what can happen even in sleepy little towns with white-steepled churches. Crocuses and grape hyacinth and snowbells appeared alongside the road, poking like lost souvenirs of some long-ago festive occasion from the dark heath of rotting leaves and fallen tree limbs. The first of the spring seed packets appeared on a wire rack in front of the Newberry five-and-dime. And swallows and nuthatches could be seen building their nests alongside the orange-crowned warblers in the wooded area just south of Sandy Creek.

The first week in May no one was particularly surprised when the Sunday edition of the *Register* announced the engagement of Noelle Van Doren (née Jeffers) and Dr. Hank Reynolds. Though she and Hank had been fairly quiet about it, everyone knew they'd been keeping company. A few of the older and more hidebound remarked that it was a bit soon for someone so recently widowed, and under such ghastly circumstances, but most were genuinely happy for the newly engaged couple, not to mention relieved for themselves. For deep in their minds and hearts, where guilty thoughts sprouted like toadstools in the dark, those who knew Noelle silently acknowledged that they could have done more to help, that perhaps they'd been a bit too quick to judge.

A quiet wedding was planned for the end of June, when the weather was expected to be nice but not too hot. Reverend Joe Wilcox, a confirmed bachelor who'd recently begun to think seriously of tying the knot himself, would officiate. These past months he and Trish

Quinn had been spending a great deal of time together, enough for him to appreciate what a truly special woman she was. He'd pretty much made up his mind that by Christmas, if all went well, he'd surprise her with an engagement ring.

Mary made plans to spend the week of the wedding in Burns Lake. Business had been good lately, despite a rough patch near the end of last year, when several of the clients, feeling less than fully appreciated, departed in a huff. The firm's bookkeeper had left as well, taking with her nearly thirty thousand in embezzled funds. But with the Rene's Room fund-raiser, which despite its many setbacks had been a spectacular success, Quinn Communications turned a corner. Mary had taken on several new clients in the past month alone. She was even thinking of making her assistant, Brittany Meehan, a partner. There was only one problem: Charlie.

She missed him. Most of all, she missed *talking* to him. Not just on the phone but at night curled up beside him in bed or seated across from him at breakfast. She missed chatting with him in the kitchen while they fixed supper, and taking an evening stroll along the lake. She missed the life they *could* have had—and almost did. Twice.

Now she was going home for their daughter's wedding. Driving west on Route 23, Mary felt a little shiver of anticipation. Or was it dread? The rolling patchwork of farmland and green hills reminded her of last summer. So much had changed since then. Her mother gone...Noelle getting married. An eternity seemed to have passed since she'd made this journey only a year ago.

A pulse throbbed at the base of her throat, measuring out the miles and minutes. Greedily she drank in the familiar landmarks of her childhood: cornfields and tire dealerships and Agway franchises, weathered barns leaning like old drunks, roadside eateries with names like Big Bob's and Aunt Susie's and Udderly Delicious (Dairy Queen and McDonald's had yet to stake their claim in these parts), a store with an elaborate display of lawn statues out front that resembled the Land of Munchkins.

It dawned on her that over the years she'd lost, or misplaced, something vital, which now seemed to glint at her here and there amid the passing scenery like flecks of buried gold. Something of herself, or perhaps the life she might have led had she remained in Burns Lake. Would she have been the worse for it? For a long time she'd thought so, but she knew now that that wouldn't necessarily have been the case. Her life would have been different, that's all. Not better or worse, just slower and on a smaller scale. Also, there was Charlie to consider. Always Charlie, tugging at her like an invisible cord.

*I'm not the first woman who's ever had to choose between her career and the man she loves. But why does it have to be so hard? Why is there no such thing as a clean break?*

There was another question niggling at

her. Was he still seeing Paula Kent? She wondered if Paula was as pretty in person as in that photo on the real estate flyer Mary just so happened to have come across the last time she was up for a visit. *Just who do you think you're fooling? You practically scoured every store in town until you found one.* Mary imagined her to be as pert as she was blond, a perfect size six, with indestructible nails and hair that never frizzed in humid weather. While gradually infiltrating every aspect of Charlie's life, Paula would have set out on a campaign to win Bronwyn over as well. Naturally the girl would have resisted at first, but with time and persistence she'd have come around. Because Paula Kent, aside from being perfectly positioned, had one thing Mary didn't: all the time in the world.

Mary was so caught up in imaginary scenarios of Charlie's love life that she missed the turnoff for Route 145 and had to double back through Middleburgh. By the time she arrived at her mother's house, the sun was setting and the table laid for supper.

Hank fixed spaghetti and meatballs while Noelle puttered about the kitchen, looking every bit the blushing bride. Over supper he regaled them with a story about a patient at the hospital where he'd interned, an elderly Guatemalan woman with a persistent cough for whom he'd written a prescription for penicillin. The instructions had read, "Take three times daily with water." But instead of getting it filled, the ill-educated woman had soaked the prescription in water instead and faithfully downed three glasses a day from the jug.

"And the damnedest part was, she got better," Hank added with a chuckle, tipping back in his chair with his hands linked over his chest. His merry brown eyes found Noelle, and the two seemed to share a secret smile of their own. He looked, Mary thought, every bit as much at home as a man about to be married ought to.

Then it was bedtime, and Emma insisted on Mary's tucking her in and reading story after story. By the time Mary tiptoed back down to the kitchen, Noelle and Hank had gone off to bed as well. She made herself a cup of tea and headed back upstairs, stopping in the living room only long enough to pluck at random a volume of the *Reader's Digest* condensed books that lined the bookshelves, a surefire cure for insomnia. She was asleep before she'd turned the first page.

In the room across the hall Noelle and Hank quietly made love. Following the trauma of her ordeal, Noelle had discovered that in addition to the many wonderful qualities he possessed Hank was a superb lover. He was everything she'd ever wanted without knowing she'd wanted it: a man who never hurried and never seemed to mind when she occasionally faltered in her self-consciousness. Over the months since they'd become intimate, she'd gradually blossomed, seeking his attentions now as often as he sought hers. Opening herself to him in a way she wouldn't have

517

dreamed possible. They'd even talked of another child, one born of true love who would be as much a sister to Emma as she was to Bronwyn.

Mary spent the next two days with her daughter, shopping and running errands for the wedding. They drove up to Albany to buy a dress for Emma that she insisted had to be pink with sparkles and lots and lots of ruffles. They finally settled on white organdy with puff sleeves and a ruffled collar, which Emma, with a sigh of resignation, deemed acceptable. Afterward they lunched on pizza and chicken Caesar at California Kitchen before heading off to Nordstrom's in search of a pair of shoes to go with Noelle's gown.

Mary had never seen Noelle so content. If she fretted over Emma a tad more than necessary, her gaze anxiously tracking the little girl's every move, it was only natural after what she'd been through. That would fade in time. In the weeks after her ordeal, Noelle had seen a therapist for several months. Now she was ready to put the whole ordeal behind her, and Mary saw no evidence to the contrary. Noelle smiled a lot these days. She'd even put on a few pounds since Mary's last visit. It suited her. She simply glowed. *If love doesn't heal all wounds,* Mary thought, *it sure does work wonders for the complexion.* She realized to her chagrin that she was more than a tiny bit jealous. She'd have given anything, no pun intended, to be in her daughter's shoes.

"Hank's the best medicine anyone could have

prescribed," Mary observed, watching Noelle wiggle into yet another pair of ivory-colored pumps. Emma, on the floor nearby, was absorbed in wedging her own foot, shoe and all, into a flesh-colored stockinet.

Noelle looked up in sudden radiance. "He *is* pretty wonderful, isn't he?" She cocked her head, brushing back a lock of springy dark hair. "You know something, if the subject had come up beforehand, I doubt I'd have asked him to move in. It's funny how things work out, isn't it? Just when you think you have it all mapped out, along comes something that's better than anything you could have figured out on your own."

Out of old habit, Mary bent down to pinch the toe of Noelle's pump. "They look a little tight. How do they feel?"

"Like shoes I'll have to wear only once," Noelle replied with a laugh.

"I think I like the first pair best."

"I'm leaning more toward this one."

This time they laughed in unison. "I guess we'll never see eye to eye on some things," Mary admitted. "But in case I haven't put it into so many words, I approve one hundred percent of your marrying Hank. Even if I didn't adore him for purely selfish reasons, anyone who makes you this happy would get my vote." The words hung in the air between them: *He'll be a good father to Emma.*

"Thanks, Mom." Noelle looked both pleased and faintly embarrassed. She slipped her feet out of the pumps and reached for another box. Her eyes carefully averted, she observed lightly, "You know, I could say the same thing about you and Dad."

Mary grew flustered. This was one subject she and Noelle had never discussed. Maybe her daughter had sensed it was off-limits but now wanted everyone to be as blissfully happy as she. Mary sighed. "Your father and I are very different people—" She stopped. No. She had to come up with something better. "We might have made a go of it," she said, struggling to keep her voice even, "but I just can't see myself living in Burns Lake. Can you?"

"Honestly? No." Noelle darted a glance at Emma, who'd abandoned the stockinets and moved on to the shoes Noelle had just abandoned. Unaware of the splinter she'd driven into Mary's heart, Noelle peeked into the uppermost box on the stack beside her before clapping its lid back on in disgust. "On the other hand," she said somewhat distractedly, frowning as she hunted through the remaining boxes, "almost nothing ever turns out the way you expect. This time last year who'd have believed I'd be getting married again?"

"You have a point." With an effort, Mary hoisted her smile back into place. "The only question now is, Which of these shoes do you see yourself getting married in?"

Noelle sank back in her chair, legs sprawled in front of her in a pose Mary hadn't seen since she was a teenager. A mischievous grin spread over her face. "Oh, Mom, does it really matter? No one will see them anyway, and Hank certainly won't care. He'll be too busy looking at *me*."

In the end Noelle chose a pair of white high-heeled sneakers that would be hidden by the hem of her long dress and comfortable enough to dance in. The gaudiest high-heeled pumps, decorated with sequins and bows, she bought for Emma, who was absolutely enraptured with them. Yes, she knew it was a lot to spend for dress-up, she confessed ruefully to Mary as the cashier was ringing up her purchase, but lately she'd been relying a lot less on good sense and more on simply what *felt* right.

Words that resonated throughout the following day and into the evening, when Mary and Charlie met for dinner at the Stone Mill. They'd be seeing each other at tomorrow night's rehearsal dinner and the wedding on Saturday, where they'd be surrounded by friends and relatives, but tonight was just for the two of them, as it had been in the beginning. Only now their time had drawn to an end.

She spotted him by the window that looked out over the millrace, where a stream made lusty by snowmelt rushed to meet the pond below. It was early still, and the tables around him were only half filled. He was wearing a dark suit and tie, which made him look dignified and even somewhat sober-sided, more like an elder statesman than the owner of a small-town newspaper. Though she ought to have been used to it by now, the gray hair at his temples still came as a small shock. But maybe that was because she couldn't look at him these days without seeing an overlying snapshot in her mind of Charlie at seventeen: tall and slightly stoop-shouldered, as if from shooting up too fast, with his Indian black hair that was always rumpled from running his fingers through it. And, oh, yes, his smile, that quicksilver smile that could go from zero to sixty in a heartbeat.

He saw her walking toward him and stood to greet her. *Always the gentleman,* she thought. He was smiling, but there was a touch of wariness in his expression as well. Wariness she perversely longed to banish the way she'd once playfully splashed away their reflections in the little creek hollow below their house where they used to sunbathe. But they weren't teenagers anymore. Maybe part of the problem was that they never really had been.

"Long time, no see." She kissed his cheek, squeezing her eyes shut for the briefest of moments against a stab of bittersweet pain. "You're looking good, Charlie. I don't think I've ever seen that suit. It must be new." She refrained from asking, *Did Paula pick it out?*

He gave his signature loose-limbed shrug. "You know me, your basic L. L. Bean kind of guy. I wear this only on special occasions."

Mary put on her best smile. "We have a lot to celebrate. Our daughter is getting married."

"That she is," Charlie echoed amiably. He pulled out her chair and waited until she was comfortably seated before settling back into his own. "What would you like to drink?"

"A vodka tonic would be nice." When the waiter had taken their orders, she recalled with a groan, "Oh, God, that first wedding. I had a splitting headache for three days afterward. Even now when I think of how it might have ended..." She shook her head, not wanting to dwell on how close they'd come to losing Noelle.

Charlie reached across the table to squeeze her hand. "She's happy now. Isn't that what counts?"

Mary squeezed back and deftly withdrew her hand. "Someone once said there're no such things as happy endings, only happy beginnings." Their drinks came, and she slowly sipped hers, staring out the window at the water rushing past, almost close enough for her to have dipped a hand into. This time of year it'd be ice cold still; the creek wouldn't be warm enough for swimming until at least the middle of July. When she brought her gaze back to Charlie, the deep lines like woodcuts on either side of his mouth and nose caused her throat to tighten unexpectedly. She smiled crookedly. "I guess we never had much of a chance, did we? It was us against the world. Now it's the world against us."

"If you're right, it's a world of our own making." Charlie spoke lightly, but his smile didn't quite reach his eyes. His hand rested on the table alongside his wineglass, curved like a question mark.

"Maybe so," she said. "But there's no undoing it, is there?"

"I'm not the one to answer that."

Mary felt something crumple inside her. Her resolve to tread lightly, oh-so-lightly, was replaced by a sudden urge to get it over with all at once. It hurt too much. She was hurting Charlie, too. "What are you asking of me?" she asked in a low, unsteady voice.

The smile dropped from his face, and he regarded her with a weary sadness that would have broken her heart if it weren't in pieces already. "I'm not asking anything of you, Mary. I don't have the right, any more than you would ask me to give up everything I've worked so hard to build here." He shook his head sorrowfully. "When I was young and cocksure, I didn't know any better, but over the years I've learned a thing or two. I know, for instance, that when you force a square peg into a round hole, either it breaks or the hole gets ground down. I wouldn't do that to you." He shot her a wry look. "Though I'll admit there's a part of me that's selfish enough to want to try."

Mary sighed. "You're right. It just wouldn't work."

He lifted his glass. "We could drink to that or simply drown our sorrows. Your pleasure." Through his joking demeanor she could see the pain that had tightened the muscles in his neck. His eyes were sad but resigned. And it was his weary acceptance—so unlike the fear and uncertainty of the first time—that hurt most of all.

"Oh, Charlie," she said, softly, her tears dangerously close to the surface. "I wish—" She paused to clear her throat before going on. "I wish things could have been different. If it helps, there's no one else. There never has been, and I doubt there ever will be."

She waited for him to say something about Paula Kent, half wishing he would, for it would have been the one concrete detail she could have used to distance herself. This felt too close. Too raw.

But Charlie, with only a touch of hoarseness, replied, "Well then, I guess we'll just have to get on with our lives as best we can. Don't worry about me. I've had plenty of practice." He offered her a bleak smile and sipped his wine. "Shall we order?"

"Suddenly I'm not so hungry," she said miserably.

"You should eat something anyway."

"Now you sound like my mother." She summoned a small laugh.

"Look." Charlie leaned toward her, and in that moment she glimpsed the flinty bedrock glittering darkly beneath the layers of pretense. "The day after tomorrow our daughter is getting married. We owe it to Noelle after all she's suffered to get through this with as much grace and humor as we can muster." He sat back, his expression softening. "Now, why don't we have a look at this menu? I've been told by our Lifestyles editor that the teriyaki salmon is the thing to order."

She felt chastened by his...there was no other word for it, his *nobility*. She pushed her empty glass aside and picked up the menu. "You're right, Charlie, I'm being selfish." In a brave attempt that sounded utterly false to her ears, she added lightly, "There's no point in my wasting a perfectly good evening with the most eligible bachelor in Burns Lake." The thought of Paula Kent once again flashed through her mind.

"That's how we used to refer to old Cuddles, remember? The most eligible bachelor in Burns Lake." Charlie laughed. "Poor guy, stuck in his pen with nothing to do but moon over the fence at the cows."

Mary laughed, too, her memory of that long-ago time cast now in a soft sepia glow. She remembered how Cuddles, who was anything but, had once escaped from his pen onto the road, where an elderly couple in a pink Buick Regal cruising north on Route 30A were shocked to find Mr. Pettigrew's prize bull coming at them down the center line. The driver, a retired telephone repairman on his way to visit his wife's sister in Vermont, had panicked and attempted to pass the bull, which promptly charged, leaving a dent the size of the claims inspector's subsequent incredulity in the Buick's passenger side door.

Mary smiled. "I don't think that old couple ever recovered."

"I'm not so sure about Cuddles either. He was never quite right in the head after that." Charlie chuckled softly. "After you left, he wasn't the only one." She caught a brief glimpse of something glinting darkly in his eyes;

then he was rolling past it with an easy grin.

"From what I can see, you've recovered nicely." The words were out before she knew it. "I hear you've been seeing a lot of Paula Kent these days."

Charlie, to her frustration, neither confirmed nor denied it. "Is that so? Well, you know how it is in a small town. Rumors have a way of spreading."

"There's truth to some rumors."

But Charlie was withdrawing, his face closing against her like a door through which she was afforded no more than a glimpse of what lay beyond it. "You can't have it both ways, Mary." His tone was cool, though not entirely devoid of gentleness. "If you want what I have to offer—which isn't much, I grant you—it's yours for the taking. I don't have to spell it out, you know that. But you've made your choice, which I respect even if I don't much like it. Don't ask any more of me than that."

"I'm sorry." Charlie was right: She wanted to have her cake and eat it, too, even if the thought of Paula Kent was choking her. "Can we start over?"

It was a poor choice of words, and Charlie winced visibly. Just as quickly he recovered and shot her his patented quicksilver smile. "You bet. What do you say about that salmon?"

"Sounds good," she lied.

And that was that—as easy as falling off a log and at the same time the hardest thing she'd ever had to do. Almost as hard as watching Charlie walk away the first time. They dined on salad and salmon followed by strawberry-rhubarb pie for which Mary had little appetite but which she ate regardless. They lingered over cups of espresso. Charlie, in particular, seemed in no hurry to go; if he found her presence painful, it didn't show. They chatted more about the wedding and about the likelihood of Trish and Father Joe making the same trip down the aisle. Mary asked after Bronwyn and was told that she'd been seeing a lot of Dante Lo Presti. Apparently he wasn't the demon Charlie had imagined him to be. On the night neither wanted to elaborate on, much less relive, the boy had proved his worth to Charlie's satisfaction.

They parted outside the restaurant before walking to their respective cars, with a decorous kiss that left Mary's mouth tingling. As she watched in her rearview mirror while he pulled out of the lot, unexpected tears filled her eyes. She could already feel him receding in more ways than one. At the wedding, surrounded by friends and relatives, they would have little enough opportunity to chat, much less speak as candidly as they had just now. Then she would be back in the city. When she returned to Burns Lake in the months to come, it was unlikely that she would even run into Charlie. With Doris gone, they would see each other only on state occasions. School plays. Emma's high school graduation. And down the line if there should be another grandchild or two (their daughter was still a young woman after all) at christenings. They would murmur the usual polite exchanges. Charlie would be accompanied by Paula Kent—or whichever lucky woman happened to snag him—and that would be hard, yes, but not unendurable. She was used to putting on a brave face.

But alone, in the privacy of her car, surrounded by the faint chirping of night insects and the stream in back of the mill whispering what she didn't want to hear, Mary didn't have to put on any kind of face at all. She could simply weep to her heart's content. Weep for what she'd lost and for the debt she would continue to accrue...yes, and for the despair that even the right choices can bring.

*Oh, Charlie,* she told him silently, *I didn't want it to end. I just don't see another way.*

Mary wept until a group of diners, boisterous with too much booze, spilled into the lot and began making their way toward the car parked alongside hers. Fearing someone would think she was ill or had gone mad, she straightened and flipped open the glove compartment in search of the box of Kleenex stashed there. Its interior light flicked on, and in the rearview mirror she caught a glimpse of her face: puffy red eyes and a forehead marked with a red crease from the steering wheel. She blew hard into a tissue and started the engine. On the drive back to her mother's—now Noelle and Hank's house—her sinuses throbbed and her head felt swollen to twice its normal size.

An expression of her mother's came to

mind: *There's a lid for every pot.* The truth of it brought a grim smile. Only why, oh, why, did *hers* have to be a man who for one reason or another was never a perfect fit?

The following day was a little easier to bear. She got through the rehearsal dinner, at which the worst thing that happened was the demise of the restaurant's elderly air conditioner. Then Saturday arrived, the day of the wedding, and there was a noticeable drop in the humidity that had been clinging to the region like water to the inside of a glass. The sun shone brilliantly, and though every little thing that could go wrong did, no one seemed to mind.

Hank got called away in the early hours of the morning to deliver Norma Hofstedder's baby, which wasn't supposed to have been due for another three weeks. By nine, when he still hadn't returned, Noelle nonetheless refused to worry. "He'll be back in plenty of time," she insisted cheerfully.

Emma's stuffed dog Bowwie, laundered for the occasion, emerged from the dryer with only one ear intact, the other a handful of shapeless brown fuzz. But after some initial whining and sniffling, she allowed herself to be consoled by Grandma Mary, who made the point that this way, when she started first grade in the fall, she could carry a piece of Bowwie tucked in her pocket as a reminder that he was waiting for her at home.

Last but not least, Noelle discovered a rip in the lace hem of her wedding gown. And then she *did* panic a bit, less confident in her sewing skills than she was in her bridegroom's ability to deliver babies. Luckily Aunt Trish, who pointed out with a twinkle in her eye that it had been *she,* not Mary, who'd won first place in the home ec spring fashion show, was on hand to repair the damage.

In Mary's old room her sister hummed as she sewed up the rip in Noelle's gown. Her cheeks were pink, and her eyes glowed. She'd never looked prettier. If Mary hadn't known better, she'd have thought her sister was the one getting married. Everything was Joe this and Joe that.

"Joe says it's a refreshing change from couples who insist on writing their own vows." Trish, seated on the bed, glanced up from her stitching. "Not," she was quick to add, "that he has anything *against* it, mind you. But there's something so nice about the old-fashioned way. What's wrong with 'love, honor, and obey' when both people say it?"

Mary, at the dressing table, stopped fussing with her hair and turned to smile at her sister. There was no reason not to smile. It was after ten, with the wedding scheduled for eleven-thirty, and Hank had just returned. A minute ago she'd heard the front door slam and the sound of his voice drifting up the stairs. The breeze blowing in through the open window smelled of lilacs. Sunlight fell over the old maple bed where Trish sat cross-legged, the satin gown on her lap a pool of molten silver. All was right with the world.

With one exception: As parents of the bride

she and Charlie would be seated side by side, but they wouldn't *be* together. For the simple but complicated reason that she'd broken off with him, once and for all. *Which you will not, I repeat* not, *allow yourself to wallow in or in any way spoil this occasion,* cautioned a stern voice in her head.

"There's nothing wrong with the old-fashioned way," she agreed pleasantly.

"I mean, of course a bride and groom should have any kind of wedding they want," Trish prattled on. "Why, just the other day I was reading in a magazine about this couple, both avid scuba divers, who exchanged vows underwater. Did you ever hear anything more peculiar? But the point is, they got exactly what they wanted." She stopped to take a breath. "Goodness, where was I? I forgot what I was trying to say."

"That when you're in love, nothing else really matters," Mary said somewhat distractedly, her gaze fixed on her reflection in the mirror, on the enamel-backed brush she was pulling through her hair, part of a prized dresser set given to her by her grandmother when she'd turned sixteen.

Behind her in the mirror, she saw her sister give a firm nod. "Well, it's true. With all the pain and suffering in this world—and God knows this family has had its share—what better to celebrate than two people in love making a life together?" The needle in her hand flashed in and out of the silvery pool in her lap. "Take me, for instance. Six months ago who'd have thought I'd be in any kind of mood for a wedding? But you know something, I think finding out about Gary was actually a blessing in disguise. If I hadn't walked in on him with that—that woman"—her lips tightened as she spit out the word—"I wouldn't have gotten to know Joe." She stopped, catching Mary's eye in the mirror. "Oh, listen to me, going on and on. You'd think *I* was the one getting married." She blushed deeply, her cheeks as blooming pink as the Cecil Brunner roses climbing up the trellis to peek in over the sill.

Mary tossed an affectionate look over her shoulder. "I have a feeling you're next," she said, causing her sister to blush even harder. "How does Joe feel about the bookstore? I always thought being a minister's wife was a full-time job in itself."

"Maybe so, but Joe's not like that. He's very supportive of my career." Trish's staunch reply had the air of a topic that had been much discussed between them. "If anything is going to get in the way, it's that disgusting mall. Did you know that Bigelow Books is already distributing flyers around town?"

She was referring, of course, to Cranberry Mall, on which Van Doren & Sons had eventually resumed construction, after an understandable delay. The grand opening was scheduled for the end of July, just three weeks away. And Trish, along with the other small downtown business owners whose livelihoods were threatened, was merely cowering in fear, waiting to see what would happen. Mary grew suddenly exasperated with her sister.

She spun around on her dressing stool. "Well, for heaven's sake, why aren't you doing something about it?"

"What *can* I do?" Her sister's shoulders sagged.

Mary's publicist's instincts kicked in. "For one thing, you could distribute a few flyers of your own—you know, like you did with the orange-crowned warbler. Remind your loyal customers that you're willing to go the extra mile."

"That's not a bad idea." Trish nodded thoughtfully.

"Then organize some sort of event. A cooking demonstration. Or getting together with the Old Rose Society to promote a book on gardening; those ladies love nothing more than an excuse for a tea party." Mary found herself warming to the idea. Excitedly she added, "You could even host some sort of regular event, like a once-a-month breakfast at which some well-known author would speak."

"Why would a well-known author come to Burns Lake?" Trish asked dubiously.

"To sell books, of course! And," she added slyly, "because you'll present it to their house publicist as the best idea since sliced bread."

"I will?"

"The way it works," Mary explained, "is you sell tickets to the event so you know how many people are coming. Say you get fifty to start with—that'll grow as word spreads—

and the entry fee includes the price of the author's book, with coffee and pastries thrown in. That's a guaranteed sale of fifty books, plus more down the line. You keep the profit margin low to promote ticket sales, and in return you get some cachet, lots of goodwill, and a steady flow of customers."

"That's brilliant." Trish brightened visibly. "There's only one catch: I'd need someone as experienced as you to help me pull it off." She held out a hand to prevent Mary from putting her two cents in. "Listen to me, before you start trying to make me over in your image. It's taken me half a lifetime, but I've finally made peace with the fact that I'm not you. Don't look at me that way. I'm serious. Do you know how easy it was growing up in your shadow? The country mouse and her city cousin."

Mary felt the wind go out of her sails. "I didn't always live in the city."

"No, but even when you were here, there was always something different about you. You were more stylish, more determined somehow. Smarter, too. Definitely smarter."

"You're selling yourself short," Mary insisted.

Trish frowned, shaking her head. "No, I'm not. I'm just telling it like it is."

"Yeah, well, look where it got me. I'm so smart I almost lost the one child I have and the only man I ever loved." A wave of loneliness washed through Mary, and the room's sunny warmth suddenly felt heavy and cloying, like a too-sweet dessert.

"Smart isn't the same as knowing how to be happy," her sister observed with the ironic air of a woman who'd spent precious years barking up the wrong tree.

"Well, if you have the secret to happiness, I'd appreciate your sharing it with me." Mary heard the caustic note in her voice and cringed. Was she becoming the very thing she'd dreaded, a clone of her mother?

Trish laughed and reached over to retrieve her spool of thread. She snipped off a length as long as her arm and squinted like a pirate into a spyglass as she poked it through the needle's eye. "Some of it's just luck, but a lot of it, I think, is opening your eyes to possibilities you never imagined."

"Such as?"

"Well, take *your* career, for instance." Trish bent once more to her task, more assiduously than necessary, it seemed to Mary, her needle flashing in and out of the silky fabric. "It wouldn't be the same, I know, but you could be a publicist somewhere besides New York City. Oh, I'm sure it'd be a huge adjustment, and I'm not saying you'd make anywhere near the same kind of money. But just for the sake of argument, you *could*."

Mary, rightly suspecting she was being led down the garden path, replied a bit too sharply, "Okay, then, just for the sake of argument, where do you see me setting up shop?"

"You were the one that pointed out the need to promote my bookstore," Trish said. "What about all the other small businesses that'll suffer when the mall opens? If we had someone as experienced as you to show us the way, it might work. Otherwise, we don't have a prayer of surviving."

"This sounds like blackmail to me." Mary glared at her sister.

"It's just common sense." Trish breezed on. "I'm always reading about quaint little towns like ours—'the town that time forgot,' that's how it's always billed—that some smart promoter figured out a way of making it into a tourist destination."

"Sort of like preserving an endangered species?"

"Exactly!" Trish glanced up wearing an expression of such bright-eyed innocence it was hard not to buy it. Enthusiastically she went on. "So you see, if someone like that were to take on Burns Lake, just think what could be accomplished."

"Why do I get the feeling I'm being offered a job I never applied for?"

Her sister's face fell. "Well, it's just a thought. You certainly don't have to take me up on it. I was just making the point that you can be happy and fulfilled anywhere you choose to live." She tied off and snipped the thread, holding the gown up for Mary's inspection. "There. Does that look straight?"

The subject was closed. And in the ensuing whirl of activity Mary hardly gave it a second thought. It wasn't until she was at the church seated in the front pew of the sanctuary—done in pale woods with simple, soaring lines much grander than suggested by its exterior—watching Noelle glide down the aisle on Charlie's arm, that her sister's words returned to haunt her. *You can be happy and fulfilled anywhere you choose to live....*

But she hadn't *chosen* Burns Lake. Quite the opposite, she'd spent most of her adult life trying to escape it.

*Are you sure you weren't just running from things that were too hard to face? From people who'd disappointed you or who you felt you had let down. Like your mother. And Noelle. And yes, Charlie.*

Mary shut her mind against those thoughts, focusing on her daughter instead.

Noelle was a vision in satin and lace, her gown as simple and elegant as the wedding itself: no bridesmaids or ushers in attendance, the only decoration the arrangement of flowers at the altar and a spray of pale pink orchids in her hand. In that moment, as Charlie and their daughter approached, Mary indulged in the memory of her own long-ago wedding, a very different sort of affair, to be sure, with Charlie looking nervous but beaming just as happily as he was now. He'd been wearing an ill-fitting navy suit and she the dress in which she'd been confirmed three years before...let out a roomy three inches to accommodate her newly expanded waistline. The ceremony, such as it was, had taken place at town hall, with only Corinne in attendance and Charlie's folks, wearing the pained and slightly guilty expressions of parents who suspect they're somehow to blame.

The only ones who hadn't seemed to notice the lack of floral arrangements, organist, and a host of teary-eyed relatives were the bride and groom themselves. And now, with all her heartache momentarily stripped away, Mary was free to remember exactly the way it had been. The way she'd felt. *I was happy,* she thought with no small measure of awe, *really, truly happy.*

As happy as Noelle looked now. Tears filled Mary's eyes as she watched her daughter glide to a stop before Hank, who looked as awestruck as a teenager coming face-to-face with a movie idol. The two waited with patient smiles until Emma, looking impossibly adorable in her ruffled organdy dress, had tired of the grand spectacle of strewing rose petals from the basket looped over her arm and had scampered the last few feet up the aisle. As Father Joe launched into the ceremony, Emma stood half hidden by the folds of her mother's gown, peering out self-consciously at the assemblage of friends and relatives.

There were Hank's parents all the way from Kansas, both as squarely solid and plain as posts, though looking at Hank, Sr., Mary could see where the twinkle in his son's eye had come from. They were flanked by Hank's aunt Mabel and uncle Ned, accompanied by their four offspring, two men and two women, all from the same large-boned, fair-haired, and freckle-faced stock. None of Noelle's neighbors from Ramsey Terrace had been invited, though several high school friends were in attendance. Lacey Buxton as well, wearing a polka-dot peplum suit, her face nearly hidden by a matching wide-brimmed hat. And Nora Lundquist, along with her sons Everett and Jordy and their wives. Mary thought with a wry smile that it was too bad her mother hadn't lived to see this; it was just the sort of affair on which Doris loved to offer running commentary.

Charlie discreetly took his place alongside Mary. Without thinking, she tucked her arm into his. He glanced at her in mild surprise, then smiled. *We're like any proud parents of the bride,* she thought. If several people happen to glance at them in curiosity—Bronwyn in particular—what business was it of theirs? At least Trish, seated beside Mary with her hands folded primly in her lap, was careful to keep her eyes averted. Though that might have had more to do with Father Joe, strikingly dignified in his surplice and collar.

*I lost him once. I don't want to lose him again.* The thought came out of nowhere, as resounding as a note struck on the organ.

Mary refused to pay it any mind. This wasn't about her and Charlie; all that had been resolved. This was Noelle and Hank's day, on which no tears but those of joy were to be shed. Any twinges of regret she might feel were perfectly normal, she told herself. She mustn't give them a second thought.

After a brief reading from the Book of Psalms, Hank and Noelle exchanged vows, then slipped onto each other's fingers the simple gold bands they'd selected. When they kissed, the entire assemblage seemed to release its breath as one. Louella Carson at the organ, a huge woman in a floral print dress, struck up a chorus of Handel's *Water Music,* signaling the joyous march down the aisle.

Mary, dabbing at her eyes, leaned close to whisper, "Did you ever think we'd see the day?"

"I had a pretty good idea," Charlie whispered back hoarsely.

"Remind me to consult your crystal ball next time. Mine seems to be out of order."

"Hope ain't the same as being able to see into the future," he drawled sotto voce, staring straight ahead with a deadpan expression as they began making their way down the aisle to join the newlyweds outside. "Sometimes you've just got to wing it."

Mary stole a glance at his stern, hawk-nosed profile and saw the smile pulling at one corner of his mouth. The warmth that rushed through her was like a current sweeping her off in a direction she hadn't foreseen. She surprised herself by asking, "Would winging it include a return ticket?"

He paused when they reached the vestry and steered her off to one side as everyone else streamed past. "I'm a little slow. You know us country boys," he said, turning to look her full in the face. He was smiling, but his eyes were serious. "Would you mind telling me what this is all about?"

"I don't know," Mary replied honestly, shaking her head in disbelief at her own sudden change of heart—if that's what this was. "I was just wondering if maybe I've been looking at this the wrong way."

"Sort of like being too close to the forest to see the trees?" Charlie, standing with his back to a stained glass window, was bathed in an ethereal glow that made her wonder briefly if she was dreaming. The stream of departing guests dissolved into a blur. They might have been the only two people in the church.

"Something like that," she said, trembling inside.

Charlie regarded her intently. "I'm listening."

Mary took a deep breath. "I still don't know if I could come back here for good," she confessed, "but one thing I *do* know is that wherever I wind up, I don't want it to be alone."

"I'm here, right where I've always been," Charlie told her, his mouth flat and unsmiling. "Just say the word."

He was asking for a sign, even if it was nothing more than a lottery ticket to what the future might hold. He was telling her in so many words that such a profound change had to be every bit her own idea, on her own terms. Otherwise, it would be doomed.

He'd already gone as far as he could go. Now it was she who had to take that first step.

Mary felt a sudden sense of buoyancy, like an empty glass being slowly filled with something sweet and cool. She recognized it as a sort of letting go, a release of the tight grip she'd held on her heart.

"They're waiting for us outside," she said, nodding in the direction of the double doors that stood open to the sun-washed steps, where a receiving line had begun to form. Her throat was tight. "Can we get together later on and talk this over?"

"You know where to find me."

"That's never been the problem." She gave a rueful smile. "The problem is I haven't always known where to find *me*."

"Maybe you haven't been looking in the right place."

"I wish I knew where that was. God, how I wish it."

"In that case, allow me." Charlie took her arm. As they crossed the vestry, side by side, she felt his heart thumping and for an instant mistook it for her own

Through the open doors just up ahead, she could see the bride and groom, poised on the front steps, surrounded by friends and family, not to mention a number of Hank's patients. Their daughter—*their* daughter!—shimmered in the sunlight like something newly minted, which of course in a way she was. At that precise moment Noelle caught sight of them and broke into a smile so blinding that everyone else looked up, too.

"Don't let go," Mary murmured in a sudden panic. "I don't think my legs will hold me."

"I've got you," he said, holding her pressed so close she could feel the flutter of his warm breath in her hair. He smelled of soap and shaving cream and the freshly laundered shirt he wore, size large, light on the starch, please.

Together, they strode out of the church into the sunlight.